"...wonderfully crafted..."

"...provides reflections on the nature of faith, religion, love and lovers (lost and otherwise), sexuality and life, dying and death."
The Mensa Bulletin

"...a very Zen piece of writing...and an enjoyable read..."
Robert Lory, author of *The Thirteen Bracelets*
and 35 other novels;
Managing Director, write-to-communicate.blogspot.com

"...strong...fascinating...moving..."
B. Kaufman, Executive Director, CACLD

"If I were to list the ways that I --as a man -- saw myself reflected in [Thomas], I'd fill another book..."

"And the story is fresh off the presses (with) a reference (in it) to President Obama..."

"Whether you are a male or female, if you want to better understand the opposite sex, you gotta read this book -- or even if you just want to better grasp the eternal mysteries of life."
The Mensa Bulletin

"This book resonates with the perspective of someone who has loved fully and deeply..."

*"The description of their lovemaking reminded me of Lawrence, in many ways. There (is) humor, fun, utter physical joy, light-hearted banter, graphic sexual detail, love ...
a touch of spirituality ... without ever once slipping into voyeurism or sensationalism. Really well done."*

"(Thomas's) passion for women is present in the book in a way that women might actually recognize and like, without shortchanging humor and male banter. There seems to be a touch of Henry Miller in the book and a touch of Saul Bellow."

-- Stephen Haven
Director,
Master of Fine Arts in Creative Writing Program
Ashland University

and

Author, *The River Lock*;
and
The Long Silence of the Mohawk Carpet Smokestacks,
collected poems

The writer wants to acknowledge here several friends, associates and acqaintances for their inspiration and encouragement to begin to write -- and/or for their support during the writing and production of -- this book. They are, in no particular order:

IJH (Olivia), Jim Pitts, Gary T. Gillan, John Irving, Aldo Arpino, Aldo Magi, Lisa Marie Riccardi, Katherine Jane (Kat/K.J.) Moore, Niffer, St. Sheila, Joseph Fernandez, Ricky Foust, J-P-2, SAL/CC, Judy V., Tad Hillery, DJA, JWL, MEG, LAM, PLP.

Thank you all.

To: my precious little petal

(I am bound to you forever)

One

The large manila envelope had arrived in the mail yesterday, two days before Christmas. It was hand-addressed, not computer-printed, and even though there was no return address on the package Rebecca Halsey realized at once who the envelope was from. It seemed to her a lifetime -- *another life, almost* -- since she last had seen that handwriting.

Rebecca had not opened the thick, 8x10-sized envelope at first -- but instead had put it away until today. Now, with William out for the afternoon on last-minute Holiday errands, she was home by herself. She took the envelope from the bureau drawer where she had secreted it yesterday under some linen before William might see it among the Christmas cards and the rest of the mail.

She considered for a moment but could not imagine why Thomas would be communicating with her again after all these years. Last night before drifting off to sleep, with William beside her, she had not been able to get thoughts of Thomas out of her mind -- and, because of William, she had felt guilty about that.

But, guilt feelings or not, Rebecca had also looked forward

to this afternoon, when she knew William had plans to be out of the house and she would be alone for a period of time and have an opportunity to see just what might be in the very bulky envelope Thomas had sent her.

Rebecca sat down and held the package, turning it over in her hands, now more conscious of its girth than she had been yesterday. She began, very deliberately, to open it. She paused for a moment and smiled to herself as she realized how slowly and carefully she was proceeding. *Why* was she being so slow and deliberate -- and why so fastidious in trying not to tear the envelope as she opened it? Did she <u>really want</u> to see and read what was in it, or was she delaying opening it because she did *not* want to see or read its contents.

And why, for that matter, had she put the envelope away yesterday to keep William (who, after all, knew about her past relationship with Thomas) from seeing it? One reason, she knew, was so that she'd be able to open the envelope and examine its contents by herself, without William beside her or looking over her shoulder. She wanted that privacy. But *why* did she want to exclude William? She could not answer that question satisfactorily.

Rebecca held the envelope in her hands and carefully withdrew its contents. Her eyes rested on the typewritten first page of the mass of material she took from the envelope. *Good Lord,* she thought, *There must be two hundred pages here.*

Two

Rebecca's eyes rested on the first page of the thick sheaf in her lap.

Rebecca did not focus on or immediately begin to read the material. For a brief moment her thoughts turned to another place and time and to what she and Thomas had shared so long ago. She continued for still another moment to gaze straight ahead distractedly. Fleeting memories of that long-ago time in her life, before meeting Thomas and then when she was with him, after she and Arthur had separated and subsequently divorced, reemerged.

She thought for another moment about the sheer emotional intensity and turbulence of that period of her life, almost shuddering as she did so.

After Arthur, what she and Thomas had, for as long as it lasted, *was* rich, fulsome and good.

A smile crossed Rebecca's face as she thought about and briefly re-lived some of the good times she and Thomas shared. He had been such a welcome relief and pleasurable change from Arthur; he was the rock upon whom she could rely as she and Arthur went through the trials of divorce.

Rebecca smiled, resting her head against the tall back of the comfortable Queen Anne chair in which she sat, her tiny frame nearly lost in the huge chair. When she sat back, her feet were almost a foot from the floor. With ankles crossed, she swung her legs back and forth and wondered again why she hesitated to read the thick sheaf of typewritten material in her lap.

Finally, Rebecca's fingertips began, almost absently, to trace the top page of the material, slowly, lightly, even caressingly. She paused for another long moment and then, abruptly and with resolve, straightened her head and sat upright in the chair.

Stop being so silly, she thought to herself. All of what happened between her and Thomas had been so very, very long ago.

"I am in love with William," she said aloud.

"He is the best thing that *ever* happened to me. And he loves *me* -- very, very much.

"He is kind, caring, thoughtful and absolutely reliable. I know I can always count on him and I know he loves me deeply. I feel his devotion everyday; he demonstrates it in every possible way.

"And he is faithful."

Yes, she thought in utter silence now, *faithful -- above all else, William is faithful.*

But what in the world can this sudden word from Thomas be about? Rebecca wondered again, *and why such a long letter -- and why now, after so many years?*

She spoke aloud once again. "Well there's only one way to find out, Becky," she said. "Read it."

And so, with William still out of the house on his errands, she began --

I close my eyes, then I drift away
Into the magic night, I softly say
A silent prayer like dreamers do.
Then I fall asleep to dream my dreams of you.

In dreams I walk with you; in dreams I talk with you.
In dreams you're mine, all of the time ...

But just before the dawn, I awake and find you gone.
I can't help it, I can't help it, if I cry
I remember that you said goodbye...

-- Roy Orbison
"In Dreams"

Three

December 25, 2012

Merry Christmas, Becky --

It has been 15 years since you came into my life and we fell in love.

It has been 10 years since we last saw, or spoke to, one another.

I realize that hearing from me again after all this time must come as a total surprise -- if not a shock! -- to you, and I apologize for that.

To the extent possible, and from a distance, of course, I have kept up with and known where you have been living and what has been going on in your life -- generally, at least -- during all of these years. I am sure you can guess from whom I've learned these things. Julie and I speak on the phone regularly(every three or four months) -- although, regrettably, she and I have also not actually seen each other since just after you said "Goodbye" to me, and you and I parted for the final time.

When good ol' Jules and I speak, we always do so at considerable length and our conversations cover just about everything from soup to nuts. Our phone calls are never short ones. You know dear Julie as well as I. Short phone calls and Julie are twain that have never met.

When we speak, there is also a very predictable pattern to our conversations. We talk first about our children and what is new in their lives. (I'm sure that parents the world over do that in conversations with old friends. One's "kids," even in their 20s and 30s, are <u>still</u> one's kids, just as they were when in diapers and as they were when teenagers. How strange it is that those of us in our 50s, even, still refer to our grown children as "kids." We are parents forever; parenting <u>is</u> a forever proposition, a lifelong 'sentence' in a manner of speaking.)

Anyway, after, and only after, we have talked about the "kids," Julie and I then share with one another more personal and other news from our own lives.

Julie and Robert continue to be very happy together. I am sure you know that. Frankly, I am surprised -- pleasantly so, of course -- that things have turned out so well for them. I was more than a little dubious at first that they'd be able to work through the daunting obstacles they faced when they began to build their relationship. But they <u>did</u> work through them and they did it well. I can't profess that I yet know Robert all that well but I do know that Julie loves him deeply and that she deserves every bit of the joy and peace that are now a part of her life. I believe she and Robert were made for one another (as corny as that might sound).

[Rebecca smiled at the phrase Thomas had written -- "made for one another" -- and at his excuse for it as a cliché, and for having used it. She remembered well that Thomas did not like and tried not to employ clichés, in speech or in writing. "I hate cliché's," he'd smile. "I avoid 'em like the plague."]

Rebecca read on --

Julie and Robert are blessed in what they have found and continue to build together. I am sure they will be happy together for many more years. I sure hope so.

Thomas's letter continued --

In any case, as Julie and I speak and our conversation moves along its predictable, usual path -- all the while as she lavishly sprinkles in high praise of Robert -- we spend a few moments talking briefly about recent movies we've seen and books we've read. This never varies. I think Julie reads absolutely every book that finds its way to <u>The New York Times</u> *bestseller list, whether it is fiction or nonfiction, a biography, social commentary or self-help (especially self-help; she never misses one of those!)*

And, on top of all of that reading, she and Robert see more new movie releases every year than I've seen probably in the last ten years. These days, unlike when you and I were together, I am not much of a <u>cineaste.</u> *Do you remember* <u>that</u> *word -- cineaste -- which you "discovered" one day in something you were reading, and that we both liked so much and subsequently overused?*

(When you and I were together we used to go to the movies a lot, too, as Julie and Robert do, didn't we? I don't see very many movies these days because, like most men, I am uncomfortable going into a movie theater by myself. For some reason, women -- unlike men -- tend not to be quite as uncomfortable going to a movie by themselves. Conversely, men more so than women are less uncomfortable going to a restaurant for a meal alone. I'm not sure, either, why this is the case but I do think it is generally true, wouldn't you agree? As far as movies are concerned, these days I wait for those I am interested in seeing to become available on DVD and then I rent and watch them at home.)

And so, after Julie and I have covered the arts and letters and cinema segments of our conversation, two topics remain on what over the years has become our almost inviolable telephonic agenda. We speak, penultimately, about current events and rue the sadness and terrible tragedies that continually abound, and surround us each day, in this frightful and still so uncertain 9/11 world in which we live. It hardly seems possible that the Twin Towers/lower Manhattan massacre happened so long ago -- and served to set in motion the terrible ensuing chain of same-date horrific and tragic events.

Just Before The Dawn

The Afghanistan/Iraq war and America's calamitous commitment there has, finally, come to an end, if we can believe and count on President Obama's pledge to pull out <u>all</u> of our troops from those two countries by the end of this coming year.

The 9/11 date continues to haunt us, of course: in 2005 it was the Sears Tower tragedy in Chicago and just last year the Golden Gate Bridge decimation on the same date. Now we must hope and pray that our good fortune in escaping any such disastrous attack this year will at last signal an end to Islamic terrorism in America on the eleventh day of September.

We all have had enough of war, violence, genocide, poverty and starvation and terrorism in this sad, tragic world of the 21ˢᵗ century. Radical Islamic extremism (or, as they would say in Johnstown, "crazed, towel-headed Ay-rabs") and mankind's merciless onslaught on one another must end and a world in which fear is omnipresent must change.

Julie gets highly emotional and, not infrequently, will sob when we speak of the terrible multi-year 9/11 events. She lost a friend in New York in that attack and another in Chicago.

Ultimately, there is the proverbial pregnant pause in our conversation as we reach the point we always reach and <u>the</u> question I always ask before our conversation completes its standard, familiar course.

Julie knows full well the question is coming but, even so, she always seems slightly ill at ease and somewhat nonplussed when, at last, I do bring it up.

Come live in my heart and pay no rent.
-- *Samuel Lover, Irish poet, (1797 - 1868)* --

Four

Rebecca resumed reading Thomas's letter --

Julie knows full well the question is coming but, even so, she always seems slightly ill at ease and somewhat nonplussed when, at last, I do bring it up.

"And so, Jules," I'll say, "What do you hear these days from Becky?"

There follows at this juncture <u>another</u> very pregnant pause...

Julie's pregnant pauses are thinly disguised attempts to cut off or redirect or retreat from the conversational thrust.

*Julie is a good and loyal friend -- of mine **and** yours. She is exceedingly mindful, and always altogether respectful, of the friendship and the confidences that I assume the two of you share. I want you to know that Julie never **volunteers** information about you and what I do learn from her is almost always in response to a direct question and, then, I almost have to **drag** the answer or information out of her. Julie always responds to this first question I ask about you and others I subsequently raise hesitantly, very briefly and only in the most general terms. As a Washingtonian, Julie has learned well the art of the no-response response. "Becky's fine," she will say*

19

with that little lilting laugh that one hears in her voice when she is nervous, trying her best all the while to connote that there isn't much more she can add to that initial response, and hoping that I will leave things right there.

But she also knows, full well, that I will not let her off the hook quite that easily. I never do. I continue, "Are she and Bill well?"

"Are they still living in Mt. Roda?"

"Have they been traveling?"

"Have they been back to Washington recently?"

"Are her children well and doing OK?"

*And Julie will respond, "Everything is fine -- with her, Bill **and** the kids."*

And then comes the loaded question.

"Are she and Bill still doing well?"

*"Yes they are, Tom. They are doing well and they are **very** happy together."*

Julie tells me this regularly and I am glad, truly glad -- for you, Rebecca -- to hear that is the case.

I know from Julie that Bill is a good man and that he has been good to you and that the years the two of you have had together have been good and kind years. You deserve that, dear Becky.

*Sometimes I wonder how I'd react and what I'd say or do if Julie were to tell me the two of you were no longer together or, even, that you were **not** doing well.*

Rebecca paused, and reread this last sentence.

She gazed out the window, briefly, and then continued reading --

To be honest, I'd probably call you in the hopes of seeing whether we might be able to resurrect what you and I once had together.

Rebecca smiled once again. That particular phrase -- "To be honest" -- was another cliché, she remembered, that grated on and irritated Thomas. It and the word "frankly" would prompt the same response from Thomas. "No, please," he might say, caustically and sarcastically, but with a smile as if he were joking (which, she knew, he was not) when someone used either phrase or construct. "Don't be honest (or frank) with me. Please don't. I'd much rather you lie."

Again, Rebecca smiled when she recalled this frequently acerbic aspect of Thomas's personality. Political correctness and Thomas often clashed to the point, Becky thought, where Thomas would sometimes, occasionally, come across to others, quite understandably, as antisocial, if not rude.

But she also thought Tom **was** honest, with her and with himself. Yes, Tom was an honest man.

Thomas's letter continued --

I also wonder -- often -- whether <u>you</u> have ever asked Julie about <u>me.</u> That, however is <u>the</u> one question I have never raised with Julie. I am almost sure I know the answer and I fear, and really don't want to hear it said aloud.

I wonder, too, whether you have known somehow that, quite coincidentally, we have actually lived very close for many of the ten years since we last saw one another and still live close today.

[Rebecca did know this. Still, she could not keep from looking at the envelope in her lap to see the city in which it had been postmarked.]

Thomas's letter went on --

If indeed this letter has found its way to you and you are now reading it and have looked closely at the envelope in which it came, you will see from the postmark that we are separated, geographically, by not more than 100 miles, no more than a two hours' drive.

I write today, Rebecca, after having given much thought to whether it is right and proper to enter your life once again, and to do so in this way. If it is wrong, I am sorry and apologize for that -- but in my heart I do not think it <u>is</u> wrong and in my heart I know it is <u>something I must do.</u>

21

Where to begin?

When you and I last spoke, ten years ago, I said I loved you and always would. That is as true today as it was then. I love you, Becky. You must know how strongly I feel that love, all love, is not ephemeral. It just <u>can't</u> be. It is -- <u>must be</u> -- forever. If it is not forever, it is something other than real love -- infatuation? sexual/ physical desire? Becky, I write today to underscore that I love you still and will love you forever.

Not a day has gone by in the nearly four thousand days since I last held you in my arms that I have not thought of you with warmth, tenderness and love.

*I feel about you as Thomas Wolfe felt when he wrote the following to Aline Bernstein, the love of **his** life --*

"I shall love you all the days of my life, and when I die, if they cut me open they will find one name written on my brain and on my heart. It will be yours. I have spoken the living truth here, and I sign my name for anyone to see."

-- Tom Wolfe

There have been so many people whom I've met and known casually, people who have come in and out of my life since you and I parted, dear Becky. I speak not of lovers but of the variety of people all of us encounter regularly in our lives' quotidian activities. Some I've met over the past ten years have become friends, some very good friends.

One -- and only one -- of all of those we meet and know in our lives becomes a "best friend," however. All of us have a -- <u>one</u> -- best friend, and only one. Most of those we meet and encounter never become anything more than acquaintances.

So many, many people enter our lives during our three score and ten years on this good earth. By far, the <u>great majority</u> of them come -- then quickly go. Some few, very few, stay and leave a permanent *mark on our lives and we are never, ever the same.*

You, dear Becky, did that to me. You made a mark on my life, and it remains and I am not the same man I was before I met you.

I think of you and ask myself how can **one** *face in my life and memory be so cherished and treasured? How can one* **voice** *be so lasting, one soul so special?*

I write to tell you all this and I write to tell you one other thing, too. It is something that I want you to hear about from me, if only impersonally, through this letter.

The other thing I want to tell you, that I want you to hear directly from me, through this letter because I cannot -- as much as I want to -- tell it to you face-to-face, is why I write today. It is important to me that you know. Telling you makes it more real, and I feel, truly, that you would want to know. This other thing that I have to tell you is the second most striking thing that has happened to me in my five-plus decades on this good earth, second, that is, to meeting and falling in love with you. I am amazed and still in awe (It is still so very fresh) that it is to become such a new and, hopefully, all-consuming and overwhelming part of my existence from now on.

But before I tell you what that *is, I must say one more thing about our love or, more accurately, my love for you --*

Do you remember the last day we saw and were with one another? I do. It is with me still. It remains part of my abiding conscious-ness, a part of my very being. I have not forgotten. I cannot forget that day.

You knew when we parted that day, that sunny afternoon in Georgetown that our good-byes were final, that they were to be forever. You knew that -- but I did not, and I would not know it until much, much later.

Rebecca thought back to that early fall brisk day. She and Thomas kissed as they parted on upper "M" Street in the fash-ionable Georgetown section of the District of Columbia, and she indeed did feel if not actually know that she would not see Thomas again. She and William were seeing one another for dinner that very evening and in fact had plans for a weekend together away from Washington in the near future.

Even so, when she kissed Thomas that day she felt something that she did not feel with William and had never felt either with Arthur during their courtship and all their years of marriage. The relationship which she and Thomas had shared during their brief, shining moment was rich, sexual and very,very sensuous. Thomas had awakened in Rebecca depths of sexuality that she had never known before, and that she reveled in when the two of them made love.

Rebecca remembered --

I kneel before your perfect body...

Five

Thomas had awakened in Rebecca depths of sexuality that she had never known before and that she reveled in when the two of them made love, and long afterward.

Rebecca remembered --

I kneel before your perfect body.

Rebecca remembered.

Often Thomas would say that to her: "I kneel before your perfect body." She remembered.

As Thomas knelt before her, as she lay on Thomas's bed (They almost always made love when she was at his place or, of course, when they occasionally traveled together, even before she and Arthur were finally divorced. Thomas had always felt uncomfortable, as had she, making love at her house in Bethesda, until after the divorce from Arthur had become final and Arthur had moved out all of his belongings and found a place of his own in the District.)

Rebecca remembered.

As Thomas knelt before her, Rebecca relaxed, feeling desirable in a womanly way that Arthur had never managed to stimulate in her. She sank into the large king-size bed, on her back, her legs akimbo.

Rebecca remembered.

Thomas would kiss her, lightly, tenderly, first on her mouth, and then on her forehead, next on her cheeks, on her closed eyes and then her mouth again. In this way he "tasted" her lips. He tantalizingly parted them with his tongue while slowly flicking it from side to side, giving her a promise that in mere moments his mouth, lips and tongue would visit other parts of her body. All the while he would caress her face and forehead with the fingertips of one hand and, very gently, with the other hand, the flat of his palm.

"I adore you," he would say to her as their lovemaking began.

Rebecca remembered.

You are so beautiful.

Rebecca did not recall Arthur ever telling her that she was "beautiful." Nor did William, now, say it very often, if at all.

Thomas once had written to Rebecca --

"You are so beautiful. And your body is so beautiful -- and so desirable. I adore you. I love the almond-golden color of your skin. I love your perfectly shaped breasts and your dark, hard nipples. I love your beautiful, perfectly shaped legs, the silky smoothness of your thighs. I love your tiny, beautiful, graceful hands. I love your smooth, silky hair -- all of your hair everywhere on your body, <u>everywhere</u> on your body. I love your body. <u>I love every inch of you, dear Becky,</u>

my Precious Little Petal. I love every inch of you. Yes I do."

Rebecca had been an athlete, a runner and tennis player, when younger and had also been a dancer (she had in fact auditioned with the Joffrey Ballet) as a young adult and she did, indeed, have shapely well-toned legs and was aware that men found them attractive. They were perhaps her most feminine and appealing physical feature. She often wore short skirts and heels to accentuate and show off her legs.

Rebecca remembered --

Thomas's lovemaking was slow, gentle, tender and giving. She felt the love in his fingertips and in the look on his face as he knelt before her and caressed her body.

Rebecca remembered --

I kneel before your perfect body.

Thomas's hands moved slowly, tantalizingly, very lightly to her breasts. He stimulated her nipples, using both hands, gently squeezing each nipple between thumb and forefinger. The nipples would become hardened and erect and he leant forward now to take each, in turn, into his mouth to suck.

As he sucked her nipples, his hands would move now, slowly to her midsection and gently caress the soft skin of her tanned, firm, youthful abdomen.

Next, his fingertips, slowly, tentatively, would move to and caress, touch and tease her at the uppermost edge of her pubic hairline.

Rebecca remembered --

Often Thomas would with his thumb and forefinger lightly grasp and hold two or three pubic hairs, gently pull-ing on and teasing them, and her. With the palm and flat of both hands then, he would caress her hips, slowly, and with just the tips of his fingers, touch and caressingly circle each of her trembling thighs.

Rebecca's breathing would quicken. She would begin gyrating, moving her hips and belly seductively, waiting for and silently begging him with her body's undulating upward movement to touch and fondle -- and kiss – the very essence of her womanhood; the apex of her physical being.

Thomas did not rush. He was a considerate lover, a wonderful lover, more interested in her gratification and satisfaction, seemingly, than his own.

Rebecca remembered --

Thomas never rushed during their lovemaking. His lovemaking was slow and deliberate.

Rebecca remembered --

Once, when she asked him about this, he replied, "Why would I *want* to hurry? I like what I'm doing so much that I don't *want* it to end -- and I absolutely *adore* your gorgeous body so much -- that I want what I'm doing to last, for as long as it and I, (he would smile as he said 'I') can last."

Rebecca remembered --

Thomas did not rush. He and his lovemaking with Rebecca were slow and deliberate. (Rebecca had never known that type of sensuousness -- certainly   not in her marriage, with Arthur, nor was it a part of the physical relationship she and Bill shared now. Bill, bless him, was direct and quick, seemingly most intent on his own rather than her gratification.) Slam, bam, thank you ma'am.

Rebecca remembered --

Thomas did not rush. Now he placed his hand on her mons and caressed her there slowly and softly with that sensuously circular motion.

(Rebecca stared into Thomas's eyes as he touched and caressed her and he looked up, gazing at her face. She saw and felt his love – a love and desire, which seemed to radiate from him, to her.)

"I love you," he whispered. "... my precious little petal."

Thomas knelt once again and lowered his face and head to her. He kissed her and began slowly stroking and caressing her with his tongue. At the same time, he inserted his middle finger, very slowly, into her vaginal opening.

Rebecca remembered --

Thomas stirred her desire and pleasure.

He had once referred to himself with a smile on his face, entirely for Rebecca's pleasure, as her 'fuckface' and her 'cunning linguist.'

Rebecca remembered.

She and he laughed more often, with healthy abandon, and with greater glee than she had ever laughed during the act of making love   -- with anyone.

Rebecca remembered.

Rebecca began to move her body more insistently as Thomas moved his tongue correspondingly more insistently as well and then found with his tongue, within her vulva, her clitoris. He titillated Rebecca and her highly aroused senses with his tongue moving quickly at first, then slowly, then quickly again as it darted from side to side and up and down, and round, the now hardened, tiny, pink protuberance.

At the same time his middle finger, then his forefinger also, moved in and out, in and out.

Slowly, slowly, the climax would build...to repeated, multiple orgastic ecstasy and release.

Rebecca remembered --

Rebecca remembered --

Fully aroused now and wet with desire, Rebecca returned to Thomas's letter.

She took a deep breath and thumbed through the pages of the material to find the point in the letter where she had stopped reading a few moments earlier before engaging in her memories and the fantasy of Thomas's lovemaking.

Before resuming, Rebecca placed her right hand into the waistband of her jeans and lowered it to feel herself -- confirming that she was, indeed, wet.

Then she began reading where she had left off moments ago.

I write today, Becky, to underscore once more that I love you and will love you forever.

Not one day has gone by of the nearly four thousand days since I last held you in my arms that I have not thought of you with warmth and with great love.

"I shall love you all the days of my life, and when I die, if they cut me open they will find one name written on my brain and on my heart. It will be yours. I have spoken the living truth here..."

Hearing a car outside, Rebecca pulled herself together and realized William had pulled into the driveway, finished with his last-minute Christmas errands.

She quickly straightened the pages of Thomas's letter, replacing them in their envelope and tucked the package under the seat cushion of her chair.

Six

Great passion had <u>not</u> been a part of her 17-years marriage to Arthur Halsey, ever, not during the early years or even their courtship. Nor was it or had it been part of her relationship and current marriage to William Winslow. On the other hand her relationship with Thomas had been passionate, unquestionably so. Theirs had been a relationship of highly charged sexuality unlike any she had ever experienced.

William walked in the front door just after Rebecca had placed the material from Thomas under the seat cushion of the Queen Anne chair in which she still sat.

"Get all your chores done?" she asked.

"Yup," said William. "And what have you been doing while I was out?"

"Oh, nothing, really," Rebecca replied -- too quickly, she thought. "Just some cleaning and a few little surprises for Christmas," she lied. She got up and went to give William a kiss on the cheek.

Rebecca realized anew how wet she was in the crotch. And she wondered why she felt she must lie in response to William's question about what she had been doing while he was out -- and why she could not or did not want to tell him about the letter from Thomas.

Seven

Thomas and Rebecca had met at the golf course, through mutual friends -- Pamela and Jack Morrissey.

It was a late summer day, overcast and with more than a strong hint of fall in the air, when Thomas met his friends the Morrisseys at the Bethesda Tournament Players Golf and Country Club in a Maryland suburban community just outside of Washington, DC.

Thomas joined Pamela and Jack, as planned, in the Golf Pro Shop to sign in for their round 30 minutes or so before their scheduled time at the first tee.

Thomas was not much of a golfer. Jack was marginally better, but Pamela was quite accomplished. She had been the women's club champion at Bethesda for the past three years. As the daughter of a club professional in her native Georgia, she had played since the age of 10 or 11. She was a six handicap. Jack's handicap was eighteen and Thomas had never actually acquired or registered an official handicap though if he had it would no doubt have been in the high 20s or might even break into the 30s.

Each of the three picked up a bucket of balls and headed

to the practice tee/driving range area to hit a few shots and to warm up for their round. The three were assigned two electric golf carts. Their golf bags and clubs were already strapped on and they drove off to the practice tee.

Ten minutes before their scheduled tee time, they left the driving range and drove to the nearby first tee. Adjacent to that tee was a practice putting green and here they stroked a dozen or more putts before their names were called over the loudspeaker to the first tee to begin their round.

As they arrived at the tee, Rebecca Halsey drove up in a cart of her own. She apologized loudly and profusely, laughing nervously, then apologizing again for being "so, so late."

Rebecca and Pamela were close friends and often golfed either together or in groups with other women at the Bethesda TPC.

As Rebecca continued to apologize for being "so late," Pamela uttered exasperatedly to Jack and well within earshot of Thomas, "So she's late -- what else is new?"

To Thomas, Rebecca seemed delightful -- and very, very attractive. Smallish, not much more than an inch or two over five feet, and she could not have weighed more than 100 pounds soaking wet. She had the most engaging, beautifully charismatic smile -- and he also noticed her extraordinarily shapely legs. He was also struck with -- and liked -- the soft, melodic sound of her sweet voice.

Rebecca, perhaps sensing Pamela's scarcely hidden disdain, and to change the subject, asked with an impish grin whether they had heard the "latest President Clinton joke."

Jack, ever the affable peacemaker, was quick to respond, as Pamela said nothing. Jack said he hadn't heard the latest Clinton joke, and asked Rebecca to "tell it to us."

Rebecca, with the vivacity and charm of a stage actress, regaled them --

"Well," she reported, "it was on the news a little while ago that the President had just returned to Washington last night from a brief trip to his native Arkansas. After deplaning from

Air Force One at Andrews Air Base, Mr. Clinton had his arms full as he walked slowly and carefully down the steps from the Presidential plane. Under each arm he carried a large, squirming pig.

"The Marine Honor Guardsman smartly saluted the president and asked: 'Are those *Arkansas* hogs, Sir?'

"The President, with his arms full, could not return the Honor Guardsman's salute, but responded: 'They sure are, Corporal, genuine Arkansas Razorbacks. That's what we call 'em in Arkansas -- razorbacks. I got one for Hillary and one for Chelsea!'

"The marine responded: 'Excellent trade, Sir, excellent!'"

Thomas had not heard the joke, nor had Jack, and both now roared appreciatively.

The four teed off and it quickly became obvious that Rebecca, like Pamela, was an accomplished golfer.

(Pamela as the current Bethesda Tournament Players Club women's champion had won the first of her three consecutive titles by defeating and wresting the championship mantle from Rebecca).

Pamela and Rebecca hit their tee shots before Jack and Thomas. The first hole at Bethesda TPC was a 375-yards par 4, from an elevated tee, with a slight dogleg to the right. There were trees and high rough patches down the right side, so most golfers tried to favor the left center of the fairway rather than risk potential trouble by cutting the dog leg. A shot too far left, however, would find a waste area and deep sand trap which made the next shot, the approach shot into the green, uncertain at best.

Pamela's tee shot was deep and perfectly placed. Her tee

shot had a pro-like bend, right to left. Today she was 245 yards off the tee, with just a solid 8-iron left to the green. Her swing was picture-pretty, as one sees on television when watching tour-event professional golf tournaments. Rebecca hit next. Her swing, like Pamela's, was practiced and fluid though her ball flight was straighter without the distance-adding slight hook/draw. It also was not as powerful as Pamela's and finished in the left center of the fairway, probably just over 200 yards out. Thomas, not much of a golfer himself, was impressed nonetheless. It was quite obvious to him that Rebecca was an accomplished golfer despite her diminutive size.

Jack hit next and his shot ended in the fairway, after getting a good fairway roll, near Rebecca's. Thomas was last to hit and, like many golfers on the first tee, he felt somewhat nervous and tense. His shot sliced (as his tee shot normally did) and wound up in the rough on the right-hand side of the fairway, and not very deep. He was not more than 170-175 yards off the tee, the shortest of the group, which would, ultimately, prove to be the case all day, with one or two exceptions. It took Thomas three more shots to get to the green (two of them hacking out of the rough to get back to the short grass). On the green, he needed two putts, for a double bogey six. Jack three-putted for a bogey; Pamela and Rebecca each two-putted for a par.

BTPC's second hole, a 529-yards par five, also proved manageable for the two women, each scoring another par. Jack picked up his second consecutive bogey and Thomas needed to drain a long putt (of 35 feet) to manage a bogey as well.

On the third hole, a 204-yards par three from an elevated tee, everyone but Thomas hit the green, but he scrambled with a good up-and-down and joined the other three in registering a par.

Thomas kept stealing glances at Rebecca all the while. He noticed her petite, desirable femininity, especially her shapely legs. He also noted, (with a silent assent to the chauvinism of this observation) that her breasts appeared to be smallish. He mentioned to Jack that he thought Rebecca attractive but then whispered lasciviously, as a male-to-male joke, that "her tits are kinda small." Pamela was comparatively big-breasted and Jack whispered to Thomas that *he,* Jack, was a "leg man." It brought to mind for Thomas the line he had heard on an episode of the popular network comedy show "Seinfeld" a few years earlier. In similar circumstances, the Seinfeld character remarked, "*Legs!* Why would I be a *leg* man? I *have* legs."

Thomas recalled a character played by Steve Martin in a Hollywood movie once said, "I could never be a woman. I'd just stay around the house all day every day playing with my breasts."

Thomas was, unabashedly, a "tit man."

(Thomas's former wife Ellen had railed against the typical male tendency to ogle a woman's chest immediately upon meeting her. Among the many, many things that regularly irritated Ellen was the male resistance to first examine a woman's face and look into her eyes. Thomas had told Ellen the only thing most men noticed about a woman's eyes was whether or not she had two of them. This was one of Ellen's rants and raves with which Thomas reluctantly agreed. Most males *are* tit men, he conceded, and *do* look first at a woman's chest before they look at or into her eyes.)

Thomas would say to her, "Ellen, there has *always* been a war between the sexes," -- then to piss her off, he would add, "…and do you know that it will never be won, by either side. Do you know why? There is just too much fraternization with the enemy." Ellen refused to take this at face value, as a joke. Quite often, everything Thomas said pissed Ellen off.

The weather worsened as the round of golf went on. Intermittent sprinkles dampened the course but it wasn't long
before a steady rain set in and the temperature dropped.
Everyone was getting a bit chilled and by mutual agreement
the round was called after the 9th hole -- known by most of
BTPC's club members as the hole in all of golf that professional star Greg Norman disliked most. Norman once said
he thought the hole should be "blown up." BTPC had been
the site for several years of the PGA's Kemper Open. The
tour came to the Washington area annually for two tour tournaments -- the Kemper and an event at the famed Congressional Golf and Country Club, nearby the BTPC in Avenel in
Virginia. Congressional had in fact over the years been the
venue for two or three of the PGA's "major" tournaments,
always a mark of honor and distinction for any local golf
club.

BTPC's 9th hole (the one Norman thought should be blown
up) was a short 149-yards par three, from a highly elevated
tee. It played some 20 yards longer when the pin was in the
back of the green. The green was long and not very wide and
had water front, back and on its right. For a pro, it was a
controlled sand wedge shot at best. Club members, depending on their skill level, would hit anything from a pitching
wedge to a half 8-iron. Even Thomas, not a long hitter at all,
typically used a 9-iron on the hole. During a Kemper tournament Norman found the water on three of the tourney's four
days, registering three double bogeys. On the one day he hit
the green he went deep to a front-tee placement and wound
up three putting for a bogey. The green slanted severely from
left to right toward the water in that direction, as was the case
with a front to back slant toward water at the back of the deep,
oblong putting surface. For members, if the pin was in the
back, the hole played as long as 170 yards.

"That hole should be destroyed - blown up, obliterated,"
Norman said to *the Washington Post* golf beat writer the Sunday
evening after the tournament ended in which he doubled the

hole three times and bogeyed it once. The Golden Boy Aussie never returned to play the Kemper in the years following when it was still held at the Bethesda TPC.

On this particular day, Pamela and Rebecca far outplayed Jack and Thomas as their round ended with just nine holes, stopping at Mr. Norman's nemesis. Pamela shot a four-over par 40, Rebecca a stroke behind at 41. Jack shot a 46 and Thomas brought up the rear at 53, though he *did* par the ninth hole.

The four adjourned to the "19th hole," even though they had only played nine, for a snack and drink. It was *still* the 19th hole. Thomas was even more taken with Rebecca at this point. Throughout the round of golf, he had noticed her smile -- bright and wide and, he thought again, the woman *does* have great legs! Thomas had also fallen for Rebecca's voice. He thought it melodic, tuneful, beautiful, lilting, gentle, enchanting, sweet, and very, very feminine.

As the four sat enjoying a beer, Rebecca announced that she had to be going, that she was leaving Bethesda later that day on a trip to Austin. Thomas was disappointed when he heard this. He thought of a line from a Rod Stewart love song "You said 'Hello,' I noticed, then you said 'Goodbye' too soon."

After Rebecca had taken her leave, Pamela and Jack told Thomas a little about her. She and her husband Arthur had moved to Bethesda a little over two years ago from Austin (where Rebecca said she was going that evening). The eldest of their three children still lived in Austin. Two younger children had moved to Bethesda with their parents. Rebecca and Arthur, also a golfer, though not as accomplished as his wife, joined the Bethesda TPC shortly after their arrival in the Washington area and that was where Pamela met Rebecca -- on the golf course. Later, Pamela and Jack met Arthur and, they both confessed to Thomas, did not find him as engaging a personality or as social, friendly or affable as Rebecca. Jack said they actually found Arthur rather dour -- to which the ever-honest Pamela added, "Whatever the hell *that* means." Pamela said she considered Arthur "uppity," superior and "kinda stuck up -- *and* pretty much stuck on himself."

"For no good reason, either, as far as I can see," she added.

Pamela and Rebecca had become close through golfing together, and a solid friendship sans golf then began to develop. Pamela respected and admired Rebecca's golfing prowess and Rebecca did, indeed, win the club women's championship during her first year in Bethesda -- a championship Pamela took the very next year and had successfully defended for two consecutive years.

Jack asked Pamela whether she had talked with Rebecca recently about the marital problems she and Arthur were having. Thomas was surprised to hear that, and Pamela appeared somewhat agitated that Jack had raised the subject. Pamela explained to Thomas that Rebecca had said she and Arthur were considering a divorce. Rebecca had learned that Arthur had a mistress -- an old girlfriend whom he knew before he and Rebecca were wed. Rebecca learned about Arthur's affair when she overheard he and his paramour speaking on the phone during a visit to their native homes in Ohio to visit Rebecca's parents. As is the case with any spouse who learns her or his mate has been unfaithful, Rebecca was terribly hurt -- and then angered. Pamela said that although Rebecca and Arthur were living under the same roof, they were sleeping in different bedrooms, and that had been the state of affairs for several months. Rebecca was devastated when she learned about the infidelity, Pamela continued, ("Who wouldn't be?"), and frequently would break down in tears, over coffee, shopping or even on the golf course with Pamela or other friends. Rebecca felt betrayed and alone and, of course, the situation was complicated by the concurrent move from Texas to a new home in Maryland.

Thomas was saddened, for Rebecca's sake, to hear of her personal situation and its attendant distress. He had gone through a painful and emotional divorce himself just a few years earlier. He and Ellen had been married 18 years, had three children (as did Rebecca and Arthur), and also had lived for a period under the same roof but in different bedrooms -- and so he knew very well how uncomfortable a situation *that* was. Thomas had been transferred by his employer to Washington four years ago, after he and Ellen had been separated for three years -- and one year before their divorce had become final.

Thomas got Rebecca's last name and phone number from Pamela and called a few days later while she was still out of town. He left a message, asking if she'd be interested in having dinner with him when she returned from Texas.

He and the Morriseys parted that afternoon and that night Thomas could not get persistent thoughts of Rebecca out of his mind. She was cute and she was beautiful, energetic and intelligent, but seemed so, so sad. He also could not erase the so vivid memories of her voice, the most beautiful voice he'd ever heard, a voice drifting above, filled with the most beautiful music ever sounded.

Her voice... her voice... her voice.

Rebecca... Rebecca... Rebecca...

Thomas remembered.

Eight

Thomas, Ellen and their daughters had lived in Westchester County, just north of New York City. When they finally decided to part, after *their* separate bedrooms existence in their family home, it was Thomas who moved out -- to a small apartment in Mamaroneck, a few minutes' drive from his office in Darien, Connecticut.

Within a few weeks he was served, compliments of Ellen, with a Divorce Court summons from a uniformed Sheriff's Office representative. Thomas was stunned. He had not expected that, or at least not quite so soon after he and Ellen actually separated and he'd established a separate domicile.

Then, and years later, Thomas could never quite fathom why Ellen wanted and decided so quickly to initiate the action. He thought their marriage was reasonably solid, or, at least comfortable and as solid as most marriages seemed on the surface. They did share a strong love for and devotion to their daughters. Then and even later as the years rolled on, Thomas never felt certain that he knew or understood why the marriage failed. There was certainly no infidelity on his side in the marriage, nor did he suspect there was any on

Ellen's. He knew that Ellen felt under-appreciated in devoting herself to Thomas's career over the years, and felt stifled at the same time in pursuing a career of her own. But divorce? It had never entered Thomas's mind and he was mystified that day when his secretary told him a sheriff's deputy was on the phone and wanted to talk with him about "an urgent matter."

Thomas took the call and asked the deputy if they could meet at a mutually agreeable location in the community instead of in Thomas's office. They agreed to meet in front of the Post Office. (Thomas had no idea what this business might be, but he certainly didn't want to risk wild speculation in his office should the situation seem suspicious to the gossip brigade that exists in most office environments.)

The two met a few minutes later in front of the Darien Post Office. Thomas was flabbergasted when he opened the envelope, and gave the required signature to acknowledge formal receipt in shocked disbelief. It was a summons to appear in Court and respond to a divorce petition against him filed by Ellen.

Thomas cried that evening. Many years later he reflected that it was one of only three times in his life that he *had* cried…as an adult.

●●●●●●●

The very next day after being served the summons, Thomas made an appointment with a divorce attorney, whose name he picked out of the telephone book yellow pages. She and Ellen's attorney began negotiating soon thereafter and within a few weeks proposed to Thomas and Ellen that they try counseling in an effort to save their marriage. The couple agreed to that proposal and met jointly with the counselor regularly for more than six months. Ellen also met with a psychotherapist during the same period to work through some painfully tragic issues she had struggled with over the years; things that went back to her early childhood.

Not quite two years later, Thomas suspected that Ellen was very unhappy and was again considering divorce. While at the office on a rainy Friday, Thomas's secretary advised him that "another Sheriff's deputy is on the phone" and wanted to speak with him and meet in the office. Thomas took the call. He knew the procedure this time and asked the deputy, solicitously, if they could meet somewhere other than his office for privacy's sake. It could be nearby, perhaps in front of a downtown newsstand. The deputy agreed and ten minutes later they went through the same process they had in front of the post office nearly two years earlier. Coincidentally, it was the same summons server. Thomas asked, "Do you remember me?" The deputy looked closely at Thomas but it was obvious the man needed his memory refreshed. Thomas added, "A couple of years ago, in front of the post office."

"Oh yeah, now I *do* remember," said the deputy. "Cheeses, is this *another* woman?" he asked.

Thomas couldn't help smiling. "No," Thomas replied, ruefully, "same woman, second time around."

The deputy seemed nonplussed and had nothing further to say. He pointed out where Thomas needed to sign and their business was done.

That night Thomas did not cry. He remembered crying two years earlier. This night he felt saddened but his emotions did not produce tears; rather, there was a feeling of relief. Thomas did not want to get divorced and had made that point over and over with Ellen and their Counselor as well as to Ellen's attorney and his own attorney.

But now he was resigned that there was no other way, no going back. His 18-years marriage to Ellen was over and a divorce was obviously inevitable and unavoidable.

"Who'll Stop The Rain"
-- Creedence Clearwater Revival --

Nine

When his employer offered him a transfer to Washington, Thomas jumped at the opportunity. The small rented room he'd been living in for nearly a year while he and his wife's attorneys were finalizing the terms of the divorce was depressing. It was in the basement of a home, an older house, owned by an elderly couple. It was dank and dark. In Thomas's small, cramped room, there was no window to the outside. Thomas referred to it as 'The Cave.' (The home from which Thomas had moved and where Ellen remained was huge -- 6800 square feet). The only 'plus' Thomas could find with The Cave was its proximity -- just a few miles -- to his office. Thomas was spending more time than ever at the office these days.

Thomas had started jogging a few years earlier and had worked up to the point where he'd begun running marathons. He jogged almost every day, rarely missing one, even in bad weather or when he traveled, which he did on business, quite often. Preparing for a business trip, the first things he'd place in his suitcase were jogging shoes, shorts and shirt.

Thomas's first full 26.2 miles race was the New York City Marathon, shortly before his 35th birthday. He subsequently ran the NYC event three more years and also ran other marathons -- in Philadelphia, San Francisco, Long Island, New Jersey and Myrtle Beach. Over the years, he'd also run the London, Dublin, Berlin and Athens marathons. He thought about but never actually did run an 'ultra' marathon, a race longer than 26.2 miles. As a runner he was not particularly fast but he *was* dogged and determined. Now he would tell friends, as his per-mile pace over the years continued to slow to the 9:00 - 9:15 range, "Hell, that's OK. I wasn't fast even when I was fast." Thomas's best marathon time, or PR (as runners referred to their 'Personal Record') was 3 hours, 42 minutes, 23 seconds.

Thomas met many other runners over the years, male and female. He generally found them non-pretentious, engaging and easy to know. He especially liked after-race gatherings -- "a lot of thin people who aren't smokers." Thomas had smoked as a younger man but now found the habit and its odor offensive.

Especially in Washington, some of the other runners Thomas got to know occasionally asked him to run with them, but Thomas preferred running alone. He'd always been solitary, a loner type and as a runner so he remained. Running with others you were compelled to either slow or quicken your own comfortable pace to stay with the other(s). Thomas preferred to run his own pace, *at his own pace,* some days a little slower than usual and sometimes a little faster -- but always, *his* pace depending on how he felt that particular day. Thomas saw running as a solitary activity. He had thought of it that way almost from the day he first jogged a tentative few hundred yards. He tended to be a loner in almost all of his activities. He had in fact felt alone all of his life, from the time he was growing up in upstate New York, throughout his marriage and to this day. He had become accustomed to his existence of isolation, solitude and aloneness.

Thomas had experienced the complete panoply of aches, pains and assorted physical problems that all runners do when they take up the activity and go beyond a short daily jog to long distance running -- knee pain, back pain, muscle pulls and strains, shin splints -- and, as most runners know, occasional ennui. "I just don't feel like hacking it today."

One of Thomas's lingering and most troublesome problems -- not uncommon to many, many runners -- was knee pain.

Thomas had served as an enlisted man in the Army during the Vietnam War. He had decided after his first two years of college to eschew waiting for the draft and joined up instead. He served for a brief period in West Germany and then volunteered for a tour of duty in America's unpopular war in Vietnam. Thomas had learned early in his basic training that he was an extraordinarily accurate rifleman, despite never having even *used* a firearm of any type before entering the Army.

[Thomas initially realized and the U.S. Army learned of his unerring rifleman's accuracy during, first, his basic training at Ft. Leonard Wood, MO., and then, later, during Advanced Infantry Training (AIT), at the same military installation. One day, at the rifle range, the range D.I. stood behind Thomas as he fired his M-16 rifle at the targets 150 - 200 yards afield. Drill Instructor Sergeant First Class Michael Scharf exhaled a slow whistling sound. "Son," he said, "looks to me like you could pick off a nit on a gnat's nut." Sgt. Scharf paused and added "at ninety yards..." And then, caught up in a self-induced paroxysm of alliteration tacked on, "...at night!"

"Sir, yes sir!" exhorted Pvt. (E-1) Gorman, as recruits were schooled and required to respond to anyone of a higher rank (which for a recruit, was, basically, everyone in the Army except their fellow recruits). The response was to be deferential and agreeable and was to both begin and end with the declarative and respectful "Sir."

In the end Thomas did respect Sgt. Scharf and never forgot his alliterative tendencies or his pithiness. Thomas remembered once, when addressing his newest class of AIT recruits, Scharf bellowed --

"Some of you sorry-ass troopers already like me and most of you don't. Some of you probably hate my guts. Well, you maggots who don't like me are better off -- because let me tell you this: likin' leads to lovin'... and lovin' leads to fuckin' -- and they ain't none of you here *ever* gonna fuck me!"]

In Vietnam, Thomas was detached on a temporary duty assignment to a Special Forces battalion and served in that unit as a crack sniper. Because of his special skill as a marksman and its high value in the unit to which he was assigned, full Special Forces training was waived for Thomas but he *did* have to qualify as airborne. He jumped military/Army-style -- static line from 3000-feet or lower, where the parachutist is actually tethered to the plane and his chute is pulled open automatically when the tether line becomes fully extended. Years later as a civilian in Washington, Thomas took up free-fall skydiving -- from 12,000 feet.

In Nam, Thomas was wounded twice, and at the end of his assignment was awarded the military honor of a Bronze Star "for meritorious service and great valor in the face of the enemy...disregarding his own safety to rescue two of his fallen and wounded comrades..." Thomas spent most of his "in country" tour in Vietnam's Central Highlands, the home of a variety of indigenous ethnic groups, particularly the Montagnards, or mountain people. Often in the Highlands the Montagnards fought alongside American forces and, because of Thomas's expertise, they trusted and admired him and he trusted them to act as guides to the best vantage points from which to execute his great skill on the enemy as a sniper.

In the Highlands, the rainy season began in early Spring and ran for six months or more. Thomas had three overriding memories from his 13-month tour in country (399 days and a wake-up of heightened nervous tension; in Nam, one's

emotions ranged from an insouciant "I don't give a shit" attitude, fueled largely by bravado, to a fear that at times would
result not so much in a 'I don't give a shit posture' but, rather,
'I think I'm gonna shit.') Thomas said years later, "At some
point or other I was scared pretty much every day -- and I'm
not ashamed to admit it." His second overriding memory
from Vietnam was, "My feet were wet pretty much for all
thirteen months." Thomas, as did many of his fellow troopers,
became quite adept at removing leeches from his body; they
were found mostly on the legs. The leeches were omnipresent in the marshes of the Highlands, it seemed. However, *the*
overriding concern and attitude of most of the men Thomas
served with, even the Montagnards, was to not show coward-
ice or fear in front of one's buddies -- and, even more than
that, to not ever let one's buddies down.

Thomas's Bronze Star, awarded under "The President of
the United States' Executive Order 11046," remained in the
bottom of a dresser drawer. No one else had ever seen it, not
Ellen or his daughters, not Paddy, not Rebecca. Olivia was
the *only* person he had ever even *mentioned* it to. No one else
knew that he'd even served in Vietnam; his family was under
the impression that his entire Army stint after basic and AIT
had been in Germany. And no one save Olivia knew he had
been awarded one of the military's highest honors for courage and bravery in combat in the face of enemy fire. Thomas
had no idea what had happened to his two Purple Hearts.

(Thomas's other Vietnam abiding memory was the pop
song "Who'll Stop the Rain" by the group Creedence Clearwater Revival. He would learn after returning from Vietnam that
the song had actually been written and performed in America
during the Southeast Asia conflict as a war protest song. In
the Central Highlands where one heard it played often on
the Armed Forces Radio network, it had quite another, very
literal meaning.)

One of the two combat wounds Thomas suffered came
from a grenade which caused extensive shrapnel damage to

his right leg. He'd been on patrol with half-dozen Americans when a woman villager threw the grenade into their midst. One never knew for sure who the enemy was in Vietnam, as was the case during America's later military forays in Afghanistan and Iraq. The old woman reached into a pocket beneath her skirt, pulled out a grenade, pulled the pin and tossed it underhanded at Thomas's patrol.

His leg often gave him trouble and, as a result, in his marathoning years, he felt it slowed his running pace measurably.

Thomas found that most runners, not only in Washington but in other places he and Ellen had lived or to which Thomas had traveled on business, were early morning devotees. Thomas preferred to run in the late afternoon or early evening. Thomas's brother -- Patrick (Paddy) -- would say: "Run in the morning!? Hell, no. Can't do it. Shit, man I don't even finish *throwing up* until nearly noon." Paddy was Thomas's best friend 'on the planet.'

Paddy was two years younger than Thomas. He was intellectually gifted with a quick wit and a razor-sharp and highly irreverent sense of humor. Paddy, too, had joined the Army during Vietnam and he, too, had served in Germany, where he met his first wife, a Dane living and working in Heidelberg. That marriage would prove to be short-lived and Paddy later met and married another Scandinavian, this time a Swede. His second marriage also ended within a few years. In their adult years Paddy and Thomas spoke on the phone regularly and Thomas knew Patrick as a dependable, rock-solid friend and confidante. Thomas never mentioned his Vietnam experiences (as frightful and distasteful as those memories sometimes were to him) to Paddy or his children or, even Ellen, or any of his subsequent lovers after he and Ellen were divorced. The one exception was Olivia. Thomas kept that part of his life strictly to himself. Vietnam was over and done with and lived, for him, only in the deep, forgettable past. The one, the *major* memory remnant that lingered stubbornly from that period of his life, surfaced strangely as a slight unease and feeling of tension when he heard the sounds of a helicopter overhead. He knew full well, in his civilian,post-Army life that the sound of a chopper in the skies above was not an Army Huey or cobra attack chopper or an armored Chinook, coming from or returning to Pleiku, but instead was a television station weather or traffic-report chopper. Nevertheless, a chopper's sonance and cadence sometimes brought back the fear he had known in Vietnam. He had known a number of Vietnam veterans over the years who carried far greater post-traumatic stress and flashbacks than he suffered and he considered himself fortunate that this particular little problem -- helicopter sounds -- was his *only* post-Nam carry-over.

Now, in Siesta Key, it was true enough that the sound overhead on a sunny afternoon was obviously not a military aircraft but only a television station observation or weather chopper. Still, the sound: a monotonous (THWACK-THWACK-thwack-THWACK) (THWACK-THWACK-thwack-THWACK) was enough to remind Thomas of what had been the ever-present dust-offs in Nam. Vietnam was the first war in which helicopters were so widely used. Some 12,000 of them from all of the U.S. military services were flown and saw action during the Vietnam War.

After his divorce, Thomas spent a lot of time reading, and he also volunteered with organizations whose mission had to do with physically and developmentally disabled children. Thomas also contributed financially to many charitable organizations devoted to helping those so afflicted -- to children's groups especially.

Thomas also had served as a hands-on volunteer for

Joseph A. Gillan

various children's special needs organizations during his
adult years. He volunteered as a "hugger" at Special Olympics events, athletic competitions sponsored and organized
by that wonderful organization. At the many races held at
such events, from the 100-yard dash to the 440 (once around
a standard-sized track), each finisher in *every* event, from the
first runner across the line to the last, even if he or she were 5
or 10 minutes behind the first runner, received a congratula-
tory embrace from a volunteer "hugger" at the race's conclusion. Each finisher, through receiving a hug, was made to feel
special and treated individually as a 'winner' in his or her
own right. Thomas volunteered for other organizations and
hospitals geared toward special needs children and adults.

After leaving Washington and settling in southwest Florida, Thomas became aware of and began to volunteer for a
day or two each week at a campus-like training facility for
adult men and women named The Loveland Center. The
Center served more than 100 developmentally and physically
disabled individuals -- with a wide range of functionality.
Some of the 'students,' as they were called at Loveland, were
quite high-functioning, others were less so. Some were able
to read and write at a very basic level. Others were totally
non-verbal. Some were non-ambulatory, others were non-
sighted. Classes were offered in a variety of areas designed
to accommodate students' differing capabilities. The classes
included discussion groups to challenge students' interper-
sonal skills, home economics and home life skills, physical education and basic computer learning skills. Loveland
also received contract work from area businesses for limited
product assembly work where students did piece work and
received payment for their efforts.

Thomas had been involved as a volunteer for much of his
adult life in organizations geared toward the physically and
developmentally disadvantaged. In Westchester, before he
and Ellen divorced, he served on the Board of Directors and
as president of the nearby Connecticut Association for Chil-

56

dren with Learning Disabilities.

He did comparable volunteer work for similar organizations throughout his business career, including his time in Washington and thereafter. He'd recruited The Croatian Creation as a volunteer for a Virginia-based group called, 'Charlie's Club,' dedicated to special needs teenagers.

When Thomas approached The Loveland Center and offered his services there as a volunteer, he told the organization's management staff who interviewed him that he did not want to serve on the facility's Board of Directors or as chairman of any "useless make-work committee, or anything else of that sort"; rather, he said, he would prefer a hands-on situation with the students in whatever way the staff thought he could be most useful.

And that is what he did for the six years he served Loveland as a volunteer. He told the staff, "I will sweep the floors if that's what needs to be done on any given day" -- and he sometimes did just that. He also on occasion wiped up, mopped up and cleaned up after various accidents and personal hygiene mishaps.

Later Thomas would contribute substantial sums of money whenever solicited by any organization serving special needs' members of the population. Besides Loveland, he also contributed generously to the Shriners Hospital for Children, The Angelman's Syndrome Foundation, Food for Poor Kids, The Make-A-Wish Foundation, The Association for Retarded Citizens, the Imus Ranch for Kids with Cancer, the Autism Society of America, Special Olympics, Cross International, St. Jude Childrens Research Hospital, The Hackensack University Medical Center's Children's Oncology Research Center, the Muscular Dystrophy Association, Smile Train, and others. He continued to contribute as well over the years to CACLD. And he also kept in touch with that organization's executive director, a remarkably dedicated woman and good friend, with a special needs child of her own who was now a young adult.

Love is not a word I use easily or lightly but I love these special souls at Loveland and <u>all</u> of the special souls among us, he wrote in his letter to Rebecca.

He told his friend Aldo in Toulouse about Loveland -- and Aldo (Thomas had worked with Aldo in Brussels and, later, in Connecticut) asked Thomas to tell him "in broad strokes" what he did at Loveland. Thomas wrote in an email to Aldo --

I get to school at around 7:30 a.m. and for the next hour-and-a-half (general assembly and roll call begin at 9, and then classes get underway afterwards, at 9:15 or 9:30) I wander around the lunch-room/assembly area as the students filter in at the start of the morning.

Steven Z. often is the first to arrive. Either his mom or his dad drops him off each morning. Steven told me about his weekend activities, his Dad's golf game and we also talked a bit about Florida's recent spate of cold weather. Both of us very much want warmer weather to return soon.

While Steven is chauffeured to and from school by his parents each day, most of the other students commute to and from Loveland via public transportation mini-buses designed and designated for the handicapped and disabled.

Kelly B. and several other students arrived on the first bus just before 8 o'clock. Kelly and I talked about how many times she and I danced with one another at last Thursday night's school Sock Hop and Pizza Party.

Marianne S. and I 'spoke' Italian. Marianne's heritage is Italian. We exchanged "Bon Giornos" and smiles, then said "Arrivederci" as we each went our separate way to socialize with other friends. I must try to learn a little more Italian to enhance my conversations with Marianne. <u>You</u> can probably help me with that.

I helped Ricky F. off the next bus and into a wheelchair (Ricky is ambulatory but only barely, and it is obviously much easier for him to get around in the chair) and I hung up his jacket in his assigned locker. Ricky dug into one of his pockets, found two quarters, handed them to me and asked me to get him a coke from the

Just Before The Dawn

vending machine. After refreshing himself, Ricky and I sat for a few minutes and he dug from another pocket a story about Governor Bush from yesterday's local newspaper. Ricky is a staunch Republican and great fan of the Governor, President George W. Bush and former President George H. W. Bush as well. Ricky refers to the elder Bush, as do the television news anchors and commentary show 'talking heads' as '41.'

The proper name Bush is one of the few **words** that Ricky recognizes and is able to read in print. All of the references in the Sunday paper to either the Governor or the President or their father are circled and highlighted.

●●●●●●●

Marilyn M. asked me to help her put her bracelet back on. She had taken it off to show to a friend and couldn't get the clasp refastened as she tried to replace the bracelet on her wrist.

Sandy H. and I exchanged niceties. Sandy's eyeglasses sat slightly askew on the bridge of her nose, as they seemingly always do. I did not try to straighten them for her nor did I say anything to her about them. I suspect Sandy must get tired of hearing that.

Joanne M. was excited about the Tampa Bay Bucs Super Bowl victory on Sunday and asked me if I had watched the game on television. I assured her I had (even though I really hadn't; I don't care all that much about football, as most sports-crazed Americans do). Joanne is a huge sports enthusiast. She swims several times a week and has won a number of Special Olympics' swimming competitions.

Henry M. and I joked with one another, as we regularly do, about his coming over to my house tonight at 7:30 for pepperoni pizza, diet cherry coke and a hot fudge sundae. Henry knows that I like pizza and I in turn know that he would much prefer, rather than pizza, a large, rare steak and a baked potato – "with sour cream," he stipulates and <u>always</u> adds. The diet cherry coke and hot fudge sundae, however, are staples in <u>any</u> of Henry's favorite meals. Henry is extremely social and gregarious, has strong verbal skills *and is a delight to talk with. He also has a wonderfully wry and quite sophisticated sense of humor. He laughs and smiles easily -- and it is always a pleasure to see and be with him because of that.*

I talked with Rosalind J. about her new doll. Rosalind almost always carries a Barbie doll around with her during her day at Loveland. It is her security blanket.

Anna H. and I exchanged hearty 'Hellos.' Anna, like Henry, is gregarious and enjoys socializing. Her voice is quite loud; she rarely modulates its volume in her conversations. Anna and I had not seen each other for a few weeks. She had been home sick with the flu. I'm glad she's better, and back at Loveland.

I asked Stephanie D. if she had acquired any new Harry Potter items recently. Stephanie is a great Harry Potter aficionado and memorabilia collector.

Scott B. and I engaged in the 'cool' handshake that I once learned from a Black friend in Washington. Scott likes it and likes to engage in it with me, as do I. Jason F. also likes to do the 'cool' handshake with me, but I did not see Jason today. (I was schooled in the handshake by someone you may once have known in Washington, Jim Williams. The handshake is one of those complicated procedures that one sometimes sees on television in which black athletes engage: a clasp, a turn of the wrist, a release, a click of the knuckles and a fist pump. Even though I had tried to learn the cool procedure from Jim in Washington, Jim once called me "the un-coolest white man I've ever known.")

●●●●●●●

Lisa S. asked me how I liked her new hair-style and color. I told her it looked terrific and said she looked more beautiful than ever. She beamed.

Tina V. came up to me with a ring she had found on the floor under one of the lunch tables in the assembly room. I spoke with G., the staff director, and she told me that Erica L. had lost a ring last Friday and was heartbroken about it. Erica was not scheduled to be in school today but G. will see to it that the ring is returned to Erica when she comes in tomorrow. I went back to Tina and told her this and thanked her for coming to me with her find.

Emilio M. told me about his new girlfriend. It is K., Loveland's new fitness class supervisor. Emilio, who is quiet, shy and keeps almost always to himself, asked me to tell K. about how much he loved her. I did. Emilio, with his head down and his eyes peering discretely upward with a faint smile on his face, watched from across the room as K. and I spoke.

Adam L. and I exchanged "Good Mornings." I admired the necktie Adam was wearing. He was pleased and said "Thank You. It's a present from my mom." Adam, like Henry, Anna, and many other Loveland students, is a bright, interesting and highly sociable young adult.

I cleaned Tim M.'s and Jared F.'s eyeglasses under the water faucet at the sink in the corner of the lunch room. This has become standard practice for the three of us on my Loveland days. I wonder how they are able to see out of their excessively-smudged glasses when I'm not there.

Lilly P. returned to Florida and Loveland from up north last week. Today was her first day back at school. I welcomed her back and told her that I and everyone else had missed her while she and her mom were away.

I told Bob H. how natty he looked. Today was a regularly scheduled Social Club meeting for student members of that organization. Club members go by bus to lunch at a restaurant nearby school and discuss current events, often with an 'outside' guest speaker. The men students wear jackets and neckties to the monthly lunches and the women also are encouraged to dress up for the occasion. Bob H. always dresses well, even when there is not a regularly scheduled Social Club lunch. On meeting days, he looks especially sharp, almost like a male GQ model. Bob is a handsome man in his 40s.

Chrissie G. came up to me and told me that she'd had a telephone conversation over the weekend with her sister, C. I have met C. She visits her sister Chrissie at Loveland regularly. C. lives with her family in New Jersey. Chrissie talks often about C.

Arthur N. walked up to me and lifted one of his legs to show that he had his cowboy boots on today. He chided me for not having mine on. Normally I <u>do</u> wear my boots to Loveland and Arthur, who is also known by the nickname 'Smokey,' checks me and my footwear out whenever we see each other. I wore jogging shoes today, much to Smokey's chagrin.

Mary P. and I exchanged niceties, as did Arlene J. and I. I asked Arlene how her boyfriend, Dave, was doing. "He's just fine", Arlene said. The two have a lunch date planned next weekend, for their anniversary. It will mark the second year they have been 'going together.'

I asked Tom W. if he had listened to any classical music, his favorite music, over the past weekend. He said he had. I asked if he still had the small J.S. Bach bust that I had given him as a gift a year or so ago. He said he still has it. He keeps it atop the dresser in his room.

●●●●●●●

A few of the Loveland students live in group homes. The great majority, however, still live at home with their parents, God bless them. I have met many of the parents and without exception they are extraordinary, loving, giving people. It has been said that when The Good Lord decides to place a physically or developmentally handicapped boy or girl on His Earth, He looks around very carefully and just as carefully chooses the parents He places that boy or girl with. It is not an accident that most parents of handicapped children are very special people, indeed. The Lord sees to that.

The students at Loveland range in age from their early 20s up to a few in their 60s. Most are in their 30s and 40s. The single most preponderant disability among the students is Down's Syndrome. My good friend Ricky F. is so afflicted.

Parents of special needs adult children have moved to homes near Loveland from cities and towns all over America so the special souls they have in their care may receive the extraordinary care, attention and nurturing that the wonderful Loveland staff offers them as their daytime charges. Loveland's reputation is that well known and *regarded throughout the country.*

The wonderful staff at Loveland are dedicated, loving, overworked and underpaid.

●●●●●●●

As the day's classes got underway -- in the main campus buildings for the majority of the Loveland students -- I walked across the compact, peaceful, green campus quad to the new "Phase Two" classroom.

The classes at the main campus include discussion groups and roundtables designed to teach and reinforce basic social skills. There is a Workshop which takes contract assignments from local manufacturers. Here, the students do basic assembly work and are paid for their efforts based upon their individual productivity. The weekly paycheck they receive is as important to them, of course, as ours is to us.

One of the most popular classes at Loveland is the Computer Lab. There the students learn fundamental, basic computer skills. For some of the students, just learning how to manipulate a "mouse" in order to play a computer game is a positive learning experience. For others, learning to type and spell out their name to appear on the screen in front of them is a notable and joyful accomplishment. Other, higher-functioning students use word processing programs to hone their spelling skills. There are also basic programs for some to enhance their math skills.

Additional classes include workshops that teach basic cooking and other home life skills. There is a well-equipped fitness room where students may ride a stationary bicycle (an activity from which even the non-sighted students are able to benefit). Some are also able to use a stair-master to enhance aerobic conditioning or other equipment to build or increase muscle mass and to promote better flexibility.

Not all of the students take the same classes, of course. There are various curricula designed and tailored to meet each student's unique needs and capabilities. Each student has his or her specially-

63

Joseph A. Gillan

tailored IEP -- Individual Education Plan.

The Phase Two classroom is situated in a small, one-story, six-room house that until just recently served as an on-campus Men's Group Home. (The six men who once lived over there have moved to another, larger Group Home). Now, the Phase Two students spend most of their day there. Phase Two is also where I spend most of my time once the more structured Loveland day begins at the main campus.

There are a dozen or so students in Phase Two. Their abilities and skills are wide-ranging but, by and large, they are either older students (two are in their mid to late '60s) or those who lack the mobility to change classrooms easily on their own at the main campus during the day. There are also a few in this group who need highly individualized motivational encouragement and much closer behavioral supervision.

Activities in Phase Two include arts and crafts, music, limited physical fitness (sometime just a supervised walk outside around the campus), discussion groups, home life skills and socialization skills.

As this particular Phase Two day began, I helped Tommy H. get started on a 25-piece jigsaw puzzle. Tommy is a quiet, gentle soul, largely non-verbal. The few words he does speak he repeats over and over again ("Tell Momma I be good?") Others in Phase Two are even more limited in vocabulary and verbalization skills and are sometimes difficult to understand. One or two are able to sign or signal for what their needs and intents are. I am trying to learn basic sign language. Craig S., a student at the main campus who also lip-reads, is my tutor.

Annie H. seemed a bit disoriented this morning and the staff suggested to her that she sit quietly alone for a few minutes. Soon, she got up from the table where she sat and joined a group of students listening to music. Annie has changed recently. She seems less sure of herself and, somehow, more lost. Just a few years ago Annie was part of Loveland's Community Work program for more developmentally and socially advanced students and spent a half-day twice a week assisting in a State-sponsored nursery school program for

64

developmentally handicapped pre-school children.

Barbara N. had some photographs she wanted to show me that had been taken over the Christmas Holidays during a Florida visit by her sister and brother-in-law. Barbara is a kind and gentle soul, patient with every one of her classmates, and extremely well liked by all, particularly staff. Everyone sees her as special. I agree. She also has a quite sophisticated sense of humor and she and I joke with one another and laugh together often. Barbara's laugh is rich and wonderful to hear and her smile is beatific and pleasing to witness. Barbara is in her early 60s. She has been a Loveland "student" for more than 20 years. Everyone sees her as someone very, very special.

I got Jackie S. started on a 100-piece puzzle. Jackie is fairly proficient at puzzles and enjoys the feeling of accomplishment when he completes one. Jackie likes to work on them and keep busy, but he does need some help or supervision. When Jackie begins a new puzzle or starts again (and again and again!) one he has done previously, he immediately wants to get right to the heart of the matter -- the center of the puzzle -- and is not the least bit interested in framing the puzzle's perimeter. I usually do that for him and he takes things from there. Jackie is in his 50s and is a bear of a man -- six feet two or three inches in height and well over 200 pounds. Jackie is also a wanderer. Unless closely supervised, he'll walk out the Phase Two front door and head toward the main campus, where he likes to visit and socialize with others. I spend a lot of my time keeping an eye on Jackie and, occasionally, chasing or tracking him down at the main campus.

I asked Carol C. if her Mom had cooked chicken for her recently. Chicken is one of Carol's favorite meals. Her mom had, of course, prepared it for Carol just this past weekend. Carol is largely nonverbal. When she does speak, she is so soft-spoken it is difficult to hear and understand what she is saying (unlike Anna H. at the main campus). Carol tends to communicate by responding with head movements, affirmatively or negatively, to direct questions we ask of her. Carol is a tiny soul. She's not much taller than four feet nine or ten inches and I don't think she weighs more than 70 or 80 pounds. Her facial expression often seems so sad, and distressed. When she smiles, which she does on the rare occasion, I think it is one of the most beautiful things one can see anywhere at Loveland. A smile from Carol can make my day a great success.

Pam J. told me about her weekend. Pam is non-sighted but spends most of her time at home, where she lives with her Mom and sister, "watching television", she says. The family watched profes-sional wrestling this past weekend, her mom's favorite show.

I asked Pam how her dog, "Ginger", is doing. "Ginger is fine", Pam was happy to say. Pam has a number of noteworthy strengths. One, like Barbara N., is great patience. Another is her marvelous clear soprano, singing voice. Listening to Pam sing can be spell-binding. Listening to her must be what it's like in Heaven listening to God's angels sing.

I walked over to where Tara S. sat. Tara is a very beautiful young woman in her late 20s. She is largely non-verbal, almost blind and physically limited. She also is largely non-ambulatory, although she is able to get up and around from time-to-time using a walker for support and guidance. I began to sing the old-time, silly Bill Haley rock 'n roll song softly to her, "See Ya Later, Alliga-tor; After while, Crocodile..." The song always brings a smile to Tara's lovely face. I'm not certain if it is the song's whimsical lyrics or my poor singing that amuses Tara most.

Bobby T., a diminutive young man with Downs Syndrome, asked me to clean his eyeglasses, as I regularly do for his friends Tim and Jared at the main campus. I also helped Bobby put a Windsor knot in his necktie and place it smartly around his neck under his shirt collar. Bobby thought he would go to the Social Club luncheon today and that's why he brought his tie to school.

I read a children's-level story to a group of seven or eight students, as we sat in a semicircle in the Music Room. The story was supposedly based on a real life incident about a whale in the San Francisco Bay that had gotten separated from its pod, became disoriented and swam, not back into the Pacific Ocean, but into the Bay -- and about the efforts by fish and wildlife experts, scores of environmentalists, naturalists and other volunteers to direct the lost sea behemoth back to the ocean.

After the story, it was mid-morning break time -- cookies and fruit juice. After break-time I played a music video from a George Strait concert for the group of students who had returned to the Music Room.

He who doubts,
Believes
(Anonymous)

Ten

Thomas's email to Aldo continued as he told him about the George Strait music video --

Strait (as you may or may not know -- stuck over there as you are in culturally deprived Toulouse) is a popular country and western singer here in The Newe Worlde. Pam and Tara and I all like his song, "I Just Want To Dance With You." When that song comes on the video, Pam and I take a turn dancing to it and singing along with it. "I want to twirl you all around the floor, 'cause that's what they invented dancin' for." Tara also likes the song and stands up, from her wheelchair, to take a turn dancing, as does diminutive Carol C. Kathy S., another of my "favorites" at Loveland, (actually, they all are my favorites) joins in on the dancing from time to time. Kathy, sadly, passed away recently -- and I hope she now is dancing with God and all the angels in heaven.

I played poker with Jim B. as he and I do every day I am at Loveland. Today Jackie S. and Tara S. joined us. Tara held the cards and Jim B. and I helped her with her hold 'em and discard choices. She is virtually non-sighted, as I said, and so she really couldn't see what she was doing and, in any case, did not understand either -- but she did, I believe, enjoy participating in what for her was

71

something new. Jackie announced with each new hand dealt that he had "two Queens … two Queens…" <u>regardless</u> of what the cards were he held. Jim B. understands and enjoys the game but he gets annoyed when Jackie joins us. 'Two Queens…' Jim and I play five-card draw for $1 million a hand. I owe Jim $7 million from today's action. He always beats me. Jim is in his late 50s. Up until an automobile accident when he was in his 20s when he suffered a severe brain injury, Jim was a perfectly "normal" functioning adult. The accident happened to Jim at a time when he was a draftee in the U.S. Army. Jim is able to recite, still, his serial number from his time in the military but cannot recall the street number of the house he lives in with his Dad and brother. He has virtually <u>no</u> short-term memory -- but has not forgotten his Army serial number from 30 years ago!

After the card game, I helped Mary, another volunteer, sink wash and towel dry 70-80 plastic ice cream sundae dishes to be used for Loveland's Ice Cream Social planned for this weekend. Mary and I went over to the main campus to complete this little chore as a favor for the overburdened teachers and staff there.

Back at Phase Two, Carol from the "Assisted Living" office staff called. Craig S. (my sign language tutor) forgot to bring his lunch with him today from the group home, and Carol wanted to know if we had anything in the Phase Two kitchen that we could prepare for Craig's lunch. I put on my Chef Thomas (make that To-Mas') hat and whipped up two peanut butter and jelly sandwiches. Craig came over from the main campus a few minutes later to pick them up. I had them wrapped and covered in clear plastic sheet wrap. I should also have put them in a small, able-to-be-carried-by-hand, paper bag. Craig, rather than carrying the wrapped sandwiches in his hand when he picked them up, instead stuffed them into a pocket in his jacket. They were probably more like peanut butter and jelly bread 'rolls' than sandwiches when he took them out of his pocket a few minutes later and sat down to eat them for lunch. Craig is not the neatest or most 'organized' of Loveland's students.

Bill B. and I went outside for a short walk. Bill always seems to have a surfeit of nervous energy, physical and verbal, and it some-

times is salutary to go outside with him for a quarter-hour walk to help burn off some of his excess fidgetiness.

At noon, I went back over to the main campus lunchroom to help Stretch Wilson, one of the staff, supervise the 15 or so main campus students who had stayed back today rather than going to the Social Club outside luncheon. G., the staff supervisor, had asked me earlier in the morning to do this today rather than stay with the Phase Two group and the wonderful head of that unit, Linda P., as I normally do. Linda had another volunteer, Mary (my dish-washing associate), to help her out during the lunch session today, so I walked over to join Stretch.

After lunch, Stretch organized a game of "Wilson's Wacky Bingo," a game most of the students relish. (Stretch is a single father, a retired career military man, in whom Thomas saw the same warm love and deep compassion for the very special souls at Loveland that he himself felt.)

As the game got underway, I sat between Shannon Y. and Kevin O. and helped them spot and cover numbers on their Bingo cards as Stretch called them, entertaining and amusing the players with the questions he asks, as an integral, learning part of the game, which he relates to the numbers he calls. "How old do you have to be to vote in Florida?" he asks. "Eighteen!" came the response from two of the players. "And so," Stretch says, slowly and with drama and suspense, "the number, under the 'I,' is eighteen.'"

"How many days are there in a week?"

"The number, under the 'B,' is seven."

"How old do you think I am?"

"The number, under the 'N,' is thirty-three." Stretch may in fact have been 33 twenty years ago!

The Social Club students began returning from their outside lunch shortly after 1:30, just after Wilson's Wacky Bingo was concluding (everybody won something today -- from 25 cents to $1), and in another 45 minutes the buses began lining up outside the Administration building on the main campus to load up the

students and take them home.

I was especially solicitous today to my friend Ricky F. as he got on his bus to head home. Ricky asked me to stop by and visit him at his home this afternoon before I returned to Siesta Key, and I did just that, arriving actually a few minutes before Ricky and the bus he was on pulled up. While I waited for Ricky's bus I talked with Ricky's dad (a widower and Ricky's sole caregiver) briefly about Ricky's health. Then, Ricky's bus pulled up outside and his dad and I met him as he exited the vehicle. Ricky and I, as we sometimes do, feigned some boxing moves and karate chops for a few minutes before we went inside. Ricky hung up his coat in the closet in his bedroom and plopped down on his back, on the bed, with his hands clasped behind his head. Ricky was home, with his terrific Dad, and he was decompressing and relaxing. Ricky picked up the television remote control, turned the set on in his bedroom and keyed in his favorite channel -- C-Span. Ever a Bush and Republican Party fan and loyalist, Ricky has no patience when the House or Senate floor action on the television focuses on a Democrat. "Bah!" said Ricky, and then he clicked off the television and said he wanted to rest for a while. His dad, Chuck, said Ricky wanted to be rested and alert for the network broadcast later tonight of President Bush's State of the Union address.

I slowly and quietly exited Ricky's room, along with his dad. "See ya next week, pal," I said. Ricky waved to me, with his eyes only half open.

I drove home to Siesta Key, a half hour away.

Ricky is one of my absolute favorites of all of my favorite Loveland students. Ricky is very ill and deserves all of the special attention and care and love that all of us who are fortunate to know him are able to give him.

As I said, I spend most of my time these days at Phase Two but I also have helped out in the past with students at the main campus on a one-to-one basis with simple math problems or with reading and writing. I read to Mark P. regularly, for example. Mark is quite high-functioning and a very popular guy among his classmates. I also have helped out in the past as a substitute for the fitness instructor, when she has been absent, and in other of the classes as well.

When I am working one-to-one on reading or math with any of the woman students, it is a pity that in this day and age one must be mindful of propriety and/or the potential appearance of impropriety. Therefore, when I do work with one of the women, I always make it a point to do our work in the most "public" place at Loveland -- the lunch/assembly room.

I often go to school dances and evening parties on special occasions, such as Valentine's Day, Halloween and so forth. I dance with as many of the women students as I can and, though I don't really know how to dance and thus can't really do it worth a damn, they don't seem to notice or appear to be at all bothered by or upset with that reality and my having three or four left feet.

I was not at all certain when I started at Loveland as a volunteer, nearly four years ago, that I could do it (would I have the patience, for example?) or that I would be _any_ good at it at all. I knew only that I did not want to be on the school's Board of Directors or chairman of some useless committee or anything of that sort. I wanted, simply and solely, to work with the students in any way that the staff thought I might be most helpful. That is what I have done, I believe, and I love it. I would -- and have -- swept floors at Loveland if that were how I could be most helpful on any given day.

The Loveland students are, for me -- all of them -- very, very special souls.

I love them all.

I have had the added pleasure, over time, of meeting many of the students' parents and, without exception (as I said earlier but it bears repeating), they, too, are very, very special people -- as are the wonderful, caring, giving Loveland staff extraordinary, special people.

I love Loveland's very name. My day or two days there each week always are the best days of my week. I head home, afterward, feeling both enervated and at the same time filled with peace and joy and love. I get so much more out of the effort than I give. But, *then, that is what love is, wouldn't you say? Love is giving – and, in giving, we truly do receive.*

But, dear friend that is not to say that there is not something about Loveland that troubles me -- and it is this. I have great difficulty, intellectually and spiritually, reconciling the concept of an all-loving, all-giving, all-merciful God and His creation of the seemingly nihilistic existence of these terribly hurt, disadvantaged souls. My heart aches for them and I cannot help but ask, Why... dear God, why...?

Why?

Eleven

After Loveland, and jogging, reading was perhaps Thomas's greatest passion and pastime. Soon after and since his separation and divorce from Ellen, before relocating to Washington, when he was not in the office or ensconced in his less than redoubtable new home, "The Cave," he made an effort to get to several of the past century's great writers that "for some reason or another I've missed over the years." He also *re-read* a number of classic novels that he had first read as far back as 25-30 years ago. He went through almost all of Charles Dickens and also went back to his favorite Hemingway and F. Scott Fitzgerald novels and some of Hemingway's short stories: "The Short Happy Life of Francis Macomber" and "Hills like White Elephants" he particularly liked. His favorite Fitzgerald novel was "Tender is the Night" and he thought it much richer and more meaningful, for him, with all of its "forgotten sorrow" when he *reread* it than he did when he was first introduced to it years ago, in college, as a young man -- as he did many of the great novels that he went back to as a more mature man. He read a fascinating biography of Fitzgerald's brilliant but troubled wife, "Zelda," by Nancy

77

Milford. He "discovered" Iris Murdoch, and wondered how he had missed *her* during his earlier years. He read her classic debut novel "Under the Net" ("Events stream past us ... [like people in crowds] and the face of each [of those persons] is seen for only a moment. What is urgent is not urgent forever but only ephemerally. All work and all love, the search for truth, like itself, are made up of moments which pass and become nothing.") He followed that by reading her novels "The Bell" and "Nuns and Soldiers." He thought Murdoch a brilliant writer, thinker and existentialist/philosopher. Her recurrent and seemingly all-encompassing solipsism also appealed to Thomas.

He read Pascal's "Pensees" and found great truth, and applicability to his own spiritual journey, in the story told in it of the philosopher in search of Christ, to whom Christ said, "You would not be seeking me if you had not already found me."

He read "Zeno's Conscience" by the Italian Proust, Italo Svevo. ("Those who have not yet experienced marriage believe it is more important than it is." ..."A marriage is far simpler than an engagement. Once married, you don't have to talk anymore about love.")

He reread Leon Uris's "Trinity" to remind himself why he, as an Irish-American, disfavored the British so much for what the Irish nationalists held was England's "occupation" of the Emerald Isle and for the British exploitation and plundering of Irish natural resources and their cruel maltreatment of the Irish people for so many decades. Thomas steadfastly refused to ever think in terms of calling Britain "Great Britain." A nation that adds the adjective "great" to its formal appellation is deluding itself, Thomas held. To Thomas it was England, and no more than that. There was certainly nothing 'great' about the way England treated the Irish. He reread his college texts of Machiavelli's "The Prince And the Discourses" and he dug out of an old box from his college days Spencer's "Paradise Lost," and "Comus" and "Lycidas." He reread

Dreiser's "An American Tragedy" and Upton Sinclair's "The Jungle." He reread Sinclair Lewis's "Main Street." He reread Faulkner's "Sanctuary," "Light in August," and "Soldier's Pay" ["… the years rieve us of sexual compulsion…" "The saddest thing about love…is that not only the love cannot last forever, but even the heartbreak is soon forgotten."] He also reread "Go Down, Moses," and "As I Lay Dying." He reread John Steinbeck's "Travels With Charley."

Thomas regretted that he had never read much of Somerset Maugham and decided to rectify that omission. He went quickly through "Of Human Bondage" and two of the four volumes of Maugham's "Collected Short Stories." Similarly, he had never read much of William Saroyan and went on to read his "The Human Comedy" ("Everybody at Bellevue [New York City psychiatric hospital] is somebody who lost love somewhere along the way." "None of us can do the one thing that's broken the human heart since the beginning of time. It [to recapture lost love] can't be done.") Thomas reread Guy de Maupassant's "Selected Short Stories." (" … [man lusts for] her breast…covering a woman's heart which he finds so satisfying that he makes no attempt to find what lies beneath it.")

He read, for the first time, Samuel Butler's "The Way of All Flesh." He reread Edith Wharton's "The Age of Innocence" and four of Jack Kerouac's novels: "On The Road," "The Town and The City," "The Dharma Bums" and "Doctor Sax."

He reread Burton's "The Anatomy of Melancholy." He loved the quote, "Tempora Labunter, Tacitisque Senescimus Annis." Translated from the Latin it was: "Time glides on, and we age insensibly with the years.") He thought that this, surely, was one of life's Universal Truths.

He read, for the third time, Gabriel Garcia-Marquez' masterpiece "One Hundred Years of Solitude" ("…the past is a lie… memory has no return… every spring gone by can never be recovered… and the wildest and most tenacious love is an ephemeral truth in the end." "... weeping from love, the oldest sobs in the history of man..." "It's as if the world is repeating itself...")

He read, for the first time, Joseph Conrad's "Heart of Darkness" and "The Secret Sharer." He read, for the first time, William Styron's "Sophie's Choice" and reread Camus's "The Stranger" ("In the depths of winter, I finally learned that within me there lay an invincible summer.") He also reread Camus's "The Fall," "The Stranger," "The Rebel," "The Plague" and "The Myth of Sisyphus."

After Garcia-Marquez, he "discovered" other Latino-Hispanic writers, little known, whom he found gifted and talented. He was enthralled with Julio Cortazar's bizarre and quirky "Hopscotch" ("He was fired from his job at the insane asylum because he is crazy." "It is raining inside of me... Oh, my love, I miss you. I feel the pain of you in my skin, in my throat, every time I breathe it's as if an emptiness came into my chest where you no longer are...") and Javier Marias' wonderfully clever work of genius, "Tomorrow in the Battle Think on Me."

He read, for the first time, Edna St. Vincent Millay -- a volume of "selected poetry," and Virginia Woolf's "A Room of One's Own." He was struck with the brilliance of Millay's "Renascence", written when she was but 19-years-old, and Woolf's "... Room..." and, again, wondered how he had missed these two wonderful writers for so many years.

He reread all of his Herman Hesse novels, "Steppenwolf," "Beneath the Wheel," "The Glass Bead Game," and "Narcissus and Goldmund," which he thought was one of the greatest achievements in the history of literature. If Thomas were forced to list what he regarded as the greatest novels ever-penned, "Narcissus and Goldmund" would be in his personal Top Ten.

In "Narcissus and Goldmund," Hesse writes about what all of the world's great novels essentially deal with, must deal with, in one fashion or another, the age-old themes that transcend all time: the conflict between flesh and spirit, between hedonism and asceticism, between the reality of the here-and-now and the mystery and quest for an answer to the unanswerable question -- is there a God and a hereafter? Hesse in "Narcissus and Goldmund" gets to and does all of this -- more elegantly and richly, Thomas thought, than anyone else in the past century has been able to do within the confines of a novel. Thomas found "Narcissus and Goldmund" a deep and thoughtful journey into the inner self. He considered it a brilliant, ageless piece of artistic creation.

He even read, for the first time, Hesse's "Siddhartha," a treasure included today on most high school reading syllabuses -- though it was not on SMI's when Thomas matriculated there. SMI's student reading list of "great literature" was parochial and limited. Thomas was taken and enthralled with the young Indian's desire in "Siddhartha" to discover the secret to end the pain of existence that he saw in everything around him.

Thomas regularly reread his favorite writer/novelist, Thomas Wolfe, getting back to one of the four of Wolfe's great novels once a year or so. "Look Homeward, Angel" was Wolfe's most widely acclaimed work but Thomas's favorite Wolfe novels were "Of Time and the River" and "You Can't Go Home Again." Thomas even became a member of an organization formed to foster and promote study and appreciation of Wolfe, The Thomas Wolfe Society, and he attended two or three of the group's annual meetings -- especially those held in Wolfe's birthplace, Asheville, NC., "one of the most beautiful spots on God's good earth," Thomas had written to Rebecca. The Wolfe Society was made up primarily of academicians who, Thomas felt, were by and large more interested in what *they* felt and wrote about Wolfe in their overblown and stuffy critiques than they were in what the great and talented Wolfe had written. Many of them suffered from a tendency to over analyze and suffered, in their daily life with "regular" people (non-academicians), an inability to interact with the hoi polloi through their self-imposed "paralysis through analysis" and, Thomas thought, their obviously ersatz scholarly intellectualism. There were a couple of exceptions in the Society, particularly in Thomas's early years as a dues-paying member of the group, renowned and brilliant scholars who had the touch of the common man that too many of the group's latter-day stuffed shirts -- too taken with their self-inflated academic credentials and their (ill-deserved) superiority complexes -- did not have. One individual in particular was "Aldo ," from Sandusky a longtime member of the Society, not an academician but a working man with a genuine love and appreciation of Wolfe's magnificent talent. Aldo, as intellectually gifted as many of the more-credentialed stuffed shirts in the Society, was a true Wolfe admirer and scholar and -- even as a non-academic -- had had published several seminal Wolfe studies and analyses over the years. Aldo also was a "real" person, Thomas felt -- not at all artificial ("bunch of fucking phonies," as Thomas once described in "Paddy-speak," to his brother some of the Society members from the academic world he had met and the few he had come to know over the years of his membership). Aldo from Sandusky was not like that at all. He was self-effacing, genuine, modest, humble and mostly, "real." Many of the academicans in the Society, a woman member of the group had once told Thomas, were seemingly as if not more interested in expense-account travel to the annual meeting venues than they were in actual Wolfe scholarship.

Thomas considered and disagreed with conventional literary criticism of Wolfe that his prose was best suited for younger, still-unformed, maturing readers -- but not seasoned, more mature denizens of society's upper intellectual strata. Thomas agreed with the way underappreciated 20th century novelist Kurt Vonnegut put it: that Wolfe "goes down easier when one is eighteen..." but, Vonnegut added, "Civilizations are built mainly on masterpieces that stun eighteen-year-olds." Thomas had read and liked a number of Vonnegut's books: "Slaughterhouse-Five," "Breakfast of Champions," [Here's to you, Dwayne Hoobler!] "God Bless You, Mr. Rosewater" -- and his final book, published just weeks before he died, "A Man Without a Country."

Thomas enjoyed and appreciated Thomas Wolfe not to try to impress others, a tendency he surely saw among many members of the Society, but because of Wolfe's sensual, haunting lyricism, because of his elegant, lush emotional prose and his consistent ability to take the English language to soaring, new heights of poetic linguistic beauty. He once read that Wolfe's lyrical, creative style represented an expression of The Life Force, and he saw it that way, too. Thomas was intoxicated by Wolfe's writing.

But by and large, as a non-academic, Thomas felt like an outsider, a "mongrel," as he referred to himself as a member of the group. Among members of the Wolfe Society, he felt, too, that they treated him as one, a mongrel and an outsider.

Thomas eventually discontinued his membership in the Society, even though he continued a great admirer of the prodigious talent of Wolfe and he continued to reread a Wolfe novel annually -- and continued an epistolary relationship with his best friend in the society, Aldo from Sandusky.

Twelve

As Wolfe was his favorite "dead" writer, John Irving was
his favorite "live" author, as Thomas put it. Thomas admired
Irving's work greatly, all of it. His first exposure to the writer
was through Irving's best seller "The World According to
Garp." After that, Thomas read each of Irving's subsequent
novels, "The Hotel New Hampshire," "The Cider House
Rules," "A Prayer for Owen Meany" (Thomas's favorite
Irving book), "A Son of the Circus," "A Widow for One Year,"
"The Fourth Hand," and "Until I Find You." Thomas also
procured copies of and read three novels from early in Irving's
career, "Setting Free The Bears," "The 158-Pound Marriage"
and "The Water-Method Man."

He wrote a fan letter to Irving after reading "Until I Find
You" and was gratified -- actually, exuberant -- when he
received a reply, much more than a polite "form letter." He
exchanged a few further letters with Irving before the correspondence exchange ebbed and ended. Irving told Thomas
that he was a fan of the great English author Graham Greene
and wrote of him as "...the most accomplished novelist in the
English language; in any language, he was the most meticu-

lous." Thomas also was a Greene admirer and had reread his "The End of the Affair" just recently. Thomas also liked Greene's "The Heart of the Matter," "Travels With My Aunt" as well as "The Honorary Consul" and "The Power and the Glory."

Thomas wrote back to Irving, "I was delighted to learn that you are a Graham Greene admirer. I am, too -- very much so in fact. In your honor <u>and his</u> I have, therefore, moved his works in one of my bookshelves of highest honor to stand next to yours."

Thomas appreciated Irving's great talent and acerbic wit. In one exchange of letters, Thomas wrote to Irving, after his novel "Until I Find You" had received less-than-stellar reviews in the *New York Times* and *Washington Post,* "I have just looked up 'literary-critic' and 'book reviewer' in my dictionary. FYI: in each case, there is a picture of an asshole accompanying the definition."

In his response Irving concluded *his* letter this way:

"Book reviewers are, for the most part, assholes -- and many of them have never written a novel, and never will. When you've written 11 novels, 14 books, the experience of being reviewed is largely one of being condescended to by your inferiors. I'm used to it."

Thomas laughed aloud at that remark: "... condescended to by your inferiors."

Greene died in the early 1990s and Thomas also learned that Irving more recently considered Gunter Grass "... the greatest living novelist today."

Thomas read the remaining three of Irving's books that he had not previously gotten to, "The Imaginary Girlfriend," "My Movie Business" and "Trying to Save Piggy Sneed."

Thomas considered Irving America's finest and most talented 20th century writer -- and 21st century as well ("<u>so far</u>", he would add). Thomas considered Pat Conroy a close second to Irving, given Conroy's ambitious grasp of the great and universal themes he had tackled and written about in *his* novels, as Irving did in *his*, and in the elegance and beauty of Conroy's style and use of language. Thomas was surprised, pleasantly so, to learn that Conroy was also an admirer of Thomas Wolfe and, too, a member of the Wolfe Society as Thomas was.

Thomas had never read any of Gunter Grass's works but, because of Irving and Irving's high estimation of Grass, decided to do just that. He bought and read Grass's "The Tin Drum," acknowledged by many to be his greatest work, and "Cat and Mouse." Thomas also read, for the first time, another of Irving's favorite writers, Canadian Robertson Davies and his "World of Wonders."

●●●●●●●

Thomas had qualified as airborne during his time in the Army -- but military jumps are largely static line, low altitude parachute "rides," and, in Washington, Thomas decided he'd like to try freefall sky-*diving*. He learned about a sky-diving "center" in Chambersburg, PA, near Gettysburg, and only about a two-hours drive from Washington. He made arrangements to visit Chambersburg and participate in a half-day training class to qualify for the freefall. The experience was indeed substantially different than static line jumping. A static line jump, Thomas learned, *was, indeed comparatively* more like a parachute "ride." A freefall *jump* -- from 12,000 feet -- was in fact a sky *dive,* not a parachute *ride.*

Becky was not in favor of Thomas going ahead with his plan to freefall jump -- nor were his daughters. But Thomas was convinced that the motor trip to Chambersburg was actually potentially more hazardous -- especially the short portion of it on the Capital Beltway -- than the jumping itself and succeeded in assuaging Becky's concerns by persuading her that this indeed was the case. In truth, Thomas wanted to do this alone and to *be* alone, as he had *always* been alone as far back as he could remember. Thomas had very few early memories from his youth but did recall, once, when he was confined to bed with a childhood scourge of the 1950s, scarlet fever. One of his sisters had the disease at the same time. She was abed and isolated in another room and Thomas remembered all of the attention she got, from visitors and his mother, while he was by and large left alone. Thomas *had* always been alone. As an adult, he thought of himself as a loner -- and, almost, as a recluse if not, increasingly as he aged, an eremite.

Most people to whom Thomas talked afterwards thought him reckless for having freefall sky-dived, but Thomas told them that the majority of the jumpers he'd met at Chambersburg were neither dare-devils nor devil-may-care macho men at all and that there were a large number of women jumpers as well -- and none of them had a death wish, either, as one of Thomas's friends had suggested Thomas might have. Thomas did not see or gather that in talking with and getting to know some of his fellow skydivers. As an Army veteran and with his static-line-jumps experience, Thomas was considered comparatively experienced as a parachutist. "At least, you've had the balls to jump out of a perfectly serviceable air plane," one of Chambersburg's trainers said to him. Thomas also found that most jumpers, curiously, like almost all marathoners, were non-smokers. Thomas had been a smoker as a young man but had ultimately broken himself of the habit, and quit -- and to this day disliked the foul smell of a cigarette being smoked near him, even outdoors.

Many of the jumpers at Chambersburg "tandem jumped" -- with a staff trainer/experienced jumper "attached" to the novice's back, the two of them diving groundward "in tandem." Thomas rejected the whole idea of a tandem jump, wanting to take the plunge, as it were, on his own. Most people who asked Thomas about the experience were curious as to how difficult -- and how much of a hard jolt -- the actual touchdown or landing was. They assumed it would be the biggest jolt in the overall procedure. Rebecca was concerned that Thomas might exacerbate his leg and knee problems, which she assumed he had acquired through years of jogging and marathon running, unaware that its genesis went back to his service in Vietnam. Thomas told her and all others who asked about the landing that it, or the touch-down, was not a jarring jolt at all. That -- a jarring landing -- perhaps *had* been the case occasionally with the military static line jumps he had made but it did not prove to be so with the freefall. The equipment used in the freefall, the chutes and the way they were designed, had eliminated the old static line hard landing that old-time military jumpers knew so well.

In the freefall, jumpers exited the aircraft at about or slightly higher than 12,000 feet (at anything higher than that, the air is too thin and there is not enough oxygen to breathe and maintain consciousness). The biggest jolt, Thomas explained to his curious questioners, was when one actually exited the aircraft -- and the rush of wind hit one smack in the face and front of one's body.

In the freefall, jumpers wore an altimeter on one wrist and part of their training -- it was *drilled* into their heads, again and again and again -- was to look at the altimeter every three or four seconds. This was to assure that they pulled the cord to deploy the chute at 4,000 feet and, as they were told, to enjoy the last third of the jump "under canopy." When the chute opened, it was a slight, gentle, uplift that straightened the free-faller to a position with feet downward toward the ground and landing zone. When the chute deployed, the jumper was trained to look up at it to be certain it *was* fully opened so as not to face the emergency situation where the reserve chute cord would have to be pulled. It was always a relief when the jumper looked upward and saw a fully-opened and deployed main chute. As the jumpers descended the last 3,000 feet groundward and were within several hundred feet of the landing zone, they were also cautioned not to look toward the ground at that point but, rather, toward the horizon -- to obviate against a stiff-legged landing. That is how an injury, the type Rebecca worried about for Thomas, might occur. Finally, at that point, looking toward the horizon, with the ground approaching, the jumper would pull down hard on the chute line toggles to further slow his descent and the landing, then, was surprisingly quite gentle. "It's as if the ground is coming up, to meet you, not you going down to it." Thomas explained this to those who asked to both demystify and, hopefully, tone down their perceived macho nature of the act.

With all of the new, more sophisticated equipment, even a relative newcomer to the sport of free-fall, like Thomas, was able to negotiate a landing on his feet, standing up, more a testament to the equipment and superb training than to the novice jumper himself.

Before touching down, Thomas was also amazed that before the chute was opened, during the freefall, in the proper position, as trained -- with one's stomach facing the ground and arms and legs akimbo and stretched out -- how just the slightest, subtle turn of one's outstretched arms enabled one to "steer" and turn, to the right or left, during the fall. One clearly had the sensation, while free-falling, of flying under one's own power and, moreover, being able to control one's flight directionally.

●●●●●●●

Thomas also was a great fan of major league baseball. He especially loved what he regarded as the unchanging symmetry of the game. Thomas had once written to a friend:

Baseball, without making too fine a point of it, can be seen in many ways as a metaphor for life itself. The game, in America at least, has been around seemingly forever. Players come and players go. Some have long, remarkable and noteworthy careers (or baseball lives). Others have less distinguished tenure. Many are red hot for a brief period but prove in the end to be not much more than a flash-in-the-pan. They and their glorious early-career achievements ultimately prove unsustainable.

But the game, the game, the game: it goes on and on and in it, as in life itself, as The Preacher in Ecclesiastes says, "there is nothing new under the sun." A sharply hit ball to the shortstop in the year 2005, fielded cleanly and thrown on to the first baseman will beat the runner to the bag by a half-step or so, for an out, just as it did a hundred years ago. And yet, at the same time, each game and each repeated event in each game has its own unique identity, its own fingerprint. I love that about baseball. Even though it is true that there is 'nothing new under the sun' in the game, it is also true that nothing which happens in a game today happens in exactly the same way it happened yesterday. The day of course is different, the weather conditions different, the venue, the teams and players are different, the circumstances and score are different.

I love, especially, that everything in the game is so neatly and precisely quantified. Give me the name of a player from the 1890s or the 1990s or any period in between and I can look up him and his record in The Baseball Encyclopedia and tell you how many games he played in every year he played and in his career, how many times he went to bat and how many hits he had and runs he scored and how many doubles, triples, homeruns and runs-batted-in he had and what his batting average was. I can tell you how many times he struck out in his career and how many times he walked and how many bases he stole and how many times he was hit by a pitch. I can tell you when and where he was born (and died). I can tell you how tall he was when he played and what he weighed and what, if any, nickname he had.

Baseball is great for nicknames.

"Dizzy" Dean, "Snuffy" Stirnweiss, Reggie "Mr. October" Jackson, "Hack" Wilson, Ted "The Splendid Splinter" Williams -- aka "The Thumper" or "Teddy Ballgame," (he was so good he had three nicknames) "Joltin' " Joe DiMaggio, Lloyd "Little Poison" Waner, "Duke" Snider, Stan "The Man" Musial," George Herman "Babe" Ruth -- aka "The Bambino", Mordecai "Three Fingers" Brown (I'll bet old Mordecai desperately wanted a nickname -- but almost certainly not the one that befell him, especially if it was literal),

Henry "Hammerin' Hank" Aaron, Ewell "The Whip" Blackwell, "Rabbit" Maranville, Vernon "Lefty" Gomez (do you suppose Mr. Gomez preferred his nickname to <u>his</u> given name as Mordecai probably did?), Marty "Slats" Marion -- American heroes all.

Marion, tall and thin, befitting the nickname "Slats" (6 feet, 2 inches, 170 pounds, according to The Baseball Encyclopedia), was also known, alternatively, as "The Octopus," presumably because of his fielding prowess. His wide-ranging, sure-handed fielding ability must have made him seem like one of those multi-appendaged sea creatures to disappointed hitters whom he so often deprived of infield singles or doubles into the outfield, through the shortstop hole.

Thomas followed baseball closely during its long season, keeping up with the daily box scores and standings. Thomas was not very much of a football fan at all though, he would concede, "I'll watch a televised game occasionally." Thomas had never been to an NFL game. He had been to numerous major league baseball games -- in many of the game's great and fabled stadia -- Yankee Stadium, Fenway Park, Wrigley Field, Forbes Field, Dodger Stadium and others. In Florida, he regularly went to Spring Training or Grapefruit League games.

Thomas found that baseball fans, generally -- there always was the exception -- were less rabid and manic than football fans. He was bemused at how so many of the pigskin fanatics he saw everywhere seemed to have their entire lives, almost, wrapped up in their favorite team and its performance during each season. They painted their faces and torsos team colors, showing off their artwork by going shirtless at games; they wore absurd head gear that related in some fashion to the team or its nickname or mascot, they plastered their automobiles with team decals and insignia, flags and bumper stickers. They spent hundreds of dollars every season to purchase team sweatshirts, jackets, hats and other accoutrements and memorabilia -- for one year only, to do it all again the next season.

They would become ecstatic and often downright giddy -- or depressed -- over their team's Sunday performance depending on whether their Redskins, their Cowboys or Giants or Browns or Forty-niners or Chiefs or Bucs won or lost. Their mood and outlook for the entire week hinged almost entirely on how their team fared on Sunday. In Washington, the lives of *so many* -- restaurant workers, street vendors, Congressional aides -- seemed to Thomas to be tied directly to the won-loss record of the Redskins. On Monday morning, if the Skins had lost the day before, Thomas would note (with silent, disguised glee) the somber expression on the faces of those all around him as he traveled to work via the Metro. Thomas often would tell those whom he considered the most devoted and rabid Skins' fans that *his* favorite team was "whoever's playing the Redskins this week." The comment, predictably, outraged them. Thomas carried this same attitude to, and voiced the same comment in, southwest Florida, when he moved to Sarasota, after leaving Washington, as it applied to the Tampa Bay Buccaneers. People who lived 60-70 and 100 miles or more away from Tampa were fanatic, diehard Bucs' fans. "Get a life," Thomas would think.

Thomas did not see what he considered comparable lunacy among baseball fans, except among many of those who pledged their allegiance and lives to the Boston Red Sox. Red Sox followers, Thomas thought, were the football fanatic 'nut cases' of major league baseball fandom.

Thomas was a great fan of the Washington-based national print columnist and television political commentator George F. Will, particularly after learning that Will also was an avid baseball fan. Thomas read and enjoyed immensely Will's book on baseball, "Men At Work," an erudite examination of "the craft of baseball."

Will apparently also was, like Thomas and most major

league baseball devotees, a "stats" fancier, Thomas learned. In a column on baseball in *Newsweek* magazine about the game and The Elias Sports Bureau, whose "business is to examine the statistical histories of ...major professional sports," Will wrote in 2002 --

"It is incessantly said that pitchers (in today's modern-day baseball) do not pitch inside as aggressively as they did in the rough-and-tumble past. Elias says: oh? In 1941, one in every 309 batters was hit by a pitch. In 1951, one in 214. In 1971, one in 179. In 2001, one in 99. Mickey Mantle, a power hitter, was hit 13 times in his career. The Astros' Craig Biggio was hit 28 times last year."

"When asked if any pitcher faced both Babe Ruth and Mantle, Elias reported: *Al Benton pitched against Ruth for the 1934 Philadelphia Athletics and against Mantle for the 1952 Red Sox."*

*"Elias knows **everything** worth knowing,"* Will concluded.

After reading that column by Will, Thomas went to *his* Baseball Encyclopedia to look up Benton (as he had gone to the same source to look up Marty "Slats" aka "The Octopus" Marion).

Thomas found that John Alton (Al) Benton pitched in the major leagues for part or all of 14 seasons. His rookie year was 1934, the year he faced Babe Ruth and his final year was 1952, the year he faced Mantle. He missed the years 1943, 1944 and 1945. (Thomas assumed, though the Encyclopedia did not so state it, that Benton was in the Armed Forces during that World War II period). Benton's career won-lost record was 98-88, a winning percentage of .527. His best year was in 1941, with Detroit, when he won 15 games and lost only six. He pitched a total of 1688 and 2/3 big league innings in his career and gave up 1672 hits during those innings. He struck out 697 batters, walked 733, and compiled a creditable earned run average for his career of 3.66. In those days of baseball (before the dreadful designated hitter rule,) Al went to bat, as a pitcher -- something pitchers, in the American league, do not have an opportunity to do today -- 512 times, got a career total of 50 hits (none of which was a home run; all were singles) and had a career batting average of a less-than-lusty .098. In the year he pitched against Babe Ruth, 1934, Al's won-loss record for the A's was a modest 7-9. In 1952, the year he pitched against Mantle, his record with the Red Sox was an even more modest 4-3. After his stint with the A's and then the Tigers, before he joined the Red Sox, Al pitched for two years with the Cleveland Indians.

John Alton ("Al") Benton was 6 feet 4 inches in height when he was in the majors and weighed 215 pounds. He was a right-handed pitcher and also swung his non-threatening bat from the right side.

His career fielding percentage was .939.

Al Benton was born on March 18, 1911 in Noble, OK. He died on April 14, 1968 in Lynwood, CA.

What Elias *doesn't* know, the Baseball Encyclopedia *does*, Thomas concluded, in a silent one-upping of the revered George F. Will.

●●●●●●●

Thomas had played baseball as a youngster. He loved the game even then, but was never very good at it.

Self-deprecatingly, he told his friends these days "I loved baseball so much that I'd be a retired major leagues shortstop right now, instead of a retired lobbyist -- had I had the talent, that is.

"Unfortunately, for me, the Peter Principle kicked in as far as my baseball ability was concerned shortly after Little League competition."

The Baseball Encyclopedia also included "career" information on the Little League umpire in Johnstown who Thomas remembered, as did almost every former Little Leaguer in Johnstown of Thomas's generation, one Jake Reisigl. Jake was a squat, cigar-smoking curmudgeon who puffed on his stogy during games. The cigar, belching dark, odoriferous smoke, protruded from Jake's mouth through one of the iron face-guarding rungs of his umpire's protective face mask/guard. If the cigar went out, the kids of the day feared, Jake would call a halt to the game until he got it fired up again.

Jake, the story went, as a young man actually had "had a cup of coffee" in the Majors.

And that was the truth, Thomas learned in later years, thanks to The Baseball Encyclopedia.

Jake, according to The Encyclopedia, pitched for the Cleveland Indians in 1911, at the age of 24. His big league career was remarkably short-lived, however. Jake pitched in just *two* games that year, for a total of 13 innings. He never pitched in the majors again.

Jake surrendered as many hits as innings pitched in his cup-of-coffee single season; he walked three hitters and struck out twice that number. Jake was charged with a loss in one of his two games. Thus, his career won-loss record was 0-1. Jake went to bat five times in his two games and was hitless, for a career batting average of .000. Jake had three fielding chances in his two games, all assists -- presumably taps back to the mound -- and handled them flawlessly, for a career errorless fielding percentage of 1.000.

Jake "Bugs" Reisigl was born Dec. 12, 1887 in Brooklyn, NY. He died Feb. 24, 1957 in Johnstown.

That's right. Jake had a nickname in the majors -- "Bugs" -- according to The Encyclopedia. Thomas did not recall that anyone in Johnstown's Little League population, players or parents, had ever known about that sobriquet while Jake was alive.

When he was playing, for Cleveland, Jake stood 5 feet 10 and ½ inches (the Encyclopedia is *that* specific -- 5-10 and *one half*) and weighed 175 pounds.

Thomas hesitated to guess or even imagine how and where Jake's nickname came about -- or what, possibly, it might have been based upon. It was, however, a very good thing, Thomas thought, that it was not widely known in Jake's day as a little league umpire in Johnstown. The possibilities for fun with it were endless, Thomas felt.

●●●●●●●

Thomas did indeed love baseball -- the sport and the poetry and the metaphor-for-life aspect of its universality and unique, never *exactly-the-same* repetitiveness. He thought that those few who covered the sport and wrote intelligently and well about it, like George Will -- and Roger Angell -- were artists of the highest order in the pursuit of their largely underappreciated endeavors by the public at large.

Angell for many years wrote about baseball in the highly respected and quite literary *New Yorker* magazine. His annual end-of-the-year baseball season recaps in the 1960s, '70s and '80s were works of art and collector's items. Angell was acknowledged by those in the know to be the "best baseball writer ever." Other of the cognoscenti had written "It is difficult to imagine anyone writing better about anything." Angell also authored a number of books about the sport. No less than *The New York Times Book Review* wrote about one of Angell's books: *"It is much more than a book about baseball. It is a book for people who miss good writing, who miss clarity, lucidity, style, passion."*

(Angell's mother was Katherine White, herself a longtime *New Yorker* employee. She was the magazine's fiction editor; Angell's stepfather was E. B. White, who wrote "Stuart Little," "Charlotte's Web," and other time-honored, well-known children's books.)

Thomas read Angell's baseball books, "Late Innings," "The Summer Game" and "Five Seasons." He followed and read almost religiously Angell's annual baseball seasonal wrap-ups in the *New Yorker*. Recently, Ellen had sent Thomas as a Christmas gift a copy of a non-baseball book by Angell, "Let Me Finish."

Thomas and Ellen, after the initial discord following their divorce, had established a "working" and reasonably amicable relationship in the years thereafter and they often exchanged modest and inexpensive gifts and Holiday remembrances. "After all," Thomas said, "even though we're divorced we will remain forever -- jointly -- the parents of three very special children." He once said to her, "You know, we might disagree on certain things, but that's no reason for us to be disagreeable."

The Angell book "Let Me Finish" was just such a gift from Ellen to Thomas. The book was not wholly baseball-oriented but more of a personal memoir, and Thomas enjoyed it and, as usual, also enjoyed and appreciated Angell's elegance with the written word. In it, Thomas read that Angell was a fan of an English novelist whom Thomas had never heard of, Rosamond Lehmann (1901-1990). Thomas sought out, acquired and read two of Lehmann's most notable novels, "Dusty Answer" and "The Weather in the Streets," the latter, according to one reviewer, "...a classic account of the agonies and joys of being in love."

"Dusty Answer," Miss Lehmann's most renowned and best-selling novel, Thomas thought a work of pure genius. Miss Lehmann understood well and had lived through and written beautifully and elegantly about the agonies and the ecstasies of man/woman love.

As he had done with John Irving, Thomas wrote a fan letter to Angell and was gratified and pleased to receive a response. He and Angell continued to correspond periodically after that -- about baseball and other, deeper, more existential subjects as well, subjects and issues *almost* as important as baseball. Angell was a wonderful correspondent.

"Time does not bring relief; you all have lied
Who told me time would ease me of my pain!
I miss him in the weeping of the rain;
I want him at the shrinking of the tide;
The old snows melt from every mountain-side,
And last year's leaves are smoke in every lane;
But last year's bitter loving must remain
Heaped on my heart, and my old thoughts abide.
There are a hundred places where I fear
To go, -- so with his memory they brim.
And entering with relief some quiet place
Where never fell his foot or shone his face
I say, 'There is no memory of him here!'
And so stand stricken, so remembering him."

-- *edna st. vincent millay* --

Thirteen

Rebecca remembered.

She had *her* 'Dusty Answer.'

She'd heard William drive up outside and just before he walked into the house she had placed the material from Thomas, once again, under the seat cushion of the chair in which she sat.

"Get all your chores done?" she asked, as William opened the front door and came into the living room.

"Yup." He walked across the room to where she sat. "Sure did. " He bent down and kissed her on the cheek.

"But, damn," he said, "the crowds were awful...

"...but I do think I'm finally organized and done and ready for the big day.

"And what have *you* been doing while I was out?" he asked.

"Oh, nothing, really," Rebecca replied -- too quickly, she thought. "Just some cleaning and a few last minute Christmas surprises," she lied. She got up from where she sat now and realized anew how wet she was in her womanhood after reading Thomas's letter and her rememberance of his orally pleasuring her. She felt guilty for a moment -- about her thoughts about that and about lying to William about what she had been doing in his absence.

She also felt guilty as she thought about Thomas's letter, and the sexual memories she had had while reading it, that she still could not or did not want to tell William about the letter.

Rebecca remembered. **She had *her* 'Dusty Answer.'**

●●●●●●●

"Want to go out to eat tonight?" William asked.

"Honestly, dear, I think I'd like to just stay in. I can put my Suzy Homemaker cap on and whip us up some spaghetti -- angel hair, with plain tomato sauce, if you'd like."

After dinner, William helped Rebecca clean up and straighten the table, as he generally did, and put the dishes and cookware in the dishwasher.

"I'm about ready to call it a day," he said. "Ready to come to bed?"

"In a few minutes, dear," said Rebecca. "There are just a couple of things I need to do. You go ahead. I'll be up in a minute."

Rebecca made some noises in the kitchen, to feign activity, and then went back to the living room and sat in the same Queen Anne chair she had earlier.

●●●●●●●

Rebecca remembered.

"Stop this," she told herself. "The man you love -- and who loves you -- is waiting for you upstairs in the bedroom the two of you share together.

"Get upstairs and get to bed with your husband. Thomas, and all of that part of your life, is over. It's in the long-ago past. Tomorrow is Christmas. Straighten up, girl."

Rebecca, determined now, went upstairs. She went into the master bath off the bedroom, did her nightly routine, put on a nightgown and slipped into bed next to William. He was snoring slightly.

Rebecca remembered.

Rebecca turned on her side, away from William, and drifted into sleep. William snored but did not otherwise stir.

Arthur also had been a snorer; Thomas had not. Rebecca remembered.

Fourteen

Christmas went well for William and Rebecca. They spent the day alone, very quietly, but with phone calls from friends and children and some few visits from neighbors.

Two days later, on the 27th, Rebecca sat alone, again in the living room Queen Anne chair with the thick envelope under its seat cushion containing the letter from Thomas.

Rebecca remembered.

She had *her* 'Dusty Answer.'

Rebecca had grown up as an only child in a small Midwestern industrial city. Her parents had been married for more than a dozen years before she came along -- and surprised them. They doted on her from the beginning, as most parents of only children do. From the very beginning, she was a motivated and excellent student, far surpassing her peers academically. In high school she became a cheerleader, popular among her classmates, and turned in her free time to an interest in dancing. She also met Arthur in high school and they began dating seriously almost immediately. Arthur was one year ahead of Rebecca when they met and, thus, when she was in her senior year Arthur had already gone off to college. Rebecca encouraged him to date while he was away and, he told her, he did that occasionally -- "but there is no one here anywhere near as special as you," he told her in one of their weekly telephone conversations.

Rebecca spent most of her free time during her senior high school year dancing. She was encouraged by one of her private dance instructors to audition for the Joffrey Ballet Company -- during a call publicized in the local Lima newspaper for dancers at a Joffrey company performance in Cleveland, some two hours away from where Rebecca lived. Her dad drove her there for the performance and her audition. She was mesmerized by the show and, afterward, reasonably satisfied at how well she thought she had danced during the trial -- and she had been encouraged by the reaction to her performance by those managing the audition.

Rebecca went on to college to study Fine Arts after graduating from high school and longed and lived for the summers when she and Arthur would have all the time they wanted for the two of them to be together.

Arthur was studying Business Management -- at another university, out of state and too far from where Becky had enrolled, for either of them to even consider weekend travel to see each other.

Rebecca remembered.

Christmas had been a week ago and Becky still had not had another opportunity to get back, privately, to Thomas's letter, as much as she had wanted to do just that -- and she chose, still, not to mention its existence to William.

William seemed to be getting out of the house more often than usual during the last few days, however, and -- without wondering why that was the case -- she had looked forward to today when he had said he had some gifts to "return and exchange" and would be away for most of the afternoon.

Rebecca decided to take out Thomas's letter once again, for the first time since two days after Christmas, though she had thought about it, certainly, every day since it had arrived.

She sifted through the opening pages of the letter to find the place in it where she had left off the first day she opened it --

I write today, Becky, to underline once more that I love you and I will love you forever.

Not one day has gone by of the nearly four thousand days since I last held you in my arms that I have not thought of you with warmth and with great and tender love ...

I feel about you as Thomas Wolfe felt once when he wrote the following to Aline Bernstein, the love of <u>his</u> life --

"I shall love you all the days of my life, and when I die, if they cut me open they will find one name written on my brain and on my heart. It will be yours.   I have spoken the living truth here, and I sign my name for anyone to see."

-- Tom Wolfe

I write to tell you this and I write to tell you one other thing, too ...

The other thing that I want to tell you, that I want you to hear directly from me, if only 'impersonally' through this letter rather than face-to-face, is why I write today. It is important to me that you know this. I feel you would want to know it...

It...is the second most striking thing, after meeting and falling in love with you, that has happened to me in my five-plus decades on this good earth ...

Rebecca went back and read that portion of Thomas's letter once more.

She could not imagine what Thomas might be referring to, what that "one more thing" might be.

Rebecca remembered.

Fifteen

Rebecca remembered …the day she learned about Arthur's infidelity. They had traveled from Austin for a short visit with her parents, in Ohio, and she happened, quite accidentally, upon Arthur their first day there, in the kitchen, speaking on his cell phone. As she entered the room and heard her husband's voice and saw the phone held to his ear she assumed at first that he was on a business call. She hung back in the doorway and, listening to Arthur's half of the conversation (as cell phone conversations overheard in so many venues these days, in restaurants, on the street, in department stores and supermarkets and doctors' offices, all are -- *half* conversations), she realized that the half-conversation she had stumbled on that her husband was engaged in was not a business call at all, but quite a personal one.

Rebecca confronted Arthur a few minutes later, and he denied that the call had been personal. Rebecca knew clearly, what she had heard, Arthur's conversation - closing "Love you." She did not let go of the issue and learned a few days later that Arthur had been having an affair for three years with an old friend from his college days whom he met up with again quite by chance in an airport while on a business trip. He told Rebecca that he and Nora realized when they met anew that there was a spark between them that had never gone out.

●●●●●●●

Rebecca and Arthur had married shortly after his graduation from college, before she herself had graduated or gotten her B.F.A. degree, and they then moved to and settled in Austin, Texas. There they met William and Nancy Arnold at a neighborhood summer Holiday get-together and the two couples became close friends. Arthur, at that time, had not yet rekindled his relationship with Nora. Rebecca became pregnant soon after marriage and within five years she and Arthur had a family of three children.

Rebecca gave up her dream to dance professionally but did launch, with Arthur's blessing and all the moral and financial assistance he was able to provide (grudgingly, she felt), a private dance studio in the basement of her and Arthur's home; at the same time she also began to devote more of her free time to golf. She had learned early on that, despite her diminutive size, she was quite good at the sport and she soon won the Women's Championship at the golf club she and Arthur had joined in Austin, the same club where the Arnolds were members. Rebecca felt that Arthur was somewhat envious of her golfing achievements. He was a decent golfer but nowhere near the top of his peer group, as she was -- at the very top.

Less than ten years after settling in Austin, Arthur was offered a promotion and transfer to Washington as the children approached their teenage years -- and the family relocated cross country to Bethesda. Their good friends, the Arnolds, also had moved from Austin at about the same time -- to San Diego. Rebecca faithfully kept in touch with them, while Arthur seemed to lose interest in maintaining the friendship on a long-distance basis.

Rebecca remembered.

On her trip to Austin, to clean up some personal issues and to get away from the tension that now flooded and overwhelmed the home she and Arthur lived in together in Bethesda but did not really share, together, she thought about the friend of the Morrisseys she had met on the golf course a few days ago. He seemed like a nice enough gentleman, she thought. She knew from Pamela that he was divorced and 'available.' Tall and thin, he also cut a reasonably presentable figure, an important consideration for Rebecca. She was intrigued. She also was pleased that he had called and left a message asking her to go to dinner with him when she returned from her short trip, and she planned to do so once she got home.

Sixteen

Rebecca called Thomas upon her return to Bethesda, responding to the message he had left for her the day they had met at the golf course the previous week. She called his home number during the day, when she assumed he'd be at his office in the District, and left a message saying she'd be delighted to have dinner with him sometime.

Thomas returned her call that night.

… And their long, slow dance of love began.

They spoke on the phone for nearly two hours the night of Thomas's call. She told him about her trip to Austin and the time she spent cleaning up some lingering chores related to her and Arthur's and their family's move from Austin, and the time she had spent with old friends -- William and Nancy Arnold. The Arnolds also were involved in a move from Austin. They were headed to the West Coast, to San Diego and, coincidentally, had returned to Austin when she was there, and for the same purpose -- to wrap up a few last details in connection with their move and relocation. William's wife Nancy, Rebecca had learned on the visit, had recently been diagnosed with breast cancer, but she and William were optimistic that her physicians had gotten an early start in detecting and diagnosing her problem and would be effective in treating and dealing with it and helping her to manage it successfully.

● ● ● ● ● ● ●

Rebecca and Thomas met, for their first date, at a little Italian restaurant ("Has anyone ever heard of or been to a *Big* Italian restaurant?" Thomas joked.) The restaurant was not far from Becky's and Arthur's home. Thomas did not feel comfortable -- while Becky and Arthur were still married, at least legally and formally so -- picking her up at her home. She felt the same way.

Delluci's was indeed a small restaurant -- not more than 12-15 tables in an intimate, single room/dining area. There was no bar.

Thomas and Rebecca ordered the same entrée -- angel hair pasta with a meatless red sauce, along with a mixed garden salad with Italian vinaigrette dressing. They both also liked the crunchy-crusted, soft-on-the-inside, warm Italian bread. They both also were fond of red wines and this night shared a bottle of California Merlot.

They had agreed to meet at the restaurant at 8 o'clock, and both got there a few minutes early. Rebecca was the first to arrive (giving lie to Pamela Morrissey's contention that Rebecca was "always late for everything.")

The night went on -- well. The conversation was easy and not at all forced, as it sometimes is between people who have just met or are having a conversation together for the first time or, certainly, as it is, too frequently, between longtime married couples. Thomas thought of how often he would see a couple across the table from one another in a restaurant --

presumably spouses? -- who, seemingly, had nothing to say to one another. It was always uncomfortable for him to even observe such a scene. Do most marriages come to that?

Rebecca chose not to tell Thomas more than he already knew about her domestic situation. But Thomas could see a sadness and unhappiness in her face and eyes. Rebecca talked about her just concluded trip to Austin, about her children, about her golf game and about their mutual friends, the Morrisseys. She talked about her upbringing and how she and Arthur had met in high school and married very young. She talked, but only briefly, about her love of dancing and the little studio she had once run out of her home in Austin.

The conversation flowed and ran long, long into the evening. The couple realized, shortly after midnight, that they were the only patrons left in the restaurant. The tables around them had been cleared and cleaned. A maintenance man vacuumed the carpeting. Thomas and Rebecca began to feel some slight pressure to leave in order to permit the cleaning staff to finish its work and, in turn, to leave the restaurant themselves.

And so it had begun -- their long, slow dance of love. Reluctantly, they both pushed their chairs back from their table and stood to leave.

Thomas walked Rebecca to her car. They stood beneath a parking lot lighted lamp post, facing one another and clasping each other, arms extended, with both hands. Thomas looked into Rebecca's eyes. He placed his two hands on Rebecca's face and he kissed her, lightly, on her lips. At 6 feet, 2 inches, Thomas was a full foot taller, at least, than Rebecca and he had to lean forward as he kissed her. She placed her arms round his waist. He placed his arms round her back and shoulders.

They hugged, gently, tenderly. Their embrace lingered. Neither wanted to let go of the physical contact with one another. Neither wanted the evening to end.

Finally --

"Thank you," she said softly.

"The pleasure was mine, pretty lady."

Thomas drove home and thought about Rebecca and that first kiss, long, long into the quiet night. Unlike most men looking back at the beginning of a love relationship, he could still remember, many years later, that first kiss with Rebecca.

Thomas remembered.

And so did she.

Rebecca remembered.

Seventeen

Thomas was scheduled to leave on a business trip the following day, coincidentally to Austin, from where Rebecca had just returned. He awoke early, after thinking about her and their evening together and their conversation, late into the evening before. He wanted to call her that morning, before leaving, and hear again her voice, her angelic voice, but he thought it best not to call because, after all, she was still living under the same roof as her husband, estranged or not.

Thomas returned from Austin the following Friday. He had missed Rebecca while he was away and had thought of her every day, often several times a day. Thomas, he admitted to himself, was smitten -- or on his way to that state.

Their long, slow dance of love was now well underway.

They began to speak on the phone daily, but it was almost a week before they met once more -- again for dinner.

They agreed to meet at a spot Thomas's daughter called a 'yuppie' restaurant a few steps down the street from where

Thomas lived, in Arlington, just two miles on the Virginia side
of the Potomac River and three miles from the heart of DC. It
was a delightful, small, informal restaurant that Thomas and
his daughter often went to -- "Pizza de Resistance." Thomas's
daughter also called it a "designer pizza joint."

It was another night of easy, endless conversation. Rebecca
often would reach across the table and touch Thomas's arm
or hand when she was speaking. He began to do the same to
her. They both were gratified that when they spoke the other
party actually listened. "Arthur never listens to anything I
say," Rebecca said. She laughed when she said it but Thomas
could see the undercurrent of sadness in her when she tried to
make light of her comment.

They spoke again about their friends, the Morrisseys, and
how they'd have to plan another golf date with them soon.
Rebecca spoke, too, about her friend Julie, whom she also had
met at the Bethesda TPC.

Julie was a widow who had had, Rebecca said, "much
more than her share" of sadness and pain in her life. She had
undergone a cancer operation, while still in her late 30s, and
seemed well on the road to full recovery when she was struck
with another of life's cruel blows. Her husband was diagnosed with a severe, rampant type of cancer and died within
a year of he and Julie getting that devastating news.

Rebecca suggested that she and Thomas meet Julie for
dinner sometime soon at the restaurant in Bethesda, where
she and Thomas had dined on their first date.

They met Julie at Delluci's two nights later. Thomas was
enthralled. Julie was a delight. She had indeed been through
a good deal of personal turmoil and pain. She had been a
widow at this point for nearly five years, and had just begun
dating -- "for the first time since I was a teenager," she said,
blushingly. Julie wanted another relationship, if she could
find one, "half as good as my marriage." She had joined BTPC
and was taking golf lessons (though, Rebecca whispered to
Thomas, she was not very good -- to say the least -- at the

sport.) She had taken up golf because she thought that it would increase her chances of meeting eligible men. Julie, seemingly, was trying everything to meet anyone she would judge to be a compatible, "eligible" male. She had even taken a course offered by a Bethesda Women's Group on "Fly-fishing." Unfortunately, that avenue turned into a dead end for her. She never learned to cast a fly-fishing line and did not meet any eligible men enrolled in the course or at any area fishing spots.

●●●●●●●

In any case, Thomas and Rebecca and Julie agreed to play a round of golf together the following weekend. They met Julie in the clubhouse and she was "decked out," thought Thomas, with enough designer golf clothing to appear as a model in the next issue of the Lady's "PGA Journal" magazine. Men rarely feel the need to make a fashion statement with the way they dress at a golf course; women often do.

Thomas and Rebecca had begun talking with each other on the phone every day by this time. Their slow dance of love continued.

After going to the practice tee to warm up, Thomas feared that the day ahead would indeed be a long one. Julie, <u>very</u> obviously, was not a golfer. Thomas thought that if she fly-fished, and cast, as poorly as she swung a golf club, she someday might very well wind up hooking herself while fishing and attempting to cast her line into a pond, stream or lake.

On the first tee, Julie swung and missed three times before her club head finally (accidentally? law of averages?) met the teed-up ball. The shot was a soft shank that traveled not much more than 50-60 yards. Julie, ever cheerful and not easily discouraged, was pleased, actually, that she had finally successfully struck the ball and that it had gone *forward*, in a manner of speaking, toward the first fairway and green.

"This *is* going to be a long day," Thomas whispered to Rebecca. She shook her head affirmatively, and smiled gently.

Julie got to the first green after 13 strokes. Her 4-putt green gave her a score of 17 for the hole.

Rebecca did her best to encourage Julie and, patiently, to give her pointers and tips on her swing, but by the time the three had finished the third hole they had decided to no longer keep score. "Let's just make this a practice round," Rebecca suggested. "Let's just have fun."

They had agreed after the 7th hole that they would only play the front nine and then have lunch. The back nine would have to wait for another day.

They arrived at the 9th tee. Rebecca floated a perfect 8-iron to the center of the green, with the pin in the back. Thomas's 6-iron was somewhat long, but found the putting surface nevertheless.

Julie walked to the tee. After teeing up her ball, she took her stance and waggled her club (a 5-wood) three-four-five-six times. "Hit the damn ball," Rebecca whispered to Thomas.

Thomas whispered to Rebecca: "If there's a God in heaven, she'll hit this green and end the day on a high note."

After her multiple waggles had, blessedly, ended, Julie wound up once again with her 5-wood, almost wrapping it around her neck in a corkscrew swing, lashed out and down at her ball on the tee, and, thank God, connected with it. Julie's golf ball took off on a line drive -- like a "frozen rope" in baseball -- down the elevated tee toward the green. Its line of flight and trajectory changed suddenly from a straight shot, straight ahead to a downward dive, like a dying quail, and the ball smacked into the flagstick dead in its middle, at its base, ricocheting backward, just slightly, and coming to rest on the green not more than a few feet from the cup.

After heading down the steep slope from tee to green, Julie tapped her putt dead center into the hole for a birdie two.

"Take that, Greg Norman!" cheered Thomas. Rebecca

smiled; Julie did not understand the meaning or significance of the comment, but she was inordinately pleased with her play and her shot and score. She smiled broadly. It was the first birdie of her golfing career. Thomas once, years later, wondered whether she ever had had another.

Rebecca remembered.

Eighteen

Thomas and Rebecca began seeing each other regularly, even before her divorce became final. Thomas joked about what to call what people "their age" were doing when they started "seeing each other." Was it in fact "seeing"; or was it, more accurately, "going with"; or was it what most of society would term "dating?" It seemed to Thomas that with the latter term -- dating -- the word itself was somehow attached to and more naturally, linguistically and demographically, applicable to the sexes under the age of 35 or 40, not to those of an age older than that, as he and Rebecca were.

In any case, Thomas laughed that he wasn't really sure how to actually define it nor did it matter very much to him, he said. After a while he no longer really cared or spent much time at all thinking further about how to define it or what to call it, even in a lighthearted way. He knew only that "I like it." He and Rebecca settled in to whatever it was they had easily and comfortably.

The two began not only seeing each other regularly, but talking on the phone daily, often multiple times each day. They spent most of their time together out, at restaurants or movies, at the theater or at Thomas's place but in any event away from Rebecca's and Arthur's home, with some very few exceptions. Once they were there, in bed, when they heard the front door open and someone walk through the room outside where they lay together. They both froze for a few moments, almost holding their breath, thinking that it might be Arthur. They remained motionless for a further few moments. After a while, Rebecca got up from bed to investigate, to see whether it might have been Arthur. It turned out to be Louisa, the maid.

Rebecca began jogging and once went with Thomas on a favorite route of his -- down the hill from where he lived, in Arlington, at Court House, into Roslyn, Arlington's main commercial district, across the Key Bridge into Georgetown and along the canal toward the Lincoln Memorial, one of Thomas's favorite Washington monuments. From there they crossed the 14th Street Bridge back to the Virginia side of the Potomac and ran along the river's edge, back toward Roslyn and Arlington. Now the hill from Roslyn to Arlington was upward, and considerably more difficult to run and maintain one's pace. Rebecca slowed to a walk and was apologetic, in her competitiveness, seemingly embarrassed that she could not keep pace. Thomas was secretly glad for the break, and said nothing. They walked up the hill, hand-in-hand, returned to Thomas's place and put on a pot of coffee. And then they made love.

I kneel before your perfect body.

Rebecca remembered.

Nineteen

After making love, that afternoon they went to see a movie at Court House Plaza.

Thomas remembered ... the delicacy of Rebecca, her beautiful perfectly-shaped oval face, the delicate, tiny nose, her full lips, her silky-smooth hair, both atop her head and "down there," her beautifully-textured skin, her tiny, gorgeous, finely-shaped hands and long, thin, graceful fingers. (She once told Thomas that more than a few people in her life had suggested to her that she could be a "hand model" for print advertisements and on television as well.) And her voice: "God, the voice," thought Thomas, as delicate as the first light of dawn -- and her smile, as gentle as a seraph -- *and* the inexpressibly beautiful womanly body with which she had been blessed.

Once when Thomas traveled on business to Houston for a few days, Rebecca stayed at his condominium home in Arlington, and was there when he returned home late of an evening. It was the first time he had returned home after a trip that he could remember when he *wanted* and *longed* to return home, and was greeted with a warm and inviting welcome. Thomas began to fall very much in love with Rebecca that night. It was good to come home to *her*. It was good *not* to be *alone*, as he always seemed to be.

Rebecca began staying more frequently at Thomas's for weekends or a few additional days at a time during the week. Their long, slow dance of love began to crescendo daily. They ate frequently at the "designer pizza joint." Both liked their pizza plain, or with pepperoni; no sausage, no mushrooms, no vegetables, only pepperoni or plain cheese.

Julie meanwhile had met someone -- a British citizen visiting in Washington on business. They fell in love soon after they met and Rebecca was concerned that Julie was jumping too soon, that she wanted to be in love for the sake of *being* in love. Thomas suggested that Rebecca allow Julie -- and Robert -- to worry about that themselves. "It's not really your concern, even as a friend," he said gently. "They're both adults and seem to be doing quite OK without you or me. Let's just wish them well and nothing more than that."

Julie was obviously very happy with Robert, and he with her. They planned a trip together to his home in London. They had dinner with Rebecca and Thomas at Delluci's the weekend before their scheduled departure. Julie had never traveled overseas and planned and packed her clothing weeks in advance. She sent postcards to both Rebecca and Thomas while she was away. She and Robert were "having a great time."

Rebecca told Thomas that since moving to Bethesda she had wanted to go to   the Wolf Trap Performing Arts Open Air Arena in nearby Virginia, but Arthur had never shown any interest in it. She and Thomas went there for a concert featuring The Neville Brothers and noticed that many of the attendees brought picnic lunches with them to spread on a blanket on the grass before show time. She and Thomas did that, along with a bottle of Merlot, for the next concert they attended -- The Righteous Brothers: "You've Lost That Loving Feeling," "Unchained Melody," "You Are My Soul and My Inspiration" were three of their best recordings. Thomas would later see the duo in concert once again, in Sarasota, with Lu-Ann.

Thomas and Rebecca took a rail trip from Washington's Union station to Manhattan's Grand Central station. Neither could remember the last time they had ever traveled any distance by train. They stayed at the Waldorf-Astoria for the weekend and saw some Broadway shows, "Cats" and "Phantom of the Opera." They had dinner at Sardi's and also visited the Plaza's Oak Room and strolled hand-in-hand through Central Park.

They took a weekend trip to southern Virginia, to Occoquan, staying there in a rustic, but modernized Bed and Breakfast facility. "Arthur would never have wanted to stay in a B&B, only five-star hotels for him," she told Thomas the last night of their stay, as they sat in a hot tub off their room and sipped champagne.

They took a trip to Nantucket, "The Grey Lady of the Sea," staying *there* at a delightful five-star hotel, The Jared Coffin House, in the village's central downtown district. They walked the cobble-stoned streets of Nantucket hand-in-hand and made love in their hotel room in a super king-sized four-poster bed. The next morning they made love again and then had room service breakfast in bed.

"Arthur would *never* have eaten in bed," said Rebecca.

"I do," said Thomas. "I like to eat in bed -- breakfast, <u>and</u> you!"

Rebecca remembered.

●●●●●●●

They went to Florida to play golf and to escape to a warmer

clime during Washington's winter. That trip had some rocky moments. Rebecca and Arthur still had not reached final agreement on their divorce and Rebecca while in Florida with Thomas began to have second thoughts on whether she *really* did want to end her marriage. Thomas was deeply saddened and distraught the night, at dinner, when they had this conversation. He had sensed and felt a change in her during the trip. She seemed obviously preoccupied. At dinner, Rebecca said, "I think I belong in my marriage." Thomas suspected at the time that financial considerations -- worries -- were a big part of Becky's newly-surfaced concerns.

Much later, after that disconcerting comment and disappointing Florida trip, they took a weekend trip to Johnstown, the first time since his divorce Thomas had 'brought' a girlfriend "home." Paddy, when learning of Rebecca's dance background, dubbed her "Goody Two Shoes." Paddy later would bestow sobriquets on other women Thomas dated, after his divorce. Rebecca 'Goody Two Shoes' was the first so christened, primarily because of her love of and background in dance. Another lady friend, from Washington, after Thomas and Rebecca had stopped "seeing" one another, once also accompanied Thomas to Johnstown. She, Stefania, had relatives in Eastern Europe, in Croatia. Paddy christened Stefania "The Croatian Creation." Still later, Millicent, a Pennsylvania native, was dubbed "Quaker State Annie." Years later, Patricia, a vice president and bank manager in Sarasota, became "Tillie the Teller." Olivia, a red head, was christened "The Scarlet Harlot."

When Thomas and Rebecca were in Johnstown, Thomas's aging mother was in the hospital, terminally ill. They visited and spent time with her there. When she died, a few months later, Rebecca never called Thomas to offer her condolences or comfort --- a hurt, for Thomas, that still stung. Thomas had been devoted to his mother, widowed young with four children and then beset to deal on her own with breast cancer while still a relatively young woman. Thomas, who was not self-congratulatory about very much in his life, *did* feel that he had been a good son to his mother as he also felt that during his marriage he had been a good *father*. "I define myself as a father, first and foremost," he said often to friends. He did wonder if he had not spent *enough* time working at his marriage, short-changing Ellen, and too much time trying to be the best father he could be -- the father he lost when he himself was 13 years old, the father he never really had. Thomas's father traveled often when Thomas and his three siblings were growing up.

Thomas cried at the funeral home in Johnstown where his mother was waked on the day of the funeral. He wept when the funeral director closed the coffin to ready it for the trip via hearse to St. Mary's Church for a funeral Mass. It was the second time in his adult life that Thomas had been unable to hold back tears.

Twenty

It was late in January, a month after Rebecca had received the long letter from Thomas. She had, eventually, gotten back to reading it and occasionally would go back to parts of it to reread. It still rested under the seat cushion in the living room Queen Anne chair, and she still had not mentioned it to William.

She was not sure why she still had not yet told William about the letter. She knew that she did not want to hurt him but she also did not want to release -- to anyone -- her own personal, very private recollections of Thomas and the love they had shared.

Rebecca remembered.

Of late, William seemed to be spending more time out alone during the day on weekends, ostensibly on errands and various assorted chores.

She took out Thomas's letter and went to a page she had read before.

Do you remember the last day we saw and were with one another? I do. It is with me still. I have not forgotten, I cannot forget ...

You knew when we parted that day, that sunny afternoon in Georgetown, that our good-byes were final and that they were to be forever. You knew it -- but I did not, and would not know it until much, much later.

Rebecca remembered.

Do you remember our talks about how <u>all</u> man-woman relationships have two things in common? First, there is always more love on the part of one of the two. One of the two <u>always</u> loves more than the other. But even more than that, the overriding thing that <u>all</u> relationships have in common is this: in one way or the other, <u>they end</u>. They run their course and end. One way or the other: 'til death do they part, literally or figuratively. They end. <u>All of them</u>. Love is not forever, as much as the two -- every two -- believe, initially, with all of their heart, that <u>it</u> will be forever for <u>them</u>. They are wrong. All relationships, one way or the other, do end. And it is always a sad, tragic and unhappy thing when a love that once burned so brightly is, finally, extinguishable.

Do you remember those great lines that we each found so thoughtful from "One Hundred Years of Solitude" about "weeping from love ... the oldest sobs in the history of man..." "...the wildest and most tenacious love (is) an ephemeral truth in the end."

Is love an ephemeral truth only? Neither of us wanted to believe that. We, like all lovers, believed that <u>our</u> passion and love would never die, that ours was eternal and would last forever. We believed in that old Chinese proverb that you once read and told me about which holds that there is a cosmic belief that an imaginary thread connects those people who are meant to be together, and that nothing can ever break that line (thread), not time nor distance nor circumstance.

The difficulty with this is complicated when it leads to the inevitable -- marriage. And here is that marriage-exacerbated complica-

129

tion about which you and I have spoken and, I believe, about which we agree: women marry thinking their husbands will change; men marry thinking their wives will never change. Both are wrong.

Rebecca remembered.

Do you recall our discussions about whether people can love more than once in a lifetime? It seemed to me that true love was a one-time occurrence. It could happen anew in the event a former or current love passed away, but not following a "break-up" or divorce. Love, it seemed to me, was indeed eternal and for someone to love again soon after being in love with someone else cheapened the meaning and sanctity of it. Is love, indeed as Marquez wrote, an "ephemeral" truth? You thought that someone could love again, after a love had ended for a reason other than death, and I think now, as I age, that I may finally agree with you on that. Love can happen again.

Rebecca heard William's car outside and once again put Thomas's letter back under the seat cushion.

To all the girls I've loved before
Who traveled in and out my door
I'm glad they came along
I dedicate this song
To all the girls I've loved before

To all the girls I once caressed
And may I say I've held the best
For helping me to grow
I owe a lot I know
To all the girls I've loved before

The winds of change are always blowing
And every time I try to stay
The winds of change continue blowing
And they just carry me away

To all the girls who shared my life
Who now are someone else's wives
I'm glad they came along
I dedicate this song

To all the girls who cared for me
Who filled my nights with ecstasy
They live within my heart
I'll always be a part
Of all the girls I've loved before

To all the girls we've loved before
Who traveled in and out our doors
We're glad they came along
We dedicate this song.

-- *To All The Girls I've Loved Before*
(Willie Nelson)

Twenty One

Thomas thought back to that fall day in Georgetown, when he and Rebecca last saw one another. As he wrote to her, *You knew when we parted that day that our good-byes were final, and that they were to be forever. You knew it -- but I did not, and would not know that until much, much later.*

Thomas left Georgetown that afternoon and drove to the District, parked his car on 22nd street near the U.S. State Department, and walked to the Lincoln Memorial where he sat on the steps, as he had so often done. It was a contemplative spot for him and, he thought, one of the most beautiful sites in a city of startling monumental beauty.

He thought about what had just happened and the realization began to dawn on him that Rebecca had perhaps hinted at and been adumbrative about what lie ahead for them.

Thomas sat on the next to last step going up to the great statute of President Lincoln. Thomas's back was against a pillar. He looked out at the Mall and the Washington Monument, its image shimmering in the Mall's reflecting pond. Off to the left he gazed at the somber, sacred Vietnam Wall. There are nearly 60,000 names etched on that black marble edifice, the names of the now gone men and women who had made the ultimate sacrifice for their country, most of them 18, 19, 20 and 21-year-olds, youths, really, not quite adults chronologically, who had died, alone and frightened, in a rice paddy or strange and remote village far from their home in Iowa or Missouri or upstate New York. Thomas remembered one young soldier in particular who died in front of him, in tears and crying for "mommy." Thomas saw no shame in that. The 18-year-old had been remarkably brave in battle and, Thomas later had learned, was posthumously awarded the Silver Star, the second highest decoration for valor in battle. Others died stoically, without a word. All died bravely -- 60,000 of them.

Thomas sat on the steps of the Lincoln Memorial that afternoon for nearly an hour. He was bemused, as always, by the tourists and visitors who daily climbed those steps, cameras in hand, and as they neared the top where he so often sat, he would offer, as he did countless times, to take their pictures using their cameras "if you'll show me how to use it, which button to push." The Asian visitors always seemed to be the most grateful, bowing effusively to Thomas and uttering over and over their obviously heartfelt appreciation for his gesture of kindness. "Thank you, thank you, thank you," all with a wide smile accompanying their bow. Thomas also was inspired as a witness to the many African-Americans he saw each time he was there who were visiting the Memorial. He was able to discern or intuit which were from the Capitol District area and which were from further away -- from the Deep South, perhaps. Those from distant points were the visitors, it seemed to Thomas, who climbed the steps more slowly toward the great stone statue of Lincoln seated in a chair, all the while looking up, in reverence and obvious awe, at the stone edifice of The Great Emancipator. It was something terribly personal for them, more so than for most visitors.

As he stood to leave that afternoon, Thomas took a final glance at the Vietnam Wall and the area surrounding it. He noticed, as he usually did at the Wall, a number of "tree huggers" (this was a time in America before this term was used deprecatingly by ultra-conservatives to refer to staunch environmentalists). The tree huggers at The Wall were men, by themselves, who stood at a distance from the tableau with 60,000 names on it. These tree huggers stood near a row of elms and sycamores, 75 feet from The Wall. These men, presumably veterans of that terrible conflict in Southeast Asia, could not bring themselves to actually approach and stand on the walkway next to The Wall. This, for now, for them, near the tree line, was as close as their memories and hearts would permit them to stand -- near but not immediately next to the names of so many of their fallen comrades. Most of the tree huggers, Thomas noted, would, if they were wearing hats -- mostly baseball caps, with the bills worn frontward -- remove those hats out of respect and in tribute to the dead of their war, as they stood at their distance, 'hugging' the far-off tree line.

Thomas remembered.

Becky, meanwhile, drove from Georgetown to Bethesda. She was meeting William tonight for dinner -- at Delluci's.

She thought about Thomas.

Rebecca remembered.

Thomas walked back to where he had parked his car and drove home the short distance to Arlington and called the Croatian Creation. "Hey, I know this is short notice, but I was wondering if you've made any dinner plans yet." The Creation was always good that way, adjusting on the run and adapting to whatever might come along. "I'll be there in an hour," he said. "Great," said the Croatian Creation. "I'll be ready." They went to a Chinese restaurant, where they had been before, close by to where Stefania lived, in McLean.

At home that evening, after having dinner with Stefania,

Thomas considered again what he now thought Rebecca may have been telling him with her actions, not her words, that afternoon in Georgetown. He asked himself, too, that if he did not ever see her again, did he -- and would he -- still love her? Thomas's thoughts turned to the questions about man/ woman love about which he and Rebecca had had discussions: is human love, on this great spinning planet in space, this unavailing star, if it is real and true and deep, a one-time phenomenon -- or can one love richly and truly again? More so, thought Thomas, does love *happen* again?

Thomas thought about the women in his life he had 'loved' before, or *perhaps had loved*, depending on how one defines that amorphous, elusive, fleeting, mysterious, finite emotion.

Before Thomas walked back to his car, he looked again at the tree huggers as they continued to stand there, at a distance -- stoically, silently -- amidst the rows of elms and sycamores. A mild, barely noticeable late summer zephyr stirred and the trees, swaying slightly, stood serene and stately as silent sentinels to the now-stilled spirits of those so many thousands of fallen soldiers named on The Wall, safe, at rest and home, at last, from southeast Asia.

Thomas paused briefly as he walked toward his car, and looked back at The Wall once again.

Welcome home, brothers, he thought, mouthing the words silently to himself.

And then , aloud, "Welcome Home."

Thomas remembered.

135

Twenty Two

Thomas had met Ellen in college, when he returned for his junior year, after his Army enlistment had ended. They met in a college hangout, where Thomas had found work as a bartender. On that night, which was not a busy one in the bar, Thomas and a fellow bartender were going through the "Mr. Boston" Bartender's Guide, alphabetically, selecting and mixing in turn an alcoholic concoction they either were unfamiliar with or had never before tasted. They had only gotten through to the letter "J" before they realized that with "B" they had found a drink they both liked and wanted more of -- a "Blood and Sand." Thomas and his associate, a non-student town resident, mixed another Blood and Sand and made this one somewhat healthier and more copious than a drink for just the two of them. They gave the extra portion to Ellen (sitting at the end of the bar by herself), serendipitously it would turn out, since the drink's base was scotch and Ellen was a scotch drinker. (It would be many years before Thomas would have another Blood and Sand cocktail: he and Olivia shared one during her visit to Siesta Key in Florida. They ordered one in an upscale hotel bar; that bartender, too, was

136

unfamiliar with the drink and was forced to resort to *his* "Mr. Boston" Guide to see what the drink's ingredients were, and how to make it.)

When Thomas met Ellen the 'Blood and Sand' night when he was tending bar, he learned that she was a freshman transfer student from a college in Michigan. She and Thomas married in Thomas's senior year. Ellen at that time was pregnant. Love certainly was a part of their relationship early on, Thomas remembered. Ellen was pretty and sweet. She knew Thomas had just gotten out of the Army; she did not know -- she would never know -- that Thomas had served in Vietnam in combat.

After six years of marriage, two additional children had blessed their lives. Numbers two and three came along just a year apart, following a five-year hiatus after their first-born.

The family grew in economic worth over the years and also relocated a number of times as Thomas continued to receive promotions and job assignment transfers.

When the marriage ended, after 18 years, Thomas was devastated. He had been born, raised and educated as a Roman Catholic and never considered for even a moment that a divorce would become part of his life. He remembered when he traveled to Johnstown to tell his mother, in person, that he and Ellen were ending their marriage. She was not as upset as he feared she might be. It turned out, she confided in him, that she had never really liked Ellen over the years. She had found her "snippety," she said, and kind of "highfalutin."

Thomas took seriously his marriage vow of fidelity. When he mentioned, once, to Paddy that he had never been unfaithful in his marriage, Paddy was dumbfounded. Paddy had been married four times and, he said, had cheated in all of those marriages, several times.

"You never did it? Never? Not even once?" Paddy asked, incredulously.

"Nope," said Thomas. "But don't canonize me just yet," he told Paddy. In reality, Thomas added, he had never faced a situation where infidelity *might* have happened and, thus, he had never even been *tempted* to break that most sacrosanct of all the marriage vows.

●●●●●●●

After the second time Ellen had Thomas served with a divorce summons, and Thomas had come to terms with the fact that his marriage was indeed ending, he contacted a divorce attorney whose name he had picked out of the telephone book yellow pages, Betty Allen, "specializing in difficult divorces." Another reason Thomas hired her had to do with simple logistics. Her office was close by his.

Betty and Thomas became friends during the process and Thomas often confided in her about the pain and hurt he was experiencing. She was very good at keeping Thomas from surrendering too many of the joint marital assets, which he had, initially, wanted to do in totality, to give Ellen <u>everything</u>, "just to wrap this up and end things once and for all."

Betty again cautioned Thomas against this attitude and protected and championed his rights in negotiations with Ellen's attorney and in court. The divorce, finally, was said to have been amicable. Ellen's primary emotion during the process was anger -- along with retribution and a clawing desire to acquire as much materially as she could; Thomas's overriding emotions were destitution and a sense of betrayal and abject loss and failure. He still could not understand or articulate how and why the marriage had soured.

In the end, after four years of negotiations and back-and-forth, Ellen got much more than half of the Gormans' joint assets, and Thomas did not much care. In the end, for him, all he wanted, finally, was to move on. Ellen could have <u>all</u> of the material items, and money, that she wanted. Thomas wanted to be fair about all of it, but, primarily, he wanted more than anything for the pain of it to cease.

Thomas wrote to Aldo in Toulouse about a subsequent course of events —

"I appreciate full well what you say about material items and monetary assets and the inevitable reality and need to downsize when one goes through a divorce. My former home in Westchester, which you once visited, was nearly as big as a junior high school. It contained something on the order of 6800 square feet of living space. Ellen kept it and almost all of its furnishings when she and I were finally, and irrevocably, divorced. I moved from my furnished single room, "The Cave," to a 1000 square foot condominium apartment outside of Washington and took with me only my clothes and books and some personal items along with a few additional, assorted other items which Ellen in her magisterial munificence had put into a cardboard box for me to take along -- one fucking box, Aldo -- ONE, the contents of which I did not discover until I opened and unpacked the box some six weeks later when I moved from temporary living quarters in Washington to my palatial Arlington abode.

"Ellen had kept the house and all of the furnishings and furniture in it, of course, but had also claimed 'custody,' as it were, of all the "crockery and vases and pots and bric-a-brac" (as you put it), not to mention all of the artwork and the three to four dozen Lladro porcelain pieces she had purchased in Spain as well as the $40k silverware that the two of us had purchased in your native land, Italy, and the gold from Egypt and the fine dishware from Holland and the crystal from Sweden and all of the finery, lace et. al. from Belgium and every other fine item we had purchased together during our years living in Europe.

"When the day came for me to transition from my temporary living quarters in Washington to my newly-purchased condominium in Arlington, and after my few pieces of Salvation Army furniture had been spaced throughout the apartment, I opened my box from Ellen the evening of my move to find in it only a few odd, assorted and inexpensive dishes and water glasses, 25 years old, along with a meager few dented, mangled and/or rusted kitchen miscellanea. There were a half-dozen stainless steel knives and forks, a corkscrew -- and one spoon. The spoon was the type one uses to eat a cut of grapefruit. It had a ragged, serrated, cutting edge. I suppose it was symbolic in some way of what Ellen felt toward me that she packed that one particular spoon in my take-away box, but I wasn't then, and have never since been, able to figure out just what its symbolism may be. In any case, I still have the spoon. It is my <u>favorite</u> piece of 'silverware.' Make that 'stainless steel.'

"It was late on a Saturday afternoon when my move-in to my new living quarters had been accomplished and I was altogether unfamiliar with my new neighborhood and its environs. I walked a few city blocks to find a small convenience store. Most of the other, larger commercial establishments and supermarkets in the area by that hour had closed up for the weekend. I went into the convenience store and purchased a bottle of cheap wine (red, of course) and a pint of chocolate chip ice cream for my supper. Back home, I employed the corkscrew I had gained custody of in the split of marital assets and goods to open the wine bottle and free its contents from their encyst and, with a sense of freedom and a measure of pleasure, jubilance and insouciance, such as I had not felt in many years, chose to use it, rather than my grapefruit spoon, to dig into and eat my ice cream meal. The apartment was dark; the only light came from the refrigerator door when it was open. In my take-away box I found a single, 60-watt light bulb and I took it with me from room to room to the few lamps I had spotted around my Palais de Versailles. I moved about my new home that first evening, drinking my wine directly from the bottle and eating my chocolate chip ice cream with the business end of my corkscrew -- and burning the fingertips of my right hand each time I moved to another area along with my light bulb.

"I treated my serrated-edged spoon that evening with condign disdain though I have since, over the years -- as I implied earlier -- become quite fond of and attached to it.

"Meanwhile, back in Westchester, Ellen had the $40,000 silverware from Italy -- enough to accommodate a party of 24 -- and the gold from Egypt and all of the crockery, vases, pots and pans and other bric-a-brac from our two-decades' life together. I had a corkscrew, a light bulb and my spoon."

Over the years after their divorce, Ellen and Thomas learned to get along with one another, partially out of the requisite necessity of shared parenthood. In reality, their relationship was actually quite civil. "After all, divorced or not," Thomas said, "we will remain together as the parents of our three daughters. They will be a part of the two of us forever."

Twenty Three

Thomas began to consider dating even before the divorce with Ellen was finalized. He asked his attorney Betty about this, wondering whether it would work against him in the final court judgment. Betty assured him it would not but advised him that if he *did* begin to "see" someone, that he not "rub it in Ellen's face." He needed to be "circumspect" and "discreet," Betty advised.

Thomas's first 'date' since he was a teenager was dinner with a woman, divorced, who worked in his company, but in another department. A Hungarian immigrant, Julia and he found they could talk easily with one another and enjoyed each other's company as well. Julia was taller than average for a woman, nearly six feet, thin, dark, quite prepossessing. Her figure and womanly charms were regal and striking enough to turn men's heads on the street. When he told Paddy he was going to start "dating," Paddy asked him why ("Jesus, Tom, you just got rid of one cunt and now you want to hook up with another? What, are you fucken nuts?") In all honesty Thomas replied, "Because I'm horny, Paddy. I *need* a woman. My right hand is getting tired."

"Can you cook yet?" Paddy asked.

"What the hell difference does <u>that</u> make?" asked Thomas.

"Well," Paddy retorted, "it's something you gotta learn to do so your dick doesn't talk your stomach into getting married again."

●●●●●●●

In Washington, Thomas's first date after he had settled in Arlington, with his grapefruit spoon , lightbulb and cork-screw, was with The Blind(s) Lady. Carol came to his condo-minium apartment in suburban Virginia to measure for "window treatments," a descriptive that Thomas considered comically 'fancy-schmansy' and that his dear mother might have termed 'highfalutin.'

Thomas shortened Carol's sobriquet to The Blind Lady, singular. She was an attractive, chesty divorcee with two pre-teen children and she and Thomas dated for a period of only a few weeks before parting ways. Thomas liked Carol, found her attractive, but, as he told Paddy, he also found her some-what intellectually deficient. "I don't think <u>her</u> light bulb has come all the way on yet."

Thomas also began dating single women he met during the course of his work on Capitol Hill. He went out with probably a dozen or more in his first 18 months in Washing-ton. Until this period, he still had not "honeymooned" (as his secretary, Arlene, referred to sexual intimacy -- "And have the two of you '*honeymooned*' yet?" she would ask, with a leer-ing but fun smile on her face) with anyone since his marriage had ended -- not Julia, not the Blind Lady, and not any of the 'Hill' ladies he had met -- until Maria.

Maria, also a lobbyist, represented a competitor company to the company Thomas worked for. (Thomas, since Julia "The Hungarian," had tried to never date again anyone who worked in his own company. "Don't dip your pen in company

143

ink," was his, and others' prevailing wisdom on <u>that</u> matter.) Thomas actually had known Maria casually before moving to Washington, having met her there in industry trade association meetings on day and overnight business trips from Connecticut, even before he was divorced.

Maria had never been married. With Maria, the relationship culminated, eventually, in a 'honeymoon.' Strangely, Thomas felt a twinge of 'guilt' when he went home early the next morning. It was the first time since his marriage, two decades ago, that he had been with another woman. He knew, in his head, that he was not being 'unfaithful' to Ellen but felt, in his heart, that somehow he *was* being unfaithful. He ascribed the feeling to his Catholic upbringing and a moral hangover from that strict, multi-year, regimented, moral indoctrination.

The Jews do not have a corner on the guilt game. Catholics are right in there, too, thought Thomas.

Twenty Four

In Johnstown, Thomas had gone to the same school, St. Mary's Institute, for thirteen years, from kindergarten through senior high school to graduation. All of the grades at SMI, from the elementary to the senior high school level, *were in the same building.*

The school building was a few steps, two streets, away from St. Mary's Church, where Thomas served for many of those 13 years at SMI as an altar boy and where the funeral Mass for his mother had been offered.

The Roman Catholic Mass when Thomas served as an altar boy was still offered in Latin. Thomas remembered, into his adult years, some of the rote phrases that constituted an altar boy's role in the playing out of the sacrament.

"Dominus Vobiscum."

"Et cum spiritu tuo."

"Mea culpa, mea culpa, mea maxima culpa."

"Et in saecula saeculorum,"

Amen.

He remembered, in those days, having to sound the hand-held bells device thrice, on two occasions, during the Mass's

Consecration, once when the priest held his hands up holding the bread to be consecrated as Christ's body, the other when he held up the chalice of wine to be consecrated as Christ's blood. As an adult, that (the bell-ringing) -- along with the Latin Mass -- had become a thing of the past in the modernized Catholic Church.

●●●●●●●

Even as a pre-teen, Thomas was troubled and thought not infrequently about some of the great questions of life that were answered too cursorily and easily by the nuns and priests in SMI's Catechism classes.

Is there a God? How do we know -- how *can* we know -- that He exists? Is there life after death, a Heaven, Hell and Purgatory? What *is* Purgatory?

"Always was and always will be..." That was an especially difficult concept to fathom, particularly for a young mind. The 'always will be' was easier to grasp for Thomas than the 'always was.'

Is God all-loving? Why, then, does he condemn a person and a soul to eternal pain and damnation in the fires of Hell?

And for that matter, what is "Limbo?" -- is that, really, a place where, as the Church holds, non-baptized babies must go for eternity? And was that God's idea originally or an idea cobbled together in the two millennia since Jesus's time by Church "leaders."

Questions like those did not seem to trouble Paddy, who, actually (in a manner of speaking), was on the Church's payroll. Paddy was a paid altar boy and Mass-server at a Catholic shrine/tourist attraction -- Auriesville -- nearby Johnstown. Auriesville honored a young Indian girl -- Kateri Tekakwitha -- who had gained sainthood after spending her early years as a pagan before converting to Christianity and subsequently being martyred at the tender age of 18 or 19, according to Auriesville lore. Thomas's and Paddy's mother drove Paddy there every Sunday to "work" and, during the summer vacations, two or three additional days a week to serve during the many Masses offered at the Shrine during the day for the tourists/faithful.

Paddy even told of a priest at the Shrine who tried to be overly friendly to him on a couple of occasions. Sexual abuse by the clergy in those days was almost unheard of or, as Thomas theorized later as an adult, probably under-reported.

Thinking back to the days of innocence at St. Mary's and Auriesville, after he had left Washington and settled in Siesta Key, Thomas was deeply saddened and the foundation of his longtime faith substantially weakened by the sexual abuse scandals that were widespread in the Catholic Church in the United States during the last decade of the 20th century and the early part of the 21st.

Twenty Five

To the Bishop -- (Thomas wrote) --

May 10, 2002

I write, sir, after deep soul-searching and prayer.

I ask myself if it would be best to keep the thoughts and concerns that I express herein to myself -- and to my God? And I ask, will expressing them and committing them to paper in this letter to you serve any useful, positive or salutary purpose?

I do not want to seem impertinent and it certainly is not my intent to insult you or anyone else through this letter. Also, I do not want to be judgmental or come across as self-righteous. I, too, am a sinner and I do not want to seem, either, as overly critical, destructive or negative toward the Church or abjuring of my and our Roman Catholic faith. I want, above all, to be honest and constructive. I hope, and pray, that my heart is in the right place as I compose and post this letter to you. I believe that it is.

I write, sir, because of the criminal sex abuse scandal and resultant crisis facing the American Catholic Church today. Make no mistake about it: it is a scandal and a crisis. Let us not mince words here. Let us eschew, sir, the euphemisms being bandied about by Church representatives these days when speaking with the press. Some of them allude to this terrible scandal, simply, as 'a problem' or term it 'the current situation.' Others -- and, regrettably, there have not been very many Church spokesmen in the base case -- refer to the scandal as a 'tragedy.' <u>That</u> , in my opinion, is the only descriptive that has been issued publicly by a Church spokesman that comes even close to being truthful and honest and not an attempt to excuse or semantically disguise what has taken place, what has been perpetrated by too many sick priests on too many helpless, hapless, innocent youth.

What the Church is facing today, very clearly, is much more than a 'problem.' It is, unquestionably, a tragedy, albeit an undeniably self-imposed tragedy. Mea culpa, mea culpa, mea maxima culpa.

And what the Church -- and you, Bishop Norris -- have <u>not</u> done, and what you <u>must</u> do, is acknowledge and deal with it as such. All of you in the church hierarchy need to get off your high horses and stop trying to minimize and trivialize the charges that are coming forward every day by abused people who have been in pain for <u>years</u> about what was done to them when they were youngsters by men who the abused victims saw in their innocence and regarded as Men of God.

Once that mindset takes hold -- on your part and that of your counterparts across the United States -- then and only then can this tragedy and all of the ugly, emerging aspects of it be morally and properly addressed.

Then and only then can and must the attendant ramifications of the tragedy be properly and exigently redressed -- the many lawsuits, for example -- and the need to compensate the victims in some fair and appropriate manner, and the <u>urgent</u> need to treat and prosecute as criminals those terrible priests who have sinned so grievously.

Then and only then can the Church come to grips with the urgent need to revamp and reconstitute the overall composition of the priesthood, to deny a path to that Holy Office to those who avowedly assert to be homosexual. Then and only then will the

Church be able to come to grips with the very real fact that there has been long-term (for decades, at least), rampant and widespread, criminal pedophilia and sexual abuse sinfully and pervertedly perpe-trated by <u>priests</u> upon those among us who are the most vulnerable and the most innocent and trusting.

The Church hierarchy (including you, Bishop Norris) must come to terms with and acknowledge that they and <u>you</u> have allowed the abuse to continue through the abrogation of their and <u>your</u> responsi-bility to those young children and through their and <u>your</u> woefully, pitifully inadequate remedial reform (instead of what it is that you <u>have</u> done -- simply transferring culpable priests in anonymity to other parishes), or, in too, too many cases, through their and your head-in-the-sand sinful inaction.

*Just one instance of sexual abuse of a child by a priest ("I, for one, could never be a pedophile," said Paddy once in his typi-cal irreverence. "I don't even **like** feet.") would be one instance of sexual abuse too many. And there have been thousands, if not tens of thousands of instances of that reprehensible crime in and by priests of the Church.*

(When Thomas, on the rare occasion, would get "serious" with Paddy about metaphysical or theological questions, Paddy would brush the subject aside and likely ask: "Did you hear about the agnostic, dyslexic insomniac who stayed up all night wondering whether there really is a dog?") Paddy was not an overly contemplative man.

Thomas's letter to the Bishop continued ---

Hundreds of such instances and probably more -- and the thou-sands or tens of thousands of victims, wounded irreparably, for life -- constitutes a scandal so widespread it takes on epidemic and endemic proportions. The Church must stop insisting or 'suggesting' (as you have) that 'the situation' is or has been an isolated problem 'here and there.' The Church must stop its specious, feeble attempts to rationalize and/or excuse what has happened under its very nose by citing statistics and data that the Church says suggest comparable proportions   of pedophilia and abuse in the general population or among doctors, or lawyers or Indian Chiefs. _That_ is not relevant.

Dear God, Bishop Norris, it is _Catholic priests_ who have engaged in these unthinkable acts of sexual perversion.

That bears repeating: _it is Catholic priests who have engaged in these unthinkable acts of sexual perversion._

If the Church does not acknowledge the reality of this criminal sexual abuse by its priests, mostly in America, as the fundamental and most critically serious problem with which it must deal as it moves forward in the 21st century, if the Church through its hier-archy continues to do what it seems clearly to be doing today -- refusing to recognize and confront the severity and urgency of the crisis by soft-pedaling and referring to it (this criminally scandalous crisis), only, as a 'problem,' -- if the Church continues not to discuss it in other, more accurate and _honest_ terms and continues to not do this openly in the only forum where we masses of Catholics can hear what the Church has to say on the crisis -- _in the pulpit on Sunday_ -- the downside potential, I believe, is enormous. I suggest that the very real possibility exists that this crisis may prove catastrophic with respect to the very survival of the Church in America as we know it today.

Significant numbers of Catholics have already left the Church and have given up entirely on going to Mass on Sundays. They, like me, do not want to continue to hear the deafening silence from their clergy who, obviously, do not have the courage to speak to their flocks about this terrible crisis. I believe that many more Catho-lics are today on the verge of leaving their Church not only because of this widespread crime but also _because of this sinful silence on the part of the Church hierarchy._ These Catholics are angry with their priests, not only for what the priests have done but because the priests and their hierarchal leaders will not speak of it. They are leaving the Church because they are, to be sure, angry but they are leaving also, and even more so, because of their profound feeling of sadness and loss and a feeling, too, that _they_ have been abandoned and betrayed by their priests. They look at the sins and the crime, the deceit and duplicity, the cover-up, lies and hypocrisy and they ask in bewilderment: <u>what has happened to their Church and those who lead it?</u>

What, dear God, has happened -- to <u>all</u> of us? I was never abused, per se, by a priest when I was a child and altar boy growing up, but I feel now that I, too, have suffered from the effect of all of this.

I am terribly, deeply troubled by these despicable, horrific, heinous revelations that we read of now every day in the press <u>and</u> by the Church hierarchy's imperious attitude toward them as evidenced by its woefully inept and sinful non-handling of them.

I read in the current issue of <u>Newsweek</u> magazine about American Cardinal Law of the Boston Archdiocese asserting in court papers filed in connection with abuse charges brought against a priest in the Boston area that the abuse victim "was responsible for his own alleged abuse through 'negligence.'" The VICTIM's <u>own</u> ALLEGED abuse?" Is this not head-in-the-sand, blatant <u>denial</u> on the part of the Cardinal? Worse, the victim in question was six years old when the abuse began. And Cardinal Law suggests that he, the 6-year-old victim, was "responsible" for what happened to him through (<u>his own</u>!!) "negligence."

<u>Shame on you, Cardinal Law. Shame on you.</u>

It seems quite obvious, to me, that the Church leadership, as epitomized by Cardinal Law, wants all of this -- the scandal and the crisis -- to just go away so that it may tuck its head deeper into the sand and hide from it until, the leadership hopes, it does just that: goes away.

Well, sir, it will <u>not</u> just go away, not unless and until it is acknowledged and addressed more openly and <u>honestly</u> by the Church for what it is -- a criminal sex abuse crisis of huge proportions.

At the recent meeting in Rome between the Pope and America's Cardinals, the Cardinals and others from the American Church who attended that historic, unprecedented gathering outdid themselves -- and would have outdone <u>any</u> Washington spin-doctor -- in the way they danced and dodged and failed to answer <u>honestly</u> the quite legitimate questions directed to them by the Italian media and, too,

152

by media from the rest of the world who covered the meeting. The Church's putative leaders failed abjectly and completely to represent themselves as leaders in every conceivable respect. They seemingly were either unable, or chose not, to explain and/or to clarify what they had discussed in their closed-door meetings and what they were planning to do to address the crisis in their Dioceses and churches when they returned home.

The manner in which the highest members of America's Catholic Church ducked and bobbed and weaved and fell all over themselves in contradicting one another while trying to say nothing and at the same time desperately trying to project and portray their own unquestioned innocence was almost comical to watch. In fact it would have been comical had it not been such a dishonest and tragically sad spectacle.

Is there not anyone in the Catholic Church hierarchy today willing to stand up and be counted?

Twenty Six

Thomas's letter to the Bishop continued --

I am sad and I feel empty. Something has been taken from me. It has been torn from my very soul. I feel almost as if I have been spiritually disenfranchised. The Church's predatory, perverted pedophile priests have done that to me. And so has the Church hierarchy. As with the victims of the abuse themselves, whom the Church seemingly ignores, so too does the Church ignore me and other forlorn Catholics as it continues its ostrich-like approach and its arrogant refusal to respond publicly and <u>honestly</u> to the crisis. The victims have been damaged and scarred and so too have many other Catholics like me. In military terms, this would be called "collateral damage." Ho-hum -- collateral damage.

The criminal pedophilia question aside, I am also stunned by the concomitant, startling revelation that has been reported in the press recently that as many as 40-50 percent of U.S. priests are homosexuals. That, to me, is shocking. I believe, fervently, that this cannot possibly be what The Good Lord had in mind when he founded His Church under Peter.

It is exceedingly difficult for me to write that last sentence. For me to say what it is that *I* believe Jesus may, or may not, have wanted is of course extremely presumptuous. But let me charge ahead none-theless. Can anyone seriously believe that He would want His church run and led by a clergy that is almost preponderantly homosexual? I hardly think so.

If indeed as many as one of every two priests in the Ameri-can church today is a homosexual, I am no longer sure that I ever again want to go into a Confessional. "Bless me, father, for I have sinned."

I do not want to confess my heterosexual transgressions to -- and there are many, many transgressions -- and seek spiritual guidance from a homosexual priest, who may or may not be celibate and who, I seriously doubt, has even a foggy understanding of what a heterosexual struggles with in today's secular-progressive society. If my Confessor is *not* celibate, I do not want to even think about the behavior in which he may be engaging -- pedophilia or "fudge-pack-ing?" How in the world can he possibly consider himself worthy to hear Confessions, to offer Mass or to administer the church's sacra-ments? Why is he not treated as a second-class citizen by the Church -- as I and all divorced Catholics are so treated?

I ask once more: why is he permitted, how can he be permitted to continue, to administer the sacraments? His hands are dirty.

I am not homophobic, Bishop Norris. God Bless those who struggle with their sexual orientation. But I repeat: the Catholic Church's clergy should not, cannot, must not be comprised of 50 percent homosexual priests.

The silence on *this* issue, as it is on the sexual abuse crisis, is also deafening.

In addition to the pain and sadness and sense of loss I feel in the wake of the terrible sex abuse scandal, I also am angry that this infusion of homosexuals into the priesthood has been allowed -- yes, allowed -- to happen in the Catholic Church by its bishops and Cardinals.

The irony here is staggering: perverted, predatory, pedophile priests have preyed upon innocent children and then have been protected and sheltered by the Church. And at the same time, homo-

155

sexuals in large numbers have been welcomed into the priesthood and have also been protected and sheltered by the Church. Who will protect -- and shelter -- the abuse victims?

We were taught as youngsters in parochial school in our Catechism classes that homosexuality is unnatural and sinful. I do not recall that any distinction was made by our tutors (the nuns and priests who led our classes) between a practicing and a celibate homosexual. Homosexuality was wrong, we were told. Period. End of discussion. (And, just for the record, what percentage of homosexuals -- and homosexual priests -- today are indeed truly celibate?)

The Catholic Church in America today should not be a haven for homosexuals, as it certainly appears to be.

My pain and anger obviously seethes here, though it is not totally un-tempered. Last Sunday as I walked through the Church parking lot to attend Mass, I saw one of the parish priests at my church, his head bowed, walking slowly, far across the other side of the parking lot. He looked so alone and so lonely. I prayed for <u>him</u> at Mass that day as I prayed for <u>all</u> of the good Catholic priests who are not pedophiles or homosexuals. And then I prayed, too, for those priests who have sinned. Let he who is without sin cast the first stone.

Before I conclude this too-long letter, Bishop Norris, let me hasten to say that I do not want to misrepresent myself in this letter as an overly religious or prayerful man. I am not. I am far from that. That should be clear from some   if not many of my comments herein. But let me also say that I believe I am (occasionally and sometimes often) a reasonably decent and fair and generally good human being.

I implore you, sir, do not, yourself, and do not allow your colleagues, to continue to sweep this crisis under the rug by not mentioning it at Sunday Mass.

After the Gospel reading, when the lector recites the list of "intentions" for which the congregation is asked to pray, prayers are sought frequently for national and international political leaders and heads of state struggling to lead their nations and constituencies and prayers for those leaders to be just and honest as they do so, an unfathomably difficult balance to seek and achieve in these troubled times with war and so much unbridled crime and horrific, merciless terror throughout the world. But not one word has yet been uttered, that I have heard, in my church, for the Church hierarchy or for the priests who have sinned through sexual abuse of the innocent or, most importantly, for those who have been abused.

May I offer a suggestion?

Consider, sir, dictating that the following three intentions for prayer be offered each and every Sunday in each and every Catholic Church in your diocese for the next year --

1) Let us pray for Holy Mother the Church and her leadership that she and they and all of us together as Catholics will find our way out of and away from the terrible sexual abuse scandal by priests that we are dealing with in America today.

Lord, hear our prayer.

2) Let us pray for the sinners among the priesthood in America today and for what they have done in perpetrating the events for which we all are so sorry have happened.

Lord, hear our prayer.

3) And let us pray -- _especially_ -- for the victims whom those priests have sinned against, and for the victims' families, for all of the pain and suffering that has been heaped upon them.

Lord, hear our prayer.

And please, sir, don't term what we are facing a "problem" or employ any other such weak-kneed euphemism. _It is a sex abuse **scandal** and **crisis.**_ Please don't dress up the language any differently. Say it straight and say it _honestly_. We, _all of us_, need to acknowledge and talk openly and honestly about this sinful scandal. We need to pray, publicly, about it. _All of us need to get our heads out of the sand._

The Church and all of us who are (still) a part of the Church need to heal and the healing process needs to -- and will -- begin only with acknowledgement ("Bless me, Father, for I have sinned") and open discussion of the terrible things that have been done and the sorrow and pain and shame that all of us feel as the result of these terrible, perverted acts.

I said earlier that I struggled with the question of whether or not I should write and send this letter to you. I concluded, finally, that <u>not</u> to do so would have been no more moral on my part than the Church hierarchy, including you -- and your colleagues -- <u>not</u> talking about this crisis that all of us as Catholics face today. It is not the time to sit back, say nothing and blindly and blithely hope that everything will just go away. I believe that would be a conscious, willful sin of omission. And that is why I wrote and am sending this letter to you.

We need to heal, Bishop Norris, all of us. This scandal and crisis will <u>not</u> just 'go away' until we acknowledge, talk openly and honestly about it and pray <u>together</u> to find the way forward <u>together.</u>

In closing, let me say once again that I offer this letter and the comments and thoughts contained in it respectfully and deferentially. I sincerely hope I have not offended you or anyone else in the Church who may have occasion to read this.

Please pause for a moment and read, once again, what I have said here. <u>Read the pain and anguish and sorrow and sense of spiritual abandonment in every word.</u>

Lead, sir. Please lead.

Very sincerely yours,

Thomas never received a response from the bishop.

Twenty Seven

Growing up in Johnstown, Thomas had indeed been an altar boy and server at Mass at St. Mary's Catholic Church and a student for 13 years at St. Mary's Institute under the tutelage of the Sisters of St. Joseph (The 'Penguins').

Now, he had been away from Johnstown for more than three decades though he did still visit every year or so to see Paddy and his sister, a sweet, religious, gentle, giving and lovely lady -- "a saint on earth," as the Catholics would say. Paddy and Thomas referred to her, to her face (which always embarrassed her), as 'St. Sheila.'

"How in the hell did she come out of the same gene pool as we degenerates did?" Paddy would ask.

Thomas's religion and religious knowledge in those early days, as was the case with most of his classmates, was largely by rote.

Thinking back, he did not recall certainly any reported instances or even rumors of sexual abuse by priests in those days; certainly no priest had ever tried to do anything to him personally.

"The only abuse we had in those days," he once told

159

Rebecca, "was physical abuse by the damned nuns."

Sisters of St. Joseph Superior, Mother Grace Madeline, in particular wielded a sharp stick -- literally. Her weapon was a yard stick (36 inches in length from stem to stern), one inch-thick and dark green in color, as Thomas remembered. ("maybe with a few crimson blood stains on it, too"). Discipline for recalcitrant boys at SMI was a good smacking on the backs of their bare thighs by Mother Grace wielding her menacing green yardstick. The punishment was administered in the privacy of her office, after she would tell the boys to drop their trousers so that she could strike their legs without any clothing cushion to protect against or mitigate the force of her whacks. Girls, as far as Thomas and the other boys knew, were spared the yardstick. Instead, they got smacked on their knuckles with Mother Grace's ruler. Yardstick or ruler? What was it, Thomas would ponder in later years, that Mother Grace -- a "bride" of Christ -- thought she was accomplishing with these forms of corporal punishment? Did she receive anything from it that to her was personally satisfying? Thomas wondered.

The boys were creative in their efforts to foil Mother Grace and her henchwomen on Fridays during Lent for 'Stations of the Cross' devotions when all St. Mary's Institute classes were marched from the school during the early-to-mid afternoon hours, down the steps via the subway from Forbes Street, through the subterranean bowels of the subway to the steps at its other end leading up to Main Street, one city block south of Forbes Street and to the church. It became a matter of pride and skill to "escape" from the student formation before it was herded into the rear of the church to its assigned class location in the massive and richly ornamented (obscenely so) enclave. Some of the boys opted to try for an early getaway immediately upon exiting the school, named Dugan Hall, while the nuns were more or less at ease for having gotten their class out of the building and in formation, at least, before heading to the subway and before they fully homed in on guarding and closely watching their formation of students to prevent breakaways.

A half-dozen or more boys in Thomas's class banded together to form a sports-like, stations-skipping 'league' replete with officially recorded 'wins/losses.' A 'win' was a successful escape and a loss occurred and was chalked up on the negative side of the record ledger and league standings when the attempted escapee was spotted, apprehended and halted -- and forced, more or less, to attend and participate in the services after all. Thomas and friends Peter Persico, Martin Mulcahey, Patrick Quinn, Bill Slomkowski , Dick Cocker, Rico Danielli and Ernie Donatelli were official league members. Thomas was the league's statistician and score-keeper.

One of Thomas's escape techniques helped him to lead the league standings during his sophomore year. He eschewed an *early* escape attempt, when the nuns were much more alert to possible malfeasance, and waited until he and his classmates were actually in Church, which they always entered via the wide center stairway, before cutting quickly to the left or right, depending on the position of the nun/guard, and then quickly exiting the church through one of its two side stairways. The technique succeeded beyond his and his rivals' expectations. Thomas had an unblemished record that year, seven escapes, no captures -- 7-0 -- beating out and leading the league 'standings,' topping all of the rest of the reluctant stationers.

●●●●●●●

Confessions were another matter altogether. It had been drummed into the heads and hearts of SMI students that to go to Communion without having confessed one's sins, particularly those of the 'mortal' variety, was compounding one mortal sin with another and could very well lead to eternal damnation in hell if one were to die before having an opportunity to wipe the slate clean via a 'good' confession --

which enabled one to gain the sought-for and desirable 'State of Grace.' There was some disagreement and non-clarity -- a blurring of the line as defined by various of the priest and nun tutors -- on the liturgical distinctions between a mortal and a venial sin. When in doubt, consider it mortal was a safe rule to follow.

"Bless me, Father, for I have sinned... It has been two weeks since my last confession. I lied four times, I stole candy from John's Confectionary twice, I disobeyed my mother six times, I cheated on my Arithmetic test when I copied off of Mary Jane Picarsik's paper, I had six impure thoughts" (The priests were much more insistent on drumming into the boys' heads the inviolable requirement to confess this sin, when it was one of the good fathers leading the Catechism class, than were the nuns; the nuns tended to gloss over the 'impure thoughts,' transgression, perhaps out of embarrassment. The priests, however, were consistently quite definitive on this: if you looked at and 'thought' about a girl in school in 'a certain way,' then *that* was an impure thought, a sin and, under the rules, had to be 'confessed,' no question about it -- no ifs, ands or buts to be considered. 'Buts?' Paddy once asked.

●●●●●●●

Thomas thought about and chuckled in his later years about a Catholic 'confession' story in Frank McCourt's wonderful memoir, "Angela's Ashes."

As a boy in Limerick, McCourt remembered being taken to Confession by his grandmother and, when she asked him upon his emergence from the confessional whether he had told the priest about a certain occurrence, presumably a sinful one (its specifics are not important), he said that he had not, that he had forgotten to mention it. Fearing that he had not therefore had a 'good' confession, Grandma "...pushed me back into the confessional."

"Bless me, Father, for I have sinned, it's a minute since my last confession."

"A minute! Are you the boy that was just here?"

"I am, Father."

The priest, blessedly, gave Frank a pass that time around.

In Johnstown, once, Peter Persico was in the confessional with Father Gilmour and had gotten around to the 'impure thoughts' part of his recitation of sins. "I stole candy four times, disobeyed my aunt (Pete's mother had died when he was six, so in his case it was an aunt who was subjected to his numbered disobediences) five times; I was disrespectful to my teachers five times and I had six impure thoughts."

At that moment, Therese Ann Feherty walked up the aisle past the confessional booth. Pete looked out of the wood-slatted/windowed sinner's spot in the booth in which he knelt and saw Therese Ann sashay by. Almost all the boys regularly had 'impure thoughts' about Therese Ann. Pete decided, as a safeguard, to correct the record then and there (precluding the necessity of having to make another confession one minute later?)

"Make that <u>seven</u> impure thoughts, Father," he updated himself and his report.

As far as confessions were concerned, there also was inside information on which priests gave light and which gave stiffer sentences, or penances. Three Hail Marys and three Our Fathers were light and acceptable, from Father Gilmour; five rosaries from Monsignor Welch meant that *he* was to be avoided as a confessor. With Father Sheehan, you never knew just what you were going to get, depending on his mood and energy level, and to be safe he, therefore, also was to be avoided. He, for crying out loud, sometimes imposed Stations

163

of the Cross as a penance. For Thomas, in particular, *that* just wouldn't do.

It was Martin Mulcahey who came up with what Thomas and his friends considered a novel and creative approach to the exercise. "Bless me, father, for I have sinned.... I lied... once." Martin's thinking was that the entire confession and the omission of all sins could 'count' as a lie -- and in that way, by confessing to 'one lie' you were covered and absolved and need not unburden yourself of the times you cheated, lied, stole, swore, were disobedient or had 'impure thoughts' -- about Therese Ann Feherty or any other girl. "It's 'official,' as far as I can see," held Martin.

Father Carroll might have been handling confessions at St. Mary's on a piece-work basis. In and out, period. He dispensed with most of the formalities. "Did you miss Mass?" A "No, Father" got one an immediate parole and a non-challenging two Our Fathers and two Hail Mary's, even less often than Father Gilmore's usual light sentence.

Malapropisms also were a large part of life in Johnstown. "Absolve" often was said, "absorb." Thus the priest in confession was able to 'absorb' one of one's sins.

Another common confessional practice for the Johnstown SMI boys was to traipse over to the Italian church on Market Street, St. Dominic's. There, the priests often seemed to be napping in the confessional box and, frequently, they neither understood well nor spoke English very proficiently. At St. Dominic's, one could confess, almost, a multiple ax murder (Bless me, Father. I hacked six people to death...") and not get any questions about it or a lecture before being dismissed and 'absorbed,' and get only a light penance as well -- maybe just a Father Carroll-variety of two Our Fathers and two Hail Marys.

The city where he was born and in which he grew up, Johnstown -- its education, social customs and mores -- framed, shaped and indelibly stained the man Thomas became.

When he was just 13, Thomas won the city-wide straight pool junior championship held each year at 'Louie's Billiards Parlor.' Proficiency at billiards and pool (straight, 9-ball or 8-ball) in Thomas's formative years was widely viewed by most adults in town as a sign of a misspent youth. One should not have that much time on one's hands -- to learn and become so accomplished and expert at such a disreputable pursuit as pool. Instead, one should be delivering newspapers (Thomas indeed did, for many years, have a paper route) or one should be volunteering at the Church after school hours to sweep the floors between the pews, or, of course, help one's mom at home.

Thomas's mother was mortified when the <u>Johnstown Evening Recorder</u> ran a story on Thomas's winning the city's junior pool championship; on the other hand, Thomas's father was exceedingly proud of his son's feat. "That's my boy," he told his friends at the Elks club.

Twenty Eight

Rebecca remembered. She had been thinking a lot lately about Thomas and, once again, re-reading parts of the long Christmas-season letter he had sent to her, and which she had still not yet told William about....

This Saturday, she and William were planning a weekend trip to Florida's west coast, a two-hour drive from their home in Mt. Roda. Rebecca had the strangest dream last night. She dreamt that she saw Thomas walking down the sidewalk, strolling casually and slowly, across the street from where she stood. He was gazing distractedly at store window displays. He was dressed in blue jeans and a black t-shirt. He was as slim and trim as he had been the last time she actually had been with him. In the dream, he did not spot her watching him from a distance.

William had been spending more time, on his own, out of the house since Christmas, on one errand or another, and Rebecca looked forward to being with him on the drive cross state. She thought she might tell him that day about the letter from Thomas, which she had been keeping from him since it arrived just before Christmas. She and William planned to tour Sarasota, which neither had ever visited, and to take a look as well at Siesta Key and its world-famous white quartz sand beach. "It's so delicate and so fine and soft it's almost as if you're walking on talcum powder," a neighbor in Mt. Roda had told them. Since Christmas Rebecca had looked into finding where in Florida Thomas had settled, and she learned through "googling" him that his residence was in fact on the barrier island of Siesta Key, offshore at Sarasota.

It was William, quite unexpectedly, who brought up the subject of Thomas -- and, surprisingly, "the" letter -- during their drive west on Florida's infamously traffic-congested I-4.

"I saw that letter from Tom that you've been keeping in the living room since Christmas," he said.

"Thomas is the last person I ever expected to hear from -- especially after all these years," Rebecca responded calmly despite her surprise that William obviously knew about the secret she had been keeping from him, her motive for which she still did not understand.

"Does he live in Florida now, too?" asked William.

"I'm not sure," Rebecca lied.

"Why do you suppose he wrote?" William went on.

"And why, Becky, didn't you *tell* me about the letter? What did he have to say in that very long letter -- and why were you hiding it, and keeping it from me?"

"I don't honestly know Bill. I suppose I didn't want to hurt you in any way."

Silence between the two ensued for a few miles.

Rebecca asked, "And you, dear, have been spending a lot of time out of the house on your own since Christmas. Any particular reason for that? Are you OK?"

After another few miles' pause in the conversation, William glanced at Rebecca:

"And are you now trying to change the subject that we were beginning, finally, to talk about, dear?" He smiled as he said this.

It was unlike William to use the word "dear."

167

Whatsoever ye do for the least of my brethren
So shall ye do for me

Twenty Nine

In Washington, after Thomas had begun dating, or "seeing" women, and after his first "honeymoon" experience with anyone other than Ellen since before he went into the Army, he met Jane Stone -- and, he believed at the time, fell in love with her.

Before Jane and after Julia, The Blind Lady, and his one-time honeymoon affair with Maria, Thomas dated other women who were also interesting, intelligent, kind and always -- always -- attractive. As a healthy, libidinous male, Thomas enjoyed sex and was also enjoying his new-found freedom to seek access to it in great variety. Just about every woman in Washington was interesting, intelligent -- and attractive. Moreover, the ratio of single, available women to men in the nation's capitol was highly slanted in favor of the male of the species. There were many, many more single women in D.C. than single men.

And so for Thomas, after Julia, The Blind Lady and Maria and before Jane, there were , among others -- Susan, Lenore, Betsy, Cynthia, Judy (and Judi), Christine, Joan (and Joanie), Terri, Jennifer, Jeanne, Caroline, Kristin, Kersten, Frances,

Christine (ii), Audrey, Rachel, Irene, Mimi, Nancy, Pamela, Marilyn, Sherry, Stephanie, Elizabeth, Yvonne, Denise, Linda, Sharon, Kathy (Chlorine Kathy), Debbie, Lucy, Bonnie, Linda, Jo, Mary, Mary Anne, Irene (ii), Tammy, Sue, Barbara, Susan (Howdy Doody), Clarissa, Melissa and Paige, et al. -- and, of course, Velvet.

Thomas met Velvet in an art supply/custom-framing shop nearby the condominium he bought and moved into in Arlington. He had a number of prints that he wanted to get framed and hang on the walls in his new domicile. Velvet (Judi) worked in the shop and gave him several framing ideas which he liked and asked her to implement. They went out on a date, and then another and another, shortly after their meeting on a customer/supplier basis. Judi knew, of course, that Thomas was a newcomer to the area and he mentioned to her that he had begun dating, serially, a number of women since moving to Washington and was occasionally having trouble keeping their names straight. Judi offered what he thought was a brilliant suggestion -- never date a woman with the same name of anyone he might have dated previously. Thomas told Judi that might mean *she'd* have to be eliminated because he had already dated not only someone named Judy but also another woman who spelled her name 'Judi.' Art-shop Judi said that was no problem at all -- and she rechristened herself with a name unique in the list of names of women Thomas had previously dated in Washington. Judi became and was forever thereafter known, and referred to by him, as "Velvet." Thomas told Paddy about this in a telephone conversation a few days later and Paddy was so taken with the idea that *he* rechristened his current lady friend, in Johnstown, "Jasmine." Jasmine had up to then been known by her baptismal name of Arlene. Both she and Paddy, however, now much preferred Jasmine. Thomas once met Arlene/Jasmine on a visit to Johnstown and liked her very much. She was pretty, smart and very funny.

Most of Thomas's early Washington connections were merely dates, some just once, others ranging from three to six or seven get-togethers (dinners, social events, theater and movies -- like Velvet) and some, a few, but only a few, became 'honeymoon' affairs.

●●●●●●●

Thomas found Washington and its environs a delightful place to work and live. He was struck, however, with the great number of "street" people and panhandlers one encountered in the city. It seemed fundamentally antithetical to him that there were so many people in dire straits -- and in need -- in the capital city of the world's most powerful and richest government. Thomas early on realized he could not help all of Washington's street people with a financial handout, as much as he wanted or would have liked to do, but he did befriend one particular street person, an African-American man, whose regular street post was near Thomas's office. As he got to know the man, greeting him daily on the two-blocks walk from the metro stop to his office, Thomas began to give the man sums of money on a regular basis. Their daily schedule did not always perfectly mesh, however, and they would occasionally miss seeing one another, sometimes for days at a time. During those periods, Thomas would miss and worry about his friend, fearing that something unfortunate or catastrophic might have happened to him. One day, after having not seen his friend for two weeks, and to compensate for the missed days, Thomas gave his friend a $10 bill and began thereafter to proffer that amount on a regular basis instead of the $1-$2 he had been giving him previously. However, Thomas began giving his friend the increased stipend only on a once-a-week basis.

Thomas and his new friend very soon came to know each other on a first-name basis -- he was Lindsay -- but as Thomas's 'contribution' practice evolved from a $1 or $2 whenever

Thomas and Lindsay saw one another to the larger sum of $10 on Mondays, usually, Lindsay began to address Thomas from time to time, always with an ear-to-ear smile on his face, as "Mr. Once-A-Week."

Lindsay was about 30-35 years old, a few years younger than Thomas and quite similar to Thomas in physical stature: tallish and trim at 6 feet, 2 inches, and not more than 165 pounds. His appearance generally and usually gave the impression of reasonable health though often Lindsay's eyes would appear to be flooded with red -- perhaps, Thomas thought, from abuse of a controlled substance of one sort or another? On those occasions Lindsay's speech was halting and slurred and his usual broad and friendly, outgoing smile was absent. Thomas did not know enough about 'controlled' substances to even begin to guess what Lindsay may have been "on" though he guessed and believed it was probably something other than alcohol. Thomas had never taken a drug -- except on one occasion, in Vietnam, when he smoked some marijuana, and had had a bad reaction, unsettling enough so that it cured him of such transgressions for the rest of this life.

Lindsay, when he wasn't 'under the influence,' was verbal, articulate, social, up-to-date on world and Washington political events, and quite intelligent.

As Lindsay began to occasionally greet Thomas as Mr. Once-A-Week, so too did Thomas bestow a sobriquet on Lindsay -- "Mr. Mayor," of the city block of the District of Columbia's "I" Street thoroughfare between the 19th and 20th St. cross streets. Lindsay, as far as Thomas ever saw, was the only panhandler who did business with passersby on that block. Thomas assumed that territorial imperative was part of the street world's code of conduct in Washington -- perhaps it is in every big city -- and it did appear to Thomas to be honored rigidly, at least in Lindsay's case. Thomas never saw any other panhandlers in Lindsay's territory, when Lindsay was present, nor did he ever see Lindsay anywhere else

172

in D.C. in another panhandler's territory. Only occasionally would Thomas see other street people panhandling on Mayor Lindsay's block, but that was only when Lindsay wasn't there that day.

As Lindsay was about the same height and weight as Thomas, and the clothes Lindsay wore were often tattered, Thomas began giving Lindsay some of the clothes that *he* no longer wore -- pants, jeans, shirts, sweaters, jackets, even running shoes. To Thomas, it was startling, occasionally, of a morning when he would be on his two-blocks walk toward his office, after exiting the metro, to approach Lindsay from that distance and see him wearing apparel that Thomas himself had once worn. In a surreal sense, thought Thomas, it was almost as if he were seeing himself in Lindsay. "There but for the grace of God go I," he thought, inescapably.

Once, during Christmas week, Thomas gave Lindsay a religious greeting card (Lindsay later told Thomas it was the only Christmas card he had received in twenty years or more). Thomas included a larger than his usual once-a-week sum in the envelope with the card. A few days later, Lindsay told Thomas that he had used the extra money to buy medicine. He beamed as he said it. Lindsay, it seemed to Thomas, was seeking approbation, and Thomas gave it to him. Thomas told him that that was making very good use of some extra dollars and said that he was proud of him. Lindsay beamed again. He felt good about himself.

The early part of the next week, before New Year's Eve, Lindsay told Thomas that he badly needed "more medicine" and that its cost would be equal to the sum ($50) that had been enclosed with the Christmas card. It was obvious to Thomas that Lindsay was trying to hustle him, and Thomas called him on it. Thomas told Lindsay that he was sorry but that he would have to wait until next week when the two of them would get back on their regular schedule. Lindsay smiled broadly, but with his head down and his eyes averting Thomas's. Lindsay realized that *he* had been had and that his

173

attempt to put one over on Thomas had not worked.

"OK, Mr. Once-A-Week," he said, still smiling. "You're right." In his heart, Thomas wanted to believe that Lindsay may have been even a little ashamed that he had tried to hustle a friend.

On those few occasions when Thomas was away from Washington for several days or a few weeks at a time -- on a vacation or an international business trip -- Lindsay kept a running tally in his friend's absence and would present him upon his return with an orally delivered "bill" for how much Thomas "owed" him. "You've been gone for three weeks, Tom, that's 30 dollars."

The once-a-week rule had become sacrosanct -- for Thomas -- and for Lindsay.

Occasionally, after a meeting at his company when pastries had been served to the attendees in morning gatherings and cookies in the afternoons, Thomas would gather and bag up the left-over uneaten items and bring them downstairs and carry them a block away to Lindsay's street station. The Mayor shared the unexpected goodies with *his* friends from street "territories" that abutted his.

Over time, Thomas introduced Lindsay to a number of people from his office, to other non-company associates of his and to his youngest daughter who had, now, finished college and was settling into her career in Washington.

Sadly, some months before Thomas left Washington, Lindsay stopped appearing at his customary station on Washington's "I" street. Lindsay, previously, was sometimes gone for a week or two or even, on the rare occasion, for a longer period of time. But this time he never came back. He was gone for months, and Thomas never saw Lindsay again. Thomas always feared the worst -- or maybe, for Lindsay, it really *wasn't* the worst. Maybe Lindsay was now in a far better place than Washington's "I" Street with his hand extended. If he were, Thomas hoped he had gotten there easily and painlessly and that he no longer had to subsist by panhandling.

●●●●●●●

Years later, after Thomas had left Washington and was living in Florida, he met and befriended another of America's homeless street people -- Rollie, who brought back to Thomas memories of Lindsay and the sad plight of him and so many others in America, the richest country in the history of the world, who have no place to put their head down at night and no roof over their head when they do close their eyes, outside under the stars, to rest for their next day's struggle to sustain themselves and to survive.

Thomas first met Rollie paused in front of a magnificent, wonderful Banyan tree, halfway down Midnight Pass Road, south from the Stickney Point Bridge, in Siesta Key, a barrier island offshore Sarasota in southwest Florida, where Thomas had settled, ultimately, after leaving Washington. Rollie was Walter Raleigh (Rollie) William Edmondson III, formerly of Akron, OH and various other parts of the United States and the world.

Rollie lived and slept at the beach pavilion/rest room area at Turtle Beach on south Siesta Key or, alternatively, at the comparable pavilion area at Siesta Beach, three miles further north on the island. Siesta Beach was a much bigger draw than Turtle Beach, and the crowds of day-visitors there were always much more dense than they were at Turtle Beach. Rollie preferred the less-crowded venue of the two, spending most of his time at the southern end of Siesta, at Turtle Beach. Unlike Lindsay, who was quite thin and lanky, Rollie did not look as if he'd missed too many meals during his homeless-ness. Rollie was a *big* man, two or three inches over six feet in height and weighing, probably, close to 270-80 pounds. Rollie commuted the distance between his two beach "homes" -- Siesta Beach and Turtle Beach -- on a bicycle. Other than his clothes, the bicycle was Rollie's only material possession. It was several months after Thomas met and had gotten to know him well that Thomas learned Rollie was homeless.

Rollie was reluctant to tell this to Thomas initially -- Thomas supposed -- out of embarrassment. Early on, he had always implied to Thomas that he lived in a small condominium "a little place in Gulf Gate," a modest community/neighborhood on the mainland, just off Siesta Key

Rollie, like Lindsay, was not unintelligent. Rollie told Thomas that he had been born into a well-to-do family and after graduating from high school "eschewed" college to go into the family business, real estate sales -- in Akron. He was initially quite successful as a realtor but tired of "the game," -- and the need to be "obsequious" -- to have to "brown nose and boot-lick the guy selling" *and* "the guy buying." Lindsay, like Rollie, was not intellectually vacuous but Lindsay did not have the same rich vocabulary Rollie had and would not have used words like 'eschewed' and 'obsequious.' Rollie left Akron when he was not yet 25-years-old and moved to Chicago. There he began a career in real estate development, a step up from sales, he said -- but he tired quickly of that as well. By now he had been married and divorced twice, and he decided to "change everything." He packed up his old Chevy and drove to Miami, where he signed on as a crewman on charter fishing and short-term travel/vacation ships. He moved to, settled and lived in the Caribbean for a few years before returning to Florida and migrating to the state's southwest shore. He married again -- "a rich bitch in Long Boat Key" -- and tried his hand at selling automobile insurance. His third marriage was no more successful than his first two -- and he disliked and also gave up on the "car insurance game." Rollie took full responsibility for all of his failed marriages. "I should-a never been married in the first place, Tom. I like my damn freedom too much." During all of his marriages, Rollie told Thomas, he "drank a lot." Even as a homeless drifter, now, he always had enough money to buy bourbon, vodka and beer. Rollie drank, excessively, every day.

Thomas liked Rollie and tried to keep an eye on him, particularly during the colder stretches of weather in Sarasota and Siesta Key, in January and February. Thomas could not give Rollie any of his old clothes (they obviously would not have fit), as he had done with Lindsay, but he did give him a woolen blanket on two occasions during cold spells which Rollie said he used as a mat when he slept, inside, on the floor of the men's rest room at the beach pavilion overnight.

Siesta Key is touched on its south by Sarasota Bay and on its north by The Gulf of Mexico, which Rollie called "the Gulf of America."

"It is *here*, in Sarasota, in the U-S-of-A, it is here *legally*, it is not unemployed and it does not carry a shiv or eat tacos."

"It's the Gulf of <u>America</u>!"

"I see nothing Mexican about that body of water at all."

Rollie was well known, and liked, by all of the Sarasota County Sheriff's Department deputies who patrolled Siesta Key. They frequently received and responded to citizens' complaints and calls about a "vagrant" at the pavilion at the beach. Once, when he had not seen Rollie for a period of several days, Thomas went to the Sheriff's Office to ask if anyone there knew where Rollie might be, and he was told that Rollie had been picked up drunk and passed out three or four days prior and taken to the hospital Emergency Room. Thomas tracked him down there and learned that Mr. Walter R. Edmondson III, no known address, had been admitted to the hospital the previous Thursday. Thomas called on Rollie during visiting hours. Sarasota was in the midst of a winter cold snap at the time and, Thomas thought, it was a good thing Rollie was not outside all day and sleeping in the cold, unheated rest room on the floor all night. In the hospital, Rollie told Thomas when he visited, "Hell, man, this ain't *too* bad. I've got three hots and a cot and the damn nurses are prettier 'n hell."

Thomas visited Rollie every other day for the next two weeks until, one day, Rollie was no longer in the room he had been occupying. Thomas was told at the Patient Information Desk in the hospital's main lobby that Rollie had been discharged from the hospital the day before, at his own insistence, "AMA." Thomas learned that those initials, in hospital-ese, stood for and meant "against medical advice." The only context in which Thomas had ever heard the initials until then were as they referred to the American Medical Association.

Thomas drove to the beach pavilion upon leaving the hospital to see if Rollie had returned to his familiar habitue there -- and he had, to Thomas's great relief. Thomas <u>liked</u> Rollie and when he went to the Sheriff's department had been asked *why* he wanted to find out where the big man with the bike was. "Because he's my friend, homeless or not...and he is a fellow human being," Thomas added, as the Deputy stared back at him with a look of puzzlement on his face.

On the day Thomas found Rollie at the beach, when he first had feared that Rollie may have passed away while in the hospital, only to learn that Rollie had left the hospital "AMA," Thomas and Rollie had as honest a conversation as any Thomas thought they'd ever had. Rollie, always reluctant to talk about himself and his 'situation' on Siesta Key ("Hell, man, I've got everything under control. Don't worry about me."), was not reluctant to talk this time. Rollie was genuinely concerned about what they had told him in the hospital about the results of all the blood and other tests that had been run on him, and he seemed uncharacteristically eager to talk about himself and his worries. Thomas listened to his friend. Rollie had a host of medical problems -- a blood infection that had turned the outer epidermis of his lower legs and his feet and toes a dreadful, ugly, sickening-to-look-at dark blue/black hue. Rollie's condition and his health were complicated at the same time by diabetes (Rollie never knew before his recent hospital stay that he *was* a diabetic) and edema in his legs, and Thomas (and Rollie) knew not what else. Thomas asked Rollie if he had been given any prescriptions when he left the hospital, and why he chose to leave when he was indeed getting "three hots and a cot." ("Hell, Tom, I was goin' stir-crazy; I *had* to get out of there.") Rollie still had the written prescriptions but, not surprisingly, hadn't yet filled them. ("I just haven't had the time, man!") The prescription orders were in one of Rollie's pockets.

Thomas cajoled, urged, almost dragged Rollie from the bench where he sat, walked him to his car -- not without some difficulty (Rollie's feet were swollen and painful for him to walk on) -- and drove him to the supermarket pharmacy. Rollie didn't have the funds to pay for the prescription medicine, so Thomas paid for it. Thomas drove Rollie back to the beach pavilion, at Rollie's insistence, where Thomas saw to it that his friend took the first dosage of his medications, before leaving and telling him he'd be back to check up on him tomorrow.

Rollie, because of the problems with his legs and feet, and associated pain, told Thomas he had not yet been able to "get around" on his bike.

"I'm pretty much stuck right here -- so I'll be here when you come by tomorrow."

Rollie told Thomas he did not like being confined, "without transportation" (his bike) and asked Thomas, "How's our banyan tree doing? I miss seeing it."

On one of his daily jogs along Midnight Pass Road, Thomas once ran into Rollie standing next to his bicycle next to, and gazing upward, almost wondrously, at the great Midnight Pass Road Banyan tree. (Banyan trees are native to Asia; seeds for the magnificent trees were brought to America and to Florida, Thomas had read, by the circus magnate John Ringling; Ringling Bros. Barnum and Bailey circus had been headquartered in, and wintered in, Sarasota for much of the 20th century; the Ringling baronial mansion on Sarasota Bay is now a tourist attraction in the city). Many Banyan trees dot the vast grounds surrounding the Ringling Mansion, but not one of them is as stately or grand as the one Thomas and Rollie stood next to, and looking up at, that day on Midnight Pass Road in Siesta Key.

The Banyan can reach heights of 100 feet or more and, as it grows, new roots descend from its branches, dropping, reaching and stretching downward to the ground, pushing inward at that level to form new trunks. The roots grow relentlessly and a single tree might have dozens of trunks, some ten to twelve feet in diameter, some just two or three feet wide, most of which intertwine with one another and the original trunk, though it is almost impossible to tell *which* actually is the original. Thomas seemed to recall that John Steinbeck, in writing about great and magnificent trees (though Thomas did not recall that Steinbeck wrote about a Banyan), said that 'great trees' were "noble" The Banyan tree is a *noble* tree, Thomas thought.

That he and Rollie each was taken with and a great admirer of this magnificent and noble Banyan tree on Midnight Pass Road served as one further link in the bond that linked Thomas Anthony Gorman and Walter Raleigh William Edmondson III and formed their solid, unlikely friendship.

A year later, Thomas's Rebecca -- and her William -- would stand in awe one afternoon in front of the same tree, not a mile-and-a-half from where Thomas lived and from where that same afternoon at about that same time he was just beginning his daily jog, heading out in that same direction.

Thirty

In Washington, Thomas thought back to the beginning and subsequent development of his relationship with Jane Stone. She was the most beautiful, dressed or undressed, the most startlingly and stunningly attractive, woman he had ever seen or, certainly, ever been with -- connubially, that is, in the Biblical sense -- or 'honeymooned' with -- as his secretary Arlene would have said.

Recently divorced when they met, with two young daughters and, Thomas was to learn later, having just recently gone through a miscarriage, Jane and Thomas met during his visit to the office of a North Carolina Senator, for whom Jane worked as a legislative aide. She and her Senator boss each was highly regarded on the Hill and in the District generally as well as in the Senator's home state. Jane's forte was the environment and legislative environmental issues. She was an acknowledged expert in particular on the recently enacted U.S. Clean Air Act. Jane had come to the Hill and Sen. Cousins's office directly from a mid-level management position at the Environmental Protection Agency.

There was attraction on the part of each during their first

(business) meeting as they sat facing one another from opposite sides of a conference room table in an ante room of the Senator's office.

Thomas called Jane and asked her out on a dinner date, ostensibly to further discuss the legislative issue they had been exploring in their "official business" meeting. They met in McLean (where, later, the Croatian Creation also lived). They drove to the restaurant separately. It was an inauspicious first dinner date. They had pizza and then went back to Jane's home. The girls were with their father that night, and Jane and Thomas, with the attraction and spark from their business meeting still sizzling, 'honeymooned' that very first evening. The celebration went on long, long into the night and the next morning, for several hours, almost non-stop. Jane was as libidinous as Thomas. Thomas left Jane's home just before 7 a.m., and drove to Arlington, 10 minutes away. It was a Saturday and he called Jane as soon as he returned home. They both were still excited from the long evening and early morning of love-making. Jane asked Thomas if he'd like to have dinner again that evening -- "and..." (she added, suggestively). Jane said she'd be happy to prepare a meal for them at her McLean home.

They made love for long hours again that evening and into the next morning.

The relationship was off to a physically meteoric and fiery start. The flame for them ignited quickly and fiercely and it burned brightly -- too soon? Jane and Thomas *liked* each other immediately and got along well immediately, out-of-bed but, mostly, in bed.

Tall, thin, striking (like Julia) but unhappy (as many extraordinarily beautiful women are -- with one aspect or another of themselves and their physicality), Jane thought her breasts were too small, and had had an augmentation done, forebodingly so? [as another beautiful woman Thomas would meet after he left Washington, Lu-Ann, had done; Lu-Ann went back to the well, as it were, twice after the initial

182

reconfiguration for a total of *three* boob jobs."Does she have three tits" the irreverent Paddy cracked.] Jane had her boobs reconfigured only the once.

"The District Digest" magazine, a chronicler of the Washington social scene, once featured Jane as part of a cover story it entitled "The Ten Most Beautiful Women in Washington."

Jane was an identical twin, though her sibling Lyn, compared to her sister, was rather ordinary in appearance and physical stature and attractiveness.

"It's a twin thing," Jane would often say when referring to her sister when Jane and Lyn thought alike or decided similarly on things to do or not do, or even on certain personal actions. These phenomena happened often -- only for the twins to discover the similarity and coincidence after the fact. Jane told Thomas that she once, only recently, had decided to shave her pubic area -- and learned a couple of weeks after having done just that, that Lyn had decided on and done the same thing herself -- amazingly, on the same day that Jane had. "It's a twin thing," Jane said laughingly to Thomas.

The physical relationship Thomas shared with Jane was charged. They both delighted in their sexuality and in the physical aspect of their relationship. Jane was the first woman Thomas had known intimately who seemed to enjoy oral sex as much as he, both the giving and receiving of it.

(Paddy had two questions when he learned that Thomas was involved in a new relationship. "Does she have good tits?" And, "Does she swallow?" Jane scored positively on both counts, Thomas told his brother.)

But Jane, Thomas thought, always seemed so sad (like Rebecca.) At least one reason Jane's marriage had failed, she told Thomas, in tears, was that her husband was not as interested in sex as she was. She tried to interest and entice him in ways she thought might "stir a fire in his loins" but "with him, nothing worked." She served him breakfast topless (as she later would do with Thomas as well); she did housework in the nude and purchased and wore all of the latest, most alluring undergarments offered in the Victoria's Secret catalogue. Jane was beautiful enough, with a figure striking enough, to be a Victoria's Secret model herself.

But the marriage for Jane continued to feel empty and she began to have doubts about her femininity and her womanly sexual appeal. Her self-esteem suffered.

When she and Thomas met, she had been divorced for three years and had had three or four intimate relationships during that period. But Jane also seemed, to Thomas, from their very first business meeting and well into the intimacy of their relationship, always to look and feel and act sad and unhappy. Her eyes, and her voice, always seemed inexpressably sad.

Thomas and Jane traveled to Manhattan for a long weekend. They stayed at the then-renowned Plaza Hotel on 57th Street, near Central Park. They saw three Broadway shows, ate at the Plaza's Oak Room, strolled the avenues and cross streets of Manhattan, which Thomas knew well from his nine years of having worked in midtown New York.

They took a wonderful weekend trip to Virginia from Washington, to historic Williamsburg. They attended festive events at The Kennedy Center and started to become known in Washington as a "couple."

Jane was a spectacular "head-turner." She was *gaspingly* beautiful. Once in Union Station on Capitol Hill, as they wandered slowly through the commuter throngs, Thomas realized that a smallish group of a dozen or so people was following them. The group gawked and grew in number as the whispering of the crowd increased in intensity and volume that the beautiful woman in the cavernous main lobby at Washington's grand and immense main train station was no one else but Great Britain's Princess Diana. Jane was *that* beautiful and that striking. Later, as Thomas reflected on this and the crowd's reaction to Jane, he wondered fleetingly who the crowd might have thought *he* was that night. "No way that they could have imagined I was Prince Charles," he concluded in his private thoughts. "My ears just aren't big enough."

Years later, in Florida, when he was "seeing" Lu-Ann Irene Edwards, Thomas began to notice and draw unmistakable parallels between Lu-Ann and Jane and their personalities. Lu-Ann also was startlingly, physically beautiful, had just come out of an unhappy marriage and bitter divorce, was unhappy with her breasts (Lu-Ann had augmentation surgery done and then a few years afterward done again and still a third time). Lu-Ann, like Jane, also was a prevaricator and a sleep-around "easy lay." Lu-Ann, Thomas saw as their relationship developed, was -- it seemed to him -- a pathological liar. Lu-Ann almost *could not* tell the truth. Thomas saw the way she lied to her sons, to their father and her ex-husband, on the phone, to her mother and sister, both of whom lived nearby, and to her employer when she called in to beg off from coming in to work, which she did often.

There was no precise parallel between Lu-Ann and Jane on this, however. Jane, it seemed to Thomas, in the beginning, at least, was painstakingly honest. (He would find out differently later). Lu-Ann was anything but honest. The truth and Lu-Ann were strangers. Lu-Ann <u>was</u> the quintessential pathological liar.

●●●●●●●

Jane, on a weekend trip with Thomas from Washington to Florida, performed fellatio on him in their rental car on the drive back from dinner to a condominium Thomas owned at that time in Venice, south of Sarasota -- to where he would eventually settle after leaving Washington. Years later, Lu-Ann initiated the same act -- driving back home after having had dinner *at the same restaurant* -- (preposterously, Thomas thought). Was it something in the water at that restaurant? Lu-Ann was "an excellent cock-sucker," she was proud to say. She uttered the phrase mimicking Dustin Hoffman in his role as Raymond in the movie "Rain Man" and *his* line in the film, "I'm an excellent driver." (Her tone and inflection were exact replicas of Raymond's.) And, Thomas had to agree with her on that point. She did not lie about her ability as a fellatrix, Thomas would concede. On that, she -- for a change -- told the truth. She *was* an excellent cock-sucker.

●●●●●●●

Jane and Thomas loved each other, or so Thomas thought. But it soon became inescapably clear to Thomas that Jane was, concurrently, seeing two former lovers -- one in Rehoboth, at the Maryland shore, another on weekend trips to New Orleans, one of Jane's favorite U.S. cities. Thomas drew another parallel here, later, between Jane and Lu-Ann: their promiscuity. Jane began breaking weekend dates with Thomas, and he became increasingly suspicious then that she was cheating on him. He asked her point-blank about a weekend they had planned to be with one another that, at the last minute, she had cancelled and spent at Rehoboth "to get some alone time" where, she later said, she had stayed with an "old friend." Thomas continued to ask questions and she admitted, finally, that the "old friend" was a male. After further discussion and probing by Thomas, Jane admitted that the friend she had stayed with for the weekend was also a former lover. She told Thomas, at first, that she and the ex-lover slept in separate bedrooms during the weekend. Thomas asked if there had been "any intimacy" despite the fact that they were in different sleeping quarters. Jane began to cry and then admitted that they *had* slept in the same bed and there *had* been "some contact" (as she put it) but "nothing like what you and I have."

Thomas was crushed. He had never in what he saw now as his naivete given much thought to the possibility -- probability? -- that women, like men, could be guilty of infidelity. He had always thought of that ugly inconsistency and inconstancy as being almost solely in the province of men.

Women were much more constant and they were pure, he had always thought. "Some contact." Thomas thought that Jane's response to his question was particularly creative and self-absolving -- and, in a strange way, *admirably* creative. "Contact." Hmmmm --- "I wonder *what* came into 'contact' with *what*?"

The relationship at that juncture, as far as Thomas was concerned, had run into a brick wall -- and it was over, and he told Jane that he did not want to "see" her any longer. Thomas had always been faithful in all of his intimate relationships -- in his marriage and in the relationships and intimacies since his divorce. He had been intimate with many, many women, to be sure, but he was also always a monogamist in his various relationships, and he thought of himself in that way: as a monogamist, albeit a *serial* monogamist. But he was *not* a "cheater."

Jane's remarkable beauty, her insecurity, and, now, her half-truths and lies, her dissatisfaction with her body and physical image -- and *especially now* her infidelity -- all presaged and foreshadowed for Thomas what he would once more experience in the near future, with Lu-Ann Irene Edwards.

Crushed and saddened, quite understandably, Thomas had, he thought, truly loved Jane -- but infidelity for him was a non-negotiable element of a loving relationship. Thomas went through a several weeks' period of being, feeling and seeming down, to those who knew him well, though, to a loner such as he was, those who knew him well were few in number. He was unable to hide his low mood from his secretary/assistant, Arlene, however, and one afternoon confided in her, when she asked directly, that he was indeed "down," and told her the reason for it. "And I thought she was as pure as the driven snow," Thomas said.

Arlene countered, "Obviously, she's not that at all; she's about as pure as the driven slush."

Arlene had the ability to snap Thomas to reality from both a business and a personal viewpoint and she succeeded once again in doing so, with this remark. It brought a smile to Thomas's face, and then an audible laugh.

He would thereafter think of Jane by the sobriquet "Slush." Even Paddy endorsed this one. *Pure as the driven slush.*

Despite the unhappy conclusion to their brief affair, Thomas made an effort to keep in touch with Jane in the ensuing years. She was a good mother to her two daughters, she worked hard in her career, she was intelligent and wanted, desperately, to be married again.

But he had learned from "Slush," most of all, that not only men but women, too, could be unfaithful -- something the nuns and priests back at SMI in Johnstown had never covered in their Catechism classes. Females, too, undoubtedly so, had "impure thoughts." Johnstown and SMI, for all it had given him, also had short-changed him, in not preparing him for the sad and cruel *realities* of "real life." Thomas increasingly realized this as he grew older.

And as the years passed and he aged, Thomas also began to think more kindly toward Jane. He remembered her birthday and periodically would send her a card or flowers on that June occasion. She responded once, to tell him that she was "with" someone, and very happy. Thomas was happy for her that this was the case.

When One Does Not Love Too Much,
One Does Not Love Enough
-- *Blaise Pascal* --

Thirty One

And then there was Olivia.

Thomas and Olivia began to "look" at one another twenty years before they, one day, touched hands, twenty-two years before they embraced and kissed for the first time, and twenty-three years before they made love for the first time.

Olivia, Olivia, Olivia …

In Thomas's mind, it seemed like there had always been Olivia...that he had always been moving toward her for a long time, a very long time, that he had been moving toward her *always*. Over space, over time, in ways known and unknown, *they had been moving toward one another, inexorably, slowly, surely, ineluctably.*

Thomas: *Every time I think of this woman, I am in love with her. Every time I hear her voice, I am in love. Every time I see her, I am in love. Every time.*

Time spent with her is precious and priceless, every minute like a rare diamond.

●●●●●●●

Thomas remembered.

Olivia.

Thirty Two

As Johnstown and the nuns and priests at SMI had not prepared Thomas for the painful reality that hit him so hard with Jane -- that women, too, are capable of infidelity -- neither did they prepare him for a great love such as Rebecca -- and *another*, in Olivia. And as much as Thomas wanted to believe in *one* true love -- a love of one's life -- neither was he prepared for the reality -- it was almost as painful to him as unfaithful love -- that love *can* happen more than once in one's three score and ten in this earthly vale of tears.

Olivia, Olivia, Olivia...

...dear, dear Olivia.

Thomas remembered.

●●●●●●●

Johnstown had been a mill town for nearly a century before the two large carpet manufacturers that had made the sleepy little city their home for so long announced one day, almost without warning, that they were moving south in the U.S. to avail themselves of a less expensive labor force. Johnstown never quite recovered. Almost everyone in Johnstown either worked in one of the carpet mills or had a relative who did or knew someone who worked in one of them -- either for Mohawk Mills ("Carpets from the looms of Mohawk") or Bigelow Sanford Company. Moving to a place with a labor force cheaper than Johnstown? How could that be, Thomas wondered. There weren't any people in town that he knew of who were getting rich working hourly-paid jobs in the mills. How were the carpet manufacturing moguls able to find anyone *anywhere* willing to work for less?

A high percentage of Johnstown's population was born, brought up and died there. Many never ventured forth more than 20-30 miles from their home, perhaps a trip down the New York State Thruway to Albany to see a rock concert (Thomas as a teenager had once gone to Albany to see an Elvis Presley concert), or to tour the State capitol building. Some of Johnstown's more worldly and well-traveled citizens had made the 191-miles trip down the Thruway all the way to New York City. For some of those few, it was a honeymoon trip -- a once in a lifetime adventure that they and their spouse would talk about for the rest of their lives, seemingly incessantly -- their exciting excursion to the Big City, the Big Apple.

Everyone in Johnstown matriculated at either the parochial school, St. Mary's Institute, or at the *"non-catholic"* school (as the Catholic population referred to it) Johnstown High.

As Thomas had not been prepared at SMI by the sisters of St. Joseph nor the priests for much of what life in his later years would present to him (the sad reality of a woman's infidelity, for example), neither had many of the nuns been prepared for the likes of Thomas and his friends.

There were some nuns who, despite themselves and their

idiosyncrasies, were student favorites. Sister Ann Bertrand was one of those. Sister Ann was a big-time University of Notre Dame football fan. Known by the students as "Bertie," on Monday mornings during the college football season, Sister Bertrand would play on an old gramophone she kept beside her teacher's desk in front of her sixth-grade classroom the Notre Dame Victory march.

Cheer, cheer for old Notre Dame ... Wake up the echoes cheering her name... Send the volley cheer on high... Shake down the thunder from the sky...What though the odds be great or small, old Notre Dame will win over all...While her loyal sons are marching... Onward to victory.

The class was expected to sing along with the words on the gramophone while also marching, single file, around the classroom. Now, this assumed that Notre Dame had vanquished its "non-Catholic" opponents on the previous Saturday in South Bend. If the Irish had *not* gone 'onward to victory,' the song and the student march were put off until the following week, though Bertie was sure to be in a foul mood all that Monday after a Notre Dame defeat. Her mood continued sour through Wednesday or Thursday, but would gradually take an upward turn as the next football Saturday approached and her optimism resurfaced that victory for the Irish was in the offing once again.

Bertie also regularly raffled off to her classes blessed Rosary beads. Ticket chances cost ten cents. Thomas and his friends occasionally wondered what Bertie did with the proceeds she realized -- some wine for her room in the convent? a donation for the Church poor box? a secret personal retirement fund? That the nuns, in all likelihood, lived a life of rigorous asceticism was a thought that did not occur to Thomas or his friends.

Bertie also was a strict disciplinarian, though she did not, as her superior -- Mother Grace Madeline did -- engage in corporal punishment. Bertie's approach to discipline was restricted to a single form of non-physical punishment. Without a trial or an independent, impartial judge, miscreants in Bertie's class were sentenced to time "on the box." (Bertie was the <u>only</u> judge and jury, and she ruled with an iron fist. There was no chance of, or for, an appeal.) Bertie was the sole judge of what constituted a cause for punishment: sometimes it had to do with nothing more serious than her *perception* that the cut-up's crime was, simply, not paying attention to her lesson and he (convicted criminals in Bertie's class were, almost always, boys; girls rarely received box-time sentences) would have to move from his desk and occupy instead one of the four wooden-crate boxes turned upside down in each corner of her classroom. The *length* of the sentence, sitting on the crate, depended, again, on Bertie's judgment only. Talking to one's neighbor, or laughing -- or, worse, snickering while trying to stifle laughter -- or pestering one of the girls in the class, in a desk in front of or across the aisle from where the miscreant sat, might rate an entire morning or afternoon "on the box." (A harbinger (?) of the Paul Newman movie, "Cool Hand Luke," where solitary confinement punishment was time sentenced *"in the box"*). Not paying attention, while still quite serious -- especially if it was a first offense (most of the culprits were, however, repeat offenders/recidivists) -- might rate a sentence of only an hour or two "on the box."

Even though she was disliked -- and laughed at, but only *behind* her back -- Bertie was feared and respected, grudgingly. The boys would not have dared to pull on her what they did to poor Sister Jean Veronica.

Poor Sister Jean. She looked to be the youngest in age (and, thus, presumably, the one with the least teaching experience) of all of the SMI Sisters of St. Joseph penguins.

It was Thomas who thought of the team bobsled idea that the boys implemented to torment poor, young, inexperienced Sister Jean.

The boys had watched a recent telecast of a team bobsled racing event at the Winter Olympics and Thomas and they were taken with the manner in which the Olympians on the four-man sled racing down a snowy mountain trail moved in unison, leaning forward, then back, then to the left and then to the right, as the course took them and their sled in that direction. At the conclusion of the course, the rider in front (Thomas) would shake and shimmy and then lean back with his arms outstretched in front of him as he "braked" the vehicle to a stop.

Thomas led Peter Persico, Dick Cocker and Chet Zalewski through a simulated 4-man team bobsled race in the desks they sat in, in a single row, one behind another in Sister Jean's class. They kept it up with a race a day for several days. They did show *some* mercy to Sister Jean, however. A race would begin and then conclude in no more than three or four minutes. Sister Jean was nonplussed. She never said a word, obviously wanting the affront to end expeditiously and for the entire exercise to just end.

Poor Sister Jean. She always seemed on the verge of tears in class.

Olivia had also had the experience of a parochial school education led by nuns. Her experience was a few years later (Olivia was three years younger than Thomas, an age differential that Paddy did not approve of: "Why in the hell would you want to date anybody *your* age?") in a school a half continent away, but her school and her nuns were no less rigid, closed-minded and stultifying than Thomas's.

Olivia had a sense of humor that Thomas found to be more 'masculine' in its ribaldry than it was feminine, and he appreciated and enjoyed that, as he did almost everything about Olivia.

Olivia remembered, in her school, Sister Bonaventure and Sister B's oft-uttered refrain to her English grammar class whenever any of them would make, orally, any of four inexcusable mistakes that Sister B. just would not tolerate:

Sister B's mantra: "Never say knowed, throwed, busted or blowed."

Olivia acceded to Sister Bonaventure as far as 'blowed' was concerned. Olivia gave "great head," she was proud to say. Thomas agreed. Thanks to Sister Bonaventure's influence, Olivia would never, ever speak of having 'blowed' him. It was either 'blew' him or "sucked your cock dry." Olivia was an expert fellatrix. She loved, she said, to suck Thomas's cock. At first, she was a "spitter" but over time became a "swallower." She told Thomas that she even experienced orgasm herself while sucking him off. She never "blowed" him. (Would Sister Bonaventure have been pleased that Olivia had never said 'blowed'?) Olivia was hard-pressed to find the right tack with "busted," however. She was exceedingly well-endowed in the chest -- big tits -- and would ask Thomas if he felt that *that*, in adhering to Sister 'B's' guidelines, would mean that she, Olivia, were "big bursted." Olivia made Thomas laugh -- aloud -- as much as any woman he had ever known.

As Jane had told Thomas about the snatch-shaving episode with her sister as a "twin thing," Olivia -- "The Scarlet Harlot," as Paddy christened her -- was not a natural red head. She achieved that coiffure tincture through drug store hair dyes. Once she told Thomas that she was considering, the next time she colored her hair, "to get an extra batch for a snatch to match." Thomas laughed aloud at that one, too.

Olivia... Olivia ...Olivia...

●●●●●●●

It was *always* Olivia. Olivia eased Thomas's pain and his disappointment, sorrow, heartache and disillusionment over Slush, Rebecca -- and "LIE."

Olivia... Olivia ... Olivia

Thomas remembered.

Thirty Three

Thomas often referred to Johnstown as the land that God forgot. It seemed to him that the city was mired in the last century and would never, he thought, escape the economic depression that defined it after the carpet mills abandoned the city and shut down their plant operations. The dozen or more huge mill buildings throughout the city -- in the East End and up on Polack Hill stood vacant today, with windows broken in many of the four and five-story brick-faced structures by rock-throwing youths. The city and its environs and its broken-windowed, abandoned mills *looked* depressed -- and destitute. Johnstown: the *city* that God forgot.

Paddy and Thomas also saw Johnstown, sardonically, as the land of malapropisms. Paddy was in a unique position to hear and mentally catalogue "the latest beaut" in his capacity as bartender and manager/franchisee of the clubhouse bar and restaurant at the town's municipal golf course.

The most recent "beaut" was a conversation he had overheard between Joey and Louie as they sipped Bud lights, from the bottle, sitting at the end of the bar early one rainy afternoon. The golf course was closed because of a rainstorm

-- a veritable downpour ("The rain was sweepin' down the first fairway like a ragin' inferno," Joey told Paddy, mixing his metaphor in a creative Johnstown-ism. "Can't play golf in this shit -- there ain't fuck nothin' to do now *but* drink.")

The conversation that Paddy strained to listen in on, while he concurrently tried to pay attention to other drinkers seated at stools along the rest of the long clubhouse bar, then turned to ornithological matters. The river that ran through Johnstown was the Mohawk. It dissected the city, and one either lived north of it *in* the city or south of it, still technically and geographically, *in* the city but, more precisely to Johnstonians, "over the river." Louie elaborated on his ornithological observations. Last Saturday he said was the "second or tird" time in the past month he had seen eagles "over the river" in the same place. Joey, suitably impressed, paused for a second and then remarked, "Yeah, I've seen some of 'em there lately myself. I think they're fucken startin' to come out of extinction."

"... *startin' to come out of extinction...*" Paddy swore that that is what he heard Joey say.

It was not only malapropisms that Paddy delighted in overhearing during Joey-Louie conversations. The two buddies -- mostly Joey, it seemed -- also had problems on occasion with syntax. The two were decrying the overexpansion and development alongside Route 30, the highway just north of town. "Yeah," summarized Joey, "the buildings up there are gettin' too close apart any more."

A friend of Paddy's told him about the conversation *he* had overheard between the two Grammatical, Sociological and Astrological magnates when Joey, Paddy's friend swore, told Louie that he had seen the eclipse of the moon last week, all the way to its conclusion, when, at the end, Joey said, the moon "... like magic very slow came out of ecliption."

Joey and Louie were also participants in the Saturday afternoon and evening and night and Sunday morning poker game at the Clubhouse bar. It was at those events, at a table just off the bar near where the cash register, behind the bar, was situated, that the conversations became even deeper, more philosophical, existential -- and personal.

Joey, Louie, Ralphie the Leech, Two-Ton Tony, Danny the Rat, Asshole Al and Sammy the Snake, during the course of their weekly game of seven-card stud poker, were discussing marital fidelity and infidelity.

Joey allowed that he had been unfaithful "only two or tree times" during his 14-year marriage and seemed to be looking for approbation for his constancy and chastity. Louie was next. Louie said he had cheated only once in his marriage, "but, cheeses, that was Rory Lou Connolly."

"How the fuck you gonna pass that up?" he asked.

Next was Ralphie, to be followed by Tony, Danny, Al and, finally, Sammy, who even though he still had a few minutes until the floor was to be his appeared to be deep in thought. He was counting, on his fingers, and silently moving his lips as if in a one-sided conversation. Sammy seemed nervous as his turn to address the subject at hand inexorably approached.

Tony, like Louie, said he had strayed only once during his 20-year marriage, but that was with Mary Jane Petrosino, with whom, he said, "I'm in love." That, for Tony, seemingly, was exculpatory. "Hell Mary Jane and I have been gettin' it on regular since the week after I married Carm -- and I ain't never cheated on Mary Jane yet," Tony concluded, his self-felt honor intact.

Sammy the Snake appeared, now, to be perspiring slightly. He took out a handkerchief (obviously soiled) from one of his rear trousers pockets and wiped the sweat from his forehead.

Danny took the floor next, as Ralphie lost his turn through inattention and inebriation. Danny asked first if they could finish the poker hand they were playing. He had pocket Aces and did not want to forfeit his chance for a big pot with conversational distractions.

Sammy sweated even more.

Danny picked up another Ace and won the hand and pot easily.

"C'mon, Danny, how many times d'ju do it to somebody else since you and Lori got married?" pressed Ralphie, alert and relieved now that *he* had gotten a stay of execution -- which seemed to have held and would not, he hoped, be revoked.

The guys knew that Danny was a renowned Johnstown philanderer, though that would not have been the descriptive any of them would have used to describe Danny's extra-curricular and extra-marital sexual forays.

"Danny, you ain't *never* kept it in your pants," said Tony.

The guys were anxious to hear how much Danny would admit to. Danny spoke -- "Alright, I been married ten years now to Lori and I prolly cheated nine/ten times a year since then. How many's that make?"

"Hell that's a lot, Danny. Gotta be somewhere around tirty er forty," offered Asshole Al.

The rest of the guys had no doubt that Danny, despite his admission to, in reality, 90-100 transgressions, was in all likelihood understating his case even with that estimate, but they let their doubts go and turned their gaze next to Al the Mathematician whose mental multiplication of 10 times 10 in toting things up for Danny had suffered a miscalculation.

Sammy was obviously nervous now, and continued to sweat. His turn was to be next, as soon as Al spoke his piece.

Al told the group that he had never even once been unfaithful to Kara during their 35-year marriage.

"Yer shittin' us!" said Danny.

"Nope, that's the truth guys," Asshole Al insisted.

Al, however, tarnished his admirable truth by adding: "Ain't never had the fucken chance to do it with nobody else."

All eyes at the table turned now toward Sammy.

It was his turn to speak and it was also his turn to deal. He shuffled the cards slowly, then stacked them and put them

201

down on the table in front of him. Sammy raised the forefinger of his right hand. He was seeking a rules interpretation and clarification.

"Lemme get this straight now," Sammy intoned.

There was a palpable pause. Paddy was observing from his post behind the bar.

Sammy continued, "We're talkin' fucken around is <u>all</u>, right?"

No one spoke. Sammy took a deep breath. It was almost a sigh. There had been no objection to his clarification request.

There was another palpable pause. Finally Sammy continued once again -- with his point of clarification seemingly cleared and approved --

"Blow jobs don't count, ain't it?" he asked.

Paddy took all of this in from where he stood behind the bar and, he told Thomas, when Sammy asked his point-of-clarification question Paddy almost crushed in his hand -- the possibility of a cut glass injury notwithstanding -- a draught beer glass he was about to fill for another customer as Sammy's immortal question was uttered and floated over the poker table.

Paddy thought that if *he* ever wrote a book -- about Johnstown -- he would borrow Sammy's question and use it as his book's title.

A *New York Times* best seller?

"Blow Jobs Don't Count, Ain't It?"

●●●●●●●

Paddy told Thomas of some of the other "beauts" he had heard from his cat bird's perch behind the bar.

Without identifying the source, he had heard one Johnstonian telling another that a priest in a confessional had the power to "absorb" people of their sins -- an SMI graduate?

A man with keen eyesight who was able to see broadly and widely from right to left had "perennial" vision.

A man who had had a bad experience of some sort -- Paddy could not remember exactly what it was, only what its stated result was -- spoke about the experience having "left a bad taste in my mind."

Another Johnstonian would refer to 'gay' females as "Lebanese ladies." Gay males in Johnstown were still queers, or fags -- not gay. "They've taken that word away from me," Paddy complained. "I can't use 'gay' any more without it meaning something else that it does not mean to me and never has."

Another Johnstonian once said of something he wanted to remember and keep in the back of his mind that he would "keep it in my back head."

On another occasion -- and this was Sammy -- Paddy heard Sammy lamenting an injury he had suffered to his arm while at work. Sammy was a warehouseman. "My fucken arm hurt so bad I thought they were gonna have to decapitate it," was Sammy's learned medical opinion.

On still another occasion, Paddy overheard Sammy, when he meant to say "for all intents and purposes," say, instead, "for all intensive purposes."

Once, while watching an NCAA basketball Final Four game on the bar television set, another Johnstonian, as the game neared its conclusion, announced that "Time is now an essence."

Paddy also noted memorable bumper-sticker messages in and around Johnstown. Among his favorites were:

"Nuke The Fag Whales -- For Jesus"

"The Weather Is Here; Wish You Were Beautiful"

-- and...

"The Meek Don't Want It"

Thomas had thought of a few possible bumper-stickers of his own for use in Florida and Siesta Key, one of the few places in America where an 85-year-old is considered a fetus --
"Welcome to Siesta Key; Now Go Home"
"Florida: Abandon Hope All Ye Who Enter Here"
and --
"Florida: Death's Waiting Room"

Paddy's favorite, *unpublished* bumper-sticker that he wanted to have made up, printed and available for sale was:
"Fuck Everybody and Everything Everywhere All The Time Forever" Paddy conceded that *that* message on a bumper sticker was too lengthy to fit on a single line. "Fucker'd have to be a two-liner."

Paddy also wanted to publish several other bumper stickers, though even *he* allowed that "they probably wouldn't fly in Johnstown."

"Too obscure," he acknowledged readily. Those were --
"Eschew Obfuscation"
"I've got Mixed Feelings About Ambivalence"
"My anger management class pisses me off"
"Somehow I've Always Known I'd Never Be Psychic"
"When in Rome, Buy Bottled Water"
"Practice Safe Sex: Go Fuck Yourself"

For Paddy, February was the cruelest month. It irritated him and *offended* him aurally to no end that "nobody, especially those insipid talking heads and news announcers on television seem able to pronounce, correctly, the second month of the year." The consistent mispronunciation of this rather simple noun, Paddy held, "is fucking egregious."

204

Thirty Four

Paddy ranted --

"The television nitwits leave out the first 'r' when they say the word out loud. I guess they don't see that the word is spelled and should be pronounced with <u>two</u> 'r's' -- *one after the 'b' and the other before the 'y.'* It is Feb-ru-ary, not Feb-<u>u</u>-ary.

"Otherwise intelligent, thinking, rational people make this mistake all the fucken time and it drives *me* fucken nuts.

"And I gotta live with this shit 28 days every year, except every four years I gotta hear it for 29 days."

A friend of Thomas's, Mike Brandon, told him that the legendary Walter Cronkite annually on the first day of the year's second month looked into the camera and said, "I'm going to say the name of this month correctly one time, February" (and he got it right). "Now that we know I can say it correctly, I'll say it the way I always have for the rest of Feb-u-ary" (which he'd *then* mispronounce, the way so many others do).

Paddy, in his calmer, more charitable moments, wanted also to revoke certain modern-day changes (disguised as "improvements") in some of America's major spectator sports. Thomas agreed. Paddy was primarily an NFL and NBA fan. Thomas preferred major league baseball. Paddy wanted to ban altogether pass interference penalties in the NFL ("<u>Nobody</u> knows what the hell constitutes pass interference anyway!") and, in the NBA, he wanted to ban the three-point shot and the dunk ("That's all they do in the Negro Basketball Association," he said. "Dunk and three-point shoot. What the hell happened to <u>real</u> basketball and the 'weave?' ") Thomas, the baseball addict, wanted to revoke that sport's designated hitter rule. ("You want more offense in the game? That's easy -- eliminate the shortstop position defensively," was Thomas's take on that one.) Thomas also wanted to ban artificial turf in the game. "Play it on grass, the way God invented it!" he said, sounding perhaps like his brother or one of the guys from the clubhouse poker game.

Paddy also wanted to apply the death penalty to certain social gaffes that particularly irritated him. Close to, if not at, the top of the list were women who suggested and then insisted that their date "try" their entrée in a restaurant. "No!" was Paddy's response, always. "If I had wanted what you're eating, instead of what I have in front of me and what I'm eating, I'd have ordered the same as you. Tell you what, you eat yours and I'll eat mine."

Paddy claimed he'd never seen or heard a man suggesting or offering a 'taste' of his meal in a restaurant to his female companion. "Women," he said disgustedly.

Paddy also disdained email "forwarded" jokes. "Thought you might find the attached amusing..." or "Everybody needs a laugh now and then..."

"How the fuck do *you* know or *would you* have any idea whatsoever what <u>I</u> find interesting or what I need, a laugh or any fucken thing else?" Paddy would rail. Any 'fwd' message in Paddy's email inbox was deleted automatically. "Fucken assholes.   Forward <u>this</u>!"

●●●●●●●

    Thomas often was saddened when he looked around his Siesta Key community generally and the condominium complex particularly where he lived in Florida and saw incipient death in the faces and gait and posture of so many. Age and imminent death seemed everywhere in Florida. Thomas did not make an effort to get to know very many of his neighbors, or to socialize with them at all, any of them. As a comparatively young retiree and still an active runner, he felt he did not have very much in common with them. Often-times, Thomas would find envelopes with notes written on them taped to his front door. They were invitations, often, to next week's Social Committee meeting or Book Club discussion or "coffee and pastries with your neighbors." Thomas threw the envelopes and invitations away and never attended any of the functions. It was Paddy who gave Thomas an idea to employ to put a stop to the notes and invitations. Paddy mailed to Thomas an over-sized computer generated and printed message: LMTFA. Thomas taped the message to his front door.

    The initials were not spelled out or translated but many understood them straight off (Quaker State Annie, for example). The initialed-message stood for this: Leave Me The Fuck Alone.

    The invitations tapered off, became sporadic and intermittent and then, finally, ceased altogether.

    Though Thomas was saddened daily by the human physical decrepitude he saw all around him, he was also amused by the many busy-bodies in the two-building complex in which he lived. These were the "Condo Nazis" brigade, who made it their business to be involved in the Condo Association Board of Managers, in the Beautification Committee and

Joseph A. Gillan

the Rules, Standards and By-Laws committee -- and in moni-
toring compliance with and policing and administering rules,
standards and by-laws. One woman, a chubby little cherub
somewhat younger than her associates, took on in Thomas's eyes the well-deserved title of Chief Condo Nazi. This
woman, Thomas thought, must have an excess amount of time
on her hands, or no other life, or a combination thereof. She
involved herself in *everything*. She was also quite proficient at
obtaining Association funds to buy planters and flowers that
she placed and planted in *every* available nook and cranny
around the outside grounds of the two buildings. Thomas
told Paddy about her.

"Flowers -- who the fuck needs 'em?" "She's wasting --
squandering -- your money!" (Association monthly maintenance fees) -- was Paddy's take on that state of affairs.

Thomas was also continually amazed when almost each
time he got on the building elevator at the lobby level and
another resident or more got on with him, one always took
the role of "button pusher" as the car began to ascend. "Let's
see, you're on four -- and you two are on six and Mary you're
on seven ...and *you*, Tom...." People who Thomas could not
recall ever having *seen* before knew, somehow, not only his
name but which floor he lived on. LMTFA, please!

Thomas *did* have a *limited* number of friends in the
complex. Jack and Darrah Bagley, a delightful couple, still
handsome in their 70s, were among his closest. Jack, a retired
FBI agent and Darrah, a former New Orleans debutante, had
been married 50 years and, it was obvious to all who knew
them, were still very much in love: the solicitious manner in
which they smiled at, interacted with and treated one another;
they still frequently hugged and often Jack or Darrah would
kiss the other on the cheek, for seemingly no apparent reason.
Thomas also was friends with the Brown family: Joe, Sue and
Jake.

Thomas laughed to himself often about another resident
of the complex who seemed universally <u>disliked</u>. Alfred E.

Nilowits was also known as "Prancing Al." It was comical to see him strut about the parking lot area like a proud peacock. Almost without exception the other residents, like Thomas, laughed at Al behind his back. Among descriptives Thomas had heard applied to Al were: obnoxious, conceited, arrogant, pompous and hubristic, intellectual lightweight, ersatz/clinquant, vapid and vacuous. Al seemed to see himself, for no apparent reason, as God's gift to humanity. On the other hand, Al's wife, Melissa, was well-liked by most of the residents, but pitied.

Melissa and Al lived in Florida only for a few months each year. For the rest of the year they lived in a New England state which Thomas's brother Paddy often referred to as the People's Republic of Massachusetts.

In Johnstown, the bumper-sticker aphorisms aside, the title of the book about the town that Paddy said he would one day write would reprise Sammy's line -- "Blow Jobs Don't Count, Ain't It?" Thomas wanted Paddy to write a book about his Florida condominium complex, entitled "LMTFA."

Paddy told Thomas he had heard another bar-sitter say that his eight-years-old son thought that God's name was Howard. "Our Father, Howard be thy name..."

Johnstown: the land that God forgot and the land of malapropisms and neologisms. Siesta Key: death's waiting room.

On another occasion at Paddy's golf course bar and grill, the poker regulars were approached by a Johnstown officer of the law who was looking for Vinnie Yevoli. Each of the players around the table tried to cover for Vinnie with a lie of his own.

"He ain't here," announced Sammy, overstating the obvious.

"Have you seen him in the last day or two?" asked the policeman.

Heads around the table began shaking from side to side, almost in unison. They were not going to rat out on Vinnie, without even knowing why the police were looking for him.

Sammy decided he wanted to be helpful to the constabulary -- or, more likely, to get him out of the way so that he and his fellow players could get on with their poker game.

"He was here a little while ago," Sammy declared.

Sammy looked around the room, as did the officer, following the path of Sammy's head turn and gaze. Sammy then declared further --

"He just must-a went."

Paddy told Thomas that he recalled this *precisely* as Sammy had said it. He was able to do this, Paddy averred, by remembering that Sammy had said it *alphabetically*. It was <u>not</u> "must-a just went."

It was, for the record and Johnstown posterity, "just must-a went."

"It's gotta be in the water," Paddy would sigh, often, from the vantage point of his cat bird's seat and ear-witness listening post behind the bar.

Paddy once summed up Johnstown this way to Thomas: "The birds fly upside down in Johnstown. There ain't nothin' here that even *they* see worth shittin' on."

Thirty Five

Back in Washington, after Rebecca and after Velvet and Jane -- dear, dear Jane -- and others, Thomas soon met and dated for a period Kathy, who lived in the same building he did in Arlington. Kathy was a slim, attractive blonde, younger than Thomas, as was his wont in dating. As Thomas maintained his fitness through jogging, Kathy was also fit, as a daily swimmer and Thomas was able to detect always about her a faint smell of chlorine. He told Paddy about her, and Paddy suggested she be christened, alliteratively, "Chlorine Kathy."

Kathy became more serious than Thomas, almost immediately, in wanting to "progress" their relationship. She had marriage in mind; Thomas did not. Kathy began to call Thomas and knock on his door at all hours and he was at a loss as to how, gently, to break off the relationship. She was becoming a pest, almost stalking him.

Thomas mentioned his dilemma to Paddy and, as always, his advice was pithy and to the point.

"Move," advised Paddy.

Man in his life has many friends, but he has only one best friend. Paddy was Thomas's *best* friend.

Thomas recalled an incident one northeast wintry season when a spate of smaller, commuter aircraft had crashed within a period of several weeks. The FAA concluded, eventually, that the de-icing procedures that seemed to be effective with larger passenger aircraft were less effective with the smaller planes; the weight of ice build-up on their wings was apparently re-accumulating much more rapidly than was the case with larger passenger aircraft and this, thus, was the reason, in all likelihood, that so many of the smaller planes were crashing during the winter months in areas susceptible to and hit with ice and snow storms.

Paddy's conclusion and remedy: "Fly 'em where it's hot."

The FAA in time -- several months after Paddy's pronouncement -- issued an advisory that the smaller aircraft should not be flown in the northeast or other more frigid regions of the country from November through March. Their scientific, more learned judgment was the same as Paddy's. It just took the bureaucratic agency a little longer to get to there than it did Paddy.

Thirty Six

Rebecca remembered.

She and William arrived in Sarasota late morning and checked into their hotel downtown, at the bay front -- The Ritz-Carlton (Rebecca *was* a "high maintenance" individual). After a cup of coffee and an iced tea (William), they decided to go that very afternoon to explore Siesta Key and its world-famous Siesta Beach.

Rebecca remembered.

She wondered if somehow, by some incalculable coincidence, she would see Thomas there. She had not mentioned to William that she had learned that Siesta Key was where Thomas lived. William did not know, even, that Thomas lived anywhere in Florida. He had assumed, mistakenly, that Thomas was still in the Washington area.

Rebecca remembered.

Rebecca had been struck of late by not only the increasing number of times that William had left her at home to "go out on an errand" but also, she thought, at how many calls had been coming in for him at home on his cellular phone in the late mornings and late afternoons. William would excuse himself, always, and take the calls in another room.

Rebecca remembered, as William and she parked their car in the large lot near Siesta Beach and walked toward the sand and the blue-green water of the Gulf of Mexico.

Rebecca remembered, and she felt -- not for the first time -- a pang of regret that what she and Thomas had once had together was no more, that it was gone -- irrevocably? -- and that she and William were now tied to each other -- irrevocably?

She missed Thomas and his vitality, passion and tenderness -- and she missed his sensuality.

Rebecca remembered.

Rebecca thought about her dream of two nights ago in which she saw Thomas on the street while she and William were touring in Siesta Key. She could not know that at this very moment, as she and William approached the beautiful quartz sand beach and took off their shoes to walk in bare feet, Thomas was jogging on the same stretch of beach less than a half-mile away from where she and William walked.

Thomas remembered as he jogged -- but he thought not about Rebecca. Rather, thoughts of Lu-Ann and Olivia filled Thomas's consciousness.

Thomas remembered, and he thought about....
Olivia, Olivia...Olivia.

Thirty Seven

Paddy was indeed the best friend Thomas had ever had. Thomas was more honest with Paddy and confided more to him than he ever had with any man before or ever would in the future, even though there were a certain few subjects that were never broached between the two.

One other of Thomas's very good friends was Aldo, in Toulouse. Thomas had worked with Aldo, in Brussels and in America, in Darien. Aldo was now retired and lived with his longtime spouse Sophia in the south of France.

What's in a name? Thomas had known only two people in his life with that given name -- Aldo -- and he considered both of them his friends and respected each of them greatly. Besides Toulouse Aldo, there also was Sandusky Aldo -- Thomas's friend from The Thomas Wolfe Society.

And despite Paddy being Thomas's best friend, there *were* certain issues and subjects that he felt more comfortable discussing with Toulouse Aldo than with his younger brother. Paddy eschewed, indeed ran from, "serious" conversations -- about life and death and theological and metaphysical questions, the meaning of life and death, about morality and mortality. Toulouse Aldo embraced such issues and discussions, and Thomas often thirsted to converse about them and Aldo was the only one with whom he felt comfortable doing that.

Thomas had been considering for some time the major life's move he was to tell Rebecca about in his Christmas-season letter to her, and had exchanged letters and emails with Aldo (Toulouse) about it for a year or more before he took the step that he did.

Thomas, after three or four glasses of red wine (Thomas's "position" on wine -- "the grape," as Paddy referred to it -- was this: "I don't care about its nationality or its age, only its hue matters to me.") Paddy considered white wine more a woman's wine. "Real Men don't drink white wine."

Toulouse Aldo was in fact an oenophile -- and Thomas had learned some from him about wine when they lived and worked together in Brussels. ("I'll have an eighty-two Bordeaux, please," Thomas would respond from time-to-time during air travel when asked by a flight attendant during beverage service if he'd like a drink).

Aldo, by any definition, was truly a "European." His parents were Italian and Aldo, in his heart and soul, was very much Italian as well, and would always be that nationality first and foremost. But his European diversity was equally undeniable. His parents were living in England when Aldo was born and Aldo grew up and was educated there -- and lived there until he was in his early 20s. Aldo "looked" Italian but *spoke* like an "Englishman."

Aldo earned a degree in chemistry from Oxford. He later lived in central Europe -- in Brussels -- for 25 years (interrupted by a brief three-year assignment in America, in Connecticut, where he and Thomas worked together, once again, as they had in Brussels). Relatively short in stature, and dark-skinned, Aldo when he spoke did indeed "sound" British but most definitely did not look it -- primarily because of his heritage and genetic make-up. Dark-skinned and a handsome man, Aldo, in his physical appearance, resembled a consonant mix of Paul Newman and a young Marlon Brando -- a classic, square-faced, square-jawed, movie-star good-looking leading man direct from Central Casting, speaking, antithetically, with a veddy Oxfordian British accent. When Aldo retired, he and Sophia chose to leave their longtime home in Brussels and move, not "home" to Italy, but to the cosmopolitan Southern French city of Toulouse, which they had once visited on holiday and fallen in love with.

●●●●●●●

Aldo had written to Thomas and had asked him for his thoughts on death and dying... "if, my friend, you are not uncomfortable talking about those subjects."

In his reply to Aldo, Thomas wrote --

You write that many of your friends and acquaintances in your new home city of Toulouse are "squeamish" and seemingly reluctant, if not adamantly and immutably opposed and altogether <u>unwilling</u> to speak of death. You asked if I am willing to speak of it, and correspond about it. Yes, my friend, of course I am. I am neither unwilling nor reluctant to speak of death.

Like you, I think about death more and more as I grow older and as The Dark Lady comes ever, ineluctably, inevitably closer. Also like you, I do not believe, however, that because I have these thoughts with increasing frequency as I age that this means I am dwelling unnaturally or obsessively -- or morbidly, if you will (pun intended) -- on them. Like you once again, and as <u>you</u> say, I am merely "facing facts."

Death of course <u>is</u> the fate that awaits us all. <u>That</u> is a fact. Death is the great and consummate equalizer. <u>That</u> is a fact. The Dark Lady spares no man. She cannot. The Dark Lady and her task are immutable and inexorable. All of us, kings and commoners, will one day meet up with her and be taken into her all-enveloping arms. All of us, kings and commoners, will one day enter into the tomb *and the realm of her silent eternity. Those are all facts.*

To consider thoughts of death and its ultimate imminence, particularly when one reaches his or her 40s and 50s and beyond is, to say again, merely facing facts.

Tempora labunter, tacitisque senescimus annis

("Time glides on, and we age insensibly with the years.")

*I recently finished a collection of Maupassant short stories. In one of them, he writes about the unavoidable reality that confronts man all of his life: that of having to **live** with death's "perpetual inevitability".*

Man among all living creatures has the questionable distinction and dubious gift of knowing he is going to die. (My brother Paddy, whom I have mentioned to you, disagrees with this thought. As he puts it, sardonically, "I don't know about that. I think maybe squirrels have a hunch about it.")

Thoughts of death and our own mortality are a part of our very being. Why would we not speak of death and mortality?

It was Socrates, I believe, who wrote (I have tried to verify this quote but was unable, quickly, to do so and thus I may well be somewhat imprecise here and am -- it is quite possible -- in fact paraphrasing "No one knows whether death is really the greatest blessing a man can have but we fear it is the greatest curse.")

This has been true since time immemorial -- and it will be forevermore. To give frail, mortal man his due, it is more unnatural not to fear the Dark Lady and the Great Unknown than it is to fear it.

...always was, is now and always shall be...

It is exceedingly difficult for me, intellectually, to wrap my mind around this concept and I would like to "discuss" it -- the concept of eternity -- with you further in future correspondence, but not now within the context of this "conversation" you have raised about mortality, death and dying.

It hurts my head to think too long on it -- eternity and infinity -- and I hope we do have an opportunity to explore and exchange thoughts on this, as well, sometime soon. It would be great to do it over a fine meal and an '82 Bordeaux, wouldn't it?

In any case, as I write this (always was, is now and always shall be), the closing line of Melville's "Moby Dick" comes to mind --

"... and the great shroud of the sea rolled on as it rolled five thousand years ago."

(Nietzsche's "eternal recurrence" of all things?)

Moby Dick, in my opinion, is a work of genius, unquestionably one of the finest works of fiction ever penned, certainly in America.

Far be it for me to suggest that the close to that masterful, magnificent book might have been enriched by a single, additional sentence -- but I will nonetheless go where angels fear to tread and suggest just that.

I suggest Melville might have improved his close with this additional sentence: "Much the same, perhaps, as it will roll on five thousand years hence."

*Be <u>that</u> as it may, and leaving ol' Herm and the great white whale to rest in peace, when we <u>do</u> speak of death we always get back to <u>The</u> Unavoidable Question -- <u>the essential mystery of all creation</u> -- and that question is this: **why is man born to die?***

Please let me know as soon as you are able if you have an answer to this.

*You ask if I am hesitant to speak of death and dying. You have my obvious answer. No, I am not at all hesitant to speak of those subjects. Sometimes I think even about how, most preferably, I would **want** to die. I would prefer, I think, that I not have a drop-dead heart attack or be hit by a bus as I jog along Midnight Pass Road in Siesta Key. Sudden death would not be my top choice. My father died that way, of a heart attack, at age 53 and my oldest sister died similarly, at age 57. I would also opt out of, if I were able to do so, a long, drawn-out deteriorative illness, the slow, dehumanizing end that many cancers offer us as they chain us to our death bed. Who among us would choose <u>not</u> to have to endure that, if the choice were indeed ours? I most certainly would not want it nor*

would I want my daughters to have to go through that and see me that way.

Paddy, who is indeed the best friend I have on the planet, says that he does not fear death but adds, with a smile on his face, "...as long as it doesn't hurt." I certainly agree that a lengthy, cancer-ridden, final act phase-out would probably "hurt." My brother and I in fact have had a long-standing agreement that if, or when, either of us becomes terminally sick and the portent indicates that the end will not come about any time soon, then the one will assist the other to hasten things along by providing whatever means may be necessary and available to bring that about. As difficult as that may be, we both agree, it also would be a final act of love and kindness.

Ideally, I suppose, I would opt for a death that is not long and drawn out but one which, as cancer does, offers at least some warning and a fairly limited phase-out period, maybe a month or so, to prepare to get things in order to meet my God before -- with apologies to Tennyson -- my "crossing of the bar."

When we speak of death, and we acknowledge that it is a given -- of course -- that The Dark Lady will spare not a one of us, we must also speak of the concept of God. And for me, Aldo, I am no longer certain (as I was for most of my life heretofore) that man and his evolution on this spinning planet in space we call Earth is anything more than a grand accident. St. Augustine, St. Aquinas and the brilliant modern theologian, Trappist Thomas Merton (all three of whom I have been reading extensively of late), if I may place the latter in the elite company of the two former, speak of faith and grace as an intellectual assent   to, and acceptance of, a creed that cannot be objectively displayed or proven. Fair enough. But even with faith and with grace, as we always come back to the essential question and mystery of creation, the unfathomable conundrum -- why is man born to die? -- we also find inescapable and unavoidable this second question: if there is a God, why has He made this vale of tears He has given His creatures to inhabit so dreadfully sorrowful and why does He deign and accord for His creatures for their meager and too swift three-score-and-ten such ineffable and unutterable cruelty, pain and suffering? Please do not recite or speak to me here of the theologians' response to _this_ age-old conundrum. Do not tell me that this all-loving and all-merciful and all-powerful God has absolved Himself from all of the agony of Earth and man's individual agony because He has given man "free will" and that man, thus, brings his pain onto himself of and by himself. That for me, I am sorry to say, is a tepid, tenuous -- and blasphemous -- tenet.

Most men who embrace and follow any of the world's three major monotheistic religions move ever closer to spirituality and their God as they age. I do not suggest that I am unique or, even, all that unusual as increasing theistic uncertainty and doubt seem to be taking hold of me as _I_ age, but it does seem to me that I am, generally, moving counter-cyclically to the mainstream at this moment in my spiritual journey in this vale of tears and sorrow. I wonder why this is the case for me at this time, and I do not have a ready answer. Perhaps things will cycle back to where they once were for me in the time that remains for me. (Are you familiar with this bit of German: Ich spure nur die zeit. Translated it reads: "I feel only time"). Or, perhaps, things will _not_ cycle back for me.

Yes, of course: death is the fate that awaits us all. But what, Aldo, -- What -- if there is no God? Is there nothing more for us than, simply, to "pass and be forgotten with the rest?"

To get back to the question you raised which prompts this letter --

As 'Time glides on and we age insensibly with the years' I _do_ think about dying and death more than I ever have and I also wonder more than I ever have about the existence or non-existence of a God and an after-life. Do you have those thoughts as well?

You and I have beaten around the edges of thoughts such as these, at least in passing (and perhaps superficially) in our correspondence over the years and the impression I have is that your beliefs in God and an after-life are _stronger_ now than they have ever been. Is that not true?

Do you believe in reincarnation? Socrates the great teacher wrote, 'There is no such thing as teaching, only remembering.'

Do _you_ believe, Aldo, that we do not 'pass and be forgotten with the rest?' Or are we, rather, all of us, participants in a Socratic, endless cycle of birth and rebirth -- and remembering?

I feel only time.

Thirty Eight

Thomas's letter on the subject death and dying to his Toulouse friend Aldo continued --

I have mentioned to you on several occasions over the years my great admiration of and appreciation for the great artistic talent and genius of the early 20th century American novelist Thomas Wolfe. I am not here attempting -- once again -- to convert and enlist you into the ranks of Wolfe enthusiasts; I know you have tried to read him once or twice, as favor of sorts to me, and the "conversion" did not take. But I offer here for their relevance to the discussion in which we are engaged some Wolfe thoughts on man and his life, as indomitable and unconquerable --

Wolfe wrote:

"This is man... His life is... full of toil, tumult, and suffering. His days are mainly composed of a million idiot repetitions -- in goings and comings along the hot streets, in sweating and freezing, in the senseless accumulations of fruitless tasks, in decaying and being patched, in grinding out his life... He is the dweller in that ruined tenement who, from

222

one moment's breathing to another, can hardly forget the bitter weight of his uneasy flesh, the thousand diseases and distresses of his body, the growing incubus of his corruption. This is man who if he can remember ten golden moments of joy and happiness out of all his years, un-seamed by aches ... has the power to lift himself with his expiring breath and say, 'I have lived upon this earth and known glory.'"

Wolfe also wrote:

"There came to him an image of man's whole life on earth. It seemed to him   that all man's life was like a tiny spurt of flame that blazed out briefly in an illimitable and terrifying darkness, and that all man's grandeur, tragic dignity, his heroic glory, came from the brevity and smallness of this flame. He knew his life was little and would be extinguished, and that only darkness was immense and everlasting. And he knew that he would die with defiance on his lips, and that the shout of his denial would ring with the last pulsing of his heart into the maw of all-engulfing night."

And finally --

"Man was born to live, to suffer, and to die, and what befalls him is a tragic lot. There is no denying this in the final end. But we must ... deny it all along the way."

Thomas's letter continued --

Powerful stuff -- wouldn't you agree? Man -- frail, weak, mortal man -- who writes wonderful books and paints beautiful pictures and composes great music, and creates this lasting, eternal beauty and glory and art from the depths of his individual, lonely soul despite his frailty and his weaknesses and the pain and torment and loneliness and suffering he endures throughout "the bitter briefness of his days" and creates all of this despite the certain knowledge that he is born to die: he is a noble creature. He is indomitable and his spirit is unconquerable.

Permit me to cite one more Wolfe passage here, relevant to our subject at hand, on death and dying, before I move on. These are the closing lines of Wolfe's final novel, "You Can't Go Home Again," published posthumously following his death at the too-young age of 37 --

"Something has spoken to me in the night, burning the tapers of the waning year; something has spoken in the night, and told me I shall die, I know not where. Saying:

"To lose the earth you know, for greater knowing; to lose the life you have, for greater life; to leave the friends you loved, for greater loving; to find a land more kind than home, more large than earth --

"Whereon the pillars of this earth are founded, toward which the conscience of the world is tending --- a wind is rising, and the rivers flow.'

That, my friend, is __my__ favorite Wolfe quote -- to find 'greater life,' 'greater loving' and 'a land more kind than home, more large than earth...' "

Thomas's letter to Aldo went on --

I apologize for the profusion of references to and passages from Wolfe (relevant as they are nonetheless to our subject of conversation here) -- and I pledge here and now that beginning tomorrow (once this letter is in the mail to you) that I will cease and desist from so besieging with 'Wolf-isms' you ever again, my friend.

But before wrapping up this letter and sending it off to you, I do have some little more to say about death --

It is something I learned some 20 years ago that was for me, at that time, startling and extraordinarily revelatory. It is not quite so startling to me now, as it was back then when I was a much younger man, but its eternal verity is no less weighty. It is this: man of an

224

age and particularly when health fails, though he may still be sound of mind, often very much wants and wishes to die, to end his here and now misery, to find 'his home more large than earth.' And sometimes man is able, even, to choose when to do so -- without resorting to a physically-violent suicide. Sometimes he can choose to -- and die.

As prosaic as this idea may seem now -- as it does to me and may well to you, too -- it was when it first struck me what I thought to be one of life's Great Truths. Man sometimes can choose when he wants to die -- and can do so without necessarily resorting to suicide.

I learned this Great Truth about death many years ago when I got to know an aging, octogenarian aunt of my (now deceased) good friend Rocky the Plumber. Tanta Freda was terminally ill with cancer. A native Norwegian, Tanta had lived an active, full life in her youth in the old country and, after emigrating to America, had continued to do so in her adopted new country, the United States.

Tanta and her husband John lived in the New York City borough of Staten Island and Rocky, Olivia and I drove there from our homes in New Jersey to visit her four or five times during her illness and last days.

Frail and weak, at 84, Tanta would whisper to us in the little voice she had left, "I want to die, I just want to die."

We, in our youth, thought that what Tanta meant and really wanted when she said those sad words was for us to tell her how much she was loved and how much she still had to live for and that no one on earth and certainly none of us wanted her to die.

We said all of those things, of course, and we did not understand that Tanta, truly, was not looking for reassurance or expressions of love or validation of her continuing worth. Tanta meant precisely what she said. We did not understand that Tanta wanted nothing more than for her misery and pain to end. Tanta, truly, wanted to die. Tanta was ready to depart for the far shore; she was ready to go home.

Tanta in her youth had been the quintessential female equivalent of the hale-fellow-well-met. Rocky once joked, lightly but not unlov-

225

ingly, "If Tanta had as many pricks sticking out of her as she's had stuck into her over the years she'd look like a porcupine." Tanta had lived a life of wine, <u>men</u> and song and she could not and did not any longer want to endure, confined to a hospital bed and in much pain, what little shadow of life was then left to her.

Tanta was ready to greet and meet The Dark Lady. Neither Rocky and Olivia, nor I understood this. We did not understand that Tanta no longer found her life worth living. We did not understand, at that time in <u>our</u> lives, that <u>anyone</u> would <u>want</u> to die.

Less than a week later, Tanta closed her eyes one early evening, went to sleep, and died.

Less than four years later, Rocky, racked with cancer, would similarly choose to, and die in his sleep.

●●●●●●●

Let me speak of some other deaths that I have been close to. My dear mother died almost eight years ago, at the age of ninety-one. Her life had not been an easy one. Her own mother had died when she was not much more than a toddler and she was raised by her often too stern father and a stepmother whom she never felt love from or for.

My mother never left the small city of Johnstown in upstate New York where she had been born and lived all her life (except for one memorable late-in-life trip to Europe.) She died in Johnstown and is buried there.

As a young woman, my mother worked in one of the carpet mills in Johnstown until she met and married my father. He had moved to Johnstown from the magic, big city -- New York -- and I can imagine my mother, who at that time had never traveled more than a few miles from Johnstown, perhaps a shopping trip to Schenectady, 20 miles away, being greatly impressed with that, the aura of worldliness that the big city had imprinted on him.

They began their family; they had four children within five years.

My father died at 53 and my mother, many years younger than

her husband, thus was left widowed at a relatively young age, with four pre-teen children to raise and support on her own.

A few years after my father's death, my mother learned that she had breast cancer and she underwent a radical mastectomy, still a fairly new procedure in that era, the early part of the second half of the 20th century. She went through that and its attendant, lonely, emotional trauma largely on her own.

My mother, insofar as I am aware, never dated anyone after my father's death.

As she aged, my mother was a marvel. She ventured far, far beyond, and outside, her Johnstown comfort zone. She traveled abroad, alone, in her mid 70s to visit my brother Paddy and his family who were living in Stockholm at the time, and then flew from Stockholm to Brussels to visit with me and with Ellen and our girls in Ohain. We took auto trips when she was with us to Amsterdam in The Netherlands (the _real_ Amsterdam, she called it; the small city of Amsterdam in upstate New York is not more than 10 miles from Johnstown), and to Cologne and Paris. She rode a Rhine River cruise ship past the Lorelei. She walked through the Louvre and she sipped a glass of wine at a sidewalk café on the Champs-Elysees. She rode an elevator to the top of the Eiffel Tower, and walked round the uppermost outside pedestrian deck of that magnificent edifice. Aldo, this was a woman who had never before then ventured very far afield at all from the tiny town in which she was born, and that on just one occasion -- a weekend family motor trip excursion to New York City.

During my mother's final twenty years, except for the last one, she was as happy and content with her life as she had ever been. That her world after her wonderful European visit, a "trip of a lifetime," as she called it, began to get smaller and smaller, as it does for all of us as we age, (my mother in her last year of life never traveled more than a mile or two from where she was living, on any given day, ever), did not faze her in the least. She adjusted seamlessly to all of the changes and indignities that incipient senectitude visits upon us. She did not want to give up her driver's license, for example -- and the independence and freedom that an automobile

227

confers -- but when the time came for her to do that she recognized it and faced it and took that difficult, confining step without hesitation. My mother adapted remarkably well to her ever-diminishing world. She had always enjoyed reading -- Ellery Queen and Erle Gardner mysteries were her favorite -- and watching television, and she continued those pastime pursuits every day. She continued as well as a devout Roman Catholic, attending Mass without fail on Sundays and Holy Days and, often, on several other days each week when she was offered transportation from one of her 'younger' friends who had not yet surrendered her driver's license. My mother prayed Novenas, at home, for 'special intentions.' She would never divulge to anyone what those special intentions were, but she sure had a lot of them -- measured by the sheer volume of Novenas she prayed.

Sadly, my mother's final year was not a good one. She seemed to catch one cold after another, some of which progressed to a more serious flu. She got weaker and more feeble each day, seemingly, and she began as well to lose some of her good cheer and her mental acuity. Increasingly she began to misplace items around her small apartment and feared someone was coming in during the night and stealing them from her. After she had died, St. Sheila found a dozen or more packages of dried food stuff in the bottom of the clothes hamper in my mother's bathroom.

My saint-on-earth sister (whom Paddy and I refer to as 'St. Sheila') and Paddy, both on the ground, if you will, in Johnstown, had moved Mom to an assisted-living facility. She did not like it there at all. She failed to adjust or accommodate herself, successfully, to her new environment and 'housemates,' all the while fighting off one cold and siege of flu after another. She would tell Sheila and Paddy daily and me, too, when I called (I did that once a week, on a Friday -- and she thus began to refer to me as "Joe Friday") that she no longer wanted to live. "I pray to the Good Lord every night and every morning that He will take me."

*My mother understood full well, I believe, that her mental capacity was failing, as well as her physical health. She knew she was losing her grip mentally and **that**, more than anything, I became* *convinced, absolutely terrified her.*

    Like Tanta Freda, my mother had reached a point where she, too, had had enough travail and pain and anguish and she, too, <u>wanted</u> to die.

    The years can reive us of so many things, including family and health and, finally, the very will to live and to go on.

    During her last year, my mother would ask me every Friday when we spoke on the telephone to pray for her, as she prayed: to ask the Good Lord to 'take' her.

    Aldo, I ached in my heart and soul for her. I wept, silently, in the night, deep inside, for my mother and the agony that wracked her body and sapped her spirit.

    But I could not do as my mother asked. I could not in my heart find the resolve to pray to God for her death -- though she implored me, again and again, to do that. But I could not. I could not pray for my own mother's death. I could not do it.

Thirty Nine

Thomas's letter to Aldo on death and dying continued --

Let me speak for a moment now about Rocky The Plumber.

I have had three great friends in my life -- you, my brother Paddy and Rocky the Plumber. Paddy, a year and a half younger than I, has been and remains the best adult friend I have ever had. Rocky The Plumber was not far behind, nor are you.

Ellen and I met Rocky and his wife Olivia when we lived in New Jersey, before our stint in Europe. They lived across the street from us and when I and my family moved to Brussels we kept in touch faithfully during the years the Gormans were away.

Rocky was a workingman, a plumber.

"The only thing you need to know to be a plumber," Rocky would say, "is that shit don't go uphill."

Rocky was as strong as an ox and as gentle as a lamb and he had a heart of gold. He was a good husband, a good father, a good man and a wonderful friend. He was solid, reliable, responsible and honest in each of his roles and in all he did during his earthly journey.

Rocky's given name was Ernest. I was one of the very few people whom he allowed to call him that. When I did, he would call me

'Thomas,' never Tom, matching my formality in using his proper name with a dose of formality of his own.

The bond that formed between Rocky and me was as strong as it was inexplicable. For many years of our friendship, I was a zoot-suited lobbyist in Washington, D.C., who attended formal functions at the White House. Rocky had never gone beyond the fifth grade as far as formal schooling is concerned -- but he was one of the smartest men I have ever known.

Rocky died at the age of 75 four years ago on July 15 -- the same date, coincidentally, on which my father died a half-century earlier.

Cancer took Rocky, as it has and will so many of us.

Rocky had been diagnosed, with cancer of the colon, some two years before he died. He was operated on at that time and the doctors were optimistic that they 'got it all.' Even so, Rocky underwent post-operative radiation and chemotherapy treatments for several months.

Rocky regained some of his strength, enough to play golf again (his great love; he had never picked up a golf club until he was in his 50s -- yet he ultimately became an excellent player, with a handicap of only three), and he was healthy for another year. But the cancer returned and this time the doctors said it was inoperable.

I made a trip to New Jersey, to see my good friend. We both knew why I was there -- to see one another for the final time and to say our goodbyes -- though all of that was left unsaid between us during that visit.

During his illness, Rocky and I had spoken on the phone several times and on one of those conversations he told me that he feared death -- and the unknown. Once he told me, "Thomas, I am afraid."

But Rocky soon went beyond that fear and, I believe, reached the typical terminally-ill patient's emotional stage of 'Acceptance,' as once described by psychologist/psychotherapist Katherine Kubler-Ross (I've never really understood the difference between those two 'ists.'), in her classic modern study on the several sequential stages most terminally ill people generally pass through. Acceptance is the final stage (after Denial-Anger-Bargaining-Sadness-- (and) Depression.) Rocky worked his way through the stages quickly to reach 'Acceptance.' He never was one to waste much time.

231

Even so, and though we had had the conversation about his fear of death and dying just a few weeks before I went to New Jersey to see and spend time with him one final time, we chose not to bring up the subject again that last weekend.

When Rocky's cancer was diagnosed, the first time, he lay in a hospital bed the evening before he was scheduled to be operated on, with Olivia and their adult children in the room all around him. Rocky and Olivia raised six children and all but two of them, along with various daughters-in-law and sons-in-law and even an older grandchild or two, were there that night. The mood in the room was somber. Everyone spoke in hushed tones, almost in a whisper. That Rocky had cancer was neither acknowledged nor even indirectly alluded to.

Rocky broke the mood.

"Fuck!" he bellowed. Rocky did not have a soft speaking voice in the base case, but now he roared.

His exclamation was issued in a voice loud enough to rumble down the hospital's corridors and resonate in many nearby rooms.

His family was stunned. They sat back -- in shock. They did not speak. They did not know <u>how</u> to react or <u>what</u> to say.

Rocky let the silence stand for another moment. Then, he spoke again. This time his voice was quiet and measured.

"Now <u>that</u> is a dirty word," he said. "Cancer is <u>not</u>. Cancer is a disease -- something that a lot of people get. <u>I</u> have cancer and I'm going to be operated on for it tomorrow. And all of us can talk about that here and now and we don't have to keep pussy-footing around it."

Rocky, my good friend, the man whose formal education ended before he was 12 years old, said and did absolutely the right thing at the right time in that hospital room that night.

Rocky, my good friend, was 'smarter' that night than some people I've known with Ph. D. degrees.

When Rocky died, at home, two years later, after his cancer had

232

returned, he did it on **his** terms and it was with great grace, dignity and courage.

On the afternoon before he went to bed for the last time as a mortal, he had just two days prior started a self-administered morphine drip. Rocky had been in great pain and the severity of it had brought him -- rock of a man and stoic though he was -- to ask the doctor for something to ease, and make more tolerable, his discomfort. I believe Rocky did not want his family to see him in distress. I believe he asked for the palliative more for their sake than his.

Rocky was relatively pain free that last evening and spent his final hours, conscious and alert, with Olivia and several of their children, including his only son, Ralph, who had driven from his home in Maryland earlier that day to be with his dad.

Rocky died in his sleep that night. I believe he chose that time and that night to go not only because he had had quite enough pain and suffering but because he felt that his family had had quite enough, too. I believe Rocky wanted to relieve himself and his family of the ongoing travail. I believe Rocky also chose that very night because he knew that Ralph's presence would make things easier for Olivia when he was found dead the next morning.

Rocky's death, strangely, was unexpected.

The medical prognosis for him at the time was that he had weeks if not months more to live -- and probably would live on for a while longer. It was a matter of keeping his pain under control through drugs, the doctors said. Rocky had not lost significant weight, as many cancer patients do. He did not <u>appear</u> to casual visitors and 'outsiders' to be ill though his family certainly knew and saw that he was getting weaker and more tired each day and that he had become far less engaged in the life he had left and the life around him.

Rocky, I believe, <u>chose</u> his time to die, for his benefit and the benefit of those he loved -- who of course also loved him.

Rocky and his loved ones were spared -- he saw to that himself -- the terrible indignity that so many cancer patients suffer, a slow wasting away to emaciation and death, inevitably and ultimately, when there is, finally, little left but a skeletal semblance of the person *who once was.*

Rocky, of all people, would not have wanted that. I am so glad, and happy -- for Rocky -- that it did not happen that way for him. That it did not, I say again, was, I believe, his decision.

●●●●●●●

Do you remember Terrence O'Reilly? Terry worked for me for a period of time in Darien. When Terry died, of cancer, he -- unlike Rocky -- was little more than a living assemblage of skin and bones. Terry had once weighed, perhaps, 160 pounds. When he died, he could not have weighed more than 85 or 90 pounds.

Shortly after Terry and his family were told he had cancer and that his condition was terminal, the Company arranged a transfer for him to Houston where he could be near, and avail himself of the services and treatment offered by, the internationally renowned M.D. Anderson Cancer Center in that city.

Terry was sick for 18 months. He held on to mortal life with a fierce will and determination and a superhuman strength that far exceeded the diminished capacity of his ravaged and deteriorating body. Terry held on so tenaciously, I believe (and Ann was to tell me later that she agreed), because he was terrified of Divine Judgment and punishment after death.

Terry, I later learned from Ann, had confessed to her and then to a priest midway through his illness to having lived a criminally dissolute life for many years. Terry had managed to hide his secret life from Ann throughout their long marriage.

Ann shared this startling revelation with me soon after she had learned of it, from Terry.

I tell you this -- and I tell it to you in only the most vague way -- not to divulge deep, dark, hidden, personal secrets and scandal or rumor, and certainly not to be judgmental in any way about Terry. I would not do that. Terry O'Reilly was my friend. I tell you this because Terry's refusal to die limned for me one other factor in the human death complex equation that struck me then and still does today as remarkable and worthy of note within the context of this conversation. Terry was fearful not so much of losing the meager life that was left to him here on earth, nor did he want, necessarily, to abjure the pain and suffering of that life for peace and rest with God in the beyond. Terry feared the dreadful after-life he was certain lie before him in his eternity as condign punishment for all the sins he had committed during the three-score-and-ten of his mortal life. Terry feared hell fire and eternal damnation.

Terry, calling upon all the strength left in him, would not <u>submit</u> to death. Terry chose <u>not</u> to die. He chose his mortal life of pain and suffering rather than what he was certain was to be greater pain and suffering in the Great Unknown.

Shortly after his initial diagnosis, the medical consensus for Terry was that he would live on for not more than 3-4 months longer.

But Terry held on.

Some six months later, as the cancer ravaged him mercilessly and as Terry continued to deteriorate, the doctors at that point thought he could not possibly go on for more than another three or four weeks.

Once, during a business trip to Houston, I sat with Ann and other family members around Terry's sick bed, at home. Terry had had a terrible last few days. He asked us to move closer to him. He told each of us, in turn, that he loved us and he said 'goodbye' to each of us, also in turn, trying to smile as he did so.

He turned his head slowly and with obvious great difficulty and pain as he looked once more at each of us, in turn -- stopping, finally, at Ann. He smiled at her and closed his eyes, and he seemed at peace. Ann and some of the others -- Terry and Ann's children -- wept. All of us thought, and felt, that the end, at last, was at hand.

We sat there at Terry's bedside and watched the white sheet covering his frail body rise and fall, slowly, with each breath he took. The sheet rose slowly and fell and continued to rise and fall as all of us sat there in silence next to Terry for three hours.

The sheet covering Terry continued to rise and fall, its movement now almost imperceptible. But Terry refused to die.

●●●●●●●

I made a half-dozen or more trips to Houston during Terry's last year. Few of the trips were pressingly necessary from a strictly business point of view. Perhaps none of them was. I went to Houston, under the pretext of business, mainly to see Terry and spend time with him and Ann.

Terry and I had been friends to begin with but our friendship blossomed and grew richer and deeper during his illness. I continue today to keep in touch with Ann. Terry asked me to promise to do that, just days before he died.

Ann wrote this in a pamphlet that she had printed up and distributed at Terry's funeral mass, at Prince of Peace Catholic Church in Houston --

"I want to thank, from the bottom of my heart, all those at Prince of Peace who did so much for Terry and me during Terry's illness. Terry came back to the church last April and found the strength and spiritual courage that helped him cope so bravely these past several months.

"I converted to Catholicism this year and was able to share with Terry the spiritual fulfillment that Mass and Holy Communion at Prince of Peace offered to both of us.

"Deacon Roy Walters was so good to Terry during his illness. His frequent visits at home and in the hospital, his wisdom, friendship and love were a great comfort and inspiration. Terry suffered much during his illness but I know he is now at peace and with our God and I believe Deacon Roy helped lead him there.

"There is also one other person I must mention and that is Tom Gorman from Westchester, NY, and Washington, DC. Tom called Terry <u>every day,</u> including weekends, from the day we found out Terry had cancer to the day he died. It is often said that "laughter is the best medicine" and Tom could always make Terry laugh when no one else could. Tom, you're one in a million -- and I love you."

I include this bit of personal encomium here, not immodestly,

236

I certainly hope, but, rather to illustrate and elaborate on Ann's point.

Once during a business trip to Europe, I telephoned Terry in Houston from a hotel room in Paris to tell him of a great discovery I had just made.

"O'Reilly," I exhorted. "I'm nearly 50 fucking years old and I've just realized for the first time in my sorry life that you can't pick your nose in the shower."

There was, for a moment, trans-Atlantic silence. And then Terry roared with laughter.

We went on to discuss other more weighty but no less critically important matters during that conversation but not before, first, after dissecting the nose-picking observation and comment, concluding that it would have been more accurate for me to have said that nose-picking in the shower cannot be done <u>successfully</u>. One can certainly 'pick' -- all day if one so chooses -- but success at it, i.e., grasping and extracting the sought-after internal nasal clot (snot?), is highly improbable for the critically obvious but theretofore for me at that time unconsidered reason. That reason is, of course, digital lubricity. Digital lubricity -- quite unavoidable when one is in the shower -- obviates against pick-ability success in the nose-picking traction co-efficiency factor. Terry and I reached and settled on that conclusion jointly.

Terry and I <u>did</u> speak and we <u>did</u> laugh just about every day during his illness.

●●●●●●●

Finally, Terry could hang on no longer. There was nothing left, nothing further for him to call up from his inner reservoir of determination and fortitude.

Terry died at home on an afternoon in early May, with only Ann at his side.

My friend Rocky had died before having to endure the final indignity of physical emaciation. Terry did not. When he died, Terry was not much more than head and hands and skin and bones.

It is frighteningly strange how cancer so diminishes in size so much of the body except for the head and hands. At the end, the hands in particular seem grotesquely disproportionate to the rest of what is left of the wasted body.

I have, as I mentioned, continued to keep in touch with Ann since Terry's death. She has met another man and is happy in her new life. Ann was an Angel of Mercy to Terry during his very long illness. Ann deserves much happiness.

John Lewis Wilson was a friend, who also happened to work for me, many years ago, in the communications department of the Monarch Life Insurance Company in Springfield, Massachusetts. John also died of cancer -- and I sat with him and his family during much of his illness as I did years later with Terry.

John had had a 30+ year career at the <u>New York Times</u> before he and his family relocated to New England and a less stressful post-<u>New York Times</u> way of life. John had begun his career with the paragon of American journalism as a 16-year-old copy boy and later became a shipping news reporter. Subsequently, he established a state bureau office for the paper in Trenton, New Jersey, covering legislative and political news from the Garden State's capital city.

I still have copy of the obituary that <u>The Times</u> published on John when he died -- more than three decades ago. In it is this wonderfully descriptive and evocative paragraph --

"A tall gangling man, Mr. Wilson was once described by a publication of the New Jersey Legislative Correspondents Club as the only newspaperman in the United States who weighs less than his Sunday paper."

Thin to begin with, John -- like Terry O'Reilly -- wasted away terribly before The Dark Lady finally closed her arms around him and took him home.

John's family -- like my friend Rocky's when he was first diagnosed -- could not bring themselves to say aloud either the word cancer or death. Nor could I. I was still in my 20s and I had not been so close to the Dark Lady as far as a family member or close friend is concerned (except for some terrible times that I will mention in a moment) since my father's death a dozen years earlier.

I talked to John about the office and how much he was missed and how great things would be when he got back to work.

One Sunday evening, John recognized how uncomfortable all of us were with the situation of non-recognition of the reality confronting him and us, and he took charge -- handling the delicacy of the dilemma in his own way, as Rocky later did in his way as he lay in his hospital bed and hollered "Fuck!"

In the quiet hours of that Sabbath evening in early spring, the family, and I, sat with John in his hospital room, in Springfield. John asked his wife, Lily (a tiny little woman, not five feet tall or more than 90 pounds in weight), to hand him the Springfield city telephone directory that lay on a table beside his bed. John leafed through the book to its yellow pages. He found the page he was looking for and paused. He ran his right forefinger midway down the page and stopped there. We could not see the page to which he had opened the book. John handed the book back to Lily. His finger rested on the opened page to a listing for a funeral home. No words were spoken. Lily looked at John and nodded her head to him in tacit understanding.

John told us with that action as clearly as any words could have done that he knew he was dying and that he did not want any of us to feel, for his sake, that we had to shield him from the reality of that and its imminence by avoiding recognition and discussion of it in his presence.

As Rocky the Plumber died on the same date, coincidentally, that my father had died fifty years before, John Lewis Wilson died on the eighth day of May, the same date, coincidentally, that Terry O'Reilly would die twenty-one years later.

You asked in your email if I would be willing to speak of death and dying, and I have done that. I cannot know, of course, if the thoughts I have chosen to express in this letter approach or mirror in any way what you had in mind when you posed your question but I offer them to you, my good friend, straight and plain, unvarnished

239

and unadulterated, for whatever they may be worth. I would, of course, be very interested in having your reaction to them and in hearing more in due course about your own thoughts and experiences on this, the one common fate that awaits us all.

You wrote in your email about the dissertation you had been subjected to by the man who interrupted a conversation you were in the midst of with a neighbor and then went on ad nauseam about the comprehensive brilliance of his recent investment planning and the creative strategies he had recently implemented to assure protection of his long-term wealth, etc. etc. etc. You say you pulled him up short and interrupted his self-congratulatory exposition of his financial and economic acumen when you suggested that there might be a "key ingredient" missing from his thinking. Taken aback, he asked what <u>that</u> might be and you told him, Robert Mitchum-like, "Yep," -- that he had failed to factor into his equation that <u>he</u> was "one day going to die."

Yes, of course he will. And so will I, and so will you. And so will each and every one of us. For each and every one of us, death is -- to borrow and employ that adjective oft-used by James Joyce -- ineluctable.

In addition to the deaths described herein that I have been close to, I also have been close many, many times (I've never told you this, nor, for that matter have I ever told it to <u>anyone</u>) to violent, sudden death. That was in Vietnam, my friend, a time in my life that I just do not talk about.

And so, Aldo, my good friend, on death and dying, that is all I have to say at the moment.

I shall be in touch with you again soon to discuss an issue related to this one that has been much troubling me of late.

All the very best to you and Sophia,

Tom

Forty

Thomas kept in periodic touch with Olivia after Rocky had passed away. He and she began speaking on the phone every two or three months, and then, eventually, began to speak even more frequently. Thomas enjoyed Olivia's intelligence, great compassion and her sense of humor. And, he thought to himself, *she's kinda easy on the eyes, too.* He remembered one of the ways Rocky used to refer to her: 'a big-titted ma moo.' And it <u>was</u> next-to-impossible for any man not to notice that Olivia was exceedingly well endowed in that area. Olivia also had a classically beautiful face and features, though one did notice first her chest front. Facially, she resembled, Thomas thought, the early 20th century American motion picture star Maureen O'Hara. Olivia had a big chest and beautiful smile and teeth and once told Thomas that her late mother had said to her often, "What you've got going for yourself, honey, are tits and teeth."

Thomas and Olivia enjoyed talking with one another -- and found it easy to do so. Both admitted that they had never before shared so much -- pretty much, about everything -- with anyone else, before or during their marriages. They began to speak on the phone much more frequently.

Thomas, in Washington at the time, was dating other

241

women and would never hold back about that when he and Olivia spoke.

Once, on his way to Westchester, to visit Ellen (he and she seemed to get along much better as ex-husband and wife than they did during their marriage) and one of his daughters and grandson who still lived in that area, he stopped on his way north through New Jersey to spend a night at Olivia's. He stopped there on the way back that trip, too.

Their dance of love and symphony of intimacy began slowly and very hesitantly. Both admitted to feeling somewhat "guilty" -- as if they were, somehow, betraying Thomas's ex-spouse (Olivia and Ellen were still friends), and Olivia's deceased husband Rocky, who had been one of Thomas's best friends.

They moved slowly and very cautiously, but one night, finally, they did make love. Thomas had heard so many men over the years use the expression when speaking of an intimate relationship as "the best sex I've ever had." He now understood the intensity of the phrase and also, for him -- now -- its applicability and truth. Olivia was fantastic in bed, a wonderful lover.

The intimacy that developed between Thomas and Olivia became the best sex that *he* had ever had. It was mutually giving, rich, and always satisfying -- and extended. They often made love for three or four hours at a time. And after a nap of an hour or so they'd make love, again, for an hour or two the second time around. Their mutual appetite for each other seemed inexhaustible.

During the first few months after their physical and sexual intimacy developed, they did not see each other very often, to the dismay of each. Thomas continued to work in Washington and Olivia moved from northern to southern New Jersey to be closer to two of her married daughters and their families who lived in that part of the state.

Thomas dated other women, occasionally, in Washington. Olivia dated no one else. She wanted only Thomas.

It was during this period in Washington that Thomas
met and dated Becky, Howdy Doody (She nodded her head,
nervously and constantly), Jane Stone, the Croatian Creation
and the "left coast" Congresswoman.

Whenever Thomas was indeed dating someone else and
their relationship had developed to the point of sexual intimacy, he would not and did not communicate with Olivia. She
seemed to sense intuitively during these contact interludes
that Thomas was involved with someone else and Thomas
in a strange way did not want to be with Olivia, in any way,
when he was seeing another woman. Strangely, he wanted to
give Olivia this constancy, at the least.

He had met Carol ("Howdy Doody") in a restaurant as
she sat with a friend at an adjoining table. Thrice divorced,
she had not yet given up altogether on finding a mate for still
another marriage, the next one, "hopefully" (one of her favorite words), for the rest of her life. A beautiful, petite blonde,
Howdy was a positive, agreeable lady who smiled easily and
laughed nervously (it seemed to Thomas) often -- but also,
frequently, seemed uncertain and sad. Like Jane Stone, there
was an ever-present sadness that showed in Carol's eyes
that would not go away and which she could not hide. Carol
nodded her head in agreement at almost everything and
anything -- almost like a "bobble-head" doll or the old-time
television show puppet Howdy Doody (along with his friends
Clarabelle, Mr. Bluster, Princess Summer-Fall-Winter-Spring
and others). That was when and how Thomas came to think
of her as "Howdy."

Upon reflection, Thomas wondered what it was about him,
or in him, that seemed to attract him to women who were sad
or in emotional pain and distress.

Thomas met The Croatian Creation while on a business
trip and passing through Newark Airport. He saw her in
the passenger waiting area at the same gate where he was;
they were both processing through Newark from other stops,
changing planes there and heading back on a shuttle to Wash-

ington. Stefania was a tall, shapely, large-breasted woman in her late 30s, a brunette (Thomas in Washington had been dating blondes almost exclusively, not intentionally -- but just by chance). He was attracted to Stefania, in a way, because she was not a blonde and, for some reason he could never fathom, because she was left-handed as well. He noticed that, and liked it, as she wrote in a business notebook she carried like a schoolbook -- a left-handed, 'black-haired' woman, as he sometimes referred to her. She liked and got a laugh out of the appellation. She had some of the out-of-the-mainstream personality quirks that many southpaws have: unconventional, outspoken, highly intense, altruistic about many social inequities, brash and occasionally rash.

The Creation lived in McLean, as did Jane Stone. She and Thomas spoke and exchanged telephone numbers upon landing and deplaning at Reagan National in D.C. and soon thereafter began dating, though not for long. Thomas and Stefania became fast friends and their friendship lasted over the years, on a platonic basis. They spoke periodically on the phone even after Thomas left Washington. They exchanged Christmas and birthday cards and, once, even saw one another when the Creation visited for a day while on a business trip to Tampa, just north of where Thomas had settled in Siesta Key.

When they were in Washington, Stefania and Thomas had dinner often at a Chinese restaurant in McLean that was a favorite of hers, or they ate at her apartment in that upscale D.C. suburb. Stefania often prepared French Toast as an easy and quick meal for them, along with a glass or two of Cabernet Sauvignon. Stefania, ever playful, made the meal and served it bra-less and top-less. Their actual sexual intimacy developed deliberatively. One night, after a meal of "topless French toast," they sat together on a love seat in the living room watching a television news show. They embraced, kissed and began to touch one another intimately. Stefania unzipped Thomas's trousers, placed her hand inside, and took out his now rigid penis. She stood up from the couch, maintaining her hold of Thomas's cock with her left hand and, she first, led him by his member up the stairs to her bedroom. They had been seeing each other for several weeks at that point but that evening was the first time they made love. They laughed together about their (unusual) walk up the stairs to the bedroom, and the logistics and memory of it, for years afterward whenever they thought about how matters developed that night.

Stefania from that evening on gave Thomas a sobriquet "in honor of how I led you to bed that night." Stefania, who had never been married and was not all that sexually experienced, marveled at how often Thomas was able to "perform" sexually. She began to call his penis "Otis" -- as in "the elevator; it goes up and down and then right back up again."

"Damn, the thing is always going up and down, mostly up!" marveled the Croatian Creation.

Thomas met the left-coast Congresswoman during the course of his work as a lobbyist on Capitol Hill. The meeting was facilitated by a mutual aquaintenance, another Congresswoman, who had succeeded her father as a member of the U.S. House of Representatives from a district in Staten Island.

Thomas and the left-coast Congresswoman dated for just a few months. He served as her "escort" at many of the formal functions she was obliged to attend in her capacity as a member of the House of Representatives, including, from time-to-time, White House galas hosted by the President and First Lady. They attended movies occasionally. She said those evenings were a refreshing and relaxing change of pace for her, "in a dark room, out of the limelight and unnoticed by everybody around me."

Later, in Florida, Thomas read that the Congresswoman had remarried -- a wealthy businessman from her home Congressional district. So, too, had other of Thomas's former lady friends gotten married after he and they stopped seeing each other -- Becky, Jane Stone, Chlorine Kathy -- and after he had moved to Siesta Key, Quaker State Annie, Tillie the Teller, Julia the Hungarian (with whom he still exchanged Christmas cards), and others. He and Lu-Ann Irene Edwards stopped seeing each other because she *wanted* very much to get married, and he did not.

Forty One

When Becky and William left Siesta Key (where she and Thomas had missed encountering each other on the beach by just a few moments) they returned to the Sarasota Ritz-Carlton for the last night of their brief two-day excursion from Mt. Roda. They had dinner in the hotel's formal dining room but ate largely in silence.

Back in their room, William's cell phone rang again and he excused himself and took the call in their suite's bathroom.

The next morning they awoke, did their respective toilets, got dressed, packed, called the concierge to have their car brought, by valet, to the hotel entrance, and got into it for the two-hour drive home to Mt. Roda. They were as non-communicative during that drive as they had been during dinner at the hotel the night before.

At home, two days after their trip to Sarasota and Siesta Key, Rebecca tried -- through Verizon information services and the Internet -- to find out Thomas's home telephone

247

number. Thomas had no cell phone ("I may be one of the last few people in the Western world who does not have a cell phone," he'd said recently to Paddy. "My life just isn't _that_ urgent.") In Siesta Key, Thomas had only land-line service and he paid an extra fee monthly to the phone company for that number to be unlisted, which, to him, seemed antithetical. ("They should pay _me_ for that; it doesn't cost them dollars to _not_ list numbers. They _save_ money and realize economies by that.")

William told Rebecca the weekend after their trip to southwest Florida that he wanted a divorce. They sat in their living room (she in the large Queen Anne chair) when he told her he was in love with someone else and wanted to begin to build a life with him, a longtime business associate whom he had known going back to his and his late ex-wife's life in Austin. Rebecca remembered having met the man once or twice.

Rebecca called Julie and asked her for Thomas's phone number in Siesta Key. Julie told Rebecca that she did not have it available right then and there and would have to get back to her with it "in a few days." Rebecca did not tell Julie that she and William were getting a divorce.

Rebecca began to think more and more about calling Thomas (if Julie would ever give her his damned number!), but she continued to bide her time.

Rebecca remembered.

Rebecca did not argue with William or try to dissuade him from his desire to divorce. She took the shocking news with calm equanimity. She did not suffer great emotional turmoil, she did not spend hours upon hours weeping and feeling sorry for herself as she had when her marriage to Arthur had ended, also because of infidelity. She found it easier to deal with William's infidelity. She found it easier somehow to deal with William's infidelity then it had been with Arthur's. William's betrayal with a man, not a woman, was, strangely, less hurtful.

●●●●●●●

There was no hostility as the arrangements went forward, smoothly, to dissolve the marriage and end their relationship. Amicability was something they each strove for in dealing with one another.

Rebecca finally began to talk at length about the situation with her friend Julie and thought almost daily about calling Thomas, but she did not -- quite yet. Julie still had not given her Thomas's telephone number.

Rebecca remembered.

●●●●●●●

Rebecca and William were formally divorced just four months after their weekend trip to Sarasota and Siesta Key.

Forty Two

In Florida, Thomas met Patricia as he was settling in after his move from Washington. Patricia was a branch manager and senior investment advisor for the bank which Thomas had been affiliated with in Washington and which happened to have a branch nearby his new home.

The personal relationship with Patricia progressed quickly. They traveled together to Manhattan one long weekend to attend the marriage of one of Julie's daughters, held at the Tavern on the Green in Manhattan's Central Park. Patricia had never been to the Big City and was as a wide-eyed child during the visit. Thomas found her childlike innocence endearing and refreshing. Patricia was an early-40s divorcee, with one child, a teenaged daughter. Patricia had worked her way up in the banking system to her current position of some status.

Paddy met Patricia on a visit to Florida shortly after Thomas began dating her, and dubbed her, because of her employer relationship -- a bank -- Tillie the Teller. Patricia, a native Tennessean with a marked southern accent and drawl that Paddy mocked, was a good-natured lady and took no umbrage at the name given her by Paddy. She appreciated and accepted without reservation Paddy and his often over-powering insouciance and slap-dash irreverence. "Ah lock yer bruther," Tillie drawled.

Olivia was aware at that time that Thomas had begun a new relationship in Florida, and she and he put what she and he had together on hold. Olivia was patient and understood Thomas and his hesitance to commit since his divorce better than anyone ever had. Thomas had told Olivia more about himself and his background and fears and hopes than he had ever told anyone. Olivia knew, for example, that Thomas did not remember being hugged by either of his parents ever, or told he was loved by either of them, ever.

Olivia was patient. She would wait for Thomas to come around in his own time and at his own pace. Not only was she patient, she was also confident that he *would* come around....

●●●●●●●

Shortly after Thomas and Tillie the Teller went their sepa-rate ways he met and began to date with some regularity and intensity Millicent (Millie, or Mill) Getman.

Coincidentally, as Rebecca had once auditioned for a posi-tion with the Joffrey Ballet Company so, too, had Millie. Millie in fact was offered a dancing role with Joffrey and had actu-ally toured with the company for three years before she met and married her (now deceased) husband, a history professor at Pennsylvania State University. Millie was a Pennsylvania native and met her husband while she was on a trip home to see her parents in the state. Paddy got to meet Millie on a trip she and Thomas took to Johnstown and began calling her, related to her birth state, "Quaker State Annie."

Millie, since she had been widowed, had decided to live in Florida part of the calendar year only; her permanent home was in Massachusetts, not far from where Thomas and Ellen had lived many years before, in Springfield. Millie had given up professional dancing after her marriage and gotten a degree in nursing, a noble profession which she practiced for the rest of her adult life, most of the time as an emergency care specialist.

Another blonde for Thomas, Millie was diminutive in size, five feet, one inch in height (stretched out), and not more than 100 pounds, soaking wet. The word 'cute' was not one Thomas would ordinarily use; it was not in his lexicon but it fit Millie well. She *was* cute. From her dancing days, she remained in outstanding physical condition and had taken up jogging to go along with her fixed adherence to 'Pilates' as her primary forms of exercise. She and Thomas jogged together when he visited her in Massachusetts. She preferred not to run in the Florida heat, a condition that did not bother Thomas. "Hell, I run so slow anyway I *can't* overheat."

Millie did not like Florida. She was terrified of old age, and of all the reminders of it that one saw throughout the Sunshine State. Millie tried to deny, defy and put off the appearance of aging in her life. She had had three face lifts done. Her facial skin, Thomas once told Paddy "has more lines than a AAA road map." Millie also very much wanted to get married -- to Thomas -- (as Lu-Ann Irene Edwards would want to, a few years later); Thomas did not want to marry again. "Once is enough for me," he said to Millie once when the topic arose.

Back home in Massachusetts, Millie had a wonderful tan Labrador. Thomas and the dog became fast friends, very soon into his first visit to Mill's Massachusetts home. ("I like big, brown dogs," Thomas told Millie. "It's the little, white, yapping kind I don't cotton to, you know, the kind with their own cutesy-poo blue or pink gender-appropriate custom-fitted sweater that their owners dress them in when it's cold and they are heading outside for their morning shit.") Millie had named her dog Gracie. Thomas began calling the dog, contrarily, Lucy -- 'Loose' for short. Millie lived nearby a dog-run/open field where she took Lucy (nee Gracie) to do her daily duties. When Thomas was visiting, he (an early riser) would take the dog out first thing for her morning constitutional. "C'mon, Loose," he'd say as his feet hit the floor. The dog, which slept in a basket outside the bedroom door (she had been banished from sleeping in the bedroom per se because of her frequent and very smelly farts while she slept), would lift her head, unwind herself from her sleeping position, rise slowly to her feet, turn round in circles two or three times to test the stability of her arthritic legs, and then shuffle expectantly toward Thomas. "Ready for your morning shit, girl?" The dog, it seemed somehow to Thomas, acted hesitant and slightly embarrassed by his use of the vulgarity. Millie would laugh and tell Thomas that that was indeed the case. "Gracie is very much a lady," said Millie.

Millie was a delight, and not always a lady herself. Often she was an imp. As Thomas remembered so well the original 'Otis' incident with The Croatian Creation, so too did he remember years later a bedroom 'game' Millicent devised and originated which brought both of them on occasion to the brink of tears -- tears of laughter.

One evening, as they were getting undressed and ready for bed, Millicent was naked except for her coral-colored thong panties (Becky also wore thongs regularly; Thomas thought them sexy and alluring). Millicent stood, naked, facing Thomas, as he gazed at her small, pert breasts. He, too, was dressed only in underwear.

Millie took off her thong panties. "C'mon big guy," said Millie, "drop your drawers. Let's even things up here."

Thomas stepped out of his jockey briefs.

Millie, with the toes of her right foot, picked up her panties where she had dropped them on the floor and tossed them with her foot toward Thomas. Thomas raised his right leg and 'caught' the panties mid-air as they landed on and draped over his right ankle. "One point for you, pal," laughed Millie.

Thomas shook his leg to dislodge Millie's panties from his ankle and then, as she had done, he picked them up with his toes and foot and tossed them gently back toward her. She successfully 'caught' them -- as they landed and draped over one of her tiny feet.

"Ok, pal, that ties the score at one-one." she said.

"Let's make this four out of seven," she challenged. She toe-tossed the thong back toward Thomas.

And thus, for the ages, Naked Underwear Toe Toss was born that evening in northwest Massachusetts, invented and devised by Millicent Getman and Thomas Gorman. Millicent was the sole rule maker and arbiter whether a toss was 'legal' or not. A toss that was not far enough off the floor (it had to be at least knee-high at its apogee to qualify as an 'official' toss) or too far off line, could be and was judged by her to be subject to a 'do-over.' A recognized 'catch' had to be held for at least two seconds before shaking the panties off of one's leg and dropping them to the floor -- and then picking them up with one's toes and tossing them back to the opponent. A catch was worth one point; a miss was zero.

Millie won that initial competition that evening, by a score of four to two.

Once, Millicent tossed her panties toward Thomas and they landed on his erect sex organ. Still another toss once landed atop his head. In both cases, Millie The Official Rules Maker ruled those catches unofficial and not worthy of a point. "Nope, that's no good. A 'dick-catch' is illegal, does not count," declared Naked Underwear Toe Toss' official rules maker and arbiter.

Millie and Thomas often laughed themselves into tears when playing Naked Underwear Toe Toss. Lucy, it seemed, also loved the laughter and wanted to join in. In especially raucous matches, Loose would stand behind Thomas or Millicent as a spectator 'audience' of one. As the action heated up and the laughter decibel increased, Lucy would hop from side to side and up and down, hesitantly on her arthritic legs. She, too, was enjoying the action -- shaking her head up and down -- and 'laughing.'

Millie and Thomas saw each other for a period of several months before the sheer logistics of the relationship -- the travel to and fro of 1,000 miles to see and be with each other -- took its toll and the dating dance between the two ended as the old saw that 'long-distance' relationships are doomed from the start took hold and prevailed for them.

Mortal love is just that, Thomas thought: *mortal, ephemeral. All else, as the Preacher in Ecclesiastes refrained, is vanity. All is vanity.*

No two people step into the same stream. The stream is the same and it is not the same. It is ever-changing, thought Thomas, *"...with apologies to Heraclitus."*

Thomas thought also of Nietzsche's Zarathustra and, again, of his atavistic "eternal recurrence of all things."

There *is* nothing new under the sun. All *is* vanity.

Falsehood is a scorpion
that will sting itself to death.
-- *Percy Bysshe Shelly* --

Forty Three

After Millicent Getman and Naked Underwear Toe Toss, Thomas next met and began to date Lu-Ann Irene Edwards, as stunningly and startlingly, gaspingly beautiful as Jane Stone. Thomas was smitten with Lu-Ann, almost immediately, and, once things got underway in earnest, began very soon to see her almost every day.

Olivia became aware that Thomas, once again, was "seeing" someone and, thus, the frequency of *their* telephone contact was reduced significantly and sank into another of *their* intermittent hiatuses. Thomas, again, did not want to nor would he impose himself on Olivia while he was intimately involved with another woman. He thought of himself as a monogamist -- albeit a serial monogamist. But thoughts of Olivia (and Becky) came, nevertheless, to his mind every day.

●●●●●●●

He met Lu-Ann in a jewelry store where she worked, when she waited on him. Thomas had gone into the store looking

259

for something to send to his daughter in Texas, who had been going through some personal problems and, Thomas felt, could probably use a touch of solicitous fatherly attention to help her snap out of her depression and to cheer up. He went into the store without knowing what, precisely, he was looking for, only a piece of jewelry that he would send to her, hopefully, as he said to the pretty woman who had approached him, "May I help you, sir?" to "brighten her day, cheer her up. To give her some hope that better days are ahead."

After explaining to Lu-Ann what his mission was, she immediately took up the challenge with understanding, empathy and enthusiasm. She leafed through a number of catalogues that she brought forth from under a back counter in the store and found in one of the catalogues what struck her as, and he agreed was, a terrific idea -- a piece of jewelry shaped like a rainbow on an elegant gold chain. "A rainbow can symbolize hope and better things ahead," she opined. The piece she found in the catalogue was not in stock in the store and would have to be special-ordered.

Thomas would thereafter be known to Lu-Ann as "Rainbow Man." She would thereafter be thought of by him, as the relationship developed and he learned more about her, as perfectly befitting the acronym spelled out by her three initials, Lu(Ann) Irene Edwards. Lu-Ann was, Thomas would soon come to realize, a *pathological* liar. She was physically, psychologically, mentally and constitutionally just plain unable to tell the truth.

Paddy ultimately suggested "Lyin' Lu-Ann" as her sobriquet. But, after meeting her in person the first time, Paddy suggested she be dubbed "Slot Machine Nose." Said he, "Her fucken nose holes are big enough to take quarters." Thomas preferred to stay with the nickname for her that he first thought of as appropriate and which was underlined and revalidated each day he knew her. She was the physical, corporeal embodiment of her initials, L-I-E. That *had* to be her nickname, and Thomas vetoed and, for once, overrode

Paddy's suggestion.

Everything about Lu-Ann Irene Edwards was a lie, and her lies were brought on and brought up and exacerbated by a raging, uncontrollable anger and an all-too-often tempestuous temper.

Divorced and the mother of two teenaged boys -- who lived with her but traveled regularly on weekends to see their Dad in North Carolina -- Lu-Ann was a good mom but her underlying hair-trigger temper made her and her mood of the day difficult to read, both for Thomas and for her sons. Toward the end of his relationship with Lu-Ann, Thomas quite accidentally got to know, slightly and from a distance (telephonically), her ex-husband. Thomas learned from Ted that Lu-Ann's pathological lying was what had sunk their marriage. Her constant lying, complicated by stealing, spendthrift and wastrel habits and, most egregiously, her promiscuous infidelity, combined to make their marriage an impossibility. In retrospect, Thomas regretted that he did not know more about Lu-Ann's past and her selfish, self-centered, nature and character and personality and her unmitigated mendacity before he began dating her. He realized, in retrospect, that his dick got the better of his head as the relationship kindled and kicked off and sizzled -- before it, ultimately, fizzled and then burned out.

Following their meeting in the jewelry store, Lu-Ann called Thomas at home several days later to advise him that the rainbow pin and chain he had ordered through her had arrived and that he could drop by the store at his convenience to pick it up.

Forty Four

Thomas got an early indication of Lu-Ann Irene's irratio-
nal anger and frequent irascibility when he did not (he could
not; he was out of town, on a trip to Washington) immediately
respond to her message that the jewelry piece he ordered had
arrived and that it was ready for him to pick up.

Returning to Siesta Key from that brief trip to Washington, Thomas called Lu-Ann at the store where she worked
to tell her he had gotten her message, among many others
that had accumulated while he was away, but hadn't had an
opportunity yet to respond and to thank her for all she had
done in researching and special-ordering the rainbow pin for
his daughter.

"I'd like to speak to Miss Edwards, please," he said to the
store manager who had picked up the phone the day Thomas
called. "This is Mr. Gorman."

"Well thank you for returning my call so quickly," she
snapped icily as soon as she came to the phone. Thomas was
taken aback, but he let the comment -- and its tone -- pass.

It was not the first time Thomas would see Lu-Ann Irene's
hair-trigger temper. He saw her many, many times lose her

262

temper with her sons, often over trivial and seemingly non-consequential issues. He saw it surface when she spoke of her mother, and sister -- both of whom lived nearby -- and virtually every one of the dozen or so men and women with whom she worked -- and regularly, *daily*, he saw it erupt over issues regarding, and telephone conversations with, her ex-husband. Her residual anger over their failed marriage and her perceived slights by him at that time and ever since were constant complaints of hers. Thomas, sympathetic at first, grew weary of the same old tale of perceived slights and insults time and time again. Poor guy, thought Thomas, he can't do *anything* right in her eyes. Once (she told Thomas) Ted surprised her with a new car -- *for her*; he parked it in the driveway of their home and came into the house, took her hand and walked outside to show it to her, replete with a red ribbon and bow on its roof. LIE snapped and became angry and verbally hostile (Ted told Thomas) because Ted had not consulted with her beforehand about the color choice for the car. Ted thought he might get a pat on the back; instead he got a kick in the ass.

Ted also told Thomas about Lu-Ann's many infidelities during their marriage. He said she had once even taken up with a termite control contractor whom Ted had called to inspect their house before putting it on the market for sale.

Lu-Ann told Thomas about other of her "boyfriends," as her marriage was ending and afterwards, when she was legally single again. There were many, as many as if not more affairs, than Thomas had had.

"I should have seen it coming," Thomas thought, ruefully, one evening as he sipped a third glass of Merlot, long after the relationship had ended.

"Lyin' whore."

● ● ● ● ● ● ●

Early one morning Thomas drove from his place in Siesta

263

Key to Lu-Ann's home in North Port, 45 minutes south.
They had planned a day at the beach and had decided to
start early with a big breakfast at one of Lu-Ann's favorite
franchise restaurants, the International House of Pancakes.
Thomas had never been to an IHOP. Thomas arrived early,
just before the appointed hour, 7 o'clock, parked his car in the
driveway and rang the doorbell. The boys were not at home;
they were away with their dad. Thomas saw a light on in
Lu-Ann's bedroom and bathroom. He waited a few minutes
and rang the doorbell once again. There still was no response
from inside the house. Thomas guessed that Lu-Ann was in
the shower and could not hear the sound of the bell.

He rang again, for the third time, and when there was still
no response he sat down on the front porch stoop and waited
a few more minutes before trying the bell still once more. Lu-
Ann finally came to the front door, after Thomas first heard,
or thought he heard, the backdoor to the small ranch house
open and close. Lu-Ann launched into a diatribe. "What are
you doing here!?" she screeched. "You're way early," cack-
ling like a harpy. Thomas said nothing, but followed her into
the house -- and thought he saw a man walking through the
backyard toward a car parked across the street from Lu-Ann's
house.

Lu-Ann's screech, he thought, and he told her this when
they were inside, "could probably have been heard a mile
away." That was the wrong thing to say. It further infuriated
her and increased the decibel level of her voice by orders of
magnitude.

The screech -- and the departing guest -- were, Thomas
realized much later, harbingers that he should have paid
more attention to.

Forty Five

The day Thomas went back to the jewelry store to pick up the rainbow pin for his daughter he could not help but notice once again Lu-Ann Irene Edwards's stunning beauty. She stood about five feet seven inches tall. Slim but not anorexically so, she maintained her weight between 112-115 pounds. Thomas noticed (sorry, Ellen!) her ample chest, slim waist and curvaceous womanly hips.

Lu-Ann was extraordinarily proud of her measurements and was not bashful or reluctant to recite them: "36, double 'D,' 22, 34."

Thomas thanked her again for her assistance in finding "just the right gift." She smiled and touched his forearm with the fingertips of one of her beautiful model-like hands, long, slim perfectly-shaped fingers and well-manicured nails. "The pleasure was mine," she said.

Lu-Ann had had breast augmentation performed three times. The first two procedures failed when a leak developed but that experience did not deter her from going back to have the procedure done anew two additional times. All is vanity? That aphorism from Ecclesiastes came to Thomas's mind when thinking of Lu-Ann's preoccupation -- her obsession -- with the size, shape and firmness of her breasts.

●●●●●●●

Thomas thought about calling Lu-Ann at the store a number of times during the next week, but something, intuitively, told him not to. Something told him to "go slow on this one." He would later rue that he did not go slow *enough* "on this one."

●●●●●●●

Three weeks later, Lu-Ann *called* Thomas. She called on a cell phone while she was in her car driving back to Florida from having visited "a friend" in Alabama. The two made small talk and Lu-Ann, Thomas thought, continued to angle for encomium from him for her help with the jewelry piece she had found that he purchased and sent to his daughter. Lu-Ann seemed to Thomas to be "needy." He liked her, was sexually attracted to her, but still -- intuitively -- was reluctant and hesitant to initiate and progress a relationship with her. Somehow, he just did not trust her.

She asked him if he'd be interested in meeting her some night "after work" for a drink. The invitation was vague and Thomas responded that "maybe" they could do that some time after she was back in Florida. Thomas still did not have Lu-Ann's home or cell phone telephone number and did not that day ask her for either. The conversation ended without a date to get together being nailed down definitively.

The following week Lu-Ann called Thomas again and asked if he'd be interested in accompanying her to a work-related cocktail reception and social soiree the following Thursday night. Thomas still not feel that he wanted to get anything new, like this, started, and responded, flippantly and (he knew) inappropriately. "Sure, we can do that. But I want to ask you something first."

"Yes...?"

"Do you spit or swallow?" said Thomas, almost before he realized what he was saying. He immediately regretted having blurted out -- Paddy-like -- what he knew, in retrospect, was such a crass and boorish thing to say.

There was a click at the other end of the line, as Lu-Ann Irene Edwards terminated the conversation and hung up on Thomas without saying anything further.

The very next night, as Thomas sat eating a Papa Johns-delivered pepperoni pizza while sipping a glass of Merlot and watching on television the Tampa Bay Devil Rays lose still another game, Lu-Ann called once again.

"Hi," she said. He knew immediately it was her. He waited for her to speak further, certain that she was going to lambaste him, deservedly so for his inapropos question/comment at the end of their last phone conversation.

"I swallow," Lu-Ann Irene Edwards said.

They made plans to see each other the following Thursday.

Forty Six

At first, Becky held up well emotionally during and immediately after her divorce from William, unlike what had happened to her during and after her divorce from Arthur. But soon after William left her, alone, in their home in Mt. Roda, she began drinking -- regularly and heavily -- as she had when Arthur eventually moved out of their marital home in Bethesda. Becky began to call Julie two or three times a week (she felt she had no one else to talk with, and she desperately needed to talk with *someone* about what she was going through, with a failed marriage -- all over again). Julie was a good friend and a good listener and allowed her friend to pour out her soul to her in their hour-or-more telephone conversations. Julie could always tell when Becky had been drinking: not only did she ramble more and was her speech slightly slurred, she also was more likely to cry during conversations on those nights. When the crying became seemingly uncontrollable sobbing, Julie's heart ached vicariously for the pain her friend was suffering.

Becky asked Julie, again, about Thomas, and asked her if she knew how to contact him. Becky told Julie about her efforts

-- unsuccessful -- to find a telephone number for Thomas in Siesta Key.

Becky told Julie, for the first time, that she regretted deeply having ended the relationship she had had with Thomas and would "do anything" if she could "somehow get things back to where they once were with Tom."

Rebecca remembered.

Julie of course knew that Thomas, too, missed Rebecca but she also knew how much he had been hurt when Becky began dating and married William, and then moved from the Washington area to Mt. Roda. Julie did not give Becky Thomas's unlisted telephone number and in fact tried, gently, to discourage Rebecca from trying to find and contact Thomas. In a way, Julie thought, she wanted to protect Thomas from getting hurt again. She knew that Becky was fickle, that she craved the security in a relationship that marriage could confer (but, obviously, not always) on the bond between a man and a woman in love. She also knew that Thomas was -- at times he seemed absolutely adamant -- not interested in marrying again. After Ellen, he had said to her on more than one occasion, "once was enough."

In one conversation, when Rebecca once again brought up Thomas's name, Julie asked Rebecca to "hold on for a second. There's something I want to find and read to you."

Julie went to her desk and searched for and found in a bottom drawer a postcard she once had received from Thomas, just after Becky and William had wed -- and Thomas had learned of their marriage from the Morriseys.

The postcard from Thomas had been mailed to Julie from Nantucket. It read--

"Hi, Jules--

I mentioned to you that I was coming here for the weekend. What I didn't say is that I was coming here to try to bury a memory. Becky and I shared magic moments here, on this beautiful, isolated island and I have returned to remember one last time that magic and then, hopefully, to bury it and to move on and I am trying very hard to do that. I hope I succeed. I am trying. I am trying.

See you soon. Take care. My best to Robert.

Tom"

Julie read the message to Rebecca. Rebecca sobbed.

●●●●●●●

Rebecca remembered.

Rebecca did not share with Julie that she had received a long letter from Thomas just before Christmas, or what Thomas had said in the letter that he was planning to do.

●●●●●●●

Thomas and Lu-Ann Irene Edwards dated for nearly a year before their relationship ended, as all relationships do, ultimately, end -- one way or the other.

In retrospect, Thomas began to think through some of the factors that led to the split between he and Lu-Ann. There were many. For starters, he had to admit -- reluctantly -- that there was too much of an age gap, 19 years. (Ted once told him that many of Lu-Ann's affairs during their marriage were with 'older' men, some 20 or 25 years older than her). Thomas also knew that between him and Lu-Ann there was an undeniable educational and intellectual and cultural gap. Lu-Ann spent most of her free time watching television and "listening to my music... just jamming." Thomas did not "jam."

He was not even certain just what the hell "jamming" was or what it constituted or how one did it (unless listening to a CCR or Elvis Presley or Conway Twitty CD on his car stereo might be considered as such!) Thomas was aware that Lu-Ann had not read a book in many years. People magazine was her regular read. Thomas, on the other hand, did not go a week without finishing one book and starting another, mostly great fiction. "Why do you waste your time all the time with your nose stuck in a book?" Lu-Ann asked. Lu-Ann did glance at the local newspaper two or three times a week, looking mostly through the women's fashion display advertisements, and reading the comic strips.

Thomas also disliked her quick temper and her shrillness. Ted, again, confirmed to Thomas that Lu-Ann had been quick to anger since he had first known her, all the way back in high school. "Fucking woman has been unhappy -- and pissed off -- all her life." Ted said. Thomas found Lu-Ann banal and shallow and self-centered. *Everything* was all about her, *always.* He once asked her to accompany him to Loveland to "visit my friends." She agreed, and she tried when she was there ("I'll give her that much; she tried ...but it just wasn't in her.") to be social and outgoing with the facility's "special souls," but it did not work -- for them or for Lu-Ann. They saw right through her as insincere and disingenuous with them in her interactions with them and 'play-acting' in her strained attempts to converse with them. *She* knew, too, that the day did not go well, but Thomas was supportive and positive with her when they talked about the visit afterward. He thanked and congratulated and gave her high marks for making the effort. He patted her on the back as they left the facility that day, Lu-Ann nearly in tears. "You tried, honey, and that counts as much as anything in my eyes," Thomas told her. Later, when Thomas asked Olivia to join him for a day at Loveland, the difference between how well she 'fit in' and the disastrous Lu-Ann foray into that special world was remarkable. Olivia had great, natural and unaffected, empathy and resonance with the Loveland students. She was real -- and genuine and truly interested in the students -- and the students saw, understood and knew that intuitively.

But with Lu-Ann it always came back to the age differential. It was *the* major and obvious -- and, Thomas saw in retrospect, insurmountable -- obstacle obviating a successful and lasting relationship. Once Thomas and Lu-Ann were attending a musical concert at Sarasota's Van Wezel Performing Arts Center and they met a group of Loveland students (and their chaperone) in the theater lobby during an intermission. Thomas's good friend, the gregarious Henry M. was among the Loveland group. "Tom!" Henry said, loudly, when he spotted his friend. Thomas and Lu-Ann walked across the lobby to where Henry and a handful of his friends stood and talked. "Is this your daughter Tom?" Henry asked.

"No, she's not my daughter, Henry, she's a good friend." Thomas tried to change the subject, "Are you enjoying the show, Henry?" he asked. Henry, undeterred, responded, "Yes. (and ever the ladies' man) "...your friend sure is pretty." Lu-Ann seemed to enjoy the compliment, as she always did from *any* male of the species.

Lu-Ann was the only woman Thomas ever invited to accompany him to visit any of his daughters on a Holiday when they went to his eldest daughter's home (coincidentally, near Mt. Roda) one year at Thanksgiving. Thomas's youngest daughter and her family from Washington had flown in as well. Lu-Ann did not impress Thomas's daughters. She sat idly by on that special Thursday while the women and men, too, including Thomas, lent a hand in the kitchen getting the huge, festive meal ready and then served. Finally, Lu-Ann took it upon herself to lay out the silverware at the dining room table. That was the extent of her contribution. The husband of one of Thomas's daughters came up to Thomas and whispered, "Think we should help her out or do you suppose she can handle that all by herself?" Lu-Ann did not impress.

Thomas's nine-years-old granddaughter, he learned a few

days after Thanksgiving, assessing her grand-dad and his "girlfriend," had asked her mother: "Mom, is Grandpa rich?" Thomas's daughter told the child, "Yes, honey, Grandpa has a lot of money, but he doesn't brag about it. Why do you ask?"

"I think maybe that's why Miss Lu-Ann likes him."

"Out of the mouths of babes," Thomas thought, when his daughter told him a few days later about the incident.

In retrospect once again, Thomas realized after his relationship with Lu-Ann had ended, Lu-Ann (like Becky and other women he had dated) very much -- almost desperately -- wanted to be married. Once, she said to Thomas, "You know..." trying with all of her actress' ability, to sound casual, "...you know most of my measurements..." (and Thomas did, including the three that most women -- and men -- are most aware of: in Lu-Ann's case, as she was quite aware and proud to say, those were 36DD - 22 - 34) "double D" "... except my ring size. If you ever need to know *that*, it's four-and-a-half," said Lu-Ann.

Thomas, slow on the uptake, let the comment pass. He did not think about or realize its purpose until some weeks later.

Lu-Ann *did* want to get married and *did* want long-term financial security which she saw quite clearly that Thomas would be able to offer her. Ted once told Thomas, "Lu-Ann will deny this to the death, but she is very much of a material girl. She is status-conscious and money-conscious.... And that's pretty much all she thinks about."

Lu-Ann *was* a status-seeking social climber and saw Thomas as an easy mark to get her to new heights, at least economically.

Thomas did not want to be married again but the ultimate death blow to him and Lu-Ann amounted to three words: I love you. Thomas could not bring himself to say those words to Lu-Ann, which both distressed and angered her -- mostly angered -- nor could he ever imagine proposing marriage or, heaven forfend, actually *being* married to her, and being subjected daily to her screeching and her temper.

He thought about how he had once asked her in a telephone call if she 'spit' or 'swallowed' and how when she called him back in a day or two she said, sullenly, "I swallow." Did he 'force' her into saying that? If so, Thomas thought, in retrospect, she did not deserve it. She was a good person, looking for love and understanding -- and stability -- as we all are, as all God's children are.

He thought, now, *I love you, Lu-Ann. I did then and I do now -- but we just aren't meant to be together.*

Thomas had loved Rebecca and in fact thought that he *still* did. He had once loved Ellen -- and, now, he also loved Olivia. Moreover, he was also *in love* with Olivia.

"You, too, Lu-Ann," he said to himself. "Maybe I was -- and still am -- *in love* with you."

"Sorry it's taken me so long to actually say it."

And Thomas *was* sorry, about that, and that their affair had ended as abruptly, poorly and sadly as it had.

Forty Seven

Olivia was planning a trip to Florida. She had a long-time good friend who lived in Tampa, north of Sarasota, and she was planning to visit and stay with her friend there for a week. Thomas invited Olivia and her friend to visit Siesta Key on one of those days and have lunch, and they did. Olivia brought an overnight bag with her. She would stay with Thomas for a day and two nights and then he would drive her back to her friend Rosie's place in Tampa. Olivia had wanted to have at least a full day in Sarasota so that she and Thomas might have time to visit Loveland. Thomas had told her a lot about it and the "special souls" there.

Olivia loved Loveland, and Loveland loved Olivia. Olivia had an innate empathy and love that the students saw and understood and welcomed from her, and requited. She met Ricky F. and he and she got along famously.

●●●●●●●

Three weeks after Olivia's visit to Siesta Key and Loveland, Thomas wrote to her --

Joseph A. Gillan

Ricky F. has met the Governor!

*The visit came about quite unexpectedly. I had spoken in Octo-
ber with people in the Governor's office with whom I had been in
contact for several months -- first, to ask for a signed, personalized
photo of the Governor for Ricky and, secondly, about a possible visit
by Mr. Bush to Loveland. My last conversation with them was late
in October, and they told me that my request was still open and
under consideration but would not be acted upon, at best, until after
the statewide gubernatorial election in the first week in November.*

*The Governor's representatives spoke not with fork-ed tongue.
Barely 24 hours after the Florida elections, I got a call, on Wednesday, from the Governor's office asking if Ricky might "be available"
the very next day to meet with the Governor during a quick visit to
Sarasota for a political victory dinner (of some sort or another) that
night. The Governor would be arriving via a charter flight at the
private aircraft terminal at Sarasota-Bradenton Airport late in the
afternoon and, I was told, would be willing and would "very much
like" to set aside 10-15 minutes to meet and spend time with Ricky
there.*

*I was uncertain, initially, whether there would be others with
whom the Governor would be meeting at the private terminal that
afternoon before going on to his dinner, and did not ask about that,
but Ricky and his dad, when I called him with the proposal, were
thrilled, in any case, to accept the invitation. Even if Ricky was to
be one of many, or -- hopefully -- one of just a few whom the Governor would be meeting at Dolphin Aviation (as the private terminal at SRQ is called) before his dinner engagement, it promised for
Ricky to be a very special occasion regardless of whether there were
ten or one hundred and ten people there.*

*As it turned out, the occasion was indeed very special for Ricky
and his dad, a never-to-be-forgotten experience. Governor Bush had
set the time aside to meet with Ricky and his family only, and no one
else.*

*I believe I have mentioned to you that Ricky's dad, Chuck, is his
sole caregiver. He is a retired Navy career man, and a great guy. A*

widower, Chuck's wife, Ricky's mom, died ten years ago. Accompanying Chuck and Ricky that evening were one of Chuck's daughters-in-law and Chuck's lady friend, Evelyn. "Evvie" is a widow and an extraordinarily warm, giving, joyful and fun-to-be-with lady (from what I see). I believe she is good for, and to, Chuck, as well as Ricky. Ricky has talked to me about Evvie and he says "she's OK." That, from Ricky, is tantamount to a Hall of Fame nomination in baseball or an Oscar nomination in Hollyweird. There's no fooling Ricky. He doesn't suffer fools gladly and he sees through a façade quickly. I rounded out our little group of five.

The Governor could not have been more gracious. He had no coterie of aides with him, save one (an assistant/driver -- to take the governor to his dinner after meeting with Ricky). There were no television cameras and no print press to record the event for media dissemination. The Governor was, basically, on his own. He sat, socialized and talked with us -- mostly Ricky -- for a full 35 minutes. He listened to Ricky carefully and intently, carrying on a good back-and-forth conversation with him with none of those uncomfortable little pauses and breaks that occasionally occur when two people are meeting and conversing for the first time. The Governor understood Ricky well when he spoke, and that is not always an easy thing to do. Ricky does not consistently articulate and enunciate clearly. However, Gov. Bush communicated with Ricky as well as or even better than some at Loveland who are with Ricky on a daily basis are able to do. The Governor was engaged, and he showed it.

Ricky was on his absolute best behavior. No one had to tell him to do that; he just <u>knew</u>. He was consummately respectful and comported himself with great poise and dignity throughout his half-hour plus with the Governor.

Ricky idolizes the Bushes -- the Governor and the President -- and their dad, the former President ("41"). Ricky is a registered voter -- Republican, of course -- and through his dad is a contributing supporter of the Republican National Committee. Ricky carries an RNC membership card in his crammed-full wallet.

I believe I have mentioned to you at one time that when I see Ricky each Monday he will have with him that day, invariably, a newspaper clipping from the Sunday edition of the _Sarasota Herald-Tribune._ The clipping will have been neatly folded and creased, several times. Ricky will, very carefully, take the clipping out of his rear jeans pockets and unfold it, painstakingly, mindful not to tear or damage it. He will, next, smooth it out on the hard surface of the desk at which he sits and when he is satisfied with its smoothed-out condition, finally, will then ask me to read it to him. The clipping is always a story about the Governor or the President. All of the references in the headline or the story to "Bush" will be circled with a black-ink pen. "Bush" is one of the few words that Ricky recognizes and "reads."

And thus, that night at the airport, Ricky was indeed on his best behavior, recognizing the inherent dignity of the Office of the Governor and what that dictated and called for in his own, personal demeanor toward Mr. Bush. You can see that clearly in Ricky's face in the photograph of him and the Governor taken by Evvie. That smile has hardly left Ricky's face since that wonderful moment on that wonderful night for him.

During their conversation Ricky told the Governor that his birthday was "coming up" in just a couple of weeks. The Governor asked him what the date was. When Ricky told him, Mr. Bush took a pen out of one of his pockets and a small notebook out of another and wrote the date in it. The next month on his birthday Ricky received a Hallmark card signed "Best Wishes to my friend Ricky," -- Jeb Bush.

Ricky, after telling the Governor when his birthday was, then asked Mr. Bush _his_ own birthday. Ricky asked Evvie to write that down (apparently Ricky has more confidence in Evvie than his dad to take care of such details) so that he will be able to send the Governor a card when the time comes. Ricky is a fine manager/delegator.

Ricky had with him that night his personalized, framed autographed photos of the Governor _and_ the President. The photos were placed face up on a coffee table in front of the couch on which the Governor and Ricky sat next to one another and, after informing the Governor of the date of his birthday, Ricky then pointed to the President's photograph, and said to the Governor, "Tell him."

The Governor roared with laughter. He rocked back and forth, bending forward at the waist, and for a moment I feared he might fall in the same direction -- forward – off the couch. But then, after composing himself, he put one of his arms around Ricky's shoulders, gently, and said with obvious warmth and sincerity:

"Ricky, I'm going to be talking to the President this weekend and I will tell him."

Ricky nodded his head in silent approval. Ricky is, as I mentioned a moment ago, is a fine delegator.

When all of this began, with the thought to procure, if possible, through Washington contacts, an autographed photograph of President Bush -- made out to Ricky, personally -- I wasn't all that sanguine that it would happen. When it did, it was a relatively straightforward matter thereafter to call Tallahassee to request a similar personalized photo of the Governor for Ricky. ("After all", I told the person I first spoke to, "if the White House can do it, why not the Governor's office as well.")

The two photographs were presented to Ricky at a Loveland morning assembly. Photos of the occasion were taken and sent to and subsequently published by three local area newspapers and that -- on top of having the photographs themselves, which thereafter occupied the most prominent spot on the top of the night stand next to Ricky's bed -- was another thrill for Ricky.

Just before Governor Bush left the Dolphin Aviation private airline terminal to go to his political dinner on that special night for Ricky, he mentioned to Ricky the Gubernatorial Inauguration ceremony to be held in Tallahassee in January and offhandedly asked Ricky if he'd like to attend as his personal guest. The Governor's comment was left hanging, without a response, other than Ricky's "Sure!" as to how to set things up. The next day I talked with Chuck and asked him if he'd be interested in taking Ricky and Evvie to the event. Chuck responded enthusiastically and positively. Ergo: I sent to the Governor's office a follow-up email -- ostensibly to transmit to him a copy of the photograph taken by Evvie of him and Ricky -- but more so to say that Ricky and his dad would be _honored_ to attend the Inauguration as the Governor's guest. The Governor's *office emailed me back the very next day that Chuck's and Evvie's and of course Ricky's name and address would be passed along to the people responsible for coordinating the Inauguration VIP invitation lists.*

●●●●●●●

Following the visit by the Governor to the Sarasota airport to meet Ricky that evening, Chuck and Evvie and Ricky and I decided to go out for dinner ourselves. Ricky wanted to ride with me, not with his dad and Evvie. He did, in my little two-seater Corvette sports car. We were bound for a nearby Applebee's restaurant (Sammy in Johnstown once referred to a franchise of the same restaurant in upstate New York as "Bumblebee's"). Getting Ricky into the passenger seat of the tiny little car and buckled up was relatively uncomplicated compared to getting him out of the car when we arrived at the restaurant.

(The first thing I was told to do, incidentally, after getting Ricky buckled up and we were on our way to the restaurant was to change my car radio station choice from the "Oldies but Goodies" station that I listen to most often in Sarasota, to Ricky's favorite station, "Nine-two-nine-two." That is the local "Country and Western" radio station. Country music is Ricky's favorite. I followed Ricky's 'order' and changed stations. As I said, Ricky is a fine delegator and manager.)

After arriving at the restaurant and cruising around once or twice to find a parking spot reasonably close to the restaurant front door, for Ricky's sake, we settled in to a tight spot. I turned off the radio, got out of the car and walked round to its passenger side to unbuckle Ricky's seat belt and to extract him from the car. Ricky was settled in, almost immovably. I was on my knees, literally, in the parking lot, lifting Ricky's feet and lower legs, one at a time, out of the car's foot floor well, pulling and lifting them up and out and swinging them around to his right and out of the car as he continued to sit, like a Buddha. I was able now to turn him to the right in preparation for a final Herculean tug and lift from the low-to-the-ground *vehicle to his feet. Ricky stands probably 4 feet 10 inches in height and weighs some 150-160 pounds. He is built like a fire plug and as solid as one. When, at last, the extraction of Ricky from the car had been completed, Ricky stood without moving, or saying anything, for a few seconds. He exhaled slowly and regarded me, first, with a rather stern and unhappy look on his face, as if it were <u>my</u> fault that the extraction process had been so difficult and so laborious. Then, slowly again, the look on his face changed and his visage broke into a broad smile as he looked up at me (I'm 6-2 and he, as you know, is 4-10) and said, "Get a new car, Tom."*

Ricky was able, always, to make me smile.

The Governor's visit and meeting and all that it meant to Ricky aside, <u>that</u> moment, for me, was the highlight of the evening.

Not so for Ricky. He never forgot his meeting with Governor Bush and all through dinner, through an unending smile, and while eating fried chicken fingers and spaghetti, kept saying, "Jeb made my day."

Ricky's smile was as wide as the world, as were his dad's and Evvie's -- and mine. I still smile when I think of that evening and that smile when thoughts of my good friend Ricky come to mind.

Thomas's letter to Olivia continued --

Now that we've covered the Governor for Ricky, maybe, next, we can arrange a meeting with the Pope -- and then Vince Gill and, after that, who knows?

It was good to talk to you last night. You asked what I've been reading lately. I recently purchased "The Prophet" -- at your suggestion -- and finished it just within the past few days. Here are a few excerpts among many in that brilliant work of genius that I particularly liked --

Joseph A. Gillan

"You talk when you cease to be at peace with your thoughts; And when you can no longer dwell in the solitude of your heart you live in your lips, and sound is a diversion and a pastime.
And in much of your talking, thinking is half-murdered."

●●●●●●●

"There are those among you who seek the talkative through fear of being alone. The silence of aloneness reveals to their eyes their naked selves and they would escape."

And finally, and even more existentially:
"A little while, a moment of rest upon the wind, and another woman shall bear me."

●●●●●●●

And so it is, for all of us, as each of us moves always and ever to The One.

I also recently reread another Thomas Wolfe novel (surprise!), his debut book published nearly a century ago, "Look Homeward, Angel," and I include here a passage from the very first page of that masterpiece, which is indeed a masterpiece -- a novel for the ages, I believe, that is relative here ---

"Each of us is all the sums he has not counted: subtract us into nakedness and night again, and you shall see begin in Crete four thousand years ago the love that ended yesterday in Texas."

Wolfe articulated this Great Truth in his way, in the 1900s, as Gibran did, nearly a century later, in his way."

Love,

Tom

If there is a better cure for self-deception than solitude,
It has yet to be discovered
-- *E. Herman* --
(American theologian)

Forty Eight

As Thomas moved through his 40s toward the age of 50 *(Good Lord, 50 <u>begins</u> one's **sixth** decade!)* he thought. "… the beginning of the end of the 'three-score' portion of one's 'three-score-and-ten.' "

More than anyone he knew or spoke with, Thomas spent more time alone -- as a recluse and eremite. He was, undeniably, a loner. He sometimes went days at a time without speaking face-to-face with another human being, with the exception of the check-out person at the supermarket or a waiter in a restaurant. Thomas ate most of his evening meals, alone, in a few restaurants on the island that he liked. When he entered one of the restaurants he went to often, he was known by most of the greeters and table captains and they placed him at a corner table or a table underneath an overhead light. Thomas always had a book with him when he went to restaurants, to read and to use defensively as well. The act of book-reading usually would preclude possible conversation with a voluble diner or diners at an adjoining table. Thomas went home at night, closed his door and exulted in his aloneness. He found solitude desirable, soothing and luxurious.

What Thomas had said in his Christmas letter to Rebecca, (*The other thing that I want to tell you, that I want you to hear directly from me, if only 'impersonally' because I cannot -- as much as I want to -- tell it to you face-to-face, <u>is why I write today.</u> It is important to me that you know this. ... and I feel, truly, that you would want to know about it*) and how and why he had decided to take the step, was an action that he had been thinking about with increasing regularity, seriousness and intensity of purpose as he progressed through his 40s toward his 50s. He had been reading a great deal of the writings of St. Thomas Aquinas and St. Augustine and especially Thomas Merton for several years and thinking, a lot and often, in his solitude and aloneness, about the life he had been leading and its preoccupation for so many years with sex and women. He felt that that preoccupation defined his life as dissolute and it was time -- past time for him -- to reconsider and think anew and in depth *why* he was here and what God's plan for him might be.

In his Christmas letter to Rebecca he had also written --

When we put our head down on the pillow at night, whether or not there is someone next to us, each of us is, fundamentally, alone in this world, our world. And once we have lain our head on our pillow and before we drift off to sleep, when we are solitary and alone with our thoughts, each of us has to and must, always, answer, fundamentally, to <u>ourselves</u>.

●●●●●●●

Merton, a modern-age Cistercian monk and brilliant theologian and author, who spent most of his adult life in a Trappist monastery in the United States at Gethsemani, KY, ("the four walls of my...freedom"), wrote --

"... man becomes a solitary at the moment when, no matter what may be his external surroundings, he is suddenly aware of his own inalienable solitude...and sees that he will never be anything but solitary."

Merton's seminal published works "The Seven Storey Mountain" and "New Seeds of Contemplation" were reprinted again and again and translated into more than a dozen languages, including Chinese and Japanese.

Other passages that Thomas had underscored in Merton's writings included --

"Under the guidance of divine grace, in the school of charity, in the silence of the cloister, we are to be gradually initiated into a deep and experimental knowledge of the truth -- first as it is found in ourselves, then as it is found in other men and, finally, as it is in itself."

"It is in deep solitude that I find the gentleness with which I can love my brothers. The more solitary I am, the more affection I have for them. It is pure affection, and filled with reverence for the solitude of others. Solitude and silence teach me to love my brothers for what they are, not for what they say."

"In lumine tuo videbimus lumen" -- one of the most beautiful lines in all of the psalms. 'In Thy light, we shall see light.' "

●●●●●●●

From another theologian, Thomas once read this, also about solitude and the light -- the light of God:

"...There is deep within us a place apart... In its deep, cool darkness, sometimes illumined by a light not of our making, a moment can be a refreshing step into eternity, a coming home to the solitude of God."

For Thomas this meant and articulated what he felt all men know in the quiet depths of their soul but are reluctant often to accept, acknowledge or even discuss, because few are ever quite ready to quit the here and now and the known and comfortable for the Great Unknown. Thomas went back to this thought, often, contemplatively, when he was alone with <u>his</u> God --

In Thomas's letter to Rebecca, he wrote --

Man is born alone and he dies alone. He comes into this world solitary and in pain. He leaves this world in the same way -- solitary and in pain.

●●●●●●●

Before deciding definitively on what he had told Becky in his letter he was thinking about and in fact seriously considering -- that he would attempt to take the giant step to enter a monastery as a lay person to, perhaps, become a monk one day and live the remaining days of his life that way until *his* reunification with The Light -- Thomas wanted to deal with what he considered to have been the dissolute nature of his recent past life. He went to Confession one Saturday afternoon at St. Michael the Archangel Church in Siesta Key, where he frequently (but not *every* Sunday) attended Mass.

Thomas and Aldo had once exchanged thoughts in their ongoing correspondence about the male sex drive. Aldo had called it a curse: "It just never leaves us alone." Thomas, quite libidinous well into his 40s (Stefania had referred to his sex organ as "Otis"), was also troubled by this male preoccupation. Aldo once had told Thomas that his father, Luigi, was interested, active and involved with a number of the ladies in his retirement community in Sicily -- well into *his* 80s. Aldo, ever the Oxford man, used a word in his letter that sent Thomas scurrying to his dictionary: *obsolagnium* -- waning sexual desire resulting from age. There is always the exception -- and in this instance Luigi was it: obsolagnium had not yet kicked in for him, even as he moved through his 80s.

●●●●●●●

It was Thomas's first confession in many years.
"Bless me, Father, for I have sinned...

287

Thomas unburdened himself. The confessor was compassionate and understanding and sympathetic to Thomas's dilemma. Thomas and he had what Thomas thought was an excellent discussion -- about God, sin, faith, absolution ('absorption,' in Johnstown) and penance and " a firm desire (and intention) to amend my life..." They spoke for more than 30 minutes. Thomas considered it the most satisfying Catholic confessional experience he had ever had -- going all the way back to and beginning with grade school at SMI when, he remembered, always feeling cleansed, fresh and renewed afterwards each time he received that sacrament.

"...I firmly resolve, with the help of Thy Grace, to confess my sins, to do penance and to amend my life..."

●●●●●●●

Thomas told the priest about his seemingly unquenchable sexual desire and toward the end of their conversation, asked, quite sincerely and seriously --

"But tell me, father, when does concupiscence end?"

The priest paused for a moment before responding, slowly:

"For we men ... about ten minutes after we're dead."

Now Thomas paused, and what he said next brought on a paroxysm of laughter from the Disciple of St. Peter.

Thomas could sense almost a quaking of the entire confessional box resulting from the priest's laughter and uncontrollable body movement after *his* response --

"That soon, huh ?"

Had it been Peter Persico, from Thomas's boyhood, in the confessional that day asking that question, Pete might have requested an emendation: "Can we make that fifteen minutes, father?"

When Thomas exited the confessional, he could feel the curious gaze of the eight or ten sinners waiting in line for their sequential turn to confess. They just *had* to see who it was who had brought on such laughter from inside the Holy, secluded adytum.

●●●●●●●

(Aldo, in Toulouse, once wrote to Thomas, on the same subject: "Have you ever wondered whether love may be nothing more than a self-delusion we manufacture to justify the lengths we go to in order to have sex?" He added: "The male libido is a curse: the little head comes up, and the big head goes underground.")

Thomas always appreciated Aldo's wonderfully literate emails and his sense of humor and comedic touch.

One of his favorite emails from Aldo, which he had saved in hard copy for many years and once also shared with Olivia, had to do with modern packaging and the difficulty many people beyond their 20s and 30s experience in finding a way through the complicated outer wrap to the, more often than not, foodstuff product inside --

Aldo wrote –

"You may be surprised to learn that French packaging is even worse than Belgian. In the morning when I open a carton of milk, it requires considerable skill to do so without squirting the contents over myself. But I discovered the epitome of Frankish packaging in trying to open a container of foie gras which I was about to offer to a lady autochthon ('autochthon' was a word Thomas recalled first running across in a F. Scott Fitzgerald novel and subsequently using in one of his emails to Aldo; Aldo was now feeding it back to Thomas) guest, together with a bottle of my Premier Grand Cru Classe, Sauternes, Chateau Rieussec 1979, if you please. I trust you are not only impressed, but also envious, even if it is not red wine but white (but there is no reason to get racist about this).

"But I digress…

An office associate (an Englishman) of Thomas's and

Aldo's, when they worked together in Brussels, *frequently* would use this supercilious construct (But I digress) and it never failed to amuse and bore Thomas and Aldo.

Aldo's email continued --

"For some ominous reason (which I was shortly to discover), the foie gras lay recumbent in a glass container, so clearly the elastomeric seal between it and the lid had to be perfect.

"With debonair, fully confident nonchalance, I took hold of the container and made to lift the massive metallic cable that had been cunningly contrived to hold down the lid. It refused to budge. I grasped the items mentioned more robustly but was still unable to remove the lid. I then placed the jar on the floor, put my foot on it and, with vigor, strained to remove the offending lid, but to no avail.

"Undaunted and still fully committed to implementation of my action programme and to the achievement of my objective [here Aldo was borrowing from and using corporate jargon immediately recognizable to Thomas], I armed myself with a stout pair of pliers, but even these failed to remove the lid. After some thought, I took a large screwdriver, thrust it under a small section of the metal cable (which I now surmised was not made of steel but from a sophisticated hi-tech alloy of vanadium encased in a titanium/lithium compound normally used for the construction of nuclear warheads). This stratagem eventually enabled me to remove the offending metallic contraption. The wounds I suffered were mere scratches that soon stopped bleeding.

"With renewed confidence, I made to raise the lid. But it remained stubbornly attached to the rubber seal separating it from the main body of the container. Meanwhile, the foie gras continued to observe me unperturbed.

"At this stage, I grasped a large kitchen knife, inserted it between the rubber seal and the lid and, with vigorous determination, thrust it into the seal. The knife glanced off the seal and embedded itself in the flesh beneath the thumb of my left hand. It was merely a matter of seconds before there was blood on the kitchen floor. I emitted several exceedingly rude words in miscellaneous languages. Sophia was summoned and rapidly produced disinfectant and plasters. When I had been bandaged and was out of danger, our lady guest decided to intervene. Being an autochthon she was clearly familiar with the problem.

"She requested a pair of pincers. I offered her my pliers, but she shook her head and insisted on pincers. I obtained them from my meager tool-box where they had reclined together with my hammer, six nails, and the aforementioned pliers and screwdriver. The lady grasped a portion of the elasto-meric seal and tugged vigorously, but with no result. It was then decided that she would use both hands to grasp the seal with the pincers and that I would grasp the glass container. We both tugged. At last, there was a hiss as the seal surren-dered. There was also a clatter of kitchen chairs as I fell to the floor grasping the now open pot of foie gras.

"I felt you should be apprised of this grievous threat to (more corporate jargon) Domestic Safety Excellence."
-- Aldaccio

Thomas nearly fell off *his* chair in laughter as he read this and as he reread it from time to time laughing again and again at his friend's light wonderful humor and comedic touch.

Forty Nine

Thomas wrote to Aldo --

I have some further thoughts to offer, if I may, related to my long email to you of some weeks ago on death and dying. I want to explain a bit further than I did in my earlier message why I am having increasing doubts and difficulty accepting and embracing the putative, traditional concept of God as developed by theologians through the ages -- as I myself, a mere man, age, and as I think more and more about death, dying and God.

Please forgive the imprecisions and inexactitudes that may follow here, based on my limited study and understanding of them, as supplied by Sisters of St. Joseph Sister Bertrand and Mother Grace Madeline in a small city in America in a rural part of the state of New York almost a half-century ago --

Earliest man worshipped, first, the forces of nature -- the sun and the moon and the wind and the sea. These were early man's 'Gods.' Over time, man began to personify, or anthropomorphize his 'Gods.' Ultimately, man began to imagine and posit that 'God' was not embodied in and by nature but existed above and beyond it.

The ancient Israelites (I believe this to be the case, from the little I have read) were the first to break with their old religious allegiances and alliances and the first to adopt and embrace the concept of a monotheistic 'God.'

At roughly the same time, ancient paganism also gave way, generally, to a form of monotheism.

Thus, as man continued to evolve, so too did his concept of 'God.'
(Sister Bertrand and Mother Grace did not 'teach' this!)

●●●●●●●

Fast forward, now, to the time when the man Jesus walked the earth. Jesus was a faith-healer, self-acknowledged and recognized as such. He, himself, never claimed to be 'God.' The first full-length Biblical account of his life -- Mark's gospel -- was not even written until about the year 70, nearly 40 years after Jesus's death. In Mark, Jesus is presented as a perfectly normal man with a family that included brothers and sisters. He even is said, in Mark, to have had a lady friend.

●●●●●●●

(As an aside here, please note that my reference to the date "70" above is not appended with 'A.D.' I have a question for you, my friend: when do you suppose the world will stop feeling compelled to use 'A.D.?' The year, now, is 2010. Is that sufficient in and of itself, or do we need to write and should I have written '2010 A.D.?')

Having said that, I digress. And so I return now to the subject at hand --

Though Jesus himself never said that He was 'God,' the doctrine that He had been 'God' in human form was not postulated until the fourth century (A.D. !) at the synod in Nicaea. It was not until then, and when, the Nicene Creed was published on May 20, 325 A.D. (that was exactly the date: I looked it up) that the claim was put forth that Jesus and the Creator and Redeemer were in fact one.

That, my dear friend, boggles my mind. How could anyone have known -- for certain -- 300 years after the fact, after Jesus's death, that He had been 'God' incarnate?

And then (Wait! There's More! [as today's hawkish and too loud television marketing advertisements proclaim]), seventy years after Nicaea, another synod, meeting in France, added the idea of The Holy Ghost -- almost as an afterthought -- and, thus, the concept of The Trinity was conceived.

Augustine, who, as you may recall, I have quoted before in our correspondence and whom I have read much of and admire -- though I do not necessarily agree with <u>all</u> of his thinking -- was the theologian more than any other in the fourth century (A.D.) who defined and articulated The Trinity for the Latin church.

Augustine was a scholar and theologian, to be sure, but he also was a complex, multi-faceted human being -- and a hale-fellow-well-met. For example , apocryphal or not, there is a tale that Augustine was said to have prayed (this is a story about him that I particularly like), as he was striving to achieve and maintain celibacy, "Lord, please give me chastity ... but not yet." (Sounds like my kind of guy!)

Presumably -- or so I would make the case -- Augustine was a healthy heterosexual. But he also, from the evidence available, was a sexist and neurotic misogynist. <u>These are his words</u> --

"What is the difference whether it is in a wife or a mother, it is still Eve the temptress that we must be aware of in any woman."

(I don't believe that Augustine and Gloria Steinem would have gotten along very well.)

Augustine in his writings often seemed preoccupied with sex and the sexual act (again, my kind of guy?) -- as is much of the Roman Catholic Church seemingly similarly preoccupied yet today.

Interestingly, the theology that Jesus died on the cross as an atonement for Adam's "original sin" -- sexual congress with Eve -- did not emerge, as the concept of the Trinity also did not emerge, until the fourth century.

(And I digress here for a moment: was it only Adam who was 'guilty' in Eden; was not Eve also guilty, or does Catholic theology give her a free ride? I once asked a priest in Confession about the difference in sinfulness between male -- and female -- masturbation. When a male does it, it is a sin and a 'mortal' sin because he is 'spilling his seed' instead of propagating the faith and the race; when a woman masturbates she is not doing that [i. e., "spilling seed"], and is her masturbation, thus, somehow less sinful, maybe only a 'venial' sin? The priest that day to whom I posed this question ducked it.) In any case, so much of the Catholic religion, and all of the Christian faiths -- and Judaism and Islam, too -- while presented by their leaders as true theology and The Word of God are, in reality (it seems to me), Johnny-come-lately theology writ large. So much of it, most of it, it seems to me, is not much more than manmade bunkum.

So many Christians in today's world -- particularly the 'Born-Again' fanatics -- take Biblical scripture so unswervingly literally, and yet (and I freely acknowledge here that I am not by any stretch of the imagination a Biblical scholar though there are a few parts of it that I do like to read and reread [especially 'Ecclesiastes']), so much of it is filled with inconsistency and contradiction.

Take, for one example, the Pharisees and the treatment they receive in the Bible. The Pharisees, from what I have read (not in the Bible) were the most progressive of all of the Jews of Palestine. They were spiritualists who cultivated a sense of God and God's presence in even the smallest detail of their everyday lives. They were great thinkers and, many scholars today assert, ahead of their time, philosophically, socially and culturally. Jesus himself may have been a Pharisee. Yet in Matthew's Gospel, Jesus is made to utter violent diatribes against the Pharisees -- antithetically so, to say the least, to the charity-toward-all belief and demonstrated actions that so characterized, putatively, Jesus's mission and life on earth. Luke, on the other hand, speaks quite positively of the Pharisees both in his Gospel and in the Acts of the Apostles. And Paul spoke proudly of his Pharisaic background even after he became a Christian.

I do not pretend to understand the conflicting positions and tales, above, but they are, to be sure, there in the Gospels, as are other conflicts and inconsistencies.

I also do not understand why so many theologians continue to insist that the Bible is the incontrovertible Word of God -- to be taken by man, literally, as the 'Gospel Truth' (pun intended).

The Muslims are as errant as the Christians in this regard, it seems to me, in the way that they view and interpret the Koran. And they, and it, are comparative newcomers in human history, of course... Mohammed, after all, didn't come along until 700 years after Jesus.

In today's world it is increasingly difficult -- without the gift of Grace and Faith -- to believe in God or, more particularly, to accept and believe in organized religion. Religious fundamentalism is at the core of so much of the world's turbulence and the senseless strife we read and hear about every day. (I have an old friend in Washington, with whom I speak every three or four months, who, literally, cries when she and I talk about the hate and violence that is so rife around the world and the seeming senselessness of existence today.)

But does it not seem that radical Islamic terrorism and jihad -- and other religious fundamentalism as well -- is at the core of much of this senselessness? Intolerance of others and others' beliefs is and ever has been a characteristic of monotheism. 'Is now, always was, and always shall be.' For we mackeral-snappers, we only have to look back a few hundred centuries to see how our 'Holy Wars' scarred the history of Christian monotheism.

And then there are the Jews. For many of them today, God no longer exists. For them, God died seventy years ago in Auschwitz. Elie Wiesel has written (and I paraphrase here): if God is omnipotent, He could have prevented the Holocaust. If He was unable to stop it, He is impotent and useless. If He could have stopped it and chose not to, He is detached and He is cruel.

How does one counter that argument? Can you, Aldo? I cannot. It is beyond my feeble intellectual ability to do so.

Conventional theology for Wiesel and for other modern Jewish intellectuals ended with the Holocaust.

●●●●●●●

Now, my good friend, having said all of <u>that</u>, let me also say this within the context of this discussion: the single most perplexing Christian theological concept for me to grasp, even tentatively, by my fingertips, is the concept, the very idea of <u>Infinity</u>. My brain cannot fathom it, cannot wrap itself around it.

'... is now, always was and always shall be...'

The 'now' and the 'always shall be' are fathomable; the 'always was' concept -- Infinity -- is, to me, unfathomable.

It is unfathomable -- but it is also true. <u>How</u> could it be otherwise? But (there's always a 'but,' isn't there?)... but for <u>me</u>, as Infinity is unfathomable but true, so too <u>has</u> to be the concept of and God, Himself -- unfathomable but true.

Man through the ages has 'adapted' God and he has anthropomorphized Him when in truth the only truth, and the highest truth, we humans are able to conceive, imagine and comprehend, however imperfectly, is that <u>God must be essentially unfathomable</u> If we posit otherwise, He could not be God but, merely, a human projection (And who, my good friend, was it, first, that imagined God looked like and represented Him as a Scandinavian hair shampoo model?)

At the end of the day -- for me, Aldo -- I conclude, first, that it is impossible to apply any ratiocinative thought to this Question of The Ages, as theologians have done and do still today, and I conclude, second, finally and simply, that only a God can be Infinite and Infinity can only be because of a God.

And so, tenuously, I believe... in saecula saeculorum.

●●●●●●●

I will close now, my friend, but before I do I must share one additional God-related story –

Moses came down from Mt. Sinai dragging behind him, a few feet at a time as he took several periodic rest breaks, a very large

297

stone tablet. The stone came up to his chest and was a good three feet or more in width. Upon finally reaching the base of the Mount, he took some deep breaths, paused, and spoke to the throng awaiting him there -- to where he had descended and, finally, stopped --

"I've got good news and I've got bad news," he announced.

The crowd was hushed.

"First, the good news. I got Him to whittle it down to just 10."

[There were 613 commandments in the Pentateuch]

The assembled multitude cheered.

As the din subsided, Moses held up his right hand, pointed to the large stone tablet.

He continued --

"And now the bad news...."

The crowd stood hushed.

"The bad news," Moses intoned, somberly: "Adultery is still in there."

●●●●●●●

And that, finally, is all I have for the moment, my good friend. Please give my best to your current wife (as Aldo often referred to Sophia, his wife of 35 years).

-- Tom

Fifty

Rebecca had been drinking more regularly, and heavily, since William and she had divorced -- and she was also telephoning Julie much more regularly than she had since leaving Bethesda many years ago and settling in Mt. Roda.

Rebecca was stunned at reading in Thomas's letter what "the other thing" was that he had felt compelled to tell her. She brought it up in one of her telephone conversations with Julie and Julie, laughing nervously, professed to know nothing about it. She told Rebecca that she and Thomas had not spoken in nearly a year, quite unusual for them.

Julie was very surprised when Rebecca told her what it was that Thomas was thinking about -- if not already into the planning stage or beginning the implementation of it. Julie also felt protective of Thomas's "privacy" and told Rebecca very little about what she knew of his life since he and Rebecca had stopped seeing each other. She felt protective toward him as she had felt protective of Rebecca's privacy when Thomas would ask her about Becky in each and every one of their phone conversations over the years.

Rebecca sobbed to Julie when she spoke to her of what she

knew of Thomas's strange intent to alter his life so drastically. Thomas in his letter some months before had said something to the effect that the two of them, perhaps, might think about getting back together if anything ever happened to her and William.

Rebecca remembered.

Rebecca remembered.

"I kneel before your perfect body ..."

Rebecca remembered.

Fifty One

Thomas wrote to Olivia --

I have sad news. My (our) friend Ricky F. has died. He passed away a week ago Wednesday evening. I tried to call you, but you were not in.

Ricky was 45 years old.

Ricky's health, as you know, had been deteriorating for the past month. He had undergone MRIs periodically since his brain surgery last September, just after you were here and had the good fortune to meet and get to know him. Two spots in the brain that had been noted in the first postoperative scan after that five-hours long surgery began to show growth in November. Chemotherapy was prescribed and begun at that point -- and that regimen was not an easy one for Ricky. Is any chemotherapy ever easy for anyone?

In late November a further scan showed three additional spots, and one of the earlier spots had increased in size significantly. After all that Ricky had been through with the September surgery and its difficult and laborious recuperative period this latest development was, of course, the worst possible news. It was devastating to Ricky's family and friends, who had been hoping, against hope,

301

-- until that terrible news -- that Ricky may have been on the road to a prayed-for recovery.

The decision was taken by the family, rightly (in my opinion) and sadly, to discontinue the chemotherapy regimen for Ricky when it quite obviously was not having the hoped-for mitigating effect and was serving, only, to make Ricky weaker physically and increasingly uncomfortable generally.

The doctors ruled out further surgery. Ricky's dad and other family members, after deep soul-searching, decided, also, against the only other possible course of assuasive action: radiation therapy. The doctors had said that that procedural mode might extend Ricky's life, at best, by three months but it also was quite possible, they cautioned, that it would not. Thus, Ricky would have to undergo the rigors of radiation treatment without any assurance that it would provide him -- or his family -- with further time. Moreover, the doctors said, the radiation effects would in any case be debilitating and very likely might result in the further deterioration of Ricky's now obviously failing cognitive and motor skills and abilities.

It was at that point that Ricky's dad and other members of the family decided to subject Ricky to no further treatment other than medically prescribed palliatives to keep him as comfortable and pain-free as possible.

Ricky continued to function over the course of the next several weeks but began gradually during that period, progressively and noticeably, to appear more tired and wan. His ambulation, limited in the base-case (as you know), slowed and deteriorated markedly further. His speech skills began to suffer. Ricky's happy, ready smile began to cross his face less and less frequently. He became less gregarious.

And yet, despite all that he was going through, Ricky chose to continue to attend his classes at Loveland each day. He went to a school dance and pizza party in January and to the school Valentine's Day dance earlier this month. As was his custom at school dances, Ricky stood in the front of the room next to the disc jockey and the sound equipment from which the music emanated, and waved a baton to the beat of the music as if he were conducting the

302

music being sounded and it could not play without his orchestral leadership.

At home, Ricky continued his avid and fervent interest in politics -- strictly Republican, of course. Did I ever tell you that the television set in Ricky's bedroom was always tuned in to C-Span and its continuing telecast of U.S. House and Senate floor action from Washington's Capitol Hill? Whenever I visited Ricky at home (sometimes I'd give him a ride home after school, if he didn't feel, on a given day, like taking the county-sponsored bus service for the disabled), he would, after hanging up his jacket and stacking his school books neatly on his desk, turn C-Span on, for at least a few moments, to see what was happening in the world of Washington politics that afternoon. If a Democrat was on camera or speaking from the House or Senate floor, Ricky would react with impatience, sheer disdain and a dismissive wave of his hand: "Bah!" he would say disgustedly. And then he would abruptly click the television off. Ricky was a dyed-in-the-wool Republican loyalist. He didn't have time for Democrats.

On the Friday before he died, Ricky had a bodily function accident at school, and it embarrassed him greatly. That had never happened to him in public before. That weekend at home was difficult, Chuck told me. Ricky slept for long periods of time. He did not have an appetite, eating very little to sustain himself and he began to lose further his cognitive and motor abilities. On Monday he seemed to bounce back a little. When he awoke that morning, he got up and out of bed, said he was hungry and ate a big breakfast. But the very next day his condition began once again to deteriorate. He was disoriented and unable to stand unassisted. He cried, something Ricky hadn't done since he was a child, his dad said. "He just looked so lost when he cried, and I didn't know what to do or if there was anything I could do" said Chuck, himself almost in tears.

By the next day, Wednesday, Chuck could no longer rouse Ricky; he had lapsed into a coma. Ricky's sister, who had flown in the night before from her home in Pennsylvania to help her dad care for Ricky, contacted Ricky's primary care physician. The physician came to the house -- imagine that! -- to examine Ricky and advised

303

that Ricky be hospitalized without delay. An ambulance was called and Ricky was taken in it to the hospital, arriving at about noon. He was placed in a non-critical-care room. His vital signs were weak -- very weak -- and the doctor told Chuck and his daughter that he did not expect Ricky to live for much more than 24 hours. The family was crestfallen and terribly shaken, but also resigned to the inevitable -- and maybe even a little relieved that the inevitable was, at last, at hand. The family specified that no heroic actions be taken by hospital emergency personnel to prolong the limited life left in Ricky.

I had been in Connecticut, visiting Ellen and other friends, the previous weekend and had gotten delayed there in a major snow-storm, putting off my return to Florida for two days before I was able to get a reservation for a flight home. I got back to the Sunshine state and home at about 2 a.m. on Wednesday. Ricky's dad tele-phoned me at home early that evening and filled me in on what had been going on during the past several days and where things stood at that moment. I put down my pepperoni pizza supper and glass of Merlot and drove to the hospital, a half-hour away. I got there some-time just after 7 p.m. I sat with Ricky and his dad in the darkened room. Ricky remained in a coma, but Chuck and I both talked to him as the clock on the wall above his bed ticked -- <u>*too loudly*</u> *(time pass-ing, passing, passing). Chuck and I talked to Ricky; we touched and held his hands. We caressed him and we wiped and patted dry the perspiration on his forehead. One of Ricky's brothers, Mike, came in just before 10 p.m. Mike had been at the hospital that afternoon and had gone home, just before I arrived, to get a bite to eat and to rest for a few minutes. The three of us sat at Ricky's bedside now, largely in silence.*

Ricky never regained consciousness. At two or three points during the long, sad night Ricky had emitted deep gurgling sounds. It was his death rattle.

Chuck, Mike and I remarked on this phenomenon and spoke further for a few moments about the love we felt for the departing, special soul in front of us. As midnight approached, Mike got up from his chair and went over to Ricky as his younger brother contin-

ued to lie motionless and, now, silent. We all noticed that the sheet and light blanket covering Ricky were no longer rising and falling, as they had been, with Ricky's respiration, most of the evening. Mike bent over Ricky, now, and realized that his brother was no longer breathing. Mike attempted to find a pulse, but could not. Mike looked back across the room at Chuck and me. I left the room to summon a nurse. It was now just past 11:50 p.m. The nurse and an assistant came into the room and looked at Ricky and asked the three of us to step out for a moment.

It was only another moment before the nurse reappeared and stood in the doorway to Ricky's room. She looked toward the three of us standing in the hallway outside Ricky's room, Chuck, Mike and me. She shook her head, slowly, from side to side. She then bowed her head and walked down the hallway, quickly and efficiently, away from us.

Ricky was gone. He had slipped the surly bonds of earth; he had slipped away from us and from this world without any of the three of us who were with him that night being aware of the exact moment when his breathing had ceased and life had left him.

The three of us went back into the room. Ricky's dad and brother stood next to their dear one on either side of the bed. They held Ricky, and they wept.

The Dark Lady had put her arms around Ricky gently and lovingly. Ricky went with her peacefully and painlessly.

In his handicap, Ricky had suffered all of his life. Mercifully, he did not suffer in death as he went home, silently, to eternity and his Infinite God.

I stood in the background, in a corner of the room, not wanting to insert myself into such a highly and deeply, emotionally charged moment of _family_ sadness, loss and grief. Mike had been especially close to Ricky. His body shook as he sobbed. He held on to his 78-year-old dad, who also wept.

As I stood, at a distance, tears also welled up in my eyes. I left the room for a moment, leaving Chuck and Mike alone with Ricky. I waited in the hallway, alone, apart from the family. After a few minuets more, I re-entered the room where Ricky lay.

305

Ricky F. was my friend.

The three of us stayed with Ricky for another half-hour. We held him and talked to him and told him we loved him.

Then, finally, we left Ricky's room and we walked, the three of us, as if our legs were laden with lead, down the long, empty, quiet hospital corridors to the elevator to the ground floor and then to the exit and to our cars in the parking garage.

When I got home it was 2:30 a.m. I said a prayer for my friend Ricky and I thought about him long, long into the rest of the sad, unending night. I thought about all Ricky had meant to me and to so many others outside of his wonderful family. I remembered Ricky telling me on the night he met the Governor, "Get another car, Tom."

I will not forget Ricky nor will I forget what date it was when he went to his rest: it was the 19th day of February, my birthday.

There is a memorial service commemorating Ricky and his life planned for tomorrow at Epiphany Cathedral in Venice. I will be there, of course, along with probably a hundred or more of Ricky's friends from Venice, Sarasota and, of course, from Loveland. We will honor and pray for a very special soul and we will celebrate his life and we will be grateful to The Good Lord for having shared Ricky with us albeit for much too brief a sojourn.

I have told you about Ricky's interest in politics and in the Bush family in particular and about the personalized, autographed photos of George W. and Jeb Bush that I had a hand in obtaining that were sent to Ricky by the President's and the Governor's offices. I have also told you about the meeting Ricky had with the Governor in November, one-on-one, just two days after the Governor's reelection. It was an <u>extraordinary gesture of human</u> kindness by Mr. Bush to carve out and to spend that time with Ricky. The photograph of Ricky and the Governor taken that evening became one of Ricky's prized possessions. He never tired of showing it to his many friends at school and elsewhere. The experience helped brighten the last few months of Ricky's life.

I have been in touch this week with the Governor's office and it is my understanding that Mr. Bush will be sending a personal, hand-

*written note of condolence to Ricky's dad and family. I am trying
to see if we can manage to get a similar courtesy and note from the
White House.*

Love,

TAG (Thomas Anthony Gorman)

*P.S. Here are some lines from "Vitae Summa Brevis" by a poet
that an acquaintance of mine mentioned to me. The poet's name
was Ernest Dowson. The lines apply, I think, to Ricky F., and his
too-brief time here on earth with us --*

They are not long, the days of wine and roses:
Out of a misty dream
Our path emerges for a while then closes
Within a dream.

●●●●●●●

God Bless You, Ricky.
Rest in Peace, good friend -- with Our Lord in Eternity.

And another panegyric for Ricky--

*Great voices soared far above him, vast shapes came and went,
lifting him to dizzy heights, depositing him with exhaustless
strength. The bell rang under the sea.*

- Wolfe, "Look Homeward, Angel"

Fifty Two

Thomas had become more meditative and contemplative and -- if possible -- even more solitary after he and Lu-Ann had stopped seeing each other. For the first time in his adult life, had he been pressed, he would have admitted <u>not</u> that he was 'depressed' (Thomas had no patience for "I'm depressed" from anyone; that, to him, was a manifestation of self pity, and *that* -- self pity -- he just could not brook), but that, yes, he was 'sad.' He had been infatuated, if not 'in love' with eye-candy Lu-Ann, and he was sorry when it ended -- as all relationships do, in one way or the other, end.

The last night that he and Lu-Ann spent together Thomas heard on the car radio on his way home from her place the following morning the Beatles' Paul McCartney record hit, "Yesterday."

The disc jockey, in introducing the record, remarked that it is the "most played record on radio stations around the world." No other single recording gets more plays, not only in English-speaking nations but in all nations all over the globe --

"Yesterday, all my troubles seemed so far away
Now it looks as if they're here to stay
Oh, I believe in Yesterday

Why she had to go, I don't know
She did not say

I said something wrong,
Now I long ...
For yesterday.

Yesterday...."

●●●●●●●

Thomas regretted the end - - the inevitable end -- of his relationship with Lu-Ann. Maybe he *had* been unfair to her. And yes, maybe he *had* loved her. Maybe he still did. Perhaps, Thomas thought (could it be?) that he was in love with four women, all at the same time: Lu-Ann, Becky, Ellen (even Ellen?) -- and, of course, Olivia.

At this moment, however, Thomas missed Lu-Ann Irene Edwards more than he missed anyone.

●●●●●●●

Thomas became more contemplative and solitary. He began reading more of St. Augustine ("Yearning makes the heart deep"), St. Thomas Aquinas and even more so, *his* 'newly-discovered' modern-day theologian, Cistercian Trappist monk Thomas Merton.

He struggled to get through, and had to plod to do so, Augustine's "On the Immortality of the Soul." (Thomas found even the "introduction to the modern edition" of the volume obtuse: ("... *the ratio of analogical induction to syllogistic deduction becomes obscured or lost where specialization intervenes...*")

Thomas had written in the margin next to *that* enlightening sentence: "I agree; I know *I've* certainly always found that, in my experience, to be the case."), but he found Aquinas somewhat less mind-bending and more palatable -- his "Concerning Being and Essence" and (the) "Metaphysics (of St. Thomas Aquinas)."

Thomas considered the reference to "syllogistic deduction..." and remembered the comment Paddy once offered as an example of a syllogism: "God is love. Love is blind. Ray Charles was blind. Ergo: God is a blind, dead Negro blues singer."

Thomas went back to look at the name of the author of the introduction of the Augustine volume to see if, perchance, he or she might be a highfalutin member of the Thomas Wolfe Society. He or she certainly was <u>not</u> anyone like Paddy from Johnstown, NY.

Aquinas wrote in "... Being and Essence," more directly, Thomas thought -- "and, for me, more understandably."

What Aquinas wrote seemed to Thomas to go directly to the heart of Thomas's intellectual struggle of many years to understand and rationalize, to the extent possible, the theological concept of *Infinity* -- and God.

"It follows that there must be something which is the cause of the existence (causa essendi) of all things, because it is very existence alone; otherwise the causes would proceed to infinity, since everything which is not existence alone would have as cause of its existence, as has been said. It is clear, therefore, that an intelligence is form and existence, and that it has its existence from the first being which is existence alone, and this is the first cause which is God."

Thomas was indeed becoming more contemplative as he struggled to understand more clearly these theological concepts. He began to listen more closely to his inner voice. He began once again to attend Sunday Mass more faithfully.

310

He began to spend more time in reflecting on his past life, *when he was alone with his God.* He slogged through Augustine again and *enjoyed* Aquinas ("...man's last end, namely, beatitude, to which the whole of human life is ordered"), and began reading still more about and by Merton.

Thomas began to think about and consider more seriously what he had told Rebecca about in his Christmas letter.

As he read more of and about Merton, he felt almost as if Merton in his writings was speaking directly and specifically to him, to Thomas Anthony Gorman.

Thomas Merton was born in 1915 in Prades, France, the son of New Zealand-born Owen Merton and American-born Ruth Jenkins. Both were artists; they met at an art school in Paris. They were "non-Catholics."

Merton's mother died from cancer when he was six years old; his father died of a brain tumor ten years later.

Merton reportedly enjoyed a wild and rambunctious youth and young manhood, matriculating ultimately at Columbia University in New York, during which time he converted to Roman Catholicism. In December 1941, at the age of 26, he entered the Abbey of Gethsemani (in Gethsemani, KY), a community of monks belonging to the Order of the Cistercians of the Strict Observance (Trappists), the most ascetic Roman Catholic monastic order.

Merton spent most of the rest of his life at Gethsemani. He was ordained a priest in 1949 and published over the years some of the books Thomas had read and gotten so much out of, "The Seven Storey Mountain" and "New Seeds of Contemplation."

Merton died while on a visit to Bangkok, on December 10, 1968. The date marked the twenty-seventh anniversary of his entrance to Gethsemani. He was 53-years-old, just five years older, Thomas noted, than Aquinas was when he died, in the

13th century. Neither Aquinas nor Merton was able to realize his *full* 'three-score-and-ten.'

Thomas Anthony Gorman, pleased that his given name was a namesake of those two great theologians, began to think more and more seriously about what he had told Rebecca of in his Christmas letter. He had never had a "vocation" when he was a student at SMI or an altar boy at St. Mary's Church (as, incredibly [to Thomas], Paddy had had for a brief period of time when *he* was an altar boy at Auriesville: Paddy! -- a priest ?!), but he began at this time in his life, his spiritual journey, to think more certainly and more seriously about what he had told Rebecca of in his Christmas letter.

As he read more of Merton during this intensely contemplative period, he began to feel, strangely, that Merton in his writings was speaking to *him*, to Thomas Anthony Gorman. And Thomas began to think more and more seriously about, vocation or not, whether he might enter a monastery and embark upon a path *toward* becoming a monk -- if not a priest.

Fifty Three

Thomas Anthony Gorman *heard* Thomas Merton speaking to *him* through his books, mirroring and playing back to him his own thoughts --

In Merton's "The Seven Storey Mountain," Thomas paused when he read through a variety of sections and passages --

"God... the need to worship and acknowledge Him is something deeply ingrained in our dependent natures and simply inseparable from our essence."

"There is not an act of kindness or generosity, not an act of sacrifice done, or a word of peace and gentleness spoken, not a child's prayer uttered, that does not sing hymns to God before His throne, and in the eyes of men, and before their faces."

He *heard* Merton talk about what Thomas clearly felt was his own dissolute and sinful weakness and dependence on sexual congress with so many women --

"...the iron tyranny of moral corruption that held my whole nature in fetters..."

"...rot in the hell of my own corrupt will until I was forced at last, by my own intense misery, to give up my own will."

"For in my greatest misery, He would shed, into my soul, enough light to see how miserable I was, and to admit that it was my own fault and my own work."

"But the Lord dealeth patiently for your sake, not willing that anyone should perish, but that all should return to penance."

"...all men who live only according to their five senses, and seek nothing beyond the gratification of their natural appetites for pleasure and reputation and power, cut themselves off from that charity which is the principle of all spiritual vitality and happiness because it alone saves us from the barren wilderness of our own abominable selfishness."

"And the emptiness and futility and nothingness of the world once more invaded me from every side."

Thomas went on in his study of Merton and reread "New Seeds of Contemplation" where he paused, and contemplated, when he read the following --

"...It is not we who choose to awaken ourselves, but God Who chooses to awaken us."

Thomas reread that sentence and he felt, at that moment, *alone with his God.*

Thomas also read from "New Seeds..." --

"...contemplation reaches out to the knowledge and even to the experience of the transcendent and inexpressible God."

"Every moment and every event of every man's life on earth plants something in his soul."

["Each of us is all the sums we have not counted."], Wolfe had written.

Thomas read further excerpts and knew *his* weakness --

"...inordinate attachment to sexual pleasure, especially outside of marriage, is one of man's most frequent and pitiable weaknesses."

"If you are friends with one habit of mortal sin you live in death, even though you may seem to have all the other virtues."

"...the unquiet city of those who live for themselves... in a struggle that cannot end, for it will go on eternally in hell."

Thomas decided that he would apply -- if that was the right word -- to enter a monastery. He wanted to enter one in the Merton tradition, a Cistercian (Trappist) retreat.

He knew that, at the very least, he *had* to make the effort.

Fifty Four

Thomas contacted the very monastery where Merton had spent nearly three decades of his too-brief life, the Abbey of Gethsemani, located in Trappist, KY.

Merton had written about what he found there, in his solitude, "...the four walls of my new freedom."

"Life in a Trappist monastery is fundamentally peasant life..." Merton wrote.

There, Merton said, "I was really beginning to be ready to do whatever I thought He wanted me to do to bring me to Him."

Thomas felt the same. He was ready, ready "...to do whatever I thought He wanted me to do to bring me to Him."

The writings of the Trappist monk helped Thomas further strengthen his resolve to take what unmistakably was and would continue to be, he hoped, a life-altering decision for him.

● ● ● ● ● ● ●

"Faith is first of all an intellectual assent..."

"The whole truth of Christianity has been fully revealed: it has not yet been fully understood or fully lived."

Thanks to Merton's written words, Thomas Gorman began to pray to The Lord more and for longer periods of time each day. Merton and *his* path to God inspired Thomas Gorman on his journey.

"Our discovery of God is, in a way, God's discovery of us."

"To desire God is the most fundamental of all human desires. It is the very root of all our quest for happiness."

Merton wrote about the beginning of his life at Gethsemani --

"...walking into that deep silence was like walking into heaven."

"...taking my heart home to God."

"...true solitude is the home of the person."

Merton also wrote, with special meaning for Thomas --

"Humility contains in itself the answer to all of the great problems of the life of the soul. It is the only key to faith, with which the spiritual life begins: for faith and humility are inseparable."

"The tension between your desires and your failure generate in you a painful longing for God which nothing seems to satisfy."

"...For the world and time are the dance of the Lord ... His mysterious, cosmic dance."

And as Merton wrote when he had made the decision that

Thomas Gorman was still struggling with --

"I was really beginning to be ready to do whatever I thought He wanted me to do to bring me to Him."

And although he was still struggling with the enormity of his life-altering decision, Thomas Gorman felt that *he*, too, at last "was beginning to be ready to do whatever…He wanted me to do to bring me to him."

Fifty Five

Thomas contacted the Abbey of Gethsemani but found, to his great disappointment, that his age -- over 40 -- would, under the Order's rules, preclude his acceptance. Novices accepted at Gethsemani, he was told, are usually under 40, with many in their 20s. The monk(?) with whom Thomas spoke suggested another abbey, in South Carolina, that had slightly more relaxed age criteria for prospective entrants, and often accepted men in their 40s and even 50s Thomas called that Abbey and learned that, should he so choose, he might be accepted as a Novice there.

"Strike one," thought Thomas, disappointed but undeterred. He had wanted to go to the Abbey where Merton had been -- but, obviously, and to his dismay, it was not to be.

"Time for Plan B," said Thomas, refusing at the moment to be discouraged.

Gethesmani was out; South Carolina was in.

Joseph A. Gillan

Thomas had a long and what he considered to be a good conversation on the phone with a priest at the South Carolina abbey and, with him, developed a tentative plan that would start with a visit by Thomas, and a retreat for a period of not less than 10 days. With a stay of that duration, it was explained, Thomas would be able to get an idea of what life at the Abbey was like both during the normal "work week" as well as a weekend. Following that, if Thomas so chose and he was judged by the monastery's Prelate as a potential monk and/or priest, he could come back for a three-months period called an "Observership." During *this* period he would live and work as all of the members of the monastery -- monks and priests -- did. He would rise in the morning when they rose, pray when they prayed, work when they worked, eat meals when they ate, pray again, and retire early to do it all over again the next day.

●●●●●●●

The day began in the monastery at 3 a.m. (About the same as Army basic training in Ft. Leonard Wood, MO, recalled and thought Thomas). The next four hours were taken up with a simple breakfast of fruit, eggs and coffee followed by vigils, silent prayer and reading. At 7 a.m. followed Lauds and morning prayers, followed next, at 8 a.m., by Community Mass. Work in the Abbey garden, where the monastery cultivated and grew its own fruit and vegetables, followed Mass, until 12:15 when time for a brief prayer period was set aside before the 12:30 midday meal. Work in the fields and garden recommenced at 2:15 p.m. and ended at 5:30 p.m. for Vespers, evening prayers, psalms and hymns.

Supper began at 6 p.m., followed by time for individual prayer and reading. At 7:30 p.m. came Compline, end of the day canticles, prayer and benediction. The monks' day concluded at 8 p.m. Three o'clock the next morning came -- at the same time -- both too soon and not soon enough.

The Cistercian way of life places great emphasis on soli-

320

tude and isolation, Thomas was quick to see. Thomas brought with him for his Retreat two of his Merton books and also Aquinas and Augustine. As he prayed and meditated with like-minded men -- looking for their path on their spiritual journey, as he was his, Thomas began to find great truth, for him, in the Augustinian tenet that God was not an objective reality but a spiritual presence in the complex depths of the self and the soul (a tenet shared centuries earlier by Plato and embraced as well by the Buddhists, Hindus and Shamans in the monotheistic religions).

Augustine spoke 'directly' to Thomas and to the struggle Thomas dealt with. Augustine wrote of opening *his* New Testament to St. Paul's words to the Romans: "Not in riots and drunken parties, not in eroticism and indecencies, not in strife and rivalry, but put on the Lord Jesus Christ and make no provision for the flesh and its lusts." For Augustine -- and, thought Thomas, maybe for me, too -- "the long struggle was over." Augustine wrote, after reading the St. Paul passage, "At once, with the last words (of the St. Paul sentence), it was as if a light of relief from all anxiety flooded my heart. All the shadows of doubt were dispelled."

Thomas read some of the mystic, post-Elizabethan poets, Milton, Wordsworth and Blake, and found food for further contemplation and applicability in them as well to his possible new way of life. Wordsworth wrote in "Lines Composed a Few Miles above Tintern Abbey" --

"... that blessed mood
In which the burthen of the mystery
In which the heavy and the weary weight
Of all this unintelligible world
Is lightened: that serene and blessed mood
In which the affections gently lead us on, ---
Until, the breath of this corporeal frame
And even the motion of our human blood
Almost suspended, we are laid asleep

321

In body, and become a living soul:
While, with an eye made quiet by the power
Of harmony, and the deep power of joy,
We see into the life of things."

Forging *his* own personal and subjective vision, listening
to the Holy Word, Blake wrote –

"Calling the lapsed Soul,
And weeping in the evening dew
That might controll
The starry pole,
And fallen, fallen light renew"

Thomas related his quest, strongly, to *that* thought -- "weeping in the evening dew (and) fallen...(the) light renew."

But, Thomas *always* came back to Merton, inspired by *his*
words and *his vision* and personal spiritual journey. Merton
spoke "to" Thomas and to what was troubling him --

"...the unquiet city of those who live for themselves...in a
struggle that cannot end for it will go on eternally in hell."

Thomas began to feel, with firm resolve, that he, too, as
Merton had and had written, was at last "... really beginning
to do whatever I thought He wanted me to do to bring me to
Him."

Thomas understood clearly now that the three corner-
stones of life in the monastery, should he choose to pursue it,
were prayer, work and contemplative reading and spiritual
development. The monks pray at least seven times a day.

Thomas was pleasantly surprised when he began his
retreat to learn that sleeping arrangements in most monas-
teries were no longer dormitory style [he had had enough of
that kind of close-living quarters in the Army], as he thought
they might be when he arrived. Instead, each resident had
his own cell, affording greater solitude and peace and time
for individual prayer. The cells were by no means commodi-

ous. Each measures, roughly, 10x11 feet and, besides a bed, contains only a desk and a chair. Each cell also has its own small bathroom.

Thomas was, he felt, starting to come around to embracing this new, austere existence, what could be his new life. To be sure, he was tired, physically and mentally, as he adjusted to this new life -- even in such a finite period of only a few days. He knew, coming in, that it would not be easy, but he began to feel, in only his fourth or fifth day, a need to flee, to return not to his old life, per se, but, rather, to his home environs to process all of what he was now experiencing and considering and to decide definitively what to do next, whether to accept and embrace this new life, or not, for the rest of his mortal days.

He prayed to God and to Merton -- *and*, also, to one of his modern-day heroes and inspirations, Pope John Paul II. Strangely, Thomas felt that John Paul was in touch with him in some way and had been since his death, a time at which Thomas began to pray often to him for help and guidance. Thomas had very much admired the great 20th century Pope and the manner in which he so stoically and majestically took on and was not defeated by the many physical maladies and infirmities that broad-sided him, so that all the world could see. The once fit, active and athletic Polish-born Pontiff, an avid skier well into his 60s and 70s, had been reduced to a doddering old man before his time. John Paul took on all of the physical and other health problems besetting him and, seemingly, was undeterred by them.

●●●●●●●

After nine days at the Monastery, Thomas met once again with the Abbot and discussed with him how things might proceed -- if Thomas *were* to be accepted and if he himself, in turn, chose to return.

Thomas, if it were agreed and he were to return, would

323

begin a six-month trial period as a postulant after which, if he, again, wanted to continue and remain in the Monastery, he would be subjected to a series of interviews with resident monks and priests who would offer their judgment and recommendation to the Office of the Prelate on his suitability and potential for success as a novice. That status would be conferred after the period of postulancy. A novice's first vows came two years thereafter and amounted to what was termed Conversatio Morum, a conversion of life in which the novice vows stability -- to stay at the monastery and accept monastic life. Additional vows at this point would include a vow of chastity, a vow of poverty, vows of silence and solitude and a vow of spiritual conversion. These vows are accepted and entered into for a period of three years after which an individual, again, may either leave the monastery or choose to take his solemn vows for life. The newcomer becomes a "Brother" at that point and then, in certain cases, may ultimately move on further and study for and become ordained as a priest.

Thomas got into his car and headed south to Florida and Siesta Key. He was advised by the Prelate to take at least two to three months before deciding whether or not he wanted to return and begin his Observership. Thomas took with him a syllabus of suggested spiritual and theological reading materials given to him by Father Tim.

Kyrie Eleison

Christe Eleison

Kyrie Eleison

Fifty Six

Two months and two days later, Thomas called Father Tim, his original contact at the Abbey, and said he wanted "to try" and to begin an 'Observership.' Thomas closed down his Siesta Key condominium and drove north out of Florida on I-95 to Moncks Corner, SC. He wasn't sure what the logistics and 'regulations' were with respect to having a car at the Abbey. He knew that if and when he took a vow of stability -- to remain in the monastery -- he would not need a car and, presumably, when he took his vow of poverty, the car in all likelihood would have to be surrendered, in any case, at that point.

●●●●●●●

Thomas arrived at Merkin Abbey mid-day on a Monday, early in the month of October.

●●●●●●●

He left Merkin Abbey, early on a brisk Monday morning, mid-way into the month of December, less than two weeks before Christmas. His car was still available to him. Had he stayed one more month, it would have been required of him to relinquish it or to otherwise give it up. Thomas got into his car and drove out of the sprawling Abbey grounds and front gate to Route I-26, which would take him, in just 25 miles to the major southeast United States North-to-South artery, I-95. Upon reaching that thoroughfare, Thomas could either point himself southward, back toward Florida and Lu-Ann Irene Edwards or Rebecca, or he could turn north, toward Olivia -- or Ellen?

●●●●●●●

Thomas turned northward. He first stopped at an International House of Pancakes (bringing back memories of Lu-Ann) and had a huge breakfast, including bacon -- his first meat in more than two months. He lingered at IHOP over his second cup of coffee, read the sports pages in <u>USA Today</u> and considered again whether *this* time he had made the correct decision -- to leave the Monastery.

The world is too much with me, he thought, and I am too much with and of the world. I don't really have a 'vocation.' I *wanted* to have one, much more so than what is *really* in my heart and soul. Thomas recalled the line attributed to St. Augustine that he once had read: 'Lord, please grant me chastity, but not quite yet...'

"Did I give it a fair-enough and long-enough trial?" Thomas talked to himself aloud, as he drove. Rebecca often did that, he recalled: talked aloud to herself when alone.

Thomas headed north on I-95 toward Florence, South Carolina, continuing onward across the North Carolina state line toward Fayetteville and Rocky Mount and then into Virginia, closer to New Jersey (Olivia) and Connecticut (Ellen). He did not have a cell phone. The cell phone world maddened him -- in airports, restaurants, supermarkets, doctors' offices ["everywhere!"] we are subjected, against our will, to "vicarious participation in *half-conversations.*" Everywhere on Siesta Key people were *constantly* on cell phones, men and women walking their dogs on a leash and talking on a cell phone while waiting for the pooches to do their duty; bicyclists traversing the narrow two-lane Midnight Pass Road while carrying on a cell phone conversation at the same time. Once on a trip to Chicago, to visit and experience for the first time baseball's Mecca, Wrigley Field, Thomas was annoyed by the fans and spectators all around him carrying on cell phone conversations while *not* watching or paying attention to the game. One fool in particular infuriated Thomas. He was watching the game -- and simultaneously offering a play-by-play report and analysis to the person at the other end of his cell line call. Madness, Thomas thought. "I have seen the future," Thomas seethed silently, "and, frankly, I am not all that unhappy that I will not be a long-term participant in it."

Thomas had thrown away his cell phone(s) when he left Washington and when asked now by some -- who seemed incredulous that he did not have a cellular phone -- he would reply, "My life just isn't that urgent."

As Thomas crossed into and breezed swiftly through North Carolina toward Virginia, still on I-95, through Virginia toward Washington and around the capital on its beltway, toward and past Baltimore, he drove through Delaware hardly noticing he was even in that state as he approached New Jersey and Olivia's home.

Thomas continued to second guess and question his (too rash?) decision to quit the Monastery so quickly, but he had been deeply bothered by something the Prelate and he had discussed just a few days ago when they spoke of the potential -- long term -- for Thomas to advance through his postulancy to Novice and then Monk status, with all that that status enveloped, to include the vows of chastity, poverty, obedience and stability (once in, and here, you've vowed to stay

here was the clear message). After that, should Thomas want
to continue and the Prelate agreed that he indeed had a vocation, study for the priesthood for Thomas would be precon-
ditioned on one unalterable, major stipulation. And that
stipulation is what Thomas was simply unable to accept and
countenance.

Thomas would have to agree and follow the requisite
Church-prescribed steps, the Prelate said, to formally "annul"
his marriage to Ellen. Thomas was stunned by that. He could
not do that, not to Ellen *or* to his three daughters. Ellen, born
and raised an Episcopalian, had agreed in the first place, against
her better judgment, while bitterly disappointing her parents,
to a marriage in the Catholic Church because of Thomas's
Catholicism and she had agreed, further, that any children of
the union would be raised in the Roman Catholic faith. And,
true to her word, the children had been so raised, receiving all
of the Church's formative-year sacraments, Baptism, Penance
and First Communion and Confirmation. Wouldn't an annulment, now, in effect belittle and negate the value and meaning
of Ellen's promises to the Church and, in effect, bestow ille-
gitimacy upon the children, and make them indeed by soci-
etal norms and definitions 'bastards?'And what would that
do further to Ellen besides telling her that her previous agree-
ments, in accordance with what the Church had <u>imposed</u> on
her to sanction the marriage in the first place, against her own
faith, were now null and void and fundamentally meaning-
less. What would an annulment (silly word) now mean, in
the Church's eyes, to Ellen. What? Would that make her an
'unwed mother?' A 'whore?' We made you make a lot of
promises and pledges many years ago, the Church was, in
effect, saying to her -- and we are now wiping them, and you,
off our books.

And who was it, Thomas thought, who was making this
annulment decision but a *man*, based upon 'rules and regulations' and stipulations devised by a *man*, not, Thomas thought,
by *Jesus.* Could or would Jesus ever have sat down, sharp-

ened a pencil, and configured and written down all of this? *"Let no man put asunder ...what God hath joined together."* Isn't *that*, Thomas concluded, precisely what these *men* (not God) were now proposing? Weren't *they* (<u>men</u>) 'putting asunder' what God had 'joined together?' Where was the theology in this and where, in this, was the sense, the compassion, the justice and mercy for Ellen?

●●●●●●●

Thomas's thoughts, still muddled, preoccupied him as he headed north in New Jersey, not on the Garden State Parkway toward Olivia, but on the New Jersey Turnpike. He had gotten onto the Turnpike without even noticing the exit to the Parkway, missing the cut off from it toward the town where Olivia lived.

He continued north on the Turnpike, toward the George Washington Bridge, across the Hudson and then north on the Hutchinson River Parkway to the Merritt Parkway toward Connecticut, in Stamford, where Ellen now lived.

Strangely, he thought to himself, he was thinking, now, about Lu-Ann Irene Edwards.

●●●●●●●

Thomas found Ellen's new home, a neat and attractive two-story row townhouse, which he had not seen since she had moved there, in north Stamford, near the city border with New Canaan.

It was late of an afternoon. Thomas knocked on the front door and in a moment saw Ellen part and peer cautiously though the curtains on the window of the door.

Ellen unlocked and opened the door as Thomas stood there.

He had not planned what to say and after Ellen opened the door he could do nothing but stand there mute, not knowing *what* to say.

Ellen stood for a long moment, looked at Thomas, then closed the door, slowly, without having spoken.

Neither did *she* know what to say.

It had been several years since she and Thomas had last seen one another.

After Ellen stepped back and gently closed the door, Thomas heard the key turning and the door lock engage.

Not a word had been uttered by either of them.

Thomas turned around, his head bowed. He walked slowly to his car and headed home, back to Florida.

As he drove he pondered what had just happened and it seemed to him that Ellen's closing the door in his face symbolized and crystallized for him the very essence of their long relationship: the existence of a barrier between them, erected by Ellen and never defined and which he had never been able to break down or get through.

He drove through the night, again passing by the Garden State Parkway exit to where Olivia lived, stopping early the next morning, just after 2 a.m. at a roadside Motel Six outside Charleston. He was physically and emotionally drained, still disappointed primarily with himself at what had happened at Merkin, at what had happened (or not happened) in Connecticut and at having passed by (twice) the Parkway cut-off to where Olivia lived. He knew he could not continue to drive in his current state of physical and mental -- and spiritual -- exhaustion, and that he needed a few hours' sleep.

He checked into the motel and fell asleep almost immediately on the too-soft bed in his room without undressing. He knew that he was less than an hour away from the Monastery he had walked away from -- it seemed like months not just a few days ago.

Thomas awoke in mid-afternoon, checked out of the motel

331

and started driving south again. Upon crossing the Florida state line he used a pay telephone when he stopped to gas up his car and he called Lu-Ann. She did not answer, and he left a message that he would like to see her -- to talk.

He arrived back in Siesta Key early the following morning. He emptied his postal box of a large accumulation of mail, went inside, opened a few windows and fell asleep. He slept through the following morning.

He awoke, made a pot of coffee and decided not to call Rebecca. Instead he called Julie and they spoke, as usual, at length. Julie told Thomas, "Becky would like to talk with you."

"She's been drinking a lot lately and *needs* to talk with you."

Thomas did not call Rebecca and again -- strangely, he thought -- Lu-Ann came to mind.

Why, he asked himself, can I not get *her* out of my thoughts and mind? ("OK, ok," he said aloud, "I *do* love you, Lu-Ann.")

He remembered something he had read once about an ancient Buddhist aphorism: "If you *want,* you will suffer; if you *love,* you will grieve."

Thomas also thought about Ellen -- the mother of his three children. He did not think about Rebecca.

One day we shall all lie in the night with the ghost of a dead brother in our arms. And then, in the night, in the darkness, we shall know that Death is a flower that grows in the bed of the beginning.
"Lasso Round The Moon"
-- *Agnar Mykle* --

"In the very search for faith
an implicit faith is already present..."
--*Pope John Paul II* --
1994

"Be not afraid!"
--*John Paul II* --
St. Peter's Square,
October 22, 1978

... and the fire and the rose are one.
--*T.S. Eliot* --

Jesus said to Thomas: "Blessed are they who did not see, and yet believed." (Jn 20:29)

Fifty Seven

Thomas wrote:

December 25, 2014

Dear Olivia,

I realize that hearing from me again after all this time must come as a surprise -- if not a shock -- to you, and I apologize for that ...

On New Year's Day, 2015, Thomas answered a knock on his door to find Olivia standing there.

They smiled at each other and, without a word being spoken by either, Thomas welcomed her into his arms.

Their slow dance of love began again and their communion of spirit, symphony of synchronicity and worldly intimacy heightened once more, to soar for the rest of their time together in their earthly coil.

Thomas had been reading at the time Olivia came back into

his life and playing some soft music on a CD -- a version of the beautiful love song, "The Rose," as recorded by Conway Twitty. Thomas also liked the version of the song made popular by Bette Midler but preferred Twitty's slow, soulful, sonorous interpretation and lugubrious rendition of the deep -- and to Thomas, meaningful and lovely lyrics.

Some say love, it is a river, that drowns the tender reed
Some say love, it is a razor, that leaves your soul to bleed.

Some say love, it is a hunger, an endless, aching need.
I say love, it is a flower, and you its only seed.

It's the dream afraid of waking, that never takes the chance.
It's the heart afraid of breaking, that never learns to dance.

It's the one who won't be taken, the one who cannot seem to give,
And the soul afraid of dying, that never learns to live.

When the night has been too lonely and the road has been too long
And you think that love is only for the lucky and the strong.

Just remember that in the winter, far beneath the bitter snows
Lies the seed, that with the sun's love, in the Spring becomes The Rose.

Thomas opened his door and his heart once again as he and Olivia embraced and swayed gently back and forth and from side-to-side, as the CD continued to play, neither wanting this moment of their coming back together to ever end.

A line from Chekhov came to Thomas's mind --

"We shall find peace. We shall hear the angels, we shall see the sky sparkling with diamonds."

Eleven years later Olivia died peacefully in her sleep after having sustained a massive stroke two days before. She did not suffer. Thomas was at her bedside in the hospital when she died.

Thomas had experienced the eleven happiest years of his life with Olivia. Those eleven years made up for everything else in his life that before had saddened and pained him -- all the heartache and the grey, alone years, all the mirthless, disappointing, empty years.

Thomas thanked His God for having given him Olivia -- good, wonderful, loving, sacred, sweet Olivia -- and he sobbed, uncontrollably. It was the third time in his adult life that he had been unable to hold back tears.

A year later, not quite to the same date that Olivia died, Thomas was called home as he slept early one morning, just before the dawn. He had gone to sleep the night before thinking about Olivia and the love they had shared for those eleven wonderful years, and he also knew that night that love here on earth *is* only mortal, and that mortal love is just that -- mortal, ephemeral. It had been written in Ecclesiastes that "all is vanity."

336

Eternity, and Infinity, come to us only when we go home to Him. All else, here, in the temporal world, is indeed 'vanity.'

Thomas at last knew the answers to the two questions he had been unable to reconcile during his three-score-and-ten: why man is born to die and the great truth of infinity. Thomas knew, finally, that man is born to die to return to what he yearns for during all of his time as a mortal, to return to his God when his God calls him home -- to Infinite Love. Thomas had been given the gift of faith; faith to embrace and accept, without necessarily understanding, what was in him, in his soul and in his heart, and all that lie ahead of him. His quest, his journey, had reached new heights. He had been granted a gift -- the gift that had given him spiritual peace which surpasseth all understanding. He understood clearly now that the heart "has its reasons that the mind knows not of."

He understood that great truth now through the gift of faith.

Always was, is now, and always shall be ... in saecula saeculorum.

●●●●●●●

When Thomas had closed his eyes that last evening, he thought he heard Olivia calling to him. He died with a smile on his face. Soon he and Olivia would be dancing again, and soon the hum of their happy hymn of love would sound again, this time for eternity.

●●●●●●●

Infinity, the concept that for Thomas in his earthly coil had been beyond his grasp and mortal understanding, was suddenly clear now, granted to him through the epiphanic cynosure of God-given faith -- *the key*, sublime and illuminative, *to* the ineffable, exquisite mystery of *it all*.

337

Qui s'excuse s'accuse

-- The End

CPSIA information can be obtained at www.ICGtesting.com
Printed in the USA
LVOW040453181012

303369LV00002BA/33/P